# THE DEATH OF KINGS

BY THE SAME AUTHOR

*Code Name Sebastian*
*The Nine Lives of Alphonse*
*A Handful of Dominoes*

# *The Death of Kings*

## JAMES L. JOHNSON

Doubleday & Company, Inc., Garden City, New York
1974

ISBN: 0-385-02884-9
LIBRARY OF CONGRESS CATALOG CARD NUMBER 72–96244
COPYRIGHT © 1974 BY JAMES L. JOHNSON
ALL RIGHTS RESERVED
PRINTED IN THE UNITED STATES OF AMERICA

## AUTHOR'S NOTE

Of course, there is no country in Africa called Hamara, nor is it intended to reflect an actual country there. Likewise, there is no organization called the United for Life Mission. The incidents, characters and events so depicted have no basis in fact. The props are but the means to declare what the author hopes is a truth about the humanity of God-men. Such is the nature of storytelling.

# THE DEATH OF KINGS

And nothing can we call our own but
    death;
And that small model of the barren
    earth,
Which serves as paste and cover to our
    bones.
For God's sake, let us sit upon the
    ground,
And tell sad stories of the death of
    kings . . .
                Shakespeare's *King Richard II*


For I think that God set forth us the apostles last, as it were appointed to death; for we are made a spectacle unto the world, and to angels, and to men. I Corinthians 4:9

# PROLOGUE

Mr. Warren Larkin
Earth Satellite Resource System
Kano, Nigeria, W. Africa

This is to inform you officially that we have lost the orbit of Satellite Surveyor Eight as of 1200 hours April 5 GMT. Surveyor Eight, as you know, is newest Pioneer Satellite carrying latest in ultraviolet camera equipment. Orbits have taken it over Russian missile installations and carries valuable data needed for Pentagon assessment.

ADDITIONAL IMPERATIVE REPEAT ADDITIONAL IMPERATIVE CONCERNING SURVEYOR EIGHT TO FOLLOW UNDER SPECIAL CODE ZEBRA. INDICATIONS ARE THAT GAMMA X INFILTRATED CAPSULE. REPEAT GAMMA X.

Your assignment is to proceed immediately to recover satellite which our tracking and cross-longitudinal research reveal has landed in territory called *Terragona,* known on your maps as Tuga Spur, 1245 miles east your position and east of African state of Hamara on Sahara border. Intelligence indicates that half-ton satellite probably landed in water since surface impact would have detonated internal explosive sound censor for our seismographic pickup your station or Libya. No pickup was made.

URGENT NOTE. SATELLITE ARMED FOR SEVEN-DAY LIFE CYCLE. REPEAT SEVEN DAYS. WILL SELF-DESTRUCT APPROXIMATELY APRIL 12 REPEAT APRIL 12. IMPERATIVE SATELLITE BE FOUND AND STRIPPED BEFORE SELF-DESTRUCT OR BEFORE IT FALLS TO OTHER SOURCES. WARNING OF SELF-DESTRUCT IS RELEASE OF HIGH-

3

FREQUENCY SOUND BEAMS IN FIVE-SECOND INTERVALS TWELVE HOURS PRIOR. REPEAT TWELVE HOURS PRIOR. Terragona is occupied. REPEAT Occupied. Hostile. REPEAT Hostile. No penetration permitted from outside. Suggest you contact church mission operation in station called DURUNGU in Hamara northern province. Man named Blake runs mission flying operation to team of doctors inside Terragona. ONLY WAY IN. Use all means possible—REPEAT ALL MEANS—to ride that operation. DO NOT —REPEAT—DO NOT CALL ATTENTION TO NATURE OF YOUR MISSION AND DO NOT FOLLOW OFFICIAL PROTO-COL FOR ENTRY TO HAMARA. CONSULATE IN HAMARA WILL COVER FOR YOU. INSTRUCTIONS TO FOLLOW.

Urgency of recovery of Satellite Eight necessitates your immediate action to proceed *Durungu* under whatever cover you deem wise. *Avoid delays.* Intelligence report on Blake to follow under Code X-Ray. Consul in Hamara named Longstreet. Blake is tough. RE-PEAT TOUGH. Practical approach wise.

URGENT NOTE. Chinese tracking station at Zanzibar knows we have lost satellite out of orbit and where it has landed. May also know nature of payload. Anticipate their attempt to retrieve satellite and plan accordingly. Am dispatching assistance earliest date but antici-pate delays. It is your search, retrieve OR destroy.

Good luck. More to follow to Longstreet.

H. B. Arley
Aerospace Security
The Pentagon
170047

# CHAPTER I

He awoke with a slow rise to awareness, his eyes opening gradually against the pain of daylight, staying in slits, taking it a piece at a time, testing, feeling for friendship. The murky colors of red and yellow still spun out of his brain in peculiar gyrations, pinwheels of blinding pain, leftovers from the bad dreams, mixing as they moved. Sometimes they were like circus clowns somersaulting in a blaze of amber and gold and then snapping into pillars of flame again. He would never get the flames out of his head. He knew that.

And then, as if he'd been jabbed in the ribs, he sat up, propping himself on both elbows, feeling the sudden intrusion. The motors. Not a part of his dreams now. Real. Popping against the morning chill, hammering useless fists against cold combustion chambers, children awakened before it is time, turning cranky and irritable under the prodding. Like always. Every morning. And he was half glad they had awakened him, half sad about it too. For it was good to be free of the tyranny of his dreams, but he hated the sound of the planes too, for what they meant, like military drums ordering the march into hell. His hell. His creation.

He turned his head slowly to get the room before him, noticing how the blood-red sun splashed the rough mahogany plank walls and ran off across the rustic floorboards like volcanic lava creeping relentlessly down the mountainside, a slithering reptile of deliberate intent. What forbidden fruit today, you slimy, subtle beauty of the garden?

He continued to lie there propped up, not bothering to kick his legs over the side of the bed, taking in the room with one gasping yawn, scratching his scalp through the tangle of long hair, picking at

5

the scabs that had formed there from too much digging. He glanced around the room with a feeling of detachment, smelling the old socks turned crusty with sweat, the unwashed cups in the aluminum pan under the sink, the stink of used kerosene—there was nothing more dismal than the smell of kerosene to make a man feel gritty, or maybe that was all a part of his past?—the rickety table jammed against the far wall looking helpless and indignant on far too skinny legs, a pregnant woman with two big shopping bags in each arm waiting for a bus in ninety-degree heat . . . the two wicker chairs with the flat green cushions on them looking as promising as globs of day-old chlorophyl bubblegum slapped hastily on a leak in the plumbing. And he grunted a half laugh at the picture.

It wasn't much, never was, but today looked even worse, a roof and floorboards and a bunk too short for his six-foot-three frame. It offered nothing for his night of tortured wanderings, never had, but a hard practicality that all bachelors everywhere in the world accepted with a kind of fatalism. But for this brief moment it caught him with his glands exposed, and he wondered what it was like to awake to other things, to the smells of a woman next to him . . . or what it would be like to awake to neatness and order, delicate cups maybe, a chrome coffee pot boiling off its inviting steam, and a rose in a glass on the old rickety table like he'd seen at the D.O.'s house over in Mandawra . . . and slips and underthings hanging there on the hook maybe beside his shapeless, well-laundered khaki shorts?

But he heard the motors again, slashing across the feminine images, calling him back, now grinding out their petulance, snapping back at the mechanic's firm insistence on performance. And he turned his head slowly to look over the sill of the open window, which was nothing more than a crude hole cut out of the mahogany boards over his bunk, too big a hole for a window really, that let in too much sun or too much rain or too many bugs and now too much of the tortured, bleeding landscape. He yawned again and scratched some more, trying to climb the terribly steep face of the cliff that seemed to get higher every morning. His gaze swung around the area in a slow panning, catching the image of the outbuildings sagging like himself against the relentless pull of the morning's command.

He'd put it all there, he told himself, like it or not, it was his doing . . . the cookhouse-dining room to his left across the hard-packed clay runway made of old black Quonset sheets he'd managed to buy

6

off the Syrian trader in Talfungo, sitting there now, looking like a lop-sided bandshell, a single shaft of smoke cutting a lazy blue furrow up the red field of the sky from a bent sheet of iron chimney . . . then the infirmary, a square chunk of African red brick with colorless thatch roof looking as hopeful as an abandoned schoolhouse . . . and then the red painted Quonset that housed the nine flyers matching the sun so that it almost disappeared in the backdrop, standing there like a giant stop sign as if the flesh it contained was a kind of con-tamination to be probed at arm's length; and finally the two big hang-ars, long buildings of cement block scrounged from the ruins of the Catholic orphanage at Jeta, square warehouselike boxes in suits of gray with huge doors now sprung open to let out the planes, two beached whales with jaws gaping.

Lumps of erosion on desert sand, just so much junk dumped here, falling out of the pockets of God and left to sprout more junk maybe. But he had put it there. And God would hold him accountable for the arrangement. And then he watched the scene at the hangars, pick-ing at a pimple on his chin, as the Africans carried the metal casks of nitro between them, bouncing it in their uneven cadence as if those cans carried nothing more than water. And they were at the first yel-low Cessna, Sam and Jonathan, unlocking the plane door and set-ting that stuff down on the ground with a thump that made him wince.

*"Bonjour, mon ami!"* (As if this was shopping day and nitro was baby formula!)

*"Comment allez-vous?"*

*"Oui, très bien, merci!"*

He could envy the simplicity of the exchange. They lived for the moment of morning sun and breakfast on their stomachs—as they had learned from their long line of Sahara Africans, the Berbers or Taueg nomads out of Niger. The nitro could come in due process. Sweat then, not now. Right now they were thinking they were passing each other in Talfungo maybe, that bright city of merchandise beyond their means, and all that mattered was the proper greeting, while everything else—the world, life, death—could wait.

But this wasn't Talfungo, and he opened his mouth to shout at them . . . this was Durungu in the wild, northern desert frontier of the new African state of Hamara. A chunk of unproductive sand blown out of the Sahara's hot, mournful winds and the alchemy of African politics. Nine hundred square miles scissored out of the

7

nomadic desert land and arid steppe—camels carrying salt west on one side, herdsmen moving cattle to the green shrubs of the savannahs south on the other. Five years old, this Hamara, already a sovereign state free of the French, maybe a half million people at the most hung together far too loosely around the frail but game shoulders of its twenty-four-year-old "boy king" Premier, the Honorable Bendara Abenduko. If Abenduko had little promise of a long term in office, it wasn't because of his youth so much but his honesty, an attribute that never brought longevity to any political figure regardless of country or culture. Nobody could buy the "boy king," they said in the inner circles of government, but it was a law of politics that said what couldn't be bought could be taken by other means. As yet, no one had made the attempt, but who knew how long?

Again, Blake opened his mouth to shout to the Africans to mind that nitro, but decided against it. They had their pride too . . .

Hamara. Hemmed in by Niger on the west, smiling like a fox who knew what it was all about trying to keep the machinery running without the fuel of the colonial benefactor; Chad on the south, yawning and saying you can have it; the Sudan, poking in from the east waiting maybe for the flesh to get on the bones before accepting the new state; Libya on the north, eyeing this young upstart from a few thousand years of history and waiting for one political sandstorm to wipe out the false boundaries and all this foolishness of trying to make a state out of cowherders and date growers. Meanwhile, and Blake winced, spit sand all day and crack your molars from the cold at night, because God was trying to build His own little acre here too for Hamara and the Kingdom of Heaven.

And he grunted at that and swung his long legs over the side of the bunk, turning his back on the scene around the planes. For if it was today that Sam or Jonathan would allow their clumsy fingers to slip on one of those cans he would rather not know which one. He did not want to know. Nor would they want him to know either.

"Joseph!"

"Suh!"

"*Bonjour, mon ami!*"

"*Bonjour,* suh!" The voice came from the back, outside the door, like an actor responding to cue, delighted that it was his moment at last.

"*Musique, Joseph!*"

*"Oui,* suh!"

The shuffle of bare feet across the wooden floorboards outside, moving into the radio room, the sound of the hum of power coming up strong on the P.A. horns seconds later, then the thumping scrape of the ridges on the tape as it moved through the sprocket. Then the roll of the drums came on strong over the horns on the roof, cutting a jagged gash into the mellow morning air, even more harshly than the plane motors had done. Then the quick cadence tune of the "Colonel Bogey March" began to reconstruct the morning, pushing aside the neutral mixes of sun and sand that lay like a comforting blanket over the sleeping buildings, pounding together instead the scaffolding and timbers of a war camp. For a moment he could see Alec Guinness again marching his proud comrades to that bridge over the River Kwai while they whistled that tune in defiance of themselves and the conspiracy of war and nature. Some of that got to him as he sat there on the edge of the bed, elbows on his clumps of over-cartilaged knees, but it was never enough . . . as much as he prayed it would propel him fully to meet the day, it never did. He told himself he wasn't playing it for himself but for the others. But really, if it was for the others, maybe he should have tried to get a tape of hymns like Augie kept complaining about to the other pilots all the time. But the hymns couldn't go here either, Augie wouldn't understand . . .

He waited for the tune to run its way through once, the drums and horns and whistling playing that peculiar kind of piper, calling to the vibrant chords of men who could hardly resist the plucking on tired heart muscles, staring at his feet that jerked involuntarily with the cadence, trying to rise to the prodding like the old army veteran who could no longer march in the Fourth of July parades. Behind him, across the airstrip, he knew that Sam and Jonathan had turned to face the tower and the music as they always did and would by now be shuffling their bare feet on the hard clay of the tarmac. Soon the other mechanics would be joining them, responding to that restless African bug in them that never lay still when there was any kind of beat in the air. Over in the pilots' Quonset, he knew, the pilots would be coming up out of the deep shaft of sleep—the young never came to sunup easily—pushing against the demands of the march. And beyond the hangars, across the flat tableland of bloody sand, the herders would have paused to look his way as they always had for two years now,

9

never comprehending this kind of music but knowing by now that it was "Yellow Bird's" way of telling his world that he was awake and putting on his armor.

Then it was over and the quiet seeped in again. He stood up feeling the thump of his heart too loud in his chest, telling him he hadn't slept at all in the night—so how many nights was that, then? And the thought of it turned his tongue to the dryness of leather.

*"Comment von votre femme et familee, Joseph?"* he called loudly in the room.

Joseph laughed in a kind of whinny from the back, because the French was not good, *"Oui, très bien, merci!"*

And so the morning began officially with the music and the simple exchange with Joseph. Joseph. The mixture of how many nomadic tribes? Berber and Taueg and a long line back to the Dinka even? Who really knew what crossed in these African wilds? Right now, though, he was a free Hamaran citizen who spoke enough elementary French to become, as Joseph proudly proclaimed to anyone who would listen, "the proper *officiel interprète* for *commandant-en-chef,* Blake." And all who heard him declare it in the marketplace in Durungu laughed, because they knew that he understood no English and his French was even worse than "the big man's," if that was possible. They knew him best as a man who failed in growing dates, failed in weaving rugs and even failed as a simple cattleherder. And they would remind him that he was nothing more than a waterboy for Yellow Bird and only because the big man took pity on the most helpless and scabbiest of Hamaran riffraff; and he, Joseph, was nothing more than that. Did he forget so soon, they would chide him, poking their long sticks at him, reminding him of the day in this same Durungu market when a court of his peers was ready to chop off both his hands for stealing bread from the old woman trader, as the African law here demanded? And did he so soon forget how the big man came on them and interceded with the court to set Joseph, the *fripon,* free?

"Now you are a bond slave to Yellow Bird," they would jeer at him, not because that was so bad, but certainly a far cry from being *officiel interprète.* "And you will work your days for him until he tells you it is enough—and that is too good for you, Joseph, who has no family name and whose children run as wild goats without a name and whose wives are too ashamed to even buy fruit in the market!"

And Joseph would lift his bony finger at them and shout back, "Mark your tongue well! Someday I will drive here in a big black auto like the Premier—and you will come to me for your beans and peppers and rice!"

Again the laughter, and the sound of it would follow him all the way back to the airfield, two miles on that dusty road, and to his black pot and fire and simple lean-to shack behind his commandant's *maison*. Joseph.

Now rattling the pans and pouring the hot water from the black cooking pot into the white porcelain pan which he carried into the small bedroom of his *commandant,* setting it down carefully on the wooden crate in the corner. The smell of wood smoke and palm oil and that earthy wild smell that was African followed him. His white teeth flashed over the red stains of the kola nut that had been smuggled in through the Nigerian trade route, for kola nut was a narcotic that Hamara shunned as beneath her status as a new nation. The sheen of ebony stretched over the sharply defined lines of the Sahara nomad cheek and jaw bones and took on a glow from his perpetual grin, outlining the thin-lipped mouth even more; the old French khaki barracks cap—from which war, nobody knew—pulled close down over his tight skull against the chill of the past night's Harmattan winds gave him the appearance of being squeezed down into the long khaki French Army coat that hung on his lanky, double-jointed frame. And even when the sun moved to its forging fire in an hour or so, he would continue to wear that coat and cap as a sign of status. For it was true, anyone who possessed anything from the former French masters was said to have been favored by the colonial benefactors and could walk taller. Except, of course, Joseph got his uniform from an old French gamewarden. Only he knew that, but he was not about to lose what he had rightfully gained, despite the mockery of the marketplace crowd.

And so now he puttered through the simple ceremonies of a servant before a king, an obedience given in return for an early-morning ritual like this and a few precious francs a month to lay away for a dowry on a third wife, one in the western provinces he had his eye on, with smooth black cheeks and big breasts and wide hips; someone more *élégante* than the thin skeletons of his own nomadic breed, one who could keep him warm against the chill of the Harmattan winds at night and give him his inheritance in children for the day, one who

*11*

would someday give him honor at his side. And who knew, if all went according to plan, he would yet have enough for several more wives, then a compound, and who knew—let those jackals have their laugh! —he could yet see himself in that big black auto!

*"Le jour va être long,"* the big man said simply as he pulled on a greasy pair of khaki shorts, then the brown socks with the holes in each toe and the familiar boots that he laced up and tied but left the buckles alone so that they jingled in soft tinkling sounds as he walked, the sound the herdsmen had come to associate with him by saying, "The bull with the bells on his feet begins to walk."

*"Oui,"* Joseph said obediently and laughed again, saying he understood, but only the words, for he did not know the full meaning of the statement even after two years of hearing it.

Blake walked out of the small mud-brick quarters, letting Joseph wait, walking up the gradual incline of sand directly behind his quarters, following a path that rimmed it and down the other side to the cluster of ragged tents. As he approached, two Africans rose quickly from around the smudge fire, pulling their tattered blankets about them.

*"Bakure, bakure,"* Blake said to them in the only corrupted Sudanese dialect he knew, meaning "Peace, peace," and they returned the greeting, the large silver rings in their ears flashing the red hues of the morning sun. Blake walked to the main tent and stepped inside, one of the tall Africans following. He looked down at the woman lying on the black woolen blanket, the small naked child next to her sleeping peacefully. Blake reached down and patted the shiny rear of the child affectionately, and the woman gave him a broken-toothed smile, her dark eyes reaching up to him in gratitude and some wonder that such a man, foreign and unknown to her, should take the time for such an intimate touch. He went on from tent to tent, saying, *"Bakure, bakure,"* over and over again, viewing the dozen or more old people who stared back at him from their glazing fatigue and shrinking glands. Some spoke and tried tired smiles, faces twisted in bone tissue and pain, eyes that said they wanted to die here rather than go on the three hundred torturous lonely desert miles to Niger, the only sanctuary left for southern Sudan refugees who fled the guerrilla war there. Some were children with hacking coughs that bent them double, some were too weak from lack of food to lift their heads off the dirty

blankets. Their eyes followed him, for he represented the mountain of life to them now, the food and the medicines needed to send them on their way. But still they wondered why.

He finished the rounds and walked quickly back across the small camp area. The tall African who accompanied him stopped him and tried to press two small copper coins in his hand. Blake smiled, gently closed the fist over the coins and said, *"Bakure, bakure,"* and walked on back up the hill and the path.

Joseph watched him come down the hill, sliding with the sand, making pinkish clouds that boiled around him in a peculiar spectrum of color, a man walking in the fires of his certain suffering, and he clucked in his throat. For Joseph knew that to continue to give help to these displaced Sudanese nomad refugees was against Hamaran law. And it would catch *en chef* Blake too soon, too soon.

Blake turned at the bottom of the hill and headed for the monstrous-looking anthill that sat off to the left of his quarters facing the open airfield. It looked, as always, like the Empire State Building in miniature or like one of those fuzzy buildings at the bottom of the sea, a mark of some lost civilization. It was as if the ants built the model straight from the instruction sheet, even to the long, pointed shaft that poked skyward as high as fourteen feet to its peak, jabbing an accusing finger at God, who was prone to frown on any attempts like this that came close to the dimensions of the Tower of Babel.

The anthill had served as a john for Rudy and him in the early days. It was big enough to hold one man at a time. A hole was cut into one corner five feet deep to the limestone bed below. So acoustically perfect was its structure that pilots across the field said they could track a man's elimination patterns just by the sounds that came through that needlelike antenna. It was for this reason that Rudy called it "radio city."

Blake relieved himself, sniffing at the acrid smells of ammonia that arose out of the hole and smiling at the sound that bounced back to him from the rockbed like pieces of glass falling in there. "Lord, it is by Thy mercies we are not consumed," he said, grunting in a sigh as he felt his back muscles relax. And while he stood there, he heard the strains of the BBC news march come on the innocent morning air from the pilots' Quonset, falling in on him from that noise-gathering mud aerial above him. The tinny cacophony of bagpipes and cornets and snare drums came on louder as someone turned up

*13*

the volume, as if they expected God would come in with a news break to tell them this nightmare was over; and then the British voice came on in a dry monotone: "Good morning, this is the news . . .

"American space scientists admitted today that Pioneer Satellite Surveyor Eight, one of the most sophisticated of American space laboratories, which fell out of orbit last Tuesday, four days ago, has been lost. Officials refused to comment, however, regarding where search efforts are being carried out to find and recover what has been described as America's most expensive piece of space hardware. Russian commentary on the loss has not appeared as yet, and speculation mounts today that the Russians are carrying out their own search . . ."

As if that made any difference to those nine guys pulling in their guts for the ride upstairs today! And Blake grunted at that and turned to walk out of the anthill and back to his quarters. He paused to glance at the herders coming around the corner of the main hangar across the field, pushing their cattle ahead of them, wanting to get across the airstrip and to the gradual slopes on this side where there were still sprouts of sour grass for grazing. He lifted his voice in the quiet morning air, *"Mumba, mumba saba!"* The herders paused to look at him, for they knew that voice by now in its peculiarly distinct bellow of entreaty, never harsh or grating, but nevertheless commanding. They pulled their blankets around them as if to say for the thousandth time to him, this was the way they had done it for centuries. "Sam!"

And one of the Africans at the nearest Cessna turned and marched out six quick steps, hands stiff at his side.

"Suh!"

"Turn them back, Sam!"

*"Oui,* suh!"

Sam was the only linguist among the Africans here, because he had served in the French-American oilfields before independence. Now he turned and ran toward the hangars, waving his arms so that the cattle turned quickly in fright, bolting by their stoic herders for the bedding grounds they had occupied the night before. They couldn't understand what cowdung on this hard clay runway could do to drag on a Cessna's wheels on takeoff—and what that could do especially to an airplane carrying a chronically ugly batch of nitro under the seat. Later he would let them come across, after the planes were gone, but

14

even then he would make sure Sam had a shovel to pick up any leavings before the planes returned.

Joseph waited for him at the back door as always, for this morning ritual never was broken, and followed his *commandant* inside with the bucket of hot water off the fire in his lean-to by the door. He poured into the porcelain pan, then waited a few discreet feet away as Blake lathered his face and shaved quickly. Then Joseph handed him the khaki towel, which he held in both hands as if he had the crown jewels in it. Blake rubbed his face clean, put on a tan shirt that was almost as greasy as his shorts, gave his clump of reddish hair a swipe with one hand and walked out back, Joseph following.

They sat on small wooden crates by Joseph's lean-to, the stenciled letters still showing plainly on the boxes: HIGH VISCOSITY CRANKCASE SAE 30 and BRAKE FLUID NO. 34. Blake pulled out a battered pair of steel-rimmed glasses from his shirt pocket, hanging them on his ears so that they fit lopsided on his long, shapeless nose.

"It is good to give thanks unto the Lord and to sing praises unto Thy name, O most High," he began, reading in English because his French was so poor, his voice cracking some on the residue of sleep in his throat that had never gotten to his brain along with the tickling fingers of Harmattan dust.

Joseph sat quietly with his long legs tangled under him looking like leftover burnt sticks from last night's fire, elbows resting on his knees, his leaf-shaped hands dangling down between his legs. He chewed slowly on his kola nut, not getting much from the reading, if anything, but respectful in his attention both for the Book and the man who read so slowly, as though it was a new language to him. This man was not like the others here who read the Book so rapidly in English or in French, as if the words were stones across the river to run quickly over to get to the other side. This man was not like any of them in any way, and now after two years with him, Joseph felt some alarm by it as never before. It was not good whatever it was that rode the desert winds lately—he knew the big man was in for trouble in many ways, and soon, and it seemed as if he knew it by the way he read even more slowly from the Book, as if hunting for something there that would tell him what to expect. His step was slower too, his big frame thinner, and the shoulders seemed to bend more, as though he had been carrying wood on his back like the African women in the market; the clear blue eyes that once flashed the

*15*

sun and command were red and puffy; he did not sleep well, Joseph knew, for he would hear the big man's body thump against the wall often in the night as he turned to find rest; his long red hair that had burned like fire on the mountain had turned a dirty brownish color from the Harmattan dust, and it was as if the flame in him was slowly dying.

". . . but my horn shalt thou exalt like the horn of an unicorn: I shall be anointed with fresh oil . . ."

The sound of an airplane motor starting harshly in the still, crisp morning air caused him to stop reading, as if someone had called to him, reminding him, and a twitch came to the corner of his wide mouth for a moment while he continued to stare at the page. The engine ran up to a loud shrilling whine and then died. It was quiet again. He cleared his throat and shifted on the small wooden crate, lifting the Book closer to those crooked glasses. And he went on again, his voice muffled like the sound of drums a long way off.

Joseph was not sure he liked what was happening to the big man. He was not sure he was going to like what was *going* to happen to him here. In fact, he knew he was not. It was one thing to see a warrior die in the field standing before the enemy he could see. It was quite another to fall into the dust without knowing why or who or from which wind the blow had come.

And Joseph felt a pang of fear then, coming like the hand of his dead uncle from the grave, so that he stopped chewing suddenly as if pain had grabbed him. Was it for his *commandant?* Or fear for himself? And he strained to catch some of the words, as if this might give him some clue to the terrible omen he felt.

Across the compound in the outpatient cubicle of the infirmary, Rudy the Jew stood leaning against the frame of the open doorway, watching Emily Stewart put the last of her meager personal possessions into the cardboard suitcase. He watched her quietly, noting the bony, dartlike thrusts of fingers and wrists nervously covering over her own grave. Her thin, almost brittle body showed up starkly in the faded pink housedress. There was beauty there once—a long time ago perhaps. Two years. She had come in here in a sparkling white nurse's uniform and a doctor's black bag jammed with worm medicine and paragoric when the infirmary was a lean-to and the Hamara tribesmen had to be coaxed in for treatment with peppermint candy

16

canes that melted into blobs of sugar. The first year she had her day with the nomadic people while Blake built the airfield and the pilots did practice flights in tricky crosswinds. But in the last year she had nursed fewer Africans than pilots, did more desk work for Blake, figuring cargo weights and monitoring radio signals, than actual doctoring. And it had cut her down—her blonde hair was pulled back off her head so that it appeared that her whole face was being stretched upward. Her big, gray-green eyes which had once been full of quiet laughter were now mere slits of hard rock, and her nose had gone too sharply pointed, her mouth turning too small as her face grew thinner and gaunt. Sometime maybe the miracle of cosmetics might bring her back, but meanwhile he felt depressed watching her. It wasn't only the desert and the winds or even the frustration of working in a lonely outpost. Blake was in it too, as he had to be, as he was in everything else here. But it made Rudy feel uneasy to see what Blake meant to her even now, what the various enigmas of the man had done to drastically affect the chemistry of a woman like Emily.

"Aren't you even going to say good-bye to him?" he ventured. Somehow he had to affect the breach, dilute the bitterness in her before she got to Talfungo.

"I've said all that is necessary," she returned simply, keeping her back to him, her voice dragging on a weary, nervous edge, continuing to fidget with the clothes, probably wishing he'd go so she could be alone in this simple room that smelled of alcohol and ether.

"You just going to drive out on him?"

"I'm going to do just that, Rudy."

"Without official transfer?"

"My transfer is written all over me—you can't see that, Rudy?"

"Nothing more for Blake, then?"

"I don't have a bag of sparkplugs or ten thousand gallons of av gas on me, if that's what you had in mind, Rudy." No quip there, just a bitter shot of aimless jabbing at the shadow she could not even yet identify but which had pounded her pulses too long.

"He ought to know at least," he tried again. "Two years is a long time . . ."

She snapped the lid down hard on the case in a sound that reflected her own feelings probably. "Yes," she returned with a clip in her voice, a heart murmur thumping on empty emotional chambers, and she straightened to fold her arms and stare at the far wall as if it

*17*

were all written out there. "Two years of being his secretary, nurse, flight co-ordinator, keeping him going on Dexedrine, pouring worm medicine into his pilots and trying not to see him as anything but a walking oil can." She paused a moment and gave a shaky sigh, then added, "But he already knows, Rudy. You don't have to tell him, nor do I. He took the government flight reports out of the infirmary last night when I was at dinner—so he knows . . ."

"I know he's not easy to figure—"

"Easy?" she cut back at him quickly and turned to walk briskly the few steps to the window next to the door where he stood, her tired gray eyes taking in the row of yellow Cessnas parked there drawing the full, hot glow of the lava-colored sun on them. "He's as easy to know as a gust of Harmattan wind and twice as cold. He can't feel for anyone or anything except maybe the sound of an airplane motor running with a miss . . . Blake loves his machines of war, Rudy. He himself runs on dry cells and hydraulic brake fluid, and God doesn't have much opportunity to add to that." She paused to let the weight of her words have effect on the swollen membranes of her own lacerated heart. Then she went on, "I leave him to you, then, Rudy, you kind, considerate and lovable, Rudy the Christian Israelite, Blake's beautiful cover. I leave you to Blake's folly, his insane allegiance for airplanes and—and those Sudanese refugees he insists on treating like stray pups. I give him to you and whatever cause he thinks he has here. Now if you don't mind, I'll be going; Talfungo is three hundred hot miles south."

She picked up her cardboard suitcase and made to go by him, but she paused uncertainly on the threshold where he stood, wanting to leave something for him if not for Blake. He stood up against the frame, letting her pass, chewing as always on that spearmint gum, filling the air with the color of children's play, his homely face—big, spread-out nose that hooked slightly to the left, giving his entire head a sense of being off balance, his lips too swollen for the narrowness of his horselike face—looking even more disastrous now in this moment of confusion and disarray that he felt. Rudy was full of laughter, but when had he last laughed genuinely?

"Don't keep standing up for him, Rudy," she appealed softly to him, touching his arm lightly. "Don't go down with him, because he will go down, Rudy, his kind always does . . . they ride too high, and God lets them go for a while and then they come in hard. Don't try to figure him out as I did these two years and then get walloped in the end . . ."

"Don't get too fat in Talfungo," he said, his grin arching like the flash of a dove's wing against the smoky black of his sunglasses and the severe canopy of the stiff black brim of his baseball cap. She felt sadness for him then, for his attempt even yet to lay protective cotton over Blake. She might have stayed on for Rudy, for the gentle spring of life that he was, for his penchant to preserve every vestige of the human dimension, good and bad. But then he was, after all, a part of all this jarring environment—with its stink of fried sand, engine exhaust and cowdung that rode the Harmattan wind with an insulting jab at the dismal efforts of humanity in this place. And Blake. No incense followed him either, no sweet fragrance of holy enterprise, nothing but the fruity smell of old socks and sweat shirts and grease and that wild smell of masculine glands that teased her constantly and left her shaking in bed at night, a cruel taunt to her need. He carried the odors of dereliction on him, a foreign element at best that needed to be exorcised before this mission-flying operation grounded itself by spiritual default—and Rudy ran with him, propped him up, laid his hand to this peculiar conspiracy.

Homer Kline, the pilot of the mission's red Cessna sitting out in the middle of the field, was waiting, showing some impatience now. Emily handed him her bag, glancing just once toward the tower, perhaps to see if Blake might be coming to say good-bye. Then without further word she followed Kline out to the plane, head up, proud of her retreat.

Rudy watched as the plane moved off to the far end of the runway, swung around to catch the full hot glow of the sun and then gunned down the field, lifting easily. Rudy stayed where he was for a long time, watching the plane bank around and head south, scrawling that red pennant of loaded commentary across the new birth of morning sky. In about three hours Talfungo would have it all, because Rudy was sure Emily was not going to be exhibit A for the glories of Operation Shoestring. He spit out his gum into the dirt by the door, pulled his cap lower over his eyes, and began whistling through his teeth as he headed for the dining room. It was not promising to be a good day.

The "Colonel Bogey March" had crashed to a reverberating halt over the P.A. system and the BBC news had marched off with a squeal of bagpipes when the eight pilots straggled out of the red Quonset. They moved slowly, some in disconnected lumps of two or three, some alone, dragging out the minutes, delaying as always that moment when they had to make the flight line and go up again. They were bare to the waist, disregarding the chill yet in the air as young warriors were fit to do, khaki towels hanging around their necks like badges of valor, toilet kits in hand, wooden clogs on their feet. The muscles were young, the skin burned brown and full of the strong virile sap that oozed out in the sweat that came easily here. Yet, over their faces, beyond the puffy pockets of fatigue that clung to their mouths and eyes, was that thin glaze of hardening maturity. It was the kind of age that had come too soon, not gently over time but like a thief in the night, robbing them of their natural exuberance, their sense of adventure, their protective gloss. They had been flying nitro into Terragona territory for almost three months now.

"How do you like that?" the kid named Monk said as he scooped up his pan of water out of the barrel to walk to his place at the far end of the washstand, spilling as he went. Monk was a new replacement for Charlie Weaver, who had been killed three weeks before, trying to get into this field after dark. Monk had been in the camp only two days and had not yet caught the mood of the group, so he resorted to various pitches hoping to draw them out, to be sure. He was twenty-two years old, with ears grown close to his skull, and eyes that squinted continually so that no one was ever sure of the color. A spray of freckles ran across the bridge of his small nose and under both eyes, looking like dried cocoa, standing out even more now as the sun peeled them and pocked them over with watery blisters. He posed a picture of Boy Scout innocence and fragility, who at any moment might recite the merit-badge requirement for hygiene. Nobody bothered to engage him in his question immediately, each of them busy with getting his own pan of water, finding his place at the wooden stand and opening toilet kits with the slashing sound of zippers scraping hard on the flat surface of the morning. "They lose a satellite worth two hundred and fifty million dollars and now can't find it . . . I mean, there's got to be better ways to spend that kind of money, seems to me . . ."

"Like what?" Mundey finally offered indulgingly from his position next to Monk, in his usual, slow, intent drawl, examining a blackhead on his chin in a small cracked mirror that sat precariously on the upper ledge of the washstand in front of him. Mundey had had three tight scrapes flying into Terragona lately, and he had taken the loss of Charlie Weaver harder than the others, mostly because they had come into the operation together four months ago. He had flown the treacherous Amazon area in South America with another mission for five years before joining Operation Shoestring. He was a short, slightly built man of twenty-five who wore cowboy boots, the raised heels allowing him to gain a few more inches, thus permitting him a more reasonable command with his peers. His face still carried the pockmarks of adolescent acne, and they would flare up into clusters of fiery red strawberry patches even yet when the pressure of flying got to him. Mundey had taken to dry commentary on everyone's conversation lately, acting as a kind of straight man to draw out answers he wanted everyone to get which could be slanted to his own particular mood. "How about it, Monk?" he prodded, not taking his eyes off the mirror. "How would you spend the money?"

"A hundred cases of Lavoris," Pete Letchford offered solemnly from his place at the far end of the bench, staring at his open mouth in the mirror, afraid as always that he had trench mouth.

"Scope," someone else chimed in, then another added, "I'll take the wide-track ride . . ."

"Gasoline with octane . . ."

"Hey, what gives with you guys?" Monk derided with a half-wounded tone in his voice, pausing in his work of rubbing Mennon Menthol on his blondish fuzz. "You know what I mean . . . all that money just to experiment with a lot of gadgetry that probably won't mean a thing to anyone anyway . . ."

"Especially when you are chasing a sure thing, right, Monk?" Mundey returned dryly, swiping at his long black hair that was really too long for mission rules but which he let grow anyway because there wasn't time to worry about it.

Monk had paused again in his wielding of the straight razor over the lather, as if he was getting ready to slash at a seam rather than at his face, looking at Mundey to be sure if the remark was intentionally jocular or not. But Mundey went on rubbing Palmolive soap over his dark patches of bristles with one hand, pulling his razor directly behind it with the other, turning his body fully toward Monk so he

21

wouldn't nick himself on the neck. His quick smile was no more than a wince, as if the blade was pulling on his beard.

"Well," Monk squeaked back, holding his razor off his cheek, "if I'm flying nitro under my seat I better know why I'm doing it besides trying to prove you can bounce a Cessna without blowing it . . . I didn't come all this way to chase a shadow, see? Terragona, eighty thousand strong, is what I'm after, to plant the flag of Christ on pagan territory before the Commies or the Catholics do it . . ." And someone down the line muttered "Amen" in a tone of half parody, but Monk didn't catch it. "Now, that would be worth two hundred and fifty million in my book. You got some other reasons, Lundey?"

"Mundey," Mundey retorted, frowning into the small mirror. He didn't answer right away, because to carry on the conversation in the same half-bantering tone would sound almost profane in the light of Monk's serious intent.

So that left it open for Jeremy Potter to say, " 'Even a fool when he holdeth his peace is counted wise; and he that shutteth his lips is esteemed a man of understanding.' "

Potter seldom ever spoke a direct line to anyone except that the book of Proverbs was in it somewhere. He was twenty-three, with a long, sad face and quiet gray eyes that could dance with flecks of light at times, testifying to the strange fires banked within him, mostly humor that had never found a way out.

"So how many hours you bring with you, boy?" Mundey finally said, lifting his chin to draw the razor across the bristles over his jagged bulge of Adam's apple.

"Hundred fifty," Monk chirped like it was some kind of trophy.

Mundey paused. *"All* of a hundred and fifty?"

"Sure . . . what's wrong with that?" Monk demanded, sensing it was too quiet around the washstand.

"Oh, nothing at all," Mundey muttered and went back to his shaving.

"I got papers . . ."

"Sure, you got papers," Mundey returned, frowning now into the small mirror.

"Spins, stalls, cross-country," Monk went on, to all of them now, as if he was testifying in court. "Macdonald Aviation where Amelia Earhart once took her solos—"

"Good enough, Monk," Dirk Shannon suddenly spoke up for the

22

first time from his position opposite Mundey. Shannon was the senior flyer among them, second only to Rudy the Jew, having logged military time with the Navy in Pensacola, Florida. He was twenty-eight years old, tall, round-faced with reddish-blond hair cut close to his head and Irish-green eyes that seldom smiled but carried, instead, a watchful, intent look like a cat's around trees. "Mundey is a little testy since the umbrella school he went to would give papers to kite flyers . . ." The responsive laughs from the rest of them were to back up Shannon's deliberate attempt for lighter overlay on the conversation. Mundey's eyes locked with Shannon's for only a second or two, catching the warning of Shannon to back off and yet catching the flick of acknowledgment about the absurdity of Monk's credentials. Neither of them could fully rationalize, even in the missionary sense, how any of the rest of them could have come into this operation with so little flying experience. Men with two thousand hours in the air and military experience would have found it a test to fly nitroglycerin under these conditions. To drop a plane in Terragona without blowing it had to take a touch of a hummingbird kissing a rosebud. And yet perhaps that was the glorious audacity of men of God?

"Yeah, has anyone seen Herr Mundey in a tight turn lately?" Joe Bellinger said from the far end of the washstand, picking up the cue from Shannon. Bellinger was just six months past his twentieth birthday, but he looked older than the others, thin and wiry, with big brown eyes and narrow face with swollen lips that came from too many hours playing the harmonica.

"Nose up, power up," Tom Slater added, and he lifted his hand palm-flat, diving it in a mocking rendition of an airplane in a tight turn to the right, his lips spitting the sound of the motor and then going into spasmodic snorts as he dove his hand into the frothy water in the pan in front of him. Slater was medium build, just turning twenty-two, who looked a lot like Mickey Rooney in an Andy Hardy movie.

"Ach himmel!" Joe Bellinger yiped, putting his comb under his nose and slapping his short black hair down over one eye. "Das ist ein hundert Luftwafer Stuka Baron Von Mundey has diven in der laken—was ist dis dumbkoff in der turns, yah?"

"Yah!" everybody chorused, except Mundey and Shannon and, of course, Monk, who wasn't sure what was going on now, for they had all been this way before at Mundey's expense. "Was ist dis mit

Dumbkoff Mundey in der turns!" And the laughter followed, rising like a gaily colored balloon in the drab panorama of sand, thorn scrub and corpselike buildings, so that the Africans working on the planes paused to look toward them, wanting to get a piece of the pattern that was a rare commodity here lately. And Monk finally grinned quizzically, drawing on the mockery to bolster his own sense of diminishing accomplishment here. Mundey said nothing to the jabbing laughter, going on with his shaving in a methodical, deliberate intent, glancing now and then at Shannon across from him.

And Bellinger was intent on carrying out the German parody here that had begun some months before but nobody knew how, and he came around to Mundey in a German military strut, his shorts flapping around thin, hairy bowlegs that had the gangliness of a spider. He stopped beside Mundey and handed him a wrapper off a bar of Palmolive soap. "Baron Von Mundey," he began, holding the comb under his nose again, that shaft of black hair too short to really give the full effect, "you have receivin' das biggin' honor for deflyin' the mostin' machinin' in der laken . . . diese ist ein papier for you to be rememberin' to be cleanin' up dee turnin'—" And Mundey splashed water at Bellinger as the others popped short gasps of laughter.

"Hey!" Monk cut in again, and everybody looked at him, wondering what it would be now. Monk was looking across the field toward the shabby, squat-looking red mud building with the dumpy lighthouse-shaped structure sticking up out of it that served as the control tower. "Is that the big man comin'?"

They all looked, and then Bellinger immediately put his comb back into his pocket, the comic gone from him to be replaced by more serious intent as he went back to his place. The mood of levity had vanished as if the sun had burned it off, leaving them to hurry through their morning toilet in jerky, almost fumbling motions.

"That's him," Shannon said quietly, putting toothpaste on his brush carefully. Monk was watching Blake coming toward them from the direction of the tower, his lanky frame filling the horizon, his walk a slow, easy stride as if he was out for a relaxing stroll.

"He coming here?" Monk wanted to know, fascinated now by the growing design of Blake looming higher and higher.

"Dining room," Shannon said.

"Man, that don't look like no terror of United," Monk commented, trying the bravado again. And Mundey grunted into his pan as he sloshed water on his face. "Who's that guy in the big overcoat behind him, with the spear in his hand?"

"Joseph."

"Joseph? Joseph who? He looks like an escapee from the foreign legion. Why the spear anyway?"

"Try taking the big man sometime," Mundey offered flatly. "You'll know then why the spear."

"Kind of bodyguard," Shannon explained.

"What about the little kid half running out there in front of him with the tray on his head?"

"Mine detector," Mundey added again, rubbing his face with his khaki towel, and Monk frowned at him, realizing the bantering tone in Mundey's voice.

"Duka," Shannon went on, shooting another warning glance at Mundey. "Duka is an orphan who carries tins of dates on his head to sell. Mr. Blake buys them all from him every morning. So as the Hamaran tradition here has it, Duka will walk before him as a guard, saying he will die first if danger comes in the path."

"Mine detector, see?" Mundey had to put in again with that wincing grin at Monk.

"Not much of a trailblazer," Monk said skeptically, ignoring Mundey now. "What's the big man ever going to do with all those dates?"

"The best physic in the kit," Mundey cut in wryly, patting shaving lotion on his face. Somebody gagged a laugh down the line.

As Blake and his ceremonial "entourage" loomed larger, Blake lifted his right arm and clenched fist toward the Africans working around the planes.

"Le jour va être long!" his voice pierced shrilly in the morning air, rising above the poor acoustics of sand and increasingly mounting heat.

The Africans paused in their work and shouted the same words back, showing their right fists in return.

"What'd he say?" Monk asked, for he had not yet had his proper language indoctrination in French.

Shannon spit out toothpaste into the sand by his foot before answering. "He says to them that it will be a long day."

"Every day he says that—just like that? Clenched fist and all?"

25

"The clenched fist happens to be the symbol of Hamaran national purpose," Shannon returned patiently.

"It's the symbol of black power at home too," Monk returned with a sniff. "I mean, man, there ought to be a Christian way of saying the same thing . . . I mean, 'God be with you,' instead of, 'It's going to be a long day'?"

"And maybe the sign of vee for victory instead of the fist, hey, Monk?" Mundey came in again.

"It just happens to be Mr. Blake's way," Shannon insisted.

"Well, maybe, but am I so wrong?"

"No, you are quite right, Monk," and a new voice to Monk had cut in on them then. Augie Thornhill was probably the best physical specimen of any of them, with wavy black hair, intent blue eyes and an athletic build he liked to show off whenever it was possible—like now. But his perfect physique also bred a certain discomfort among the others, as if he had too much of the Adonis in a camp totally lacking the Aphrodite. Or maybe it was that all the rippling mound of muscle, the flashing teeth and beautiful bone torso were a little too rich for the sweaty, dirty, common job of flying this kind of operation. Or maybe it was just that the name Thornhill went with one of the biggest backers—if not the only one—of Operation Shoestring in the States, and sometimes Augie had a way of dropping the word about that. "But there's no Christian way to fly nitroglycerin either, right, Shannon?" And his voice carried certain ingredients of the sardonic, though he kept it coated with that deliberate Christian tonality that was supposed to act as a kind of buffer. "There's no Christian way to fly old airplanes beyond gas loads, or to land blind in the dark either . . . and there's no way to make Blake other than he is . . ."

"That can wait, Augie," Shannon said, not looking at Augie, who stood a few paces away making those muscles jump in his shoulders.

"Yeah, well, I hear the mission is not too happy with the big man there," Monk said, caught up in the wonder of the moment now, moved to more boldness by Augie's blunt interjection.

Nobody responded to Monk. There might have been just a few seconds during which they all, except Augie, seemed to freeze in what they were doing, as if Monk had touched every one of them with a chill. Shannon opened his mouth to say something to that, but then

Blake's voice slashed at them with the same earlier greeting to the Africans, *"Le jour va être long!"*

And all of them—except Augie and Monk, who as yet wasn't sure what to do—lifted their fists into the air and shouted, *"Le jour va être long!"* Their voices mixed in that brief salvo of sound, tearing at the tightly woven fabric of the morning with flourishing stabs, restitching it with the atmosphere of sport.

And then Blake disappeared into the dining Quonset, Joseph taking up a sentinel position at the door and Duka dropping on the lower step, his wooden tray loaded with empty sardine tins staying in perfect balance on his head.

"You see," Mundey said to Monk in that heavy drawl, lifting his voice for Augie's benefit, "maybe we're all a little crazy here for flying the short fuse every day, except maybe for Augie, who doesn't have as long a day as the rest of us because he has the shortest run to Terragona. But it's all in being the fool for Christ's sake, right, Augie?" Augie did not respond. "And anyway, Monk, so you know, that black power salute is God power here, and Blake likes to keep reminding our African mechanics of that so they don't drop a bolt on us when working over our precious airplanes. So, Monk, if you want to stay away from being a martyr before God intended it, you learn to play all this as she lays. Or else you work it like the Reverend Olympic Champion there, full of sound and fury but signifying nothing . . ."

They all tried the laugh on that, and Augie took it with a condescending grin, his blue eyes snapping in the heat as the sand flies dove down for the remnants of Colgate and Mennon Menthol. Then he stuffed the remainder of his toilet goods into his bag and strode stiffly out of the group toward the barracks, the synchrony of his muscles and bones an almost taunting disdain for them, the lesser breed.

"'A just weight and balances are the Lord's,'" Potter said then, breaking the silence, his voice rolling on a lyrical singsong. "'All the weights of the bag are his work.'"

"Augie needs to eat more dates," Peter Letchford added philosophically.

"And you need to gargle with high-test gasoline or you're going to choke on canker sores," Tom Slater put in wryly.

"Knock it off," Shannon said crisply, nipping any more of what could have followed by the others, which would only confuse Monk even more.

"Deutschland Über Alles with Baron Von Mundey!" Joe Bellinger shouted then, and the rest of them picked up the cue and shouted back, "Sig Heil!" And Mundey chased Bellinger to the barracks with a half-filled pan of shaving water, the rest of them following on his heels like a pack of baying dogs.

Only Monk and Shannon were left at the washstand. Monk stood there idly rubbing at his chin with the end of his khaki towel, his eyes following the others as they disappeared into the Quonset barracks. He would ponder it like all the others had when they had first come here, Shannon thought, like he had himself. There were very few signs of a spiritual camp here. The conversation was almost crass, too worldly even. The mixture of German Luftwaffe, laxatives, Proverbs and the strains of the "Colonel Bogey March" were hardly out of the Bible-camp codebook of identification. In time, Monk would find himself too preoccupied with flying the slim percentages here to think much on this non sequitur. That was all Shannon could hope for him—and maybe even pray for him.

"You report to the hangar at 0730 for preflight," he said simply. "You got a half hour for chow."

"Do I go up today?" Monk asked, turning to look at Shannon with some wonder in his eyes, perhaps just a trace of fear cutting over the freckles.

"Mr. Blake has you down for second seat with me the first week," Shannon said and zipped up his toilet bag. He moved on by Monk, heading for the Quonset and then paused a few feet beyond Monk, turning his head back to him but looking at the ground. "You do your job, Monk, and you don't try to figure everything out . . . you concentrate on flying, God will take care of everything else . . . okay?"

"Yes, sir," Monk said, and he cleared his throat nervously, looking a little bewildered yet, so hopelessly fragile standing there, as if he had actually shaved for the first time in his life this morning.

And he continued to stand there, even after Shannon had disappeared into the Quonset. Slowly he began to collect his shaving gear and put them piece by piece into his bag. A sudden gust of wind shot needles of sand spray against his bare, white back, and his eyes went to the parked planes waiting in the sun. He licked his dry lips and cleared his throat again noisily.

Blake's long day was about to begin.


Inside Terragona, at the main anchor hospital base called JERICHO, Dr. Bradford Rayburn had started to scrub up for what had to be a long day of surgical repairs. It was 5:30 A.M. In an hour he would start and go until sometime near ten or eleven o'clock that night. Or when the lights began to dim, which told him the light plant couldn't keep pouring the juice.

The scrub room was a ten-by-ten, airless, hot and almost asphyxiating area. It smelled of antiseptic soap and ammonia and human excrement, the latter taking more powerful control over the former with every passing day. There was something diabolical in the way the hospital seemed to be succumbing to the pressure of the forces that encircled it with longer and longer lines of waiting patients. For every one they took in, five more were there to fill the gap. There was a time—how long ago?—when he felt some accomplishment in that. But lately he began to sense a kind of victimization, as if the Terragona people had laid the trap on him, forcing him now to feel as though his godly benevolence had become overkill. He did not blame anyone for that feeling, certainly not God. But as the logistics became more and more impossible, as five thousand years of Terragona bodily malfunction became his responsibility and the eight-man staff here—plus the sixty-seven others scattered across the island—he found himself more and more marveling how he could have been so shortsighted in his plans.

He turned to the small aluminum sink and twisted the spigot once to get moisture on his hands. ONE HALF TURN EACH TIME ONLY. Rick Collins had put the sign there, warning him that boiled water was not that plentiful. Boiling and filtering the water here seemed to be a longer process, as if the bugs in it resisted to the last ditch.

He caught a glimpse of himself in the cracked mirror over the sink. His face was gaunt, cheekbones pushing up cliffs of bone under the brown eyes. A two-day-old scrub of black beard had begun to show up in dirty lines. His eyes hung out, staring back with a kind of fixed question, as if all of this was an apparition that needed explaining. He shouldn't be looking like that the first thing in the morning! He grunted. Well, where was the medical genius of Mayo's now in that

*29*

face? Where was the son of the great medical missionary pioneer, Doctor Walter Rayburn, in all of that? Where was the mighty pioneer who was going to invade a pagan, uncivilized lost tribe of the Sahara and give them God before Coca-Cola and Esso Oil set up shop? Well, it was one thing to see all of that in the gleaming antiseptics of the operating theater at Mayo's, quite another to see it work here.

"You won't find them coming but maybe ten or so at a time even after six months," the wizards at mission headquarters told him. "Primitives don't trust anyone tampering with the order of things . . ." He rubbed his hands with creamy soap that felt gritty with flecks of sand. Primitives were no different from the civilized when it came to having pain removed or adding a few years to life. One case of healing had spread the word fast—"yellow-bird magic" was too big to pass, and within a month they were lined up fifty and sixty, waiting to get in.

It was those growing lines of people that had given him the look of a man twice his thirty-four years. His staff was already reduced to walking zombies, to say nothing of himself. None of them had slept a full night in three months. They tried shifts, but sporadic emergencies in the wards brought them running like human swabbing gauze to stem the precious flow of life pouring out of bodies heaving against the strange and terrifying postoperative recuperation. Some of them ran from their beds and into the bush, tearing at bandages, moaning frightful sounds of terror at the unfamiliar pain, sometimes dragging their IV tubes that fluttered hopelessly like broken mooring lines, breaking open stitches and pouring a bloody trail all the way.

Well, it was a miracle nobody had died inside the hospital bases yet, thanks to the steady supplies of antibiotics that were flown in here every day. If anybody did die outside the hospital, they did it according to Terragona culture—crawl quietly into the jungle and wait for the hyenas. But Rayburn was worried now. Sooner or later an epidemic had to hit here. Crowded wards with people sitting in their own waste was bound to catch up with them sooner or later. And what then? If they started dying on him in droves—what then? What would that do to the good will the Terragonans extended to them all this time? Now he wished he had taken more time, given Terragona more study. But they told him at mission headquarters that "today was the day of salvation" for the Terragonans. Anyway, he had never been taught that he should wait for the more opportune

time in giving the Gospel to a people. The spiritual heroes of his
youth had barreled straight into hostile territory convinced only that
it was of God, and let the devil be damned!

Maybe only time would tell now. He glanced up at the crude cardboard sign over the mirror, done in clumsy grease pencil:

> IF YOU CAN'T THINK, MEDITATE
> IF YOU CAN'T DO IT, DELEGATE
> IF YOU DON'T KNOW, SPECULATE

It was put there by Alicia Davenport sometime ago, intended to
be humorous. Now it appeared snide, a symptom of the overlay of
the caustic that had crept into the work. Once he had laughed at
it, now it was becoming a bad joke as everything seemed to be running
cross-grain to his professional and spiritual balance.

"You're wanted in plot," he heard the voice come to him from
what seemed to be an echo chamber, thumping into his foggy senses,
which had begun to slide into the web of sleep even as he stood there.

He looked up at Alicia standing in the doorway, filling it with her
heavy form, a piece of white bedsheet wrapped around her head and
a white, blood-stained smock around her broad torso. He avoided
looking at her when she had that on—it violated his sense of medical
perfection, even though he knew it was impossible to strive for that
in this place.

He continued to lean on his hands, his head turned toward her,
but keeping his eyes on the floor. He glanced down at his hands,
still slick with the white cream. "Who?" he asked, his voice dragging
with weariness, and the day hadn't officially started yet!

"Trask and Collins, who else?" she returned, leaning her left shoulder against the doorjamb, folding her arms into a two-log fence of
flesh across her middle, watching him intently now, as everybody did
lately, to see if there were signs that he might be rethinking all of
this and maybe try some better plan. She was a big girl who had
worn her weight gracefully once back at mission headquarters in
Hamara. But now that weight had been almost cruelly stripped from
her, too quickly, leaving sagging pockets in her cheeks that pulled
on the soft tissue around her mouth, cutting away the humor that
used to be there. She was a good nurse, good in surgery, good always
with the quip to keep up morale. But lately her humor had gone

*31*

dry, almost sardonic, as she fought the endless days and nights that melted into a timeless block of painful movement.

"What's up?" he asked, straightening from the sink and reaching for a towel to wipe off his hands.

"At the expense of sounding bellicose, nothing is up," she returned tartly. "Except maybe your morning surgery . . ."

"While we are on the subject," he said, controlling himself now from sounding irritable, "you had better make sure how and where you mark the big X on those patients coming into surgery . . . I almost did a prostatectomy on that old man yesterday when it should have been a gall bladder. Good thing I looked at the workup to be sure. Even where we're running over each other, they don't deserve that kind of subtraction—"

"We got sixteen words—sixteen—in the Terragona language by which to diagnose and prognose," she came back mildly enough, but he detected the note of defensiveness. He moved on by her, smelling the antiseptic alcohol on her.

"Just don't run anybody in unless you are sure, okay?" he said to her, trying a smile to neutralize her before the subject got out of hand.

"My, aren't we off to a polite day?" she quipped as he turned to move on down past the wards, the twenty-two five-bedders that pounded out the smells and sounds of what was almost a near-chaotic atmosphere. He stepped over the tangle of black legs of the people sitting on the floor in the corridor, the big red numbers hanging around their necks indicating their position in the lineup for presurgical workup. Children. Children watching him with wonder and awe, like people everywhere viewed doctors, as if he were some giant Gulliver dropped out of nowhere to work the miracles of life. He felt Alicia's swaying movements behind him, close to his left ear, as if she wanted to say something privately to him, like, "Don't you think we ought to take another look at the instructions to make sure we put it all together right?" She had picked up a lot of Rick Collins' "cracks" lately, and he wasn't sure he appreciated it.

He pushed open the door to Trask's lab and walked in. Trask and Collins stood by the small light-table in the center of the small room. It smelled of chemistry, mold and coffee grounds. Rubber hose and test tubes filled one wall in careless disarray. Trask was not noted for his organization, and this place hardly called for it, even though

Rayburn wished for it. It was hot in the room. The one small window covered with a thin muslin screen to keep out the bugs also kept out what breeze there was. Even at eight thousand feet up, it was hot this time of year just before the rains.

"You got something, Trask?" he began immediately, because the first surgery case was probably waiting.

For a minute Trask didn't say anything, just frowned down at the glass table top in front of him as if he suspected its structure and utility. The pause was almost embarrassing, as if Trask was being asked to produce something new in a situation where nothing was really new any more. Rayburn realized that they hadn't had a conference together in a long time either. There wasn't time really, not even to pray together. They did that on the fly too. He sensed acutely at that moment that this wasn't exactly what he had promised them back at Talfungo—so long ago was it?—when they had planned this venture. They had come in here full of zap and pioneer spirit, led by his own great vision "to put God into an uncivilized territory before technology." It sounded good then. Had it gone flat since? They had jumped in here with only those sixteen words in the language that the U.N. translators had broken down from the first tape Blake had gotten when he came in here a year ago. And yet they had felt the wonder of it all, touching human malfunction never before probed and seeing the gradual opening of lives responding to their touch.

But now, though they kept recharging themselves daily as best they could, they were becoming less genteel. Their medical approach was simply a straight-on charge into the endless array of abuse and impairment. And with that, of course, had come the crusty attitude of resignation to the routine—and Rayburn felt bad now that he had not taken the time to talk more with them, encourage them, help them to keep it all in godly perspective.

"I think I've got something, yes," Trask finally said, clearing his throat in that scraping sound. "Those three cases of what looked like virus infection?" and his voice went clinical as if he was reading it straight out of a science or medical journal. "Well, they're getting away from us. Deterioration seems to be increasing rapidly . . ."

Trask looked up at Rayburn as if he expected the alarm to be sounded. Deterioration? Rayburn almost laughed. They lived with that constantly! And yet he knew too that Trask had to have something that was bothering him. And though he played it low key, that

*33*

was Trask, master of the obvious, extoller of the understatement. Doctor Milford Trask. Age forty-one. A bone man in Chicago and a good one. But in the last five years with the United for Life Mission in Hamara he had switched over to tropical and desert virology. And he had come up with a few things that had impressed the World Health people. His job here was to run blood samples and record the bugs that showed up, then find ways to treat them. He was a tall, thin man with a pointed nose jutting out from craggy eyebrows that grew undisciplined clumps of black hair, which looked like a continuation of his hairline an inch or so above. It gave him the appearance of wearing an eyeshade all the time. His eyes were blackish-blue, almost lost in the slanted lids, as if he were looking out through two narrow cracks in a fence.

"What does blood show?" Rayburn asked patiently, never liking Trask's way of dragging out the drama of his discoveries, and yet respecting the man for his thoroughness.

"I've got something of a bacterial strain in it . . . but I can't be sure . . ."

"Have you been matching?"

"For two days, yes . . . so far I've ruled out most of it . . ."

"Like eighty possible cruds known in tropical-desert bacteria, everything from gout to enlargement of the left nostril," Collins broke in with his usual droll commentary. Collins was not a doctor. He was a civil engineer. His responsibility was maintenance, power and water, and supply. He had run a motor pool in Talfungo besides supervising building. He was going on thirty-eight. He was a short man with a small face the size of a grapefruit on which was squeezed the necessary senses—a small nose and blue eyes the size of peas tucked into eye sockets no bigger than a dime. His mouth was a thin line of afterthought. His ears were too big for his face, hanging out from the sides of his head like two big shutters sagging on bent hinges. His thinning, brownish hair was cut short and close to the head, emphasizing the ears even more. Collins saw everything as a point of humor. But most of the time his attempts at jokes came out corny, sometimes in bad taste, but nobody complained. Trask had pressed him into his lab recently to help classify blood samples.

"Symptoms, then?" Rayburn went on with Trask, ignoring Collins.

"Well . . . not always constant. Sometimes there appears to be rigidity of muscle tone, some sweating—"

"Fever?"

"Up and down . . ."

Rayburn waited for Trask to go on. When he didn't, he said, "So far you could have any number of possibilities. What's the deterioration pattern?"

"Well, there's this," and Trask flipped on the battery-powered light under the glass top of the table and set down an X-ray picture. The outline of a skull showed up and the shape of the brain within in ghostly white relief.

"This is the cranial structure of that boy of twelve brought in yesterday," Trask explained in his unhurried, almost monotone voice.

Rayburn bent down to look at it closely. "Looks normal."

Trask put another picture down alongside it. "Same boy this morning." Again Rayburn peered closely at the negative, compared the two, Alicia doing the same, strands of her hair tickling his left cheek.

"So you've got enlargement of the brain tissue. Is it brain or cranial structure?"

"Brain."

"So if there is such a thing as blowing your top literally, doctors," Collins offered, "this is the closest thing to it, right?" And Collins looked at both Trask and Rayburn hopefully that they might enter into his quip.

Rayburn did not respond to him. He looked back at Trask. There was nothing in those slanted eyes that he could detect except maybe a professional smugness in his having found something nobody else knew about.

Rayburn was getting impatient. "Swelling localized, then?"

"Doesn't seem to be."

"Spinal fluid shows what?"

"Clear in appearance, sugar stays normal, polymorphs and lymphs increasing slightly . . ."

"You've ruled out meningitis or encephalitis?"

"I can't pick up that strain in the blood . . ."

"Blood count, then?"

"Well, that's funny too . . . I get a reading showing low on the white cells, then I get normal counts . . . It keeps changing . . ."

"Is the brain syndrome acute or chronic?"

"Acute."

"Hallucinatory?"

35

"There's that at times, yes. Also definite signs of emerging paranoia, beginning to border on violence . . ."

"What have you tried for treatment?"

"All the antibiotics I have . . ."

"And?"

Trask shrugged. "Nothing is grabbing yet . . ."

"What about this paranoid syndrome?"

"Well . . . the old man back there tried to get me with a bedpan last night . . . the boy went after Sylvia Pratt yesterday . . . that woman who came in last night is already straining at the straps . . ."

"We can expect some of that in brain inflammation."

"There is something definitely different about this," Trask countered mildly.

Rayburn looked at Trask, willing him to hurry it. "What?"

"There is evidence of personality shift . . ."

"Yes . . . you said there was hallucinatory—"

"No, I mean a schizoid emergence almost . . ."

"High fever can do that . . ."

"The fever is not that high . . ."

"Well, is it schizoid then or not?"

Trask frowned at the two negatives on the glass table. "The boy has been in here about thirty-six hours. He has had three hours now of normalcy or even arrest. He appears to have an identity problem. His mother is here, and she seems agitated that the boy does not respond to her, as if he doesn't recognize who she is . . ."

"You can't be saying a new personality, a new *person* is coming out, Trask," Alicia came in, with a dry, skeptical tone.

Trask shrugged.

"You must have a tumor in the frontal lobe," Rayburn tried again.

"I suspected that, but more in the anterior portion of the cerebral hemisphere . . . but nothing shows," Trask returned with a sniff. "I must have shot twenty plates on the boy and the man . . ."

Rayburn straightened from his study of the negatives and licked his dry lips with the point of his tongue. For the first time since he had come here he was conscious of an overwhelming sense of humility. It was as if Trask's discovery bordered on the cosmological, as if they had a photograph of God in front of them. Or maybe it was the first solid hint of a major unknown quantity here that could, as Trask was intimating, run amuck even.

"How does this—this personality shift or whatever manifest itself?"

"Strong psychopathic syndrome."

Trask's statement came out as ex cathedra. Rayburn could usually talk Trask out of exaggerated diagnosis, but when he put it that simply and finally, it was a point he was not going to let go of easily. Rayburn had learned to respect him when he took on that mood.

"No bacteria behaves like that—not that we know of, at least," he admitted with a sigh.

"So it has to be a neoplasm certainly," Alicia insisted, looking up at Trask, almost demanding admission.

"So three patients come in here at just about the same time with the same symptoms, so they each have tumors in the same place bringing about the exact behavior syndrome?" Trask put it back to her.

"Has Barth taken in any similar cases at his base?" Rayburn asked.

"He's got five with the same," Collins came in. Collins took all the radio calls from the other eight bases in Terragona.

"So tumors aren't contagious," Alicia put in, almost lightly, refusing yet to come up to the serious tones that Trask was building here.

"So we come back to what kind of bacteria produces this weird set of symptoms," Trask said.

"What you're saying to me, Trask," Rayburn picked it up impatiently, though trying not to sound testy, "is that we have a bacteria strain so far unknown in our listings that, the way you put it, has the ability to play with the brain?"

"I didn't say it like that—"

"Well?"

"But, yes, it's close enough to that . . ."

"It's crazy," Alicia put it bluntly, raising her elbows off the glass top of the table. "Get the fever down, relieve the cranial pressure and you'll find all this—this personality shift or whatever—is the same dementia that goes with meningitis or even malaria. There's one that could be it, malaria . . ."

Trask folded his arms and did not look at her. Rayburn knew, of course, that Trask would have run that on the slide first thing. Alicia should have known too. But then, Alicia was never quick to bow to Trask as a bona fide medical practitioner here but merely a "blood man." To her, anyone who would leave a practice in orthopedics and take on morphology and pathology had to step a long way down from his calling. Besides, Alicia had "a thing" about Trask

—as much as she maintained her Christian sense of relationship and avoided any serious altercations with Trask, the two of them usually locked horns five minutes after being in the same room.

They said nothing to each other, respecting the lines they had drawn. Down the hall the sound of someone's voice began chopping away at the language, trying to communicate to a patient in that sixteen-word lexicon, sounding as if she were driving a fence post into the ground.

"You'll need to get a blood sample out to World Health in Talfungo," Rayburn said, rubbing at the back of his neck with his right hand, trying to ease the growing ache there. "Any idea of incubation?"

"None. I don't know if I got these patients in the terminal stages, the beginning or the middle. And I can't tell how virile it is either . . . so far nobody else has caught it in here, but that doesn't prove anything."

"Have you isolated the patients?"

"I have to clean out that back room—"

"Which means I have no place for the diesel oil," Collins objected. "Speaking of that, you know we are running low—"

"Do you have any idea if this sickness is tied to any specific location?" Rayburn cut in, wiping at a sticky patch of sweat building on his forehead. It was getting hotter in the room as the glare of the bulb under the glass seemed to drill up into their faces.

"Lake Caha is what I get," Trask returned conclusively.

"How are you so sure?"

"I worked a whole day on those three people back there to get that information," Trask came back. "All three are from the Lake Caha district . . . and Barth's five are as well."

"Where is this—this Lake Caha?"

"About seven or eight miles north of us."

Rayburn looked at the rough map of Terragona beyond Trask's head on the wall behind him, the blue pins showing up the other mission hospital bases strung out across the long, thin, tubelike contour of the territory. Trask turned and jabbed his stubby right forefinger on the faint spot north of their position. The map was rustically drawn with oil paint on a piece of plasterboard. It was a duplicate of what the U.N. team had been able to put down from air reconnaissance, but it was close enough to be accurate.

"What do you know about Caha? Anything?" Rayburn went on

with this reluctantly, almost afraid to keep on unraveling this layer by layer for what it might reveal.

"Our illustrious chief, Turgobyne, has his royal country palace grounds there," Alicia put in quickly, leaning her elbows back on the glass table top again. "And as we know, gentlemen, Lake Caha is the imperial watercourse, the home of the big Terragona god, Caha, great god of iron. Turgobyne is said to draw all his powers from that lake."

"All he'd draw now is a lame brain," Collins tried, grinning impishly, almost uncertainly, at each of them. Trask shot him a warning glance so that Collins took to scratching his head in some embarrassment. Then he added, "That's enough light, doctors," and he switched off the power under the glass. "If anyone's interested, we are low on battery power as well as diesel—"

"You think maybe that lake is polluted, Trask?" Rayburn went on.

"How come all of a sudden?"

"So maybe it isn't all of a sudden . . . do they wash in it, bathe in it, dump their waste in it?"

"As they have for a few thousand years, I expect."

"So why are they all of a sudden starting to get sick on it?" Alicia asked.

"We can't be sure the lake is causing it anyway," Rayburn added. "And even so, they could have been contracting this thing for a few hundred years—"

"I don't think so," Trask contradicted. "Not with that psychopathic syndrome. They'd have killed each other a long time ago—they would have become extinct a long time ago . . ."

Rayburn stared back at Trask a long minute, still not willing to rise to the enormity of that. Alicia was looking up at him intently now too. Only Collins appeared mystified by it all.

"So what are they possibly doing to pollute the lake then, Trask?" Rayburn went on. "Or—if it's bacteria, then it has to be something natural to the lake, something that has found a conducive bed to grow in—"

"Not necessarily," Trask replied simply. "Bacteria could have entered from external sources and found the lake conducive to growth—"

"Well, those Hamaran prospectors have been blasting around up there lately, you knew that?" Collins came in with his first relevant contribution. When Rayburn turned to him questioningly, Collins went on eagerly, "I get it from those two Hamaran guys who come in here every day to pick up the nitro from our reefer boxes with that eyedropper of theirs and insulated test tubes."

"What about them?" Rayburn prodded.

"Well, they say Turgobyne told them that if they expected to find riches in the earth, they should try blowing a few holes around Caha where the ancestral spirits would show them—"

"So even our Hamaran oilmen can use the Terragona dictionary too?" Rayburn said offhandedly.

"They're sharp on the draw," Collins insisted.

"Well, their blasting wouldn't start a bacteria culture," Rayburn argued. "How many people live around that lake, Trask?"

"The U.N. air reconnaissance figured about four hundred or so," Trask said, seeming to rise on the balls of his feet now as he held forth on the anthropology of Terragona, a subject second only to virology and pathology. What "anthropology" was known on Terragona was small, but Trask had what there was. "I don't know how reliable that study is, but the U.N. people say that when Turgobyne is in residence up there, the people crowd into the main village round the imperial grounds. When he's not in residence, they are scattered around the area tending their farms. It seems those people are selected priests to be wards of the lake, nourish it, protect it and sacrifice to it regularly."

"Word I get is that Turgobyne is in residence now," Collins jumped in again. "Those two Hamaran prospectors mentioned it yesterday. So how come he's in residence?"

"He's not supposed to go there until the rains, when the ceremony with Caha is supposed to begin, a plea for good rains and rich crops," Alicia chimed in and looked up at Trask as if to say she, too, could play at the anthropology bit. "Right, Trask?"

Trask only sniffed and said nothing. "Maybe old Turgobyne knows something," Collins cut in lightly, sensing the atmosphere getting tighter in the room. "Like maybe the bottom's falling out of the Terragona stock market—or better yet, maybe he figures a gusher is about to come into his living room?"

"If that lake is actually corrupted," Rayburn said, "we'll have to tell Turgobyne to keep his people out of it."

"That won't help Turgobyne any," Trask countered. "You just don't tell him that his people can't use it, a sacred watercourse, on the fact of our insistence of its being corrupt. He'll just blame us for bringing the corruption in with us—"

"A point maybe we should consider," Alicia put in.

"Anyway, Turgobyne probably has all he can to convince his own inner circle that all we are doing is good for them," Trask went on.

"An oil well under every hut shouldn't be hard to take," Alicia said dryly.

"Yeah, but what are they going to do with oil when they do get it?" Collins jumped in, a tone of incredulity in his voice. "Bottle it? Can it? Or how about uranium or tin? Especially when it means having their land knocked apart to get it? Those prospectors, may I remind you all, are blowing tops off mountains, changing watercourses and blasting holes all over the place."

"I don't see what that has to do with us," Alicia put in with some impatience.

"Well, we carry both nitro and medicine," Collins came back.

"The Terragonans surely know the difference as to who has what by now—"

"Why should they?" Trask broke in, his voice going a shade sharper in tone.

Alicia glanced at him quickly. "Because they get healing and love and—"

"And a drastic change in their birth rate, did you think of that?"

"Not particularly, *Doctor* Trask," and Alicia's cheeks had taken on a fresh spurt of red, showing up in sharp contrast to the waxy paleness of her skin. "Because, in case it slipped your mind, that's why we came in here, remember?"

"All I'm saying is that from Turgobyne's point of view, it looks a lot different—"

"So since when did any missionary effort not have some effect on the culture, the people, even the life expectancy? We're here because we know the Gospel cuts clean across those factors, at least I *trust* you have that clear in your mind, Trask?"

"Okay, okay," Rayburn cut in, sensing now that the two of them were heading for the usual collision again. "Let's not get into matters that are peripheral." He glanced once at Trask, knowing how testy he was on all the political, cultural balances of Terragona. Trask, whenever he had the opportunity, held forth on the subject, almost as if, as Alicia suggested, he actually questioned now the basis of Christianity here. "Anyway, to keep Turgobyne's hand strong, we have to keep people alive in here. We can't afford any kind of epidemic. Maybe Turgobyne holds together, as we hold together . . . and on that we hold this beachhead . . ."

"Thank you, General MacArthur," Alicia chipped in lightly, wanting to dissipate the tension she had built with Trask.

"You better get that blood sample out on the flight later today," Rayburn said to Trask.

"I'd like to hold it until I can test some more and cross-match it with a water sample out of Caha . . ."

"I don't want to delay this, Trask," Rayburn urged, but he sensed that maybe Trask didn't want to admit he didn't know what the bacteria strain was as yet. Trask had his peculiar sense of pride in these things too.

"World Health won't crack it that fast anyway," Trask came back. Rayburn decided not to push it further.

"What about the people getting sick around Caha right now?" Alicia asked. "Can we do anything?"

"We are not allowed a hundred yards off this perimeter, you know that," Rayburn replied.

"How about flying out the critical cases if they keep sliding?"

"Until we know the contagion factor for sure, we better hold them. Besides, could anybody on the outside do better right now?"

"So when do we decide to go outside for help, then?" Alicia persisted. Rayburn hesitated. This was the crux of the matter now. They knew his intent was to hold this ground for Christianity before anybody else moved in. She had to know too that if they opened the door to outside emergency health teams, it would offer excuse for a lot of other interests to come pouring in with their own justifications. And that meant the territory could go up for grabs, which could mean defenseless Terragonans fighting and dying to hold what they had. But Rayburn wasn't sure if Alicia, or the others, actually felt the same protectiveness for Terragona as he did, especially if the issue came right down to that. Was he even sure himself?

"We're trying to hold the gate here, Alicia," he began.

"As far as I'm concerned," she came back tartly then, "when we let those Hamaran prospectors come in here with that nitro, we pretty well opened the door for other interests anyway . . . right?"

She was right, of course, but he didn't want to admit the anomaly of that yet.

"We'll wait and see how things go," he said then. "We don't have an epidemic yet. Nobody has died yet in here. And it could be we could find an answer to this thing, or even World Health in Talfungo might . . . once we know what we got, we can start working at it . . ."

"Can we increase the number of flights and that way build up additional medical supplies?" Trask asked. "I smell rain in the air, and once they start coming, our airlift won't be operational any more . . ."

"Or cut the nitro loads?" Collins came in. "You know our cooling reefers can't take much more of that stuff stacking up. We got a four-cylinder light plant bending the wires to keep those reefers down on the temperature line so that nitro won't get testy. We're going to wind up cutting our own supplies . . . or worse, if we lose power and those iceboxes start running up the heat—"

"I have no authority for either of those requests," Rayburn said, and he put that to all of them, because he knew they had been talking about the possibilities.

Alicia looked at him steadily as if she wanted to comment, maybe to tell him he'd better make it his authority, like many other areas as well.

"Looks like it's up to Blake then," Collins said. When nobody rose to that, he went on, "And the way Augie, our noble flyer, talks lately, Blake won't get his green stamps much longer."

"What's that supposed to mean?" Rayburn prodded impatiently.

"Well, Augie says the mission doesn't like the way Blake is running things in Durungu—"

"You mean *Augie* doesn't, don't you, Rick?" Alicia came in dourly again. "He's been uptight about his flying for some time now. Not that he doesn't have a right, flying that nitro in here—"

"You got to figure Blake is some kind of Vince Lombardi to get them up every day to do that," Collins came back almost in some awe.

"Every man is expendable, Rick, dear," Alicia returned almost sardonically. "The field manual is explicit on that. Anyway, someone

43

should tell Blake to visit the prayer chapel more often, get the grease off his hands, and put on a clean set of underwear . . ."

"Blake's a war jockey, not a preacher," Collins insisted, sounding now like it was very important that they all had it straight about Blake. "He doesn't wear his faith on his sleeve or carry one of those nice red Bibles." Again nobody responded and he added, "Anyway, if they pull Blake, they might as well pull our credit cards . . ."

"Don't deify him, Rick," Alicia came back as she worked over her hair, the words chopped through the hairpin in her mouth. "Anyway, if Blake wants to get the field office off his back he can stop running that VW car over here piece by piece on Augie's plane. Augie says it takes up valuable cargo space. And what's Turgobyne going to do with a VW even if you do succeed in getting it all together finally?"

"Well, figure it this way, we can say we beat Hertz—"

"Get serious, Rick!" Alicia scolded, her face going into a pattern of cracks like something had blown up underneath. It was unusual for her to show such testiness.

"Quit worrying about what you can't do anything about," Rayburn soothed, wanting to cut this off right away.

"But I mean, it's ridiculous," Alicia came back with a short laugh of disdain, finally sticking the bobbing pin into a jumble of loosely stacked hair on the top of her head. "All that chief saw was a picture of a VW on the back of a Johnson and Johnson surgical carton and he decides he wants it? We haven't got a Bible in his language yet, but we got time to put a car together for him, and with no roads at all!"

"Maybe he'll live in it," Rayburn replied, seriously, and Collins laughed, but Alicia simply stood there looking at him unamused while Trask continued to frown at the glass table, maybe wondering why he and his discoveries weren't taken more seriously. "Blake once said the car could be an ace in the hole—"

"Power symbol," Trask put in quickly.

"My eye!" Alicia said with a snort.

Again there was silence, awkward, uncertain, building up a roadblock to easy solution. Someone down the hall was calling for Rayburn now, someone from surgery undoubtedly, but he did not move. He wanted to be sure it was tied up here reasonably enough for them.

"Which reminds me," Alicia came on again, "don't you think it's time we started seriously trying to get God into their vocabulary? I mean—"

"How do you get the Atonement across in sixteen words?" Trask asked bluntly then.

"Well, I don't seem to have too much trouble getting them to use a bedpan with those same words—"

"Pardon me," Collins interjected, "but judging from the evidence at hand, I don't see that you've communicated that very well either . . ."

"They're learning," Alicia snapped with a frown. "They're learning our songs too, if that monotone hum is singing . . ."

"Do what you can," Rayburn said simply, giving her a smile of assurance, his mind still occupied by the encroachments of Trask's bacteria problem.

The conversation then seemed to have fallen into a hole abruptly. They all seemed to be waiting, wanting something more from Rayburn, the appointed leader, something to buck them up or maybe nothing more than some word that would indicate he knew where it was all going.

But he was no drum beater. He was a surgeon, period. He had no necessary charisma going for him. He had been chosen to be the wedge into Terragona on the basis of his surgical skills and his dream of putting Christianity first into an uncivilized, pagan territory.

He thought of Blake then. He wasn't too sure that the oddly shaped dimension of him could be what they needed either. And yet maybe there was in those confusing dimensions of the man some element of "Messianic" promise. If the foothold they held here in Terragona was going to be seriously threatened, it was maybe logical to look to Blake for the bold move. He knew Turgobyne better than any of the rest of them. And there was no question that he alone kept his planes and pilots in the air by the combinations of his own peculiar leadership chemistry.

Rayburn felt he knew him and yet he didn't. He remembered him from months ago when they had first come in here, as a roughly hewn piece of human texture who carried no really recognizable spiritual images. He was crass, mundane, and at times profane. And yet with his forearms smeared with grease and careless dabs of it on his face, it seemed only right perhaps that he come off in that misfit image.

And yet Rayburn sensed too that it was that image which could very well add to the growing resistance to him in Talfungo.

And Rayburn knew, as the others did, that Blake was not going to be carved down to any proportion that would fit the dimensions of this spiritual order, at least not yet. It was almost as if he fought the mold deliberately, pushing off anybody's attempts to give him all the credence necessary to keep him out of trouble with his superiors. He had come into the mission, as the story went, only six months old as a Christian, too young in the faith to know what was expected of him in a tightly knit community of the faithful. Instead of theology and vespers then, he nagged his pilots, berated them for mistakes and forced them to be perfectionist pilots while putting the habits of prayer and church into the background. And yet to Rayburn, there was something wildly beautiful about Blake in a way, like an animal running free, jumping clear of the ropes that shot out to hold him down. And as Rayburn thought about him in that image, he was tempted to pray that Blake would not yield any of it. It was perhaps selfish of him, for he knew it was that kind of spirit that had to play some kind of significant role in the ultimate bent of history here in Terragona. That free spirit maybe would have to remain free, smeared with grease instead of holy oil, if this operation with so little margin of survival was going to stay alive at all.

So now he looked at them, as they waited, not sure themselves why they waited. "Let's pray," he said. And they held hands as was their custom when they prayed. It was a long time since they had done that. Back in Talfungo maybe? And now as he felt the slim, bony twigs of Collins' fingers and the pudgy, moist twitching stubs of Alicia's, he sensed that strange feeling of spiritual wedlock again— the sense of the merging of body and spirit, the kind the people of God had, the world over, when locked in mutual suffering. People who put their feeble energies and wills on the block for whatever good they could do for mankind in the name of God. Uncertain as they were, tired as they were, a little afraid now as they were—maybe more than they would ever admit to each other, because Trask had laid out an awesome dimension here—for this brief moment they grabbed on to the poor negotiables of flesh and blood and the hope of what God could do with flimsy elements who had zeal perhaps at the expense of good judgment.

And Doctor Bradford Rayburn prayed that that thin stream of

corporate hope called Blake would not faint either, although he wasn't sure what Blake could do. And meanwhile, God, help this little band here, and those other little bands across Terragona linking hands and hearts in their own way this day, for it seemed to be getting darker in Terragona.

# CHAPTER II

Blake always ate his breakfast in the small dining room before the other pilots came in, mostly because there wasn't room to crowd everybody into the small ten-by-twelve cubicle. His breakfast was always the same—black coffee, a piece of dry toast with a dab of marmalade. Only Rudy the Jew was with him today, since Emily had left earlier that morning. The threesome gathering on other mornings had always been pleasant until the last few weeks when Emily began to show a brittle edge to her conversation, a sign that she was losing control in her inability to draw from Blake what she had come to assume.

Rudy told Blake about Emily's leaving without wanting any good-byes. Blake sipped his coffee, his face set in that mask of empty objectivity under the bill of his black baseball cap.

"She was a good kid," Rudy tried, chewing on his gum slowly and sipping at his coffee, his cap pushed back on his crewcut showing a sweat-soaked scrub of blackish-brown hair that had streaks of white icing in it. He had removed his sunglasses, and his large hazel eyes that told too much of what he felt were bloodshot from the dust and not enough sleep. He spent a lot of time at night in the hangars with Blake, stitching together what parts they could to keep the planes up to operational standards.

"Talfungo will be good for her," Blake finally said, as though he had been thinking about that for a while, although his voice sounded flat, almost disinterested.

"Exhale with joy," Rudy said then, after taking a long breath and letting it out with a rush, the smell of his spearmint gum giving the atmosphere the ingredients of contradiction.

48

"Inhale with a cough," Blake responded tonelessly into his coffee. "It must be twelve hundred grains of sand to the cubic inch out there this morning."

"Make a joyful noise," Rudy countered, almost as if this was a game each man played to checkmate the other.

Blake paused, the corners of his wide mouth twitching just a little, the only indication of a smile, reaching for another piece of toast on the plate in front of him. "Start engines," and he reached out with his knife to put a dab of marmalade on the toast.

Rudy leaned his chair back against the wall, his arms folded across his leather jacket, his grin one of athletic success spreading out to emphasize the swollen nose and chin. "We have now entered holy ground," he chirped, "and may the Lord be pleased to smile on us this day."

It was a strange but regular liturgy both men practiced with each other, but it was the embodiment of what they had learned in the two years of fighting the hopelessly thin margins here. The sweat, anxieties and tragedies they would gloss over with deliberate attempts at ebullience, because neither of them could afford to allow the mastery of those elements.

But it was always short-lived. Blake was open enough to talk, never uncivil, but there was never much of it. Not in this setting. He was at his best with the African mechanics or with the pilots in briefing; but here, even with Emily, it was as if he had been defused, as if his mental circuits had shut down and would never come to life again until he was out on the tarmac with what Emily called "his machines of war."

Rudy had never carried on any lengthy light talk with Blake since he had joined him here two years ago to prospect for a landing site for Operation Shoestring. He had been flying missionaries five years for United down south, carrying them from one lonely outpost to another, a task he found considerably boring after a while. His assignment to Shoestring he considered the biggest break in his life and yet the biggest enigma too. For four months the only conversation he could get from Blake centered on the field, equipment and logistics. Rudy, normally gregarious and having become accustomed to a Christian culture after fourteen years in it, where talk was owned as some kind of spiritual virtue, would do his best to sound out Blake on spiritual matters or even aviation. Blake, in all that time, had said nothing about spiritual things, though at times it seemed he listened carefully as Rudy spoke about God and Christ as if they were all close relatives. Only once did Blake confess that he had flown military jets in Korea, and when Rudy had said he himself had flown recon planes for the Army there, he was sure that would be a bridge where he and Blake could meet. But Blake let it drop, refusing to rise to any of Rudy's prodding.

Rudy learned to accommodate himself to the taciturnity of Blake, and Blake in turn had come to adapt himself to Rudy's eternal optimism and childlike faith in God. Both men had come to respect each other for what each could add to the other's deficiencies. To Rudy, Blake was like an old tree on a hill which no longer leaned with the wind but stood against it and yet never producing the same kind of fruit for the seasons. His spiritual life never came out in definitions of any kind, and yet strokes of compassion would appear, like with Jacob or that little orphan, Duka. He would ream out a pilot for sloppy turns, like Mundey, and yet would go to great lengths to hunt for fresh meat in the Durungu market so that they would all have something to look forward to at dinner every night. At the same time, Blake would sometimes look at Rudy in open wonder as if he could not comprehend how Rudy could float so much light bantering talk about God and life in general on the crest of that odorous spearmint gum even when conditions defied it.

But this is what had kept both men in balance these two years. They had mingled their sweat in building and shaping this airfield from what was considered to be an engineering impossibility. They had buried three pilots on the three-hundred-foot pyramid of sand at the far northern end of the runway with its crown of misplaced scrub of thorn and acacia trees the pilots had labeled "cotton hair"; they had learned to sweat every pound of weight in the airplanes, the precariousness of nitro in uncertain temperatures and the constantly changing conditions of the fields in Terragona that seemed to deteriorate every day. They lived with the dust and wind, the shortage of parts and supplies—the latter imposed on them by the austerity of the mission who seemed to believe that God worked best in poverty though they did their best. Neither of them knew each other as they ought to, but neither of them made an issue of it.

"You know Augie won't fly today," Rudy said then, plopping his chair back down with a thud and reaching for his cup on the table in front of him.

Blake waited a few seconds, then said, "What chapter and verse this time? Or is it the migraine again?"

"He's gone cold, skipper," Rudy returned, and he smiled as if he was offering a bouquet of roses to Blake, his chipped front tooth a broken font of type in an otherwise perfect line. "You know Augie, he kind of figures he's got the edge on the rest of us when it comes to certain revelations. Now me, I'm too dumb to know better—all I remember is the books of the Bible, what happened at the Council of Trent—"

"Is his plane loaded?" Blake cut in.

"Well," and Rudy sighed, "you know that they always load Augie's first, then mine—"

"Then it's too late," Blake said with finality, like he'd just clipped a hair out of his nose. "We won't have time to off-load that nitro before the temperature line gets too high . . . how about that kid, what's his name, who came in as replacement a couple days ago?"

"Monk?" Rudy said, rolling the gum around in his mouth, savoring it. "I've had maybe an hour only to brief him on the operation. He needs at least a week in second seat with Shannon. He's got a total of a hundred and fifty hours solo—"

"He'll do," Blake said, and he shouted to Ebenezer, the Fulani cook in back, "Ebenezer! Coffee!" Ebenezer, a heavy, jovial African, came out with the blackened percolator. *"Comment von votre femme et familee?"* Blake said to him, and Ebenezer opened a toothy white smile as if he'd been offered the premiership of Hamara.

*"Oui, très bien, merci!"*

"Your French isn't much better after all this time?" Rudy said lightly, holding his cup out for Ebenezer to pour into. "I don't think you should fly Monk, skipper."

"I told you we have no choice."

"He could get wiped out on takeoff—"

"So could the rest of you."

"Sure, but—"

"Have you seen this?" and Blake took out a folded sheet and dropped it flat in front of Rudy. Rudy picked it up. "That's the thirty-day diagnostic report of our nine hospital bases in Terragona."

Rudy read down the list and his lips puckered up into the shape of a whistle about to form. "Nine hundred thirty malnutrition, eight hundred and seventy cases of yaws, fourteen hundred with scurvy?" Rudy looked up at Blake. "With all that tropical fruit over there, they got all that scurvy?"

"Strictly food for the gods," Blake said.

Rudy went back to the list. "This is going to call for a lot of number-ten tins of powdered milk and orange juice." Blake lifted his cup to take the coffee in quick swallows now.

"To say nothing of antibiotics and plasma for the close to twenty-five hundred surgery cases," he added.

"We're refloating an entire population," Rudy commented in some awe.

"So you see why we got to keep airplanes in the air."

Rudy began whistling softly through his teeth, stirring his coffee idly. "You like molasses candy?"

Blake peered at him over his cup, trying to track with the change of subjects. "Last week it was Fulani fudge that we wound up drinking," he said with some detachment, glancing at his watch.

"Yeah, I know," and Rudy looked up at him from the paper and that quick grin came on, "but I noticed in Emily's medical book last night that molasses candy acts better than an apple a day."

"Quit worrying about your bowels," Blake said morosely. "Either you are trying to regulate everybody or that Mundey is trying to close up shop."

Blake got up then with his cup in his left hand and headed for the screen door, pulling on his sunglasses with his right.

"Skipper, how about talking to Augie?" Rudy called after him, scrambling to follow, carrying the statistical sheet with him. "Monk is really too green. He's been in the john since a half hour ago . . . even the thought of flying second seat—"

"I told you, too late to abort," Blake flung back over his shoulder as he moved toward the hangars, swallowing up the ground in those long strides, the buckles on his boots clocking it all the way. Young Duka was already out front with his tray of empty tins on his head, and Joseph was crowding up close on Rudy's heels.

"You know molasses candy has sorghum in it?" Rudy said, coming up alongside Blake then, trying to match the long strides and looking up into that face that had the markings of an old shoe a good foot above his own. "And sorghum is a health food . . ." Blake did not

52

answer, his eyes on the mechanics around the planes on his right. After a few more paces Rudy said, "You know they're in council meeting next week in Talfungo? You think maybe we ought to try to avoid any more flaps up here for a while?"

Rudy knew Blake was aware that Emily, soon to arrive in Talfungo, was not going to boost his stock up here. He had to know too that there was a kind of theological case building against him in the upper echelons of the mission, had been for some time. But those facts never seemed to faze him. An airplane engine suddenly kicked to life not more than twenty yards away, rocketing a hammering sound into the tugging finger of wind that came in from the higher atmospheres. Blake lifted his head into that wind, and he would note now that it was earlier today and could pose a problem with the planes taking off. Nitro did not ride easy in crosswinds. It would mean he would have to schedule the flights before dawn if the wind decided to build-up regularly at this hour. Rudy wanted to discuss that with him too, but they were in the hangar then, the pilots waiting, seated in casual clumps in the chairs in front of the big aerial blowup of Terragona.

It was said by the pilots that Blake ran a briefing like one for the Battle of Britain all over again. He would mount the platform with his bundle of cargo weight sheets and Terragona field descriptions, and in a few minutes run through it all in a rapid, commanding tone. Today, though, there was some disarray. The pilots found at breakfast that Emily had gone, and this left them feeling out of joint somewhat, since Emily was a pleasant distraction here every morning when she read the latest on the weather that had come over the Terragona frequency earlier that morning. And without her now, it seemed to leave Blake without a prop, although he carried on with all the usual exterior controls as if nothing was amiss. Further, they had also heard that Augie was not going up today, and their minds would naturally feel around that, for one man's opting out always put more strain on their commitment.

They watched Blake from under the brims of their baseball caps, seeing a rustic kind of man with knobby knees, the legs of a long-distance runner beaten a reddish brown by the sun, the arms of a blacksmith, and the face, as Mundey put it so often, "like George Washington's hanging out of Mount Rushmore," looking smooth from a distance but showing up the lumps and protrusions around the mouth and eyes on close view. He stood under the big sign of his, done up in clumsy black lettering on white plasterboard:

AIRSPEED OF 76 MPH ON TAKEOFF WITH A WIND VELOCITY OF 10 MPH WITH FULL LOAD OF 2200 WILL GET YOU OFF AND UP IN 1827 FEET. YOU HAVE 1930 FEET TO PLAY WITH—SO FIGURE IT OUT FROM THERE.

The pilots could have computed that straight out of the Cessna handbook, but it was Blake's way to spell it out for them. Later, before takeoff, he would have calculated the wind velocity in the tower, and fed them the new readings. All of this was to remind them that the margins were not really too bad in this field that appeared woefully short for full-load takeoffs.

There was another sign above that, dangling on the end of a long wire, done up in yellow with red lettering:

NITROGLYCERIN BEGINS TO DETERIORATE AT 160 DEGREES FAHRENHEIT. DESERT SUN RISES 0445 HOURS IN THE DRY SEASON AND WILL INCREASE THE TEMP THREE TO EIGHT DEGREES EVERY FIVE MINUTES BY SEVEN AM. COCKPIT TEMP, WITH WINDOW SLIDES OPEN TO TAKEOFF, WILL INCREASE RAPIDLY WHILE STANDING. THE HIGHER THE TEMP INSIDE THE COCKPIT THE EASIER FOR NITRO TO BLOW. DO NOT RIDE RUDDER. DO NOT ROLL YOUR BANK. FLY IT WITH YOUR FINGERTIPS.

That was Blake, the man who figured out everything in his slide-rule brain, who worked and reworked the percentages for them every day. The pilots had their mixed emotions about him. He was unlike anything or anyone they'd known in their priestly role in life. He rode them hard, almost callously, constantly demanding perfection in their flying. Every one of them had been dressed down for one thing or another in their flying in carefully selected language that was new, strange and jolting to them. A bad or sloppy landing at any time here would bring him out to meet the pilot before he was even completely rolled to a stop, and there would ensue a berating that had the mechanics staring with some wonder and awe. Mundey would remember one such case of a sloppy low-wing turn into the field that resulted in his making thirty passes before dark and ten more after dark "to make sure you know the difference between an airplane and a tractor." Most of them had, for weeks, smarted under this kind of treatment, for they had come to expect a mission life that emphasized devotion to God and an atmosphere leaning toward the relaxed attitude of spiritual exchange. Instead, they found themselves doing drills on the airplanes, practicing takeoffs and landings over and over again, stripping down their engines time and time again "so that if anything goes wrong you'll have yourself to blame." The motions of spiritual exercise soon gave way to airplane terminology, and the biggest achievement they could aim for was to drop their machines down on this field so softly that not one speck of dust rose from their wheels. And as time wore on, they became more and more concerned with developing flying skill, prodded constantly by Blake, whose demands became more and more abusive as time wore on.

But then there was the other emotion that rose in direct contrast with regard to him which came out right now with the smell of hot engine grease in the air. They knew Blake held the margins of survival for each of them. Those clumsy reddish-brown hands still caked with the glow of lubricating oil had worked their miracles during the night with overworked airplanes and had given each of them better than a sixty–forty chance to make it today. The fact that he had lost three men did not alter their willingness to let him command, for his strange wisdom and instincts about aircraft and flying were too valuable to tamper with. And though they all continued to put their trust in God for those extra margins needed, they also realized that perhaps God Himself was delegating His miraculous powers to Blake, after all. This had been slow to come, but not a man among them would argue the point now—and it was for this reason that they seldom discussed any more the matter of Blake's spiritual image. Except for Augie, they were content to play each day on the strength of Blake's technical know-how and leave the spiritual side of him to God. The fact that they did not know him as they knew each other didn't bother them either at this precise moment—right now he was Moses with the rod, and they would leave it at that.

"Where's Monk?" Blake said then, disregarding the other business at hand.

"Still trottin'," Mundey offered factually, and somebody chuckled, for each of them knew that kind of agony in their time here, more often of late.

"Somebody get him in here," Blake ordered, but just then Monk came into the hangar and walked uncertainly toward them, his face pale, almost green, the freckles across his nose standing out in bold relief. "Sit down, Monk," Blake said, indicating Augie's empty chair next to Mundey. Monk sat down and stared at the sandbox in front of him, perched on a small wooden stand, inside which was a clay model of Augie's field assignment in Terragona called JERICHO. The same kind of box sat in front of each pilot, each with an identifying name that matched the airplane he flew—ST. LOUIS BLUES, BLUE DANUBE, SUGAR LUMP, COFFIN CORNER, ROUTE 66, MASON DIXON, FLATBUSH—each model showing small red "X" paint marks to indicate the latest reports on field erosions radioed in periodically from the bases in Terragona. Originally the pilots had put spiritual names to their planes and the fields they flew into in Terragona; but when Charlie Weaver's plane called BLESSED AS-SURANCE smashed into the "cotton hair" hill, Blake insisted on the change to more neutral codes. To him spiritual names were taking on some kind of fetish almost, making the pilots too dependent on God to overcome their sloppy flying. Only Augie held out with JERICHO, but then Augie was carrying on his own theological tussle with Blake, as everybody knew.

"Monk, you have to fly Augie's place today," Blake said crisply.

Monk looked bewildered, swallowed hard and tried a grin to ac-knowledge he was ready—but it sank dismally into the green. "Y—yes, sir," he managed finally, fresh sweat breaking out on his forehead.

The others looked at each other quickly, knowing that to push Monk into the line this fast was to court disaster. So Mundey stood up and said, "Excuse me, but is the Reverend Thornhill suffering another attack of theological migraine?"

"No time to discuss it," Blake returned shortly, and it was always that way, Blake never allowing them to put in their opinions about such matters. "Monk, you see that model of your field in front of you in that box?" Monk nodded as Mundey sat back down next to him. "It's the main hospital base called JERICHO in Terragona, not a bad field at all and the closest in flying time. You'll find mileage and field description in that loose-leaf binder in front of you. Those little paint marks on that surface represent soft spots. Take a good look at them, memorize them and keep your plane out of those areas. JERICHO is kind of swampy so lay off your brakes when you hit, to avoid skid. Got it?"

Monk sort of half nodded, licking at his dry lips, staring at the model, trying to photograph it in his brain. "Now remember on take-off," Blake continued for all of them, his voice almost harsh, "you people aren't climbing fast enough for colder air in the higher altitudes. That nitro doesn't behave in heat, so get up to six thousand right away and open your cold-air vents. Wind gusts are coming earlier, so we go off earlier tomorrow. Any questions?"

"Mr. Blake," Joe Bellinger offered then, "that engine of mine is knocking her guts against the fire wall now in those climbs." Some of the others nodded to indicate that this was their problem too.

"Was ist mit dis Baron Von Bellinger who burnin' up der gassin' puffin' in der climbin'?" Mundey suddenly threw in with that impish kind of grin, taking satisfaction in getting even for what Bellinger had done to him earlier. The others laughed with hollow sounds, and Monk tried to grin too while continuing to rub his forehead with one long forefinger, his eyes never leaving that sandbox.

"Don't worry about the fire wall," Blake said shortly. "That engine won't land in your lap yet. Monk, it's cool enough yet out there so you can go off last and watch how the others do it . . . okay?" Monk looked up at him in some wonder yet, but said nothing.

Blake stepped back then, and Rudy came forward from where he was standing a few feet behind Blake on the platform. He took off his black baseball cap, and the pilots, including Blake, did likewise in disconnected motions just as the plane engines exploded with a slamming cough as the mechanics began the runup.

"Lord," Rudy said, lifting his voice above the engine rumble, "look on us frail creatures of dust and grant us a safe journey today . . . be with Monk on his first flight," and he hesitated, not wanting to focus on Monk's smallness in light of the task ahead, "and give us wings of the eagle and small winds on which to soar. We remember that You are our refuge and underneath us are Your everlasting arms . . . Amen."

And they were moving out of there quickly, working against that temperature clock of Blake's. In five minutes they were rolling their planes down the dusty field to the far end of the runway, turning to face the run down toward the "cotton hair" and the protective escarpment of sand barrier that cut down the Harmattan crosswinds. "Fifty-four tons of sand," Rudy the Jew would often hold forth to his other pilots, "carried by one thousand Hamaran nomads in five-pound buckets on their heads in exchange for free medical care at our base dispensary."

The planes moved heavily on frail wheels, their maximum loads of gas and cargo causing them to squeal when brakes were applied on the engine runup. Rudy, as always, was first out on the runup line, waiting there as Blake talked to him on the radio, asking for RPM readings, magneto check, oil pressure, he alone deciding whether Rudy, or any of them, should go or not, depending on the slightest fluctuation of a needle in the bay of bug-eyed gauges. And all the time Rudy was conscious of the sixty-pound metal cannister of nitro hanging from the plane's ceiling behind him in a nylon mesh bag that was designed by Blake to keep it from taking the bumpy shocks that often accompanied takeoffs and landings. And, as always, the temperature. Already the gauge showed 118 degrees as the 7:30 desert sun turned its molten brass on the aluminum roof of the plane.

And it was time then, and Rudy knew that terrible moment of exposure, the mantle of godliness hanging heavy on thin shoulders. For in this moment, as he looked down that long strip of red clay, he could see it only as a questionable piece of planking that dropped off at the end into a tangle of thorny desert. And now he suffered the pains of humanity when death pondered the delicate percentages with the intentness of a fox.

Blake stood and watched them from his place on the dumpy-looking control-tower bridge made of red mud brick, looking as skeletal and unreal as the giant anthill alongside it. He had one leg hooked over the wooden railing, the earphones hugging his ears tightly, the microphone bent down from the right earpiece to an inch in front of his mouth. One by one the planes moved on out on the runup, then opened up to rush by him, sending back the billow of red dust, sometimes fishtailing as the pilots overcontrolled and he would have to yell at them the warning. And then they were under the protection of the sand hills, lifting shakily off the ground as they came abreast of the "cotton hair," then banking in careful twenty-degree turns away from the hill and the wind, staggering up the mountain of sky, clawing for the upper atmosphere and the cool air that would calm the fevered brow of the nitro.

And then Monk was last, sitting there in the confining cabin, watching the temperature gauge creep up to 146 degrees, hearing that voice in his ears chanting to him: ". . . when you reach 2330 RPM, Monk, let out your brakes . . . flaps all the way down . . . you got a fifteen-mile wind blowing across southwest . . . pull back on your controls at seventy MPH . . . it's a piece of cake, Monk . . . now give me the instrument readings . . ."

Monk did it, feeling the plane begin to shudder and shake under him with the increased runup of RPM, holding her there until Blake would give him the green . . . and then it was cleared and Blake snapped, "Let her go, Monk!" And he felt the plane jump ahead, and his hands went wet on the wheel as he felt her balk against the wind, and that voice told him to ease up on his controls . . . then the ground was flashing by, red sand screaming the warning that matched the blood roaring through his veins, then the blur of the outbuildings, the mechanics watching with folded arms and finally that quick, double-vision glimpse of Blake going by, looking like an umpire ready to call him out . . . "Lord, You never told me," Monk yelled against the rising fist in his throat . . . and then he was under the arm of the sand hills, feeling the plane steady some now that it was not fighting the crosswind, until it responded to his much-too-eager pull on the wheel, jumping up from the ground so that voice in his ears said, "Easy, Monk, easy . . ." as if he were some kind of animal lying hurt in the dust . . . and then that big hill with the dirty leaves and silvery scrub came up on him off to his left reaching out a hairy hand to him . . . "lean her over easy to the right, Monk," that voice said, "easy does it . . ." He put the plane over into as gentle a turn as he could, feeling he wanted to swallow but was afraid to lest even that ripple of motion set off that cannister of hell hanging behind his right shoulder that sagged over with his turn, straining against the leather straps holding it to the ceiling . . . he felt the wing slip away from him, caught her and put her nose up to reach for the upper altitudes.

"Beautiful, Monk, beautiful!" that voice sang into his ears. "You're a real Eddie Rickenbacker, man!" And Monk blinked against the sweat in his eyes, the sharp spasms grabbing at his bowels again. But he didn't care. He sniffed and wiped at his runny nose. All that mat-

tered now was that he had mastered the first gigantic test . . . a piece
of cake . . . sure, a dandy, lumpy piece of cake . . .

Blake put the headset on the hook behind him, feeling that fatigue
that took him like this always after they were gone, a painful kind
of loneliness hanging heavy in the rafters of his brain. Maybe it wasn't
loneliness. Maybe it was some other nameless thing or something he
really refused to identify. He never allowed himself time to stick a
finger inside himself and feel for it. He would keep it in the dimensions he wanted it to be, like he always had.

But maybe today, with Emily gone, he felt it more. She wouldn't
be here now to pour him coffee and fill out the weight charts. With
her there, he could concentrate on her, on the light, undemanding
conversation. But not today.

Beyond that, though, was that other thing which he sensed was
beginning to come down on him. Usually it only came in the night,
mostly in horny kinds of shapes, floating on smoke and flame. Today—
right now—it was there in daylight even as he watched Monk's plane
turn into a splotch of soot on the far horizon dissolving into the sun
like a fly into the mouth of a furnace. A kid like that flying a mission
of this kind on the strength of credentials that wouldn't qualify him
to fly a picture of a plane on a blackboard was now enlarging the
awful images that he had managed to fight off for so long. And the
rest of them would be thinking about it too. When they got their
planes trimmed up at eight thousand feet so they wouldn't have to
play the controls, then they would think about it. He heard their voices
now on the frequency coming up the stairwell from the radio room,
talking to each other as if they were kids walking through a cemetery
at night, making it sound big and bold as if the dead really cared
anyway. But later, anytime now maybe, they would start to think
about Augie sitting it out over there in the red Quonset with his open
Bible on his knees, maybe rationalizing his fright with spiritual laws
while Monk fought his cramped bowels all the way to JERICHO.
And if Monk didn't make it? If he forgot in that one second before
his wheels touched over there and he set it too hard . . . what then?
And when they stopped thinking about Augie, they'd think about him.
Maybe why their own *commandant* didn't take the flight himself?
They had reason to ask that now.

But now Blake leaned his back harder against the mud-brick wall of the tower, feeling the heat bake through the leather jacket and slowly relax his muscles. He sniffed at the wind, sensing that part of it was swinging away from its natural northerly flow, the tail drifting eastward perhaps while the head kept trying to tug it back. It was hotter now too—too early to be this hot. It was only 7:45 and already he noted that the temperature on the thermometer hanging under the small canopy of mud over his head was well over eighty-five degrees. He could concentrate on that. The wind, the heat, the elements of the logistics that had to be thought of if he would keep things going. He would have to watch that wind. Too early for easterly winds, not really due for another month at least. But there were other disbalances too. He could see the herders beyond the hangars pushing their cattle on to the south, heading for the savannahs. Too early for the savannahs. Usually they camped out there until the first clouds showed in the sky, and then headed out, anticipating what the rains would do to put fresh greens in the dried-out grasses. He would have to check that out.

But now he would have to face Augie. He didn't want that. To face Augie was to face a big part of himself. "Behold we see in a glass darkly, but then face to face . . ."?

He turned and walked down the stairs. The frequency was quiet now. Only the hum and hiss with splatters of static. They were not talking any more. They'd be thinking about landing in Terragona, thinking about those red marks in the sandbox models, hoping the wind was right, not too gusty, hoping they could hold their planes from going in too fast . . .

"Joseph!"

"Suh!"

"You get Monsieur Thornhill! *Comprenez-vous?* Monsieur Thornhill!"

"*Oui, je comprends!*" And that light tittering laugh followed, and he was trotting across the sand toward the pilots' Quonset, the long overcoat flapping around his legs.

Blake knew it would be an hour before Augie appeared—at least. Augie would think about it, pray about it, prepare himself as if he was going to a high liturgical service. So Blake sat down at the rough mahogany table and took out the red logbook from the lower drawer. "Annual Log" it said on the front, one of those five-and-dime things he'd found in Durungu market a long time ago.

He opened it, letting those pages slip through his thumb as if he was fluttering a deck of cards. He studied the spare-parts listing he kept on his own on one page, then picked up the folded sheet of paper tucked inside the cover, ran over the words again:

> . . . I can only say, Mr. Blake, that Christ forgives as He has you . . . but in the end He expects you to descend into your hell as He did His. There is nothing taught in the Bible that a man, once he experiences the forgiveness of God, should run and hide from the monster that pursued him in life. You must descend to your hell, Mr. Blake, and as I see it for you it is the cockpit of an airplane. Perhaps only as you fly again will you know complete deliverance. . . . Meanwhile, seek out those who can give you help on your way, those who will lovingly guide you to that final victory. God has His people everywhere, you need not feel you fight this alone. Honor God by never taking second best or the easy way out. I can only remind you of the words in the Scriptures: "For it became him, for whom are all things and by whom are all things, in bringing many sons into glory, to make the captain of their salvation *perfect through suffering.* For both he that sanctifieth and they who are sanctified are all one; for which cause he is *not ashamed to call them brethren*" (Hebrews 2:10–11).

Blake put the letter back on the page, wondering if Bell really had it right. A lot of it made sense, but he wasn't sure about finding people who would understand.

He glanced across the page then to what he had written sometime ago:

> What makes it worse now is that I've got to protect them from me . . . I've got to build the command even higher . . . they like me to be their God-image, big grandpa to pat them on the head and spin yarns about the glory of God in history . . . I don't know anything about that . . . anyway, this operation can't afford that . . . once they start getting mushy on God, once they even get me down to know me buddy-buddy, well, then they're going to fly it in the ground . . . I have to stay away from the clinches, so I

won't show up myself either . . . Maybe they know anyway . . . God, I'm scared of airplanes! What Bell was talking about is so true . . . when do I finally whip this thing
. . . sooner or later they're going to start asking why I don't
fly with them . . . the one element of command they need
I can't give them . . . Rudy the Jew probably knows, you
can't fool that wise old owl . . .

He continued to stare down at the words scrawled out there in
his jerky handwriting, uncertain even now that he had actually written
it. He was not much on the true confessions, but it helped some to
know where he'd been in his mind. He heard a voice on the radio
a long way out just then. He waited, tensed, ready to react. The voice
faded off again. Only the wind blowing through the open doorway
in soft hissing sounds, like the tides of the universe were finally coming
in, stood out now, mixing with the hum of the radio.

He turned a few more pages and stopped to read again:

Charlie Weaver got it today. Try fancy landings with secondhand control surfaces. So what's left now is nothing
but a ball of black metal and a piece of the nose with
the words BLESSED ASSURANCE on it. They think You
fly co-pilot, God, and You will cover for their sloppy
flying . . . so they die. That's three now. Well, no more
playing church here . . . they're going to have to lose
this glorious adventure business and start thinking in terms
of nitro . . . it's a war they got on their hands, God, but
they think it's like a game of darts . . . they can only win
now when they start thinking like an army and know who
the enemy is . . .

He paused again to reflect on that. Not much of an army here
yet. They dressed alike, that was about it. But they were flying closer
to the horn now too. They were doing their praying on the fly and
learning not to mix things the wrong way. They were not so much
the typical missionary any more as they were technicians. That's what
was making the difference in keeping Terragona open. They weren't
sure either that they had made the change. When they woke up to
that fact, that they were not theologians flying on the side but twenty-
four-hour air-lift jockeys, well, what then? Well, at least they weren't

all dying on him, and he felt they might be taking some necessary feeling of accomplishment in what they were doing, beating the odds every day. But if they knew it was their effort to fly it better, they'd probably fall into the dirt and repent. He couldn't let that happen. As long as they had that sense of mastery over what could be mastered, he was sure they could keep going. Keep them busy then, he reminded himself again. Don't let them think about it too long and start asking the wrong questions of themselves. But that's what Augie was undoubtedly all uptight about. He was asking those questions, and already it was beginning to spill over on the rest of them.

He picked up the stubby pencil on the desk top then and began writing on the blank page in slow, laborious movements:

> Emily is gone. God, that sweet kid is no more! I don't think I asked too much of her. Or did I? A cup of coffee, a little clerical work—and some conversation. I think I could have shared with her my problem—maybe. Trouble is she'd spread it all the way to Talfungo. Nothing is really private in the communion of saints—I should ask Bell about that one. Well, she's going to talk plenty in Talfungo . . . but she didn't want talk here. I know what she wanted. But, Jesus, can You see me making love here? These kids don't need an Errol Flynn! Am I going to romance a woman while they're flying nitro? How was I supposed to explain that to her? Jesus, I don't want to make it tough on anyone, but there's a job to do . . .

He felt the shadow in the room then, and he looked up quickly to see Augie standing in the doorway. He closed the book, snapped the lock on the side and put it back into the drawer. He turned back quickly to the cargo sheets and began writing with a stubby pencil on the blue lines. He reached out and poured himself a cup of coffee from the small aluminum pot on the hotplate.

"Come on in, Augie," he said lightly. "Coffee isn't the best, but it's hot and has a lace of kerosene."

Augie came in slowly and sat down on a wooden toolbox, putting his back to the wall, feeling the uneven ridges of mud brick hard against his spine. The room was no more than ten by ten, littered with magazines, old parts, the roughly hewn mahogany table propped up on one leg with old *Reader's Digests*.

Neither of them said anything for a long time. Blake kept writing out the cargo weights on the sheets, with intense preoccupation, only the small point of the pencil showing under his pinched, fat fingers. The wobbly steel-rimmed glasses hung down on his nose as he worked, putting too much age into his ruddy face, and he posed a picture then of an old watchmaker growing tired with his concentration on a thousand mainsprings. To Augie, Blake seemed a broad spectrum of contradictions. He saw Blake now, not as the others did, a piece of durable, scarred chopping block on which a million pieces of kindling could be split, but in the dimensions of a disturbing audacity that bumped and scraped the walls of this holy tabernacle that was Operation Shoestring. To Augie, Blake was the incarnation of that giant Hittite who hurled the challenge eons ago across the green at the cowering Jews, thumbing his nose at the God of Israel, who apparently could not measure over seven feet tall. Blake was every hobgoblin Augie had ever seen in the Bible storybooks of his childhood, the kind that danced and roared and snaked along in their sickly green suits and brown armor. He was the composite of all the enemies of God in history from King Nebuchadnezzar to Herod, even to Caesar. He was the product of a thousand sermons delivered off the biting tongues of pulpit heroes who screamed their warnings about the Antichrist and to "beware lest this cunning beast find his way into your sanctuary by the devices of his own Trojan horse." Augie had learned all about cults and diverse spirits in seminary, and what he didn't know his father laid out for him. His life had been given to God by his father for "a ministry of trying the spirits" and "exposing the false gods," and now, though he felt some fear in this confrontation, he stirred up his Daniel's resolute determination to stand his ground, to make this his finest hour as he carried his rightful cause to the gates of hell if necessary.

Meanwhile, Blake went on writing on those cargo sheets, conscious only of Augie sitting there.

Blake was not sure which angle to take on Augie. He was aware of Augie's complaints about the operation, and he knew Augie had to be sat on sooner or later because of it. But Augie had that superior force of theology behind him, coupled with that air of self-possession that was sometimes a bit awesome. It was a known fact, too, that Augie's father, a big church leader at home, had raised the first fifty thousand dollars for Shoestring and had given sizable chunks since.

Blake had sense enough to know that squeezing Augie's emotional rib cage was to get a yelp of pain at home. Beyond that, though, was the fact established among other pilots that Augie was a theological custodian from way back. Mundey had described Augie one day, in front of Augie, as an "original member of the Inquisition who had built-in heresy detectors that blew smoke out his ears whenever anyone walked by without a full pack of doctrinal statements." Everybody laughed at that, and even Augie had smiled that window-dressing smile of his, as if he thought all these colorful statements of Mundey's were compliments. But Blake knew that Augie had a sharp mind which Mundey would not give him credit for, even though it was dedicated to detecting theological error. And Blake knew too that Augie was not a very good flyer, that inwardly he disliked flying altogether. And it was therefore harder on him to fly the percentages here. Actually Augie should have been pounding the pulpit somewhere and calling the church to pile the sandbags a little higher against the flood waters of spiritual dereliction. But in the meantime he kept sniffing the air, trying to find the trail that would lead him finally to the point of vindication . . . and now Blake knew that the time had come.

Now Augie sat there in that dark-blue sweatshirt with the golden letters, hardly even faded yet, spelling out DELAROSA SEMINARY '67 across the front in neat stencil. His light-beige gabardine tropical trousers—Augie never wore shorts like the rest, not even to wash in the mornings—were neatly pressed as usual. There was about Augie that aura that went with lifeguards at expensive beach resorts or maybe that sure demeanor of a successful evangelist carrying God's lightning bolts in each hand.

Blake paused then in his writing, dropped the pencil on the cargo sheets, reached down in a lower drawer and came up with two baseball mitts. He threw one of them at Augie, who caught it defensively, staring down at it as if it were the Koran.

"I see in your personnel record that you were a big man in Little League and college," Blake said, thumping the catcher's mitt he held in his left hand with a scarred-up old hardball, all the time moving for the door. "So let's see that big curve or whatever it was that got you those five no-hitters in your career . . ."

Augie did not move for a long time, even after Blake had disappeared outside. He kept looking at the glove, then to the door, trying to put it together, trying to fit this into what Blake had called him here for, which he was sure was the problem of his refusing to fly today. Finally he got up slowly and moved outside, bent on tossing the glove aside and getting to the issue. Because he was ready for it, for the confrontation, and he wanted it now before his resolve dissipated.

When he got outside, Blake was already taking up a station sixty feet down at the end of the tower, still thumping that mitt with the ball. Augie stood there awkwardly, the glove hanging like an unwanted clumsy bandage on his hand, staring at Blake intently, not at all sure of this dimension of the man that was being posed to him now.

And Blake finally threw the ball at him so that Augie threw up the glove to keep from getting it in the chest. The ball fell out and to the ground and Blake called, "Takes time to get it back, hey, Augie?" and his voice was almost bantering, riding a crest of the parody, as if he was saying he didn't believe Augie was any kind of pitcher like the record had said.

Augie bent over to pick up the ball, gripped it in the long tanned fingers of his right hand, feeling the jagged edges of the horsehide. He stood there like that looking down at it, remembering those endless days behind the garage, those endless years trying to rise to some measure of himself that others had set for him.

And then he heard Blake's fist thumping that catcher's mitt, the derisive call of challenge he disliked with a passion. He saw the mechanics come out of the hangar across the field to stand and watch, not comprehending this at all, because it had never been done before. He looked up at Blake again, who had squatted down showing those swollen knees like two headlights, waiting for his throw, his face half hidden under the brim of his baseball cap and sunglasses. He threw then. He wasn't in position to throw at all. But he threw, almost out of a sudden desire, off balance, so that the pain arched up from his elbow. He threw the ball as if Blake was a target or maybe a kind of symbol of a lot of things that should be destroyed.

Blake had to jump up to catch the throw, because it was wildly high. "Takes time to get the control, Augie," he called back. "So let's have it now . . . give me the old form . . . if you got it, if you ever had it, I'd like to see it . . ."

So Augie threw again, setting himself now, taking some kind of aim. And he kept throwing. Each time he threw, the ball snaked into Blake's glove with a solid thump. He threw until the sweat poured off his face in rivers, soaking his sweatshirt so that it stuck to his bare skin underneath. He threw through the blinding sting of that sweat in his eyes, ignoring the pain in his arm. Each time Blake threw it back, sometimes in a lobbing arch, other times in a snapping bullet so that it hurt through Augie's glove. And it was as if both men were testing each other, Augie's pitch growing more and more vicious and more controlled so that the sound of it in Blake's glove was like the pop of a small gas explosion . . . and each time the ball came back to him with a sting as if Blake was saying it still was not good enough . . .

And then Augie lost all track of time, intent only on finally finishing this charade, as if it was really so important after all to put that pitch to Blake that would dispel any illusion that he might have had about Augie's abilities. And every pitch brought a grunt now as Augie reared back and fired, and each return peg kept building up the resentment.

Until finally Augie threw one so hard he fell to his knees, and he didn't bother to get up. He stayed there looking at the sand that showed the black spots of his sweat and the digging furrows from his shoes. His chest hurt and his arm was a long extension of fire burning back up to his shoulder. He got up slowly and threw the mitt at the side of the tower wall and walked slowly over to it to stand with his back against it, coughing on the phlegm that stuck in his throat, flicking at the sweat that ran off his long nose.

Blake stood up from his crouching position and walked toward him, still thumping that ball into the mitt. He stood a few feet from Augie, and Augie noticed that the sweat had soaked his khaki shirt to black smears and left the hair on his arms tangled and matted with it. They said nothing for a long time, Blake continuing to slam the ball into his mitt over and over again as if he was trying to make a deeper pocket. Across the field Augie could see the mechanics slowly turning back to the hangars, almost reluctantly, still waiting perhaps to see a first-class duel of some sort. Augie did not speak for a long time. It seemed strange to be sweating as he was now, for he seldom allowed himself that kind of exposure here. He felt perplexed by it as it ran down his face, as if he had proof at last that he was made up of the chemistry common to all men. He had been nurtured in an atmosphere that denied the acceptance of flesh or its functionality—he was totally God's possession and God was Spirit. And it was obvious now too that the game of catch had disarmed his own cause. Whether Blake intended it or not, throwing a ball to a man had a way of building a scene of camaraderie; it revealed too much of the wrong things. There was now no ready confrontation that Augie had prepared for.

"You got a home-run pitch, Augie," Blake finally said, staring at the ball in the pocket of his glove.

"I didn't come here to pitch," Augie finally returned sullenly, looking down at his shoes. They were a black, soft leather, always highly polished. They were "special ceremony" shoes that went with red carpeting and concerts and ordination services. Were they the kind of shoes the Lord would wear if He walked on earth? But now they were scuffed with dust. He was confused by the dirt on them, and he reached into his back pocket, took out a crumpled white handkerchief and began rubbing at them.

"You didn't come here to fly either?" Blake said, watching him work on one shoe, then the other, intent on keeping the image intact.

"No more nitroglycerin with the Gospel, Blake. It's contradictory, unholy." It wasn't the way he had rehearsed this at all.

"Your argument is with Talfungo, then, not me," Blake replied quietly, twirling the scuffed baseball in his right hand, watching it carefully.

Augie gave a big sigh and put his handkerchief back into his pocket, reached up and flicked a ball of sweat off his nose. This was not going well now, and Blake could sense that Augie was struggling as if he had forgotten his lines.

Augie cleared his throat then, found his handkerchief again and started mopping at the sweaty grease on his forehead. The dirt from his shoes left streaks on the smooth brown cliff of his skin, which, together with the sweat, put him into a growing figure of disarray.

"I won't fly for you any more, Blake," he put it out bluntly. "I—"

"I thought you were flying it for God, Augie?" and Blake thumped the ball back into the mitt, his voice remaining on that tone of simple inquiry.

Augie hesitated, as if he knew Blake had control of the conversation. Then, "You're as much of a contradiction to God as the nitro . . ."

Blake didn't respond. He turned to look across the field toward the hangars. A hot wind gusted from the furnace of the desert and kicked up frolicking whirlpools of sand out on the runway.

"Some things you can't put back to back to God," he finally said, lifting his face toward the sun, sniffing at the air, his eyes hidden by the sunglasses. "I know this place isn't your idea of the Mount of Transfiguration . . . it maybe stinks too much of gasoline and manure when you are maybe used to incense and lilies and the things that are supposed to go with the church around the world. But sometimes you got to pull your gut in and sweat a little—"

"*We* do the sweating, *you* don't, Blake. We take the risks, we fly the short percentages . . . I don't see you taking your turn."

Blake seemed to go very still then, his head cocked to one side, still watching those ghostly dances of sand on the runway. It was as if he was listening to other sounds then—the earth breathing, the sound of the radio's loud hum inside the tower, the wind whooping around the tower in fitful gusts of exploding gas. For a second or two, Augie saw a flick of shadow cut across Blake's face, as if some strange image had passed before his eyes. Seeing it, Augie sensed a point of vulnerability and bore in with, "Anyway, I've already written Talfungo for a transfer out."

Blake turned his head back from the study of the field and looked down again at the ball in his mitt. There was no sign then of a leak in that face anywhere. It became that same hard mold of lumpy tissue around the mouth and nose, a beaten-up general's face, a chunk of armor scraped thin but still as impressive as the cutting bow of a battleship.

"No transfer without my signature," he said then, his voice taking on a note of impatience. "That's the mission rule, Augie . . ."

"How about Emily?"

"Emily was sick . . ."

"I've got the same thing, Blake."

"Not quite. What you got won't get cured by a transfer."

"You'll hold me against my will, then?"

"That's right. I can't afford to let you out, not now. Whether you appreciate it or not, there are seventy-five people, your people, over there in Terragona, who hang on because of this airlift. If I let you go, what's to keep the others from thinking about it?"

"They're already thinking about it. You can't hold them long, Blake."

"Maybe not. But meanwhile you stay, Augie. You can ground yourself, but you'll earn your keep while you're here. You can start by getting on that radio inside and sit it out for the next seven or eight hours keeping the channel open until your fellow warriors get back. Tonight you can join me on the tower and I might even let you try leading them down in the dark, because the days are getting shorter, Augie, and it's going to be a sticky wicket for them to find their way in. But maybe you've been thinking about that too in your sense of cause? And while we're at it, now that Emily's gone, you can hand out the worm medicine and aspirin to those nomad outpatients lining up over at the infirmary . . . and tomorrow morning you can wave good-bye to your comrades here with me and hope none of them blows up on you as they pass . . . yes, sir, Augie, you might just see how the other half sweats for a change—"

"I intend to protest this action all the way to the top, Blake," Augie cut back sharply at him.

"That has already crossed my mind," Blake said factually. "But right now you better take that sweatshirt off and those nice gabardines and put on a pair of shorts. It gets to a hundred and forty around noon inside that radio shack." He dropped the mitt with the ball still in it by Augie's feet. "You better work on that pitch, Augie. I don't know where you got those no-hitters, but a five-year-old could hit that curve ten miles. We'll throw at the same time tomorrow . . ."

He turned and walked out across the field, Joseph running after him, Duka already out front. The sound of his boot buckles were like muted laughter fading with him. After a while Augie picked up the mitt, stood up slowly and walked reluctantly into the tower radio room. He stood by the radio looking down at the mitt with the ball in it. It was a good pitch. It had to be! His father had always told him. And the no-hitters? He dropped the mitt on the table as if it suddenly were an incriminating exhibit, plopped himself down in front of the radio, staring at it, not making any move to do anything, because he did not want to surrender anything to Blake. He heard the voice coming in from a long way off, but he did not respond to it. It was hot inside the room. The sweat began to run freely under his shirt. Finally he took it off, flexing the muscles of his arms and shoulders, watching them jump and curl at his bidding. Then he sat there a long time rubbing his chin idly with his right hand.

Finally he reached out and spun the dial off the Terragona frequency, throwing the transmission key. When he finally made contact with Talfungo, he asked for Milt Gregson, the field director, but was told Mr. Gregson would not be in until 9:30 and did he want a return call? He said he did, and that it was urgent, and he would open the key at 9:30.

Then he turned the dial back on the Terragona channel again. There was a lot more to say to Blake directly. But he found it hard to say it straight to him. He didn't know why. He had already written to Pat Maddigan, the mission's northern superintendent, and to his father. The point now was to get the big man on this, Gregson, who was after all the top man. To get him into it, he was sure, would put the whole matter on the floor of the Field Council meeting this week.

And then he heard Blake's voice coming across the field, shouting out those clumsy French phrases at the mechanics, *"C'est la guerre, mon ami, c'est la guerre!"*

"Such is war," Augie repeated out loud to the transmitter and he smiled, shaking his head. "Have it your own way, Blake," and he pulled off his long gabardine trousers and hung them carefully over the back of his chair, sitting down again clad only in his jockey shorts, his proud muscles gleaming with sweat.

# CHAPTER III

"Steel mats, gentlemen," Henry Faber said in a tone of finality through a mouthful of fish and eggs, "steel mats are what Blake will need if he expects to put enough supplies into Terragona before the rains. And logistics beg the point, he can't possibly make it before then; he will need the mats or else his airfield will turn to an impossible quagmire in Durungu . . ."

Faber was a nervous eater, as he was a talker. He was a small, almost wizened-up man of middle or late fifties encased in a much too tight gray tropical suit that emphasized his boniness even more, giving him the stark appearance of Ichabod. His long pointed nose twitched against the Harmattan dust that filtered in even here so early in the morning in the private dining room of the Hotel Flambeau in Talfungo.

"Don't you think Blake thought of that?" Timothy Belang put in bluntly from directly across the small circular mahogany table. Belang was a rather chubby African in his thirties, with a pumpkin-shaped black face and a short stab of a goatee that did nothing more than emphasize the pointed contour of his chin. He wore white tropical shorts and shirt in the military cut of the former French colonial masters, but they were wrinkled and sweat-streaked, a sign maybe that he was wearing them for the last time. He worked inside the Hamaran Information Service as co-ordinator of government releases, a job he held even now only because the Hamaran Government felt obliged to retain him because of the secrets still locked in his head. He was committed to the National Liberation Party of Hamara but was never too much of an enthusiast. For him, Hamara could best develop in the African way and needed no Western revolutionary political designs to complicate it. His training at the French Sorbonne in Paris was in languages, not in politics, and for this he could never be fully forgiven by his more active political peers in Hamara.

"Blake may have thought of it, monsieur," Faber countered politely, pushing his half-finished breakfast plate aside and standing up slowly to turn and face the map on the wall behind him. "But Blake has not the means . . . so then what do we have here?" and he put on a pair of small black-rimmed glasses to peer at the map, looking much like a child trying to reach up to a drinking fountain. "Terragona . . . this strip of Shangri-La, as you called it, Monsieur Belang, stuck up there eight thousand feet high in that semiarid steppe of the Sahara, four hundred square miles of lush greenery fertilized by volcanic ash and the backwash of the subtropical rains off the savannahs, controlled by eighty thousand Terragona people who are a mix of Egyptian and Berber, practicing Animists rather than Muslims, and militantly hostile to outside penetration. Correct so far, Monsieur Belang?"

"You have done your homework well, Monsieur Faber," Belang admitted grudgingly, wiping at the sweat already itching in the folds of his neck.

Faber continued looking at the map as he went on, "So then, how did this Protestant mission get into Terragona in the first place?" He put it as an academic question, even though by now he must know.

"A smallpox epidemic of three years ago threatened to wipe out the entire tribe," Belang said, frowning now, for he had repeated this too many times already to Faber in the last twelve hours. "The Terragona chief named Turgobyne sent out for help, and the United for Life Mission people who had worked the northern desert frontiers for fifty years volunteered to go in. Turgobyne took his time deciding, wanting to make sure there were no political strings, and finally consented; the mission people went in by camel, stopped the epidemic, and Turgobyne was so impressed he gave them permission to put in a hospital base there . . ."

"So why do they fly everything in? They could get more in by camel . . ."

"Well, for one thing, Turgobyne knew that an overland entry with an established traffic pattern that way would open the door for others to cut into it. By forcing strictly a flight entry, he could control that

74

much easier. Second, the Hamaran Government managed to make a deal with Turgobyne, as we told you, to prospect his land for oil and uranium, provided that we did not send in more than ten people to conduct the prospecting. He agreed there was power for the taking in the dirt he was walking on. But the Hamaran Government had to have nitroglycerin in there to use for blasting—and to move that highly explosive material over the desert on camel was far too risky. So—"

"Yes, the rest I have, monsieur," Faber cut in with a sniff. "So the Hamaran Government allowed the Protestant Mission permission to use Hamaran territory for an airfield to fly into Terragona if they agreed to carry nitro . . . all of which we owe to our brilliant strategist here, Felix Mentaya, correct?" Belang did not look at the other African a few feet away, who sat quietly but watchfully, as a leopard fixed on a gazelle biding his time. "So now the mission airlift up at Durungu has grown to nine planes feeding nine hospital bases over in Terragona . . . each plane carrying twenty pounds of liquid nitroglycerin in forty-pound cannisters, leftover French material from who knows how long? Would you call that heroism or stupidity, Monsieur Belang?"

Belang hated this classroom manner of Faber's, but he said, "It's all in the way it ends," and he took a quick swallow of wine to help give him tolerance. Faber gave off with a dry chuckle. "Anyway," Belang went on, "do you think Blake is going to bow to us over landing mats?"

Felix ignored the question and turned his head to look at the other African. "Felix, how far along are your prospectors in Terragona?"

Felix Mentaya was a slow-speaking African who had been a worker for the National Liberation Party and now held a key post in the opposition side as Minister of Mines. He was not a pure Hamaran, carrying the finely sculptured lines of the Fulani and Dinka in his cheekbones, small nose and thin mouth. His skin was light, almost mulatto, which spoke of his mixed parentage. His eyes were small and almost black, except when the light hit them, and then they showed a greenish cast, recessed into deep sockets so that they often were seen as chips of hard light coming out of the shadow of his upper face. There was a disarming air of gentility about him that covered a network of bare wires underneath. Those who knew him intimately—and they were few—would testify to his low flash point especially when he was fighting for his own self-image.

There were not many who knew that Felix had been trained in a mission elementary school and had won his advanced matriculation, which got him the invitation to study at the Sorbonne, because of mission influence, particularly through an old missionary woman named Miss Drew. Only Belang knew that. At any rate, at the Sorbonne he had caught hold of the new political climate in French intellectualism—when he finished five years of study, he left God at the Cathedral of Notre Dame and carried Lenin back with him.

Now he was beginning to rise as a political figure to be reckoned with in Hamara. But it was all too slow. The country dragged in sleepy indifference to his rallying cries to "build a new order." The stroke he needed now went beyond Hamara—it lay in the timing he was trying to set in motion beyond these two bumbling idiots in the room. At thirty-two, some men could wait for events to shape the man; for Felix Mentaya it was the other way around, and that meant creating his own events.

"The prospecting is producing more than we expected," he said simply to Faber. "We are finding more treasure than we thought existed . . . and while we do it, more and more Terragonans are falling in with our cause . . ."

"Good," Faber said as he leaned his hands on the back of his chair. "So it remains for us to exploit it to the fullest. With nitro and guns, we can command half the Terragona nation and split it politically . . ."

"So what's a few guns with a ragtag bunch of rebels who don't know how to use them?" Belang argued petulantly.

Faber glanced at him sharply. "May I remind you, Monsieur Belang, that the state of mind of the Terragonans is what makes revolution. Right now they are aware of the riches under their feet over there; they know too that Turgobyne is old and can't handle what is shaping up over there now. He permits a small, useless mission to put up hospitals to dispense a foreign religion with every Band-Aid when he should be bringing in helicopters full of mining equipment. It is the same old story of greed, Monsieur Belang, of wealth corrupting the apparently incorruptible—and we will feed that corruption. We will fan that discontent and create a political vacuum we will fill for the Party . . ."

"I know the Party's strategy well enough, monsieur," Belang said in disgruntlement; he did not pretend to cover his irritation at having a European member of the Party being sent here to tell him and Felix how to get Terragona. Belang knew Felix didn't like it either, but Felix played all of it cool, planning his own strokes.

"Then, do not waste time with empty questions as to how," Faber said impatiently. He waited, then continued, "Now there's the matter of the lost American satellite, which we have been ordered to find in Terragona—"

"Nobody's sure that satellite dropped in there," Belang came back quickly.

"Our tracking stations do not lie . . ."

"Whose tracking stations? We have had no information come through here that anyone has word as to where that satellite landed—"

"*Our* information, monsieur," Faber countered bluntly, "is that it dropped in water somewhere around Terragona . . ."

"So there are nine lagoons in Terragona—"

"But only one big enough to take a half-ton satellite, which is," and Faber looked down at his notes in front of him, "Lake Caha . . . right, Felix?" Felix nodded. Belang looked at Felix, wondering how he would know.

"In any case," Belang went on, "Blake still controls the airspace. How do you intend to ride with him into Terragona?"

"We have two Cessna 206 aircraft," Felix came in, sounding bored, "that we requisitioned from the Bureau of Mines. Blake will hardly be able to resist the offer . . ."

"You are so sure of that?"

"With an operation so badly crippled as his, he cannot afford to do otherwise . . ."

"His mission will hardly consent—"

"Blake runs his own ship," Felix snapped, his eyes beginning to take on that warning glow.

"And Hamaran Government orders will be respected," Faber chimed in. "You have the necessary papers, Felix, with the signature of the Premier and Deputy Premier authorizing you to join the airlift?"

"Blake will want those signatures verified—"

"I have them," Felix went on, ignoring Belang. "I also expect the mission field director to sign them today. They will be anxious for any help they can get now with the rains moving in early—"

"Blake still controls the airspace," Belang repeated morosely.

"What about that, Felix?"

"I have a man inside Blake's operation at Durungu ready to move when I give the word . . ."

Belang grunted and tugged at his goatee, his fat face crinkling up into a smile. "There isn't a man in Blake's outfit who will go against him . . . that much I am sure of."

"And you spent too much time with the bourgeois," Felix cut back shortly. "You have lost touch with the age-old fact that money talks. I have trained my man to put silicon powder in the wheel housings of Blake's planes at the right time . . . when those planes fall apart, I will be there with my machines—"

"Sounds good here, Felix," Belang replied skeptically, refusing to come up to the warning note in Felix's voice. "But Blake won't roll over that easily . . ."

"Fleas are made to be shaken off a dog's back," Faber put in with a tone of dismissal.

"The Africans have a proverb here, Monsieur Faber," Belang replied, "that says 'a flea under the belt can worry a giant.' And Blake can be that kind of flea . . ."

"He is not Napoleonic, monsieur," Faber said, tossing his bent toothpick on the half-empty plate on the table. "When the day comes that a man of the church should be considered worthy opposition to the big plan for world revolution, I shall seek other causes. In the meantime, I expect the Americans will be sending out a space team to find that satellite. Both of you are to make certain they do not get into Terragona, is that understood?" Neither Belang nor Mentaya said anything. Faber looked at his plate again for a long time, as if trying to recollect what he had eaten, and then said, "Monsieur Belang, you have served the Party's interests well for the last five years . . . but I warn you not to complicate matters by useless forensics. I also understand that in your travels north this past year you spent two nights with Blake on his airfield in Durungu rather than use the appointed rest house at Tchari—"

"I get my information by the most direct route—"

"But just remember which side you are on!" Faber pounced back sharply. Again there was a pause. Faber hitched up his trousers, adding, "If you do not hear from me in the next twelve hours, proceed with the plan, no delays." He picked up his black attaché case then, and turned to walk out of the room.

Belang poured himself a glass of wine and swallowed it in one gulp. "Pig," he said into his glass, and he glanced at Mentaya for confirmation. But Felix was busy putting his papers back into his portfolio. "It is a sad day in Hamaran history when we have to be associated with that lowest form of hyena," Belang added. Felix got up then and zipped his portfolio closed. He was not interested in engaging Belang in any conversation. He was thinking of the Terragona conquest and what it would mean in being free from people like Faber *and* Belang. And maybe, too, if he did this right, he would be rid of that other constricting image which was growing worse, it seemed, every day. He would have to be careful with Belang, who was not so dumb as he appeared and could make a case out of the smallest ingredient.

So now, to avoid any more probings, he turned and left the room quickly, leaving Belang with his feet propped up on the table, the half-empty wine bottle in front of him.

A half mile outside the walls of the main hospital building called JERICHO, Kamako surveyed the clearing in the midst of the tangle of thick jungle. It was done now. Three months of hard work under the cover of darkness, a new "yam patch" now in the making. It had cost much—clearing the jungle, making the strong hemp lines, putting a hundred Terragonans to work. Now it was ready. The 180-foot palm tree was bent to the ground, held fast by the strong hemp lines. It had taken a hundred bush cows to bend that tree down. Now it sat there, ready to be sprung, straining like a bowline full out.

But there was no victory here yet. The yellow bird came in the morning but did not come in this way. When he had first studied its peculiar mannerisms two full moons back, it would come over the trees here very low and drop its feet onto the field just beyond. But now, ever since Kamako had taken to clearing the jungle here, it came in across the field away from the clearing. Only this time late in the afternoon would the yellow bird come in this way—like now, as he watched intently, his heart hammering as always when he watched the strange beast run toward them; and the men were ready with the stone axes, ready to cut the hemp lines holding the tree, waiting for his signal, for it had to be just right, timed perfectly.

It came with its growl growing louder, a snapping snarl almost bouncing on its spindly legs with the round feet, its wings tipping some with the wind—and then it was off the ground in one leap, too far away, climbing up over the clearing too high, its hot breath sweeping over them and leaving the trees to shake from the sound of it.

The men near the hemp lines dropped their axes, looking toward him, wondering. Had Kamako made the mistake, then? Was the old gray head operating out of his wisdom? Was all this work here for nothing, then? Aching backs, raw and blistered hands—for what? The yellow bird made fools of them all.

But there could be no mistake, Kamako told himself again, watching the yellow bird fade into the distance toward the north. There must not be a mistake, because Terragona would be swallowed up like a deer in the lion's belly, then.

"The young men grow restless," he had told his own inner council when the yellow birds had begun to fly over Terragona every day, landing in so many different places. "The men with thunder in their hands chop many holes in the earth, destroy our yam fields, and our people run to see their magic and to claim the rocks that will make them rich. Many of our elders want to rule their own villages now so that they can have the rocks for themselves. Our glorious Chief Turgobyne holds his scepter like it was a stick for digging grubworms; the men with thunder control his mind and pour water on the fires of his heart. Even his women argue with him for power. His house is full of confusion. Even now he hides in his sacred temple in Caha, afraid of his own people. Soon he will lose his power to the young men, who get bolder, for they know he does not rule his own house well.

"And what of the people of yellow bird?" he went on, jerking his chin toward the hospital base. "Our old people who are too sick and should be left in the jungle for the baboons and hyenas—where are they now? They come back from yellow bird's people chattering like children; they eat like pythons; and again they take wives or husbands, and soon children are born. The medicine in the box saves our children from death but gives life to the dead—soon there will be too many to feed and we will die fighting each other for a piece of root."

The old men on the council clucked in their throats, adding their alarm to this report.

"And our children do not tend the fields or fish," another council member spoke from the shadows. "They spend their time at yellow bird's house, singing the strange songs taught to them. And the men with thunder in their hands bring fear to our villages with their strange power. Our land now feels the curse of these people . . . and our glorious Chief Turgobyne is powerless to stop it. The gate that Yellow Bird opened into us is now soon to bring a flood of destruction on us . . ."

"What docs Kamako, son of Janus, prince of iron, now say to us?" Elpheus the elder asked, for it was in his power to act when Turgobyne was absent in council.

Kamako did not answer immediately. He kneeled down to the fire instead, picked up a half-burned stick and blew on the coals. The flame leaped up on the stick and the men in council let out long, heavy sighs, for this was the sign that what thoughts Kamako had then were right and true as the god Caha determined.

Kamako stood up tall and lean with the erect carriage of his Berber ancestry, his purple robes of council authority clinging to his body, which still showed the muscles though his head had already turned the color of the beckoning grave.

"It is time, honorable princes of Turgobyne's council," he had said then, "to bring power back to Turgobyne." The council waited in silence, anticipating the word of Caha. "We must bring the skin of the yellow bird to Turgobyne," he said then. "We must strike him from his flight, bring him down as he flies. We must show our strength over this beast of the air . . . then when we have presented Turgobyne, our honorable chief, with the skin of the yellow bird, then the Terragona people will know that power still rests in his hand. And the people of the yellow bird will know terror, and they will leave with the men who carry thunder in their hands . . . for they will not fly their birds where we lay in wait . . ."

"The people of the yellow bird, they who touch our bodies, have done us no real harm," someone spoke from the shadows. "They have made our children to sing again; they speak soft words while they take away our pain. Though our old people yet live when they should die, they can be fed if we grow more crops, for they now have the strength to work . . ."

"But not the will," Kamako had argued. "Who will work the fields when riches lie under the earth? I too feel no hate for the people of the yellow bird. But if we do not act now, then who can foresee where we shall be another moon from now? The men with thunder in their hands grow more bold, and the young follow them to get some of that terrible magic . . ."

"It will not be easy, this you do," another voice broke in. "The men with thunder in their hands have much power."

"But their life is in the yellow bird," Kamako advised. "Whoever controls yellow bird controls Terragona. And we will have our day."

"Mark it well, Kamako, son of Janus, prince of iron," Elpheus warned then, "how you do this thing, for the time grows late."

He had marked it well, Kamako thought as he crouched down in the swamp scrub of the clearing. But now it seemed as if the yellow bird knew what he planned and now teased him by coming in a different way and going out too high.

But Kamako was not to be put off. Even now he watched the red cloth on the stick there on the field he could see even from this distance as it flapped in the wind. He had watched it from even closer for many days. Before, two moons ago, when the yellow bird first came in here, the cloth stood out the other way, toward Kamako, not away from him. Why was this? And why did the yellow bird change with the way the cloth blew on the stick?

He felt the wind again as it came up hot off the desert far below, blowing away from him. When would the red cloth change its flapping again? The rains? When the rains began the wind would move against him, not away from him. Would the yellow bird follow the wind, come in against the cloth then? If it did, it would come over Kamako again, from the other direction—and he stood up to look behind him and up, tracing the path of the bird as it had to come down to the field. It comes low when it is heavy, he thought. Then it will come low again when the first winds of the rains begin. He looked at the field stretching out directly in front of him.

He could not be sure finally, but the thought of this made some sense to him and excited him—for there was hope yet, and that hope meant honor to preserve, Terragona to live. But it would yet mean time before the winds swung around with the first smell of the rains, and Terragona would perhaps suffer much before it was time. And how long could Turgobyne hold the young men?

Well, there was no other way. He would come here every day in the morning and watch the red cloth on the stick—and when it changed to snap its gay color toward him, the hour was his.

If Caha was with him . . .

# CHAPTER IV

Milton Gregson hurried the last fifty yards to the field office at 9:35, belching egg and bacon from a much too hurried breakfast, wanting to get that transmission in to Augie before anyone else. Ted Cranston's call to him about that a few minutes ago carried that extra ingredient of alarm, and he was afraid Ted would put that transmission in with the wrong party listening in.

He puffed and panted some now as he increased his pace. He was terribly out of shape. It worried him. He was big-framed but not fat. He was forty-four years old, too young to feel the constricting of the heart muscles. He was a plain, almost homely man. Twenty years of Harmattan desert winds and sun had burned his face to a reddish brown; his rather bulbous nose had peeled too often and turned a darker red than his face. His greenish eyes, red and puffy from the Harmattan dust this time of year, were hidden behind sunglasses, which he took to wearing even inside lately. His hair was still black but wiry so that it often stood up in clumps of rebellious bramble, making him look as if he'd just gotten out of bed. He spent a lot of time slapping at the cowlick twigs with meaty strokes of his left hand, so that it had become a hallmark habit with him by now. He felt the pocket of acid swell in his throat now, and he found a mint in his pocket and put it into his mouth hurriedly. Every year the tensions of approaching Field Council churned his stomach—he was not a good administrator, and his rule here was not strong enough to give him the confidence he needed. On top of that, of course, was the mounting pressure of Operation Shoestring that he knew had to come to a head this week . . .

He turned the corner of the building and headed the last twenty yards to the main door when Ted Cranston slammed out of an exit to his left, looking like bad news.

"Maddigan's been in since early last night," Ted said, trying to fall in with Gregson's long strides, his asthmatic wheeze sounding like static competing with his words.

"So I heard," Gregson said mildly, not particularly willing to soothe Ted's concerns about that right now. "When Maddigan's late, all is straight; when he's early, all is turvy . . ."

"He was with G.D. last night, real late," Ted went on, coughing on the congestion in his lungs. He was going on fifty but looked sixty, short, thin, completely bald, his dark-blue shorts and white shirt hanging limp on his skeletal frame.

"Is Augie still on stand-by?" Gregson asked then as he came to the steps. He paused there when Ted did not answer immediately. Ted's chest was heaving under the shirt as the exertion of walking so rapidly taxed his laboring lungs. He ran his hand over his mouth, not looking at Gregson.

"I thought I should tell G.D., Milt," he said then, his brown eyes wavering, carrying those same shadows of uncertainty. "I mean . . . well, you know Augie's father is coming in today . . . and I thought, well, I thought I better get G.D. to take Augie's transmission . . ."

"Couldn't go any higher than that, I guess," Gregson commented, trying to keep it light, trying to ease it for Ted. Already the word of the coming of Augie's father today was common knowledge on the headquarters compound even though the cable had only arrived a few hours ago. Ted, too quick to sense problems shaping beyond the smallest ingredient, would move to start bucket brigades before there was any hint of a spark. For Ted, whose asthma plagued him constantly, the thinner air of the plateau here was his only hope of staying alive. To stay on the plateau and away from the deadly fungus of the jungles, he felt he had to conduct the functions of his office as assistant to the field director with perfection—and any hint of trouble of any kind had to be a threat. Now the approaching Field Council, for him as well, even as it was for Gregson, loomed up as a gigantic test for them all. The humanity of God-men, Gregson thought, was not always easy to bear, including his own.

"So what did Augie have to say?" Gregson went on, feeling the burn of his stomach acids in a fresh onslaught.

"I didn't get it all . . . some pretty big words that didn't sound good about Blake . . . G.D. took most of it down . . ."

"I'm sure he did . . . did you tell Augie about his father?"

"No, the cable said not to tell him," and Ted began to dig in his shirt pocket for the wire, his bony knuckles gleaming with beads of sweat. "By the way, here's a note from Gina Roman too . . ."

Gregson took it, not knowing what that had to do with the immediate situation. He opened it and read the typed sentence.

"Every year this girl types me a note asking for transfer to the desert frontier," he commented with disinterest. "Only now she wants to take Emily Stewart's place in Durungu?" Ted did not reply, still hunting for that cable, and Gregson added, "Everybody wants to stay out of Durungu and yet this girl is dying to get there . . . anyway, I doubt Doc Barak will let her go, she's his best in surgery . . ." He paused then, trying to focus on the image of Gina Roman. Laura had told him, not long ago, that Gina was "too cold a fish for headquarters staff" and that she was showing up too often in church with that new African technician, Jonathan Bartuga. "She's doing that deliberately to get a way out of here," Laura warned. "So let her go, why don't you?"

Gregson folded the note down and put it in his shirt pocket, and then asked, "What's the mood among the other council members?"

"Well," Ted came back quickly again, abandoning his fruitless search for the cable, "Maddigan's got most of them convinced Blake has to go . . . there's even talk of halting Shoestring altogether . . ."

"Did you give G.D. or Maddigan anything on Blake?"

Ted coughed. "Well, Maddigan came in last night and insisted on having Blake's file . . . so, well, I had no choice, Milt . . ."

"Did you tell him about Mentaya's offer?"

"He seemed to know all about that."

Gregson didn't respond further. There wasn't much going between him and Ted. Both of them knew they were in their field jobs because of the influence of G.D.—General Director Martin Merriweather. Neither he nor Ted had accumulated enough administrative experience even in their eighteen years on this field to ride herd on thirty different kinds of ministries, two hundred and eighty different personality types of missionaries and twenty hard-nosed field superintendents. Both of them knew they had been elected by the district superintendents after Merriweather brought all his powers to bear. It was no secret, certainly not to Ted, that Merriweather wanted Gregson in the field leader's job because Gregson was a "model administrator," which meant he did what he was expected to do and never rocked the boat. It was also an accepted fact in the field office that Maddigan and Merriweather controlled the destiny of the mission and that everyone else, including Gregson as well as the field superintendents, yielded to that power regardless of the field manual's rules to the contrary. And Ted, of course, was conscious himself that he was in his job only because his health forbade him doing anything else and maybe because he knew Robert's Rules of Order better than most. So neither of them, though linked in their faith, could not own up much respect for each other's positions. And Gregson needed Ted's respect now and his loyalty, especially with the issue over Blake threatening to blow a hole in the field administration.

He walked inside then and said, over his shoulder, "How about the gas requisition and medical supplies for Blake? Have they been sent?"

Again Ted coughed from behind him and Gregson stopped and turned quickly around so that Ted almost bumped into him. "G.D. put a hold on all supplies to Durungu pending Field Council action," Ted said, looking at the floor.

"A hold?" Gregson said sharply, his voice rising in the corridor so that some of the staff moving by them looked at him quickly. "We can't afford a hold! I gave strict orders . . ."

"Last night he did it, Milt," Ted said with appeal, but Gregson had turned again and began walking swiftly down the corridor toward Merriweather's office at the far end.

"I mean I would have told you, Milt," Ted called after him, trying to stay on his heels, "but what can you do anyway when G.D. and Maddigan get together on these things—"

Gregson pushed the door open to Merriweather's office, swallowing against the burning pressure in his throat, knowing he had to watch himself now, that this was no place to play matador. As he walked in, Merriweather jumped out of his chair, lifting his arms in that pose of perpetual benediction, like he was trying to throw an asbestos blanket over an approaching fire.

"Well, Milt," he crowed in that jubilant, forever spiritually optimistic overture, "how's the most gifted field director in UFL history this fine morning?"

87

"Fine, G.D.," Gregson said, pausing in front of the desk, digging for his handkerchief to dab at his watery eyes under his sunglasses, waiting to let G.D. finish his overture.

"Sleep well?"

"As well as can be expected this time of year, I guess."

"Well, my boy, it's tennis, more tennis you need," G.D. sang out. "Like I was telling Mildred—Mildred, I say, what these young bucks need around here is a good hour of tennis every night. Like Barak says, it keeps the muscles toned and brings refreshing sleep . . . well, Milt, you look great anyway . . ."

Gregson knew he didn't look anywhere near that today. But that was Martin Merriweather's way. He had the public relations gift that went with his office as General Director, a cross between an insurance salesman and an army recruiter. Sometimes he became a victim of it himself, forcing too much of a mellifluous coating over situations that demanded more serious deliberation. But to Merriweather, the mission was his family—he delighted in propping up every member as his own precious deposit in the Kingdom of Heaven.

He was a surprisingly youthful-looking man for sixty-three, with a healthy tan that never seemed to fade, sharp blue eyes that missed very little from behind gold-rimmed spectacles. He had all his teeth and most of his pale-blond hair, which he combed off to one side in a youthful kind of wave. Gregson admired him for his vitality and dedication, even though the usual spray of excessive panderings toward everyone, from the groundskeeper to the Premier, was too often irritating. Yet, for all of that, Gregson never for a moment doubted the man's spirituality. Forty years of pioneering United in Hamara had taught him a few lessons on how to take his shoes off in the presence of God. And this, combined with his superior ability to relate to the thousands of potential donors at home, accounted for the million and more that went into the mission's work in Africa every year. And not a penny of that ever went into his own pocket. It was said of his power to move people at home that "once Merriweather starts to speak, Satan has to sit still with his feet off the floor."

"G.D.," Gregson began, after clearing his throat, not sure how sharp an angle of attack he should take now, "I don't understand about cutting Blake's gas . . ." He put it out carefully, not pushing.

His smile remained fixed as he stood there behind his desk. "Milt, you know how we do things in questionable operations, what's the matter with you?" he said lightly, his smile widening. "Whenever we are uncertain about how an operation should go, we hold appropriations until it's settled. No point in loading up 3,000 gallons of gasoline if we have to change the logistics tomorrow, right?"

"I wasn't anticipating any alteration of the Shoestring operation, G.D. . . ."

"Nor am I, Milt," the older man came back with that confident boom in his voice. "But Pat has his powder primed on Shoestring and Blake, so we better follow procedures on this . . ."

Gregson swallowed against the burn of the acid in his throat, feeling that funny tripping beat in his temple start up. "I'm more worried about keeping our planes in the air over Terragona, G.D.," he ventured mildly enough, feeling the binding kind of stricture across his chest. "To do that, Blake has to have gas—"

"Milt, that's what I like about you," G.D. said with that tone of effervescence. "Like I told Mildred—Mildred, I say, my man Gregson sticks by his people, you have to say that for him!" But how much more, if that, Gregson mused. Then, after adjusting his glasses with the fingers of his left hand, the older man added, "Anyway, I'm not out to cut the flights, Milt, or jeopardize our people in Terragona. Blake has enough gas to keep going for the next few days . . ."

"Excuse me, G.D., but it takes time to move that much gasoline over those roads even at their best, and if it should start raining early, as the Africans expect . . ."

Merriweather looked up at him quickly, his face still relaxed in the lines of pleasantry but just a trace of warning crossing his eyes that said he was not used to being interrupted in midsentence. "We've no choice right now, Milt," he went on, going back to his papers. "If we are going to save the operation, which I hope we can, then we play it right as procedures dictate. Anyway, we should have this settled on Tuesday at the latest—what I'm hoping for is no more than a change of command at Durungu . . ."

"Change?" Gregson said, wanting to glance over at Ted to see if his assistant knew about that but resisting it, because Ted had his own battle right now. "I don't have anything on the agenda about a change in command . . ."

"Well, Maddigan's got his case on Blake, Milt," and G.D. sounded now like this was just another one of those things. "And he's got most of the superintendents ready to go along. There's a storm building over the Durungu operation, as you must know. Our men feel we were too premature in sending our people in, too shortsighted in our agreeing to fly nitro and supplies in for those Hamaran prospectors . . . but the real issue comes down to Blake, and I don't want Maddigan coming into Council laying out this administration on what we are supposed to protect, namely the spiritual veracity of our leadership . . ."

Gregson thought of Maddigan then, seeing the awesome dimension of the man from the north who for thirty-eight years waged his holy wars side by side with Merriweather and built the pillars of Christianity in Hamara that would not be shaken easily. It was said that G.D. held the office but Maddigan carried the fuse box. Nobody stood in the way of either of them, but Merriweather, when it came down to brass tacks, would defer to him, as he was doing now.

Gregson weighed it carefully before letting the words out, but he finally said, "I have the highest respect for Pat Maddigan, G.D., but he's been highly critical of Shoestring since we launched it. I just don't think he should be allowed to use Blake's—well, unorthodox way of doing things maybe—as a means to get support for curtailing the operation—"

"Unorthodox is the right word all right," Merriweather came back quickly. "But Pat is a giant here, a spiritual giant. God has blessed him, used him in the years. At any rate, he's got momentum now . . . sometimes events are tailored for a man, and this one on Blake is cut to order for Pat. So to stay ahead of him, I think the suspension of Blake should come from you in Council, Milt . . ."

"On what grounds?"

Merriweather glanced at him sharply. The question was irrelevant to him. "Sit down, Milt," he said then. Reluctantly, Gregson sat in the wicker chair. Nobody was any good with Merriweather sitting down. He had command of any ground that was made level to him. "Now . . . I got Augie's transmission this morning. He says," and he glanced at his notes now, "that Blake is a man with definite megalomanic tendencies and Machiavellian protrusions among the Africans." G.D. smiled at that. "Augie never did say things simply . . . anyway, Milt, this means that Blake, according to Augie, is driving for the great and grandiose performance and making the ends justify the means for power—"

90

"One disenchanted pilot does not make a case, G.D.," Gregson insisted.

"Maybe not. But this disenchanted pilot has a daddy coming in here today, Milt. And that daddy has accounted for a big chunk of money for this mission over the years, to say nothing of what he's put into Shoestring. The box score up there at Durungu is not a good one for him to see: three pilots dead, a nurse suffering a nervous collapse, and now our best pilot asking for a transfer . . ."

"The box score on the miracles performed even to get those planes in the air and those kids flying nitro into Terragona every day is what I'm looking at," Gregson returned, even though he knew he was wasting his time.

"The question, though, is whether the so-called miracles Blake is performing are of God or strictly human genius," Merriweather came back pleasantly enough. "Have you read his file lately?" Which meant, of course, that Maddigan had read it to him, probably last night.

"Three years ago . . . when he first came in, when I took it to the Field Council to pass him in. Which they did . . ."

"Well," G.D. went on after a sigh, "we have a man here thirty-eight years old who has a flimsy record at best, judging by his answers to the doctrinal and theological sections," and Gregson knew that was Maddigan talking again. "His spiritual references, two in number, don't say much. This man who knew him at Global Airlines has nothing to say on his spiritual character. And Alex Bell of Seaman's Mission in New York, who was supposed to be the key man in verifying Blake's spiritual experience, is just as vague. What Maddigan is putting his whole case on, though, is Blake's description of the validity of his own spiritual experience. Let me quote:

'No man can be so brash as to be sure of everything he can see—so it is a pretty cocky view to say a man can be so sure he understands the whole mystical relationship with God. I know an airplane runs right, not by the sound of it so much, but by how it feels in the controls. Sometimes a man's life vibrates like hell'—and Merriweather paused to clear his throat on that word—'and he figures it's all in the power plant. It takes a big man with the blueprints of the entire system to find the answer. I ran out of the answers myself. If Christ means anything at all, it's that He found the short circuit and got the engines humming again—and now the controls hang loose.' "

G.D. dropped the paper back into the file folder. Gregson had read that three years ago. At that time he thought the words had a certain poignancy to them, even spiritual accuracy. But what G.D. was saying now was that when Maddigan read it in Council, void of the necessary spiritual terminology demanded of this spiritual order, it would go down as something close to heresy.

"We didn't bring Blake in for his theology," Gregson tried again, "or the right words. He was the man closest to the qualifications we needed to get the biggest airlift of this mission functional into Terragona. I doubt any other man could have done what he's done. He was a man who, by his experience with jets in Korea and being a first-line officer with Global, came up to the mark we needed. Apart from his language, he's proven the point . . ."

G.D. sighed then, and took off his glasses to rub his eyes with the heels of both hands, elbows resting on the desk top. "Milt, the point is that none of that has enough covering for his lack of spiritual credential. Maddigan has quite a list of other things here too. Like the fact that Blake plays strange music up there . . . every morning it's this 'Colonel Bogey' or whatever, and at night he finishes the day with something called 'Tannhauser,' neither one of which is in my hymn book. He calls his airfield 'Camelot' of all things, though I haven't the foggiest notion why. Worse than that, he's flying a VW sedan into Turgobyne piece by piece on our airplanes, and that's going to be hard to explain to Augie's father, let alone to me. He's got his pilots walking around up there in uniforms of black baseball caps, sunglasses and khakis. He pushes his pilots even on Sunday, Milt, ignoring the Lord's day altogether . . ."

"He's working against the rains, G.D.," Gregson said.

"And there's this other thing," G.D. came back, picking up a spool of recording tape, ignoring Gregson's remark. "Emily Stewart recorded Blake's first pep talk to his pilots five months ago . . . this is Maddigan's exhibit A you can be sure."

G.D. put the tape on the machine on the shelf behind him and hit the play switch. ". . . now I want to tell you something right out," the voice came on in a kind of muffled sound but with elements of command that were unmistakably Blake's. "I don't want anybody here gunning for quick martyrdom before God's appointed time. I don't want anyone here thinking that death is more glorious than life either. If anybody here has the sound of heavenly harps in his ears, he can take the next trolley back to Talfungo. All right, get something else straight too: You're flyers, not preachers. Up here you can't be both. You're not here to hold public prayer meetings or convert the natives. You're going to think flying night and day, and fly those machines like the Cessna people never intended . . .

"Now . . . you can pray all you want to about your flying, but not on my time or your flying time. The good Lord gave you a brain, two hands and two feet, and some ability to keep an airplane in the air. So He expects you to be flyers, not only pray-ers. So if you drop a wing on a turn or so much as raise a pocket of dust on touching down here, you own up to me, not to God.

"Now . . . you got people over there in Terragona, may I remind you, who are trying to hold on to a piece of real estate with a hypodermic and a bedpan," and somebody laughed in the background on the tape, and Blake paused, apparently to let it clear the air. "It takes guts to do that, and don't forget it . . . so you're going to have to match their guts with your own, if you intend to keep them and yourselves alive. This nitro business is not my idea, but you better remember one thing: It doesn't know the difference between God-men and anti-God-men . . . you'll splatter just as far and wide once that stuff goes up as those cattleherders out in the desert there . . .

"Now . . . you're here to win, not lose. To win you got to start thinking as a team, flying as a team. And the best way to do that is to know who your enemy is. The devil here, gentlemen, is wind and turbulence and the attitude you might have that says God will fly those planes for you. But remember this: Every time you land that airplane in Terragona without scattering yourself across a couple of miles, you kick the hell out of the devil! And we're going to keep on kicking the hell out of him until he waves the truce!" There was a pause again, but no laughter. "Okay, that's all for now. Let's get at this thing and earn our blessings . . ."

G.D. switched off the recorder. Ted coughed from somewhere behind Gregson, sounding like a feeble gasp. "Blake was new to Christianity, you know that," Gregson appealed. "He didn't have all the right language, and we didn't necessarily expect him to—"

"Why are you making such an issue of this one, Milt?" G.D. asked rather querulously. "Is this so different from other changes we had to make in leadership we felt was out of step? You got some reason for digging in like this, then?"

"Maybe I'm not arguing about doing it so much," Gregson tried again, feeling he was running out of room now, "but the timing of it. We're behind in the build-up of supplies in Terragona, the rains are expected to be early. I just don't want to short-change our people in Terragona, that's all. We cleared Blake in once, and I see no reason to tamper with the balances of the operation—"

"You will remember, too, Milt, that it was you who insisted, back in Boston three years ago, that Blake was our man," G.D. countered. "I was impressed that you were impressed. And I admit I was willing to waive his slim theological background, because we've done it before for engineers and doctors who had specialties we needed. But now it looks like we got a backfire on our hands, and if, like Maddigan says, we go into total deterioration up in Durungu, I don't want to have to explain a spiritually fuzzy leadership along with everything else. Nor do you, right, Milt?"

The phone rang, and when G.D. picked it up, Gregson walked to the window to look out across the compound. Neat hedgerows, neat lawns, neat duplexes of tropical prefab guaranteed never to "warp, mold or leak." All supposedly fitting the image, as if God built everything using a T-square. Not a brick or a twig out of place. He felt proud of it once, for the way it complemented the mission, even Hamara. But now he wasn't so sure. It seemed to look brittle, out of place, an image of plastic, a vulnerable foot of clay, carrying too much of the Western flavor in its architecture, not enough of Hamara. It begged a contrary dimension, a bold piece of architecture maybe, a feeling more of humanity perhaps, something that came closer to the spirit of Hamara.

Because Hamara had changed since independence too. Somehow he was sure the people didn't care particularly for ninety-degree corners on their houses or churches; they did not necessarily bow to water closets or slick paper magazines with God done up in 72-point Bodoni; they could do without electricity in their homes or even aluminum-pan roofs. When the French left, much of that went with them. And now Gregson sensed that the mission had to get into the new spirit of things as well. Hamara owned Christianity almost as her national religion, but it would have to become more than simply a church building. She needed a bold venture to validate God for the people, and maybe Operation Shoestring was exactly that—and maybe Blake was that spirit who could do it?

He remembered Blake again as he was that day he came down the ramp of the airplane at Talfungo three years ago or so. He sensed then that the man was not cut out of the same cloth as those who made it into the mission. He remembered his coming down that gangway with a single battered suitcase, dressed in a khaki shirt that was undoubtedly a carryover from his military days, not matching his green tropical trousers at all. He chewed on a frayed toothpick and wore sunglasses all the time. He said nothing unless directly asked. He had a habit of constantly rubbing his right palm across his mouth as if he were trying to destroy the lingering taste of something. Gregson did not think at the time that the crusty, homespun image of the man was in any way indicative of any spiritual problem within; but he should have known that in a spiritual order where externals carried such prominent credence in proving a man's rightful place in the Body, that Blake had everything going wrong for him. But at that time, Gregson, like everybody else in the mission headquarters —Maddigan included, for all he knew—was willing to ignore that image, caught up instead in the electrifying possibilities of Terragona and what Blake could do to bring about that eventuality.

Just then G.D. hung up the phone and said, "Milt, that was Maddigan . . . did you know that Blake has been sheltering Sudanese refugees up at Durungu and giving them medical treatment?"

Gregson walked back to the desk. "I didn't know."

"But you know how sticky Hamara gets on that point. It's a law, Milt, and—"

"I don't think the Premier would land very hard on him for that," Gregson continued. "It's not a law anyway, only an unwritten understanding that nobody is going to enforce . . ."

"It could get sticky, Milt, and you know it."

Gregson sighed and swiped at the brambles of his cowlick, debating whether to keep pushing. "This is no ordinary operation, G.D.," and he decided to make one more attempt. "It's not like anything we've tried before. We agreed when we decided to go with it that the man who would win it for us would not do it necessarily with charm and personality, or maybe even with a lot of theological insight. We tried to find that perfect man in every dimension, and we concluded there wasn't time to wait, that Blake was as close as we could get. . ."

"Milt," G.D. came back quickly in that tone of dismissal which said he was running out of patience with this, "I spent forty years in this mission, keeping it alive by staying one step ahead of the problems. Blake has become a problem. God knows I have no personal vendetta against him, and I want to do all I can for him once he's out of leadership up there. But right now, if we are going to keep the operation alive at all, we've got to make some kind of move on him. The Council won't release any appropriation to Durungu until we do. They'd rather evacuate Terragona totally if it came right down to it, that's how strong the feeling seems to be on him . . ."

"You know we can't evacuate our people out of there now without a military escort," Gregson insisted, ignoring protocol now.

"If it becomes necessary to do it that way, it'll be done, Milt," G.D. snapped.

"That would bring a lot of unnecessary bloodshed . . ."

"Nobody is really sure of that either, and the U.N. might be able to do it if called on," G.D. came back. "The point is here, Milt, I'm trying to avoid that possibility in any case. This has been a tremendous idea of yours from the very start. What was it that Doctor Rayburn said, 'God before technology,' something like that—well, I always did like that. To save it then, we will have to follow the procedures like any other operation of ours we felt was in jeopardy, simply change horses. So I want you to fly to Durungu tomorrow and take the elder Thornhill with you. I'll feel better if you're with him up there anyway. While you're up there, of course, you'll have to play devil's advocate on Blake . . ."

"If everyone is decided on removing him, what's the point?" Gregson asked, trying to keep it academic.

"Because it has to come from you, where it should have at the start," Merriweather retorted with a sniff. "Maddigan should not be the one calling you out on a questionable leader in the field, you know that. If there is to be a suspension, then it must come from you on Tuesday morning in Council, based on your most up-to-date, objective investigation. I remind you, Milt, that this mission stays alive as the field administration in authority maintains its primary rule. If we lose that, we could put a crack right down the entire field. Do you understand me, Milt?" Gregson wisely refrained from comment.

"And with that recommendation for suspension, Milt," G.D. went on, "I want you to recommend Augie Thornhill to take Blake's place . . ."

Gregson put his right forefinger against his temple to control the galloping beat there now. Augie would never pull it off; there wasn't a man up there who could, including Rudy Kipstein. But for Merriweather, the move would be an acceptable one with the field men and keep Maddigan at arm's length.

Gregson sighed and found his handkerchief to blow his nose. "What about those forms Mentaya sent?" he asked then, swinging off the subject, knowing it was settled anyway, feeling the dull beat of futility.

"Sign them," G.D. replied flatly.

"That's a big order. We've already committed ourselves to co-operate with the government in carrying that nitro . . . this will only get us in thicker. We've already got a dozen trade commissions, everybody from Pepsi-Cola to Texas Oil trying to buy their way into our airlift. If we go all the way with Mentaya, allowing him in, that's going to put a lot of pressure on our people in Terragona . . ."

"Milt"—G.D. took off his glasses, a sure sign that he was getting exasperated—"there are some things you have to do on your own as field leader. We can't undo our hookup with Hamara on the nitro, and there is certainly no way I know of that we can win in an argument with Mentaya . . ."

"I'd just rather wait for the Premier to return," Gregson insisted. "Somehow I feel something wrong in all this . . ."

"And we may just need Mentaya's planes if things continue to build up against us in Durungu," G.D. went on. "Sign those papers, Milt . . ."

Actually it was not for him to order it, Gregson knew. As General Director, his main responsibility was representing the mission at home among potential donors. The matters of field policy were supposed to be the field director's in consultation with his Field Council. Once a year Merriweather came to the field to sit in as "unofficial" presider over Council meetings. This did not entitle him to any kind of action other than playing the role as "spiritual father." And yet he still wielded ultimate power and influence, which nobody would question, and Gregson had no heart now to challenge him on it. He should not have asked the question in the first place.

"Okay, Milt?"

"Okay," Gregson said with a shrug.

"Good! By the way," the older man went on, picking up the tone of conversation an octave lower now, "there's a nurse over at the hospital . . . oh, what's her name now, came to see me last night, insisted God was calling her to Durungu to replace Emily Stewart . . ."

"Gina Roman," Ted put in quickly.

"That's her. Look, I don't usually get into these things, but when anyone is so certain about being led of God—well, put her transfer through, why don't you? Let her fly up to Durungu tomorrow. Any objections, Milt?"

"She hates administration, G.D., that's the only reason—"

"So?" and G.D. laughed again. "Somebody has to replace Emily, right?"

Gregson nodded, "Anything you say, G.D. . . ."

"That's my man!" and now he got up and moved for the door on springy legs. "I've got to get to Maddigan . . . I promised him a report after I talked to you." He paused at the door and turned to look back at the right leg of his desk. "Have a good trip, Milt." He never looked directly at Gregson. "I'll be praying for you." Then his voice rose an octave as he said, "Don't forget to tell your good wife to keep the coffee on . . . we have to get together more often, Milt. I always say to Mildred—Mildred, I say, I only get to the field once a year for Field Council, and we just have to drink more of Laura Gregson's superb coffee! See you Tuesday, Milt!"

He was gone then, leaving the room in a state of confusion like the passing of a tornadic wind. Gregson found a mint in his shirt pocket, put it into his mouth and chewed on it quickly. He turned then and walked out, headed down the corridor to his own office, Ted on his heels.

"Ted, I want you to get two cables off right away," he said when at his own desk, and he sat down to begin writing in his log, wanting to get it all down for the record. "One to our man Al Renfro in the Boston office—tell him to check further on Blake's background at Global Airlines, check with FAA if necessary. Two, send one to this man Alex Bell of Seaman's Mission and ask him for all the validation he can give us on Blake's actual spiritual experience. It's kind of late now, but I want it on the record. Tell him to call us if he can . . ."

"You going to oppose Maddigan on Blake, Milt?" Ted said in some awe, but Gregson did not answer that.

"Also," he said, "tell Blake on the ten o'clock transmission tonight that I'm coming, but don't tell him Augie's father is with me—"

"Maybe he should know, to get prepared—"

"And tell Gina Roman to be ready at five-thirty tomorrow morning. Also, have a plane stand by for us at the field."

Ted coughed again so that his body bent with the near convulsion of it. He looked limp, pale and drained, and his head kept bobbing uncertainly. Gregson felt a pang of compassion for him then, for he was seeing the total extension of himself.

"Get some coffee, Ted."

Ted cleared his throat and nodded, sliding out of the room as if he were leaving church.

Gregson, his mind still feeling the steady, heavy beat of that thumping in his right temple, stared at the forms of Felix Mentaya on his desk, but he was hardly seeing them. The depression had grabbed him around the heart, cutting deep to the vital core of his weak resolve, threatening to rob him of any pretense he had left. Some men rose to the battles of their office and won something in defeat anyway, but all he could do was to accommodate himself, as he always did, to the superior powers over him, with fatalistic resignation. Now it was going to be the same with Felix Mentaya's papers, and he blinked once to get his mind on them. He buzzed his secretary, ordered a cup of Ovaltine heavy on cream; when it was delivered, he sat back, pondering if he should try to talk to Mentaya about the problem he was posing for Terragona.

He sensed that Mentaya had something else in mind by asking to be in on the Terragona flights—but what? Gregson knew he had no use for missions, for reasons known only to himself. Yet, he was never overly critical and was always friendly to Gregson. If Felix had his way, though, he would probably not allow missions to remain in Hamara. The "boy king," however, took the opposite view. He knew that missions in Hamara had been the key in developing the educated leadership responsible for carrying the country through the postindependence storms. And he had expressed many times to Gregson how much he counted on those same schools and mission personnel to help develop the country for the future. Gregson wondered if he should get advice from Timothy Belang in the Government Information Office, at least about what he thought the wise thing would be to do with the papers. He had been in Timothy's home for dinner on many occasions and vice versa. Perhaps through Timothy he might influence Felix to hold off on Terragona for a little while longer.

Calling Timothy, though, on such a matter would be pushing friendship too far. He would have to talk to Mentaya himself or find a way to hold off signing the forms. But he did not want to provoke any government figure here, even as Merriweather warned. The mission, by necessity, was bound to stay clear of any sticky entanglements with the government. And yet that was already after the fact anyway: Mentaya had managed to influence the Premier to using the mission to run that nitro into Terragona, and even though the Premier called it a "co-operative venture for humanity," Mentaya undoubtedly had his own statement for it. At any rate, did he dare aggravate Mentaya further? And yet to sign those forms was to clear Mentaya's aircraft into airspace that Blake had promised Turgobyne he would keep pure. To go back on that was going to complicate matters considerably for Blake and for the missionaries in Terragona. Well, did he have any choice? The Premier was out of reach in Madagascar. And G.D. expected him to sign those papers . . .

So he signed them. And he took a sip of Ovaltine but found no comfort in it.

He played tennis with Doctor David Barak at five as scheduled. He managed to get two days in a week, not every day, like G.D. extolled. He was not a good tennis player. Today he was worse. All the backed-up frustrations he had accumulated in five years here seemed to possess him as he tried to drive the ball over the net to the nimble African, who was a pro. Now and then he drove one in bounds, and Barak deftly returned it in an easy lob. To which Gregson would address himself again with the same ferocity until the African called a halt, pleading that he did not want to be sent home to glory at the end of a tennis ball.

They sat down on the narrow bench off the court, towels draped around their necks. Barak was tall and lanky and loose-jointed with sure, slender, quick hands. He was a few years older than Gregson, with the distinct facial tracings of the Hamaran—slightly flattened nose with wide nostrils, high-ridged eyebrows, deep sockets, sharp, protruding cheekbones and the thin, delicately contoured lips of the desert nomadic. He moved with easy grace, and looking at him now, his black skin greased with sweat, he could have been any successful black athlete in the States—a good muscular frame under the white shirt and shorts and the air of a man who knew what he was doing in just about anything he tried. He was a superior surgeon, trained at Harvard Medical School under mission auspices, and for eighteen years directed the mission hospital here at Talfungo, giving it a reputation that no white doctor could have ever done. He was not talkative, but he was articulate in just about any subject, either Hamaran or American or European—on top of that, he was the most gifted Bible expositor Gregson had ever known. His love was the Psalms and Shakespeare.

Barak maintained the same relationship with Gregson as he had with the other field directors before him. He felt it his personal responsibility to guard the health of the top field officer as his own God-given charge. He had nursed three before Gregson, but none of them had cultivated the relationship with him that Gregson did. He knew that Gregson had few administrative talents, but there was more of the human sensitivity about him, maybe even too much sentiment for the job. Because of this, Barak sensed that he seemed to suffer more than his predecessors in the complexities of spiritual leadership.

Gregson, meanwhile, liked Barak because he never betrayed a confidence. There were in the African doctor, as well, qualities of wisdom and patience that Gregson needed—and more and more lately he was turning to the doctor for the therapy he needed which he could get nowhere else.

"Whose face is on the tennis ball, then?" Barak opened the conversation after five minutes of silence.

Gregson didn't answer immediately. He kept looking at the reddish glow of the setting sun beyond the date palms.

"The devil's, who else?"

"Well, it appears that the keeper of number-one pit has sent quite an embassage here to this place already, then."

"Meaning what?"

"Meaning that I am getting an unusual number of complaints from headquarters staff suffering the pains of impending councilitis . . . and you, my friend, have never hit a tennis ball like that in the years I've known you."

"So everybody's uptight. That's life . . ."

"Not quite, noble father," Barak commented with a kind of half-smile that was gentle. "Uptightness is not the heritage of the saints received from God. It would seem the people here are confused as to whom the devil has control of . . . it seems to center on Blake."

"You know him?"

Barak grunted, working at the steel strands on his racket. "I happen to man the intersection of a thousand passing rumors, remember? Besides, I gave him his physical three years ago, the only one he's had out here. He and his pilots need another, you know, to satisfy the Civil Aeronautics Board of Hamara. I have not seen him since then. But, as I remember, he was as tough as catgut . . ."

Gregson rubbed at the sweat on his forehead with the end of his khaki towel. With his eyes on the sky, he said, "You know, I never promised him a dime when I sent him up to the desert to find an airfield . . . in fact, we didn't have as much as a dime then to give him. That's why we call it Operation Shoestring. And he never asked about who was going to pay the bills. We paid him about fifty dollars a month out of the field benevolence fund for his expenses. He lived like the nomads up there on that, and seemed to like it. Later I was up there after he had spent four months hunting for a site for that airfield in those endless miles of sand and heat . . . there he was, stripped to the waist, carrying buckets of sand with those thousand or so nomads he had somehow coaxed into helping him . . . not one piece of mechanized equipment dug out that airfield, Doc, just plain sweat, and most of it his own . . . every piece of stone and cement and steel, what there is of it, he talked somebody out of up there . . . you know, he's even delivered babies around those nomad fires long before Emily Stewart ever showed up? He's been known to turn his own bunk over to some poor dying beggar making his last walk and then taking the time to bury him. No wonder they sing songs about him. But all we can do now is yank the rug out . . ."

"And he sleeps in his underwear, did you know that?" Barak broke in, bouncing the tennis ball on the cement with his racket, his voice remaining one of pleasant detachment.

"I detect some sarcasm, Doctor," Gregson returned, not sure what the African felt about the situation, or if he really knew that much, other than what Emily Stewart had probably circulated around the hospital. "And that puts you out of character . . ."

"Well, everybody around here knows you have protective feelings about Blake," Barak went on in that quiet, academic tone, unhurried. "He's your man in any case, correct? So why don't you follow your instincts then and chase the tiger for a change?"

Gregson glanced at him quickly. There was the hint of something new in the normally taciturn African now, something unusual from the many other times they had sat like this.

"Is that a prescription you're giving me?"

"Yes. And it's a good one."

"It's not that simple . . ."

"The only complication is the courage to do it."

"I didn't know you made Field Council problems your concern . . ."

"I do now, Milt," Barak came back quickly and threw the tennis ball across the court at the far cement wall. It hit with a dull crack and rolled back slowly to him down the long line of cement. "Every year I fill half a ward with people on this compound who suffer the tensions of insecurity tied to the fact that their hard-earned field positions will be changed in Council over the rightful command of their field leader. The other half suffer too but never show up, probably because they don't want this African doctor to know they, the white missionary, suffer the maladies of human chemistry . . ."

"People's glands and even morale in a spiritual order are to function according to their faith in God, not the whim and fancy of men, even their elected human leadership . . ."

"You are still their elected field leader, Milt," Barak returned blandly. "If the leader won't lead, then the entire body of faith becomes blurred, uncertain, unsure . . ."

"Sounds like you've been thinking about this for some time," Gregson commented, feeling troubled now. This was entirely unlike Barak, who never crossed over from his medical area into mission field problems. As an African, and chairman of the Hamaran Church Council, he was not under mission rule, though the church group was mission-founded and -sponsored. Still, in that role, he had the right to discuss field policy where it affected the church—but he was always very careful to steer clear of it.

"For a long time," he replied simply, frowning at his tennis racket. "Even before you showed up in office . . ."

Gregson cleared his throat. "So what's your point then, David?"

Barak looked up at him quickly as if to say he did not want to pursue this now either. "How about giving the people a field leader they can trust?"

"You've been around long enough to know that mission rules say that a field leader is a balancer, not a leader really. He implements the will of twenty field superintendents who do the deciding. Trust is developed in them, not me . . ."

"Perhaps," Barak broke in, "but you were nominated by your superintendents as the best man for the job . . ."

"You also know too that I was nominated by them under pressure from Doctor Merriweather . . ."

"But the missionaries elected you finally to be their leader. And he who will not rule invites division . . ."

"Who said that, Shakespeare?"

Barak gave a half-smile. "No, it is of my poor vintage, I am afraid . . ."

Gregson shifted uncomfortably on his seat. He felt no resentment toward Barak at all, but he sensed a growing isolation from him now. This he feared, because he did not have many genuine confidants here. More than that, he wondered how far afield the word was going about him and if Barak was now trying to tell him that the African church was beginning to wonder now too.

"Well," Gregson said in a tone of preoccupation, "you are right on one thing—Blake is my man. Shoestring is also mine. And everyone else has taken to the lifeboats." When the African did not comment, he added, "I would like to give Blake some time, yes, at least until after the rains. We owe him that much. It would be better to deal with him then, when emotions aren't so high. Anyway, I don't think that operation can run without him . . ."

Barak nodded. "Seems to me, if I recall reading the field manual, that you have a clause on which to rely to get him the time?"

"Clause 490," Gregson came back quickly.

"What your predecessors in office called the UFO, the United Fall Out," Barak added lightly, and Gregson had to smile at him on that.

"Which says," Gregson went on, "'The field director may at his own discretion claim default in Field Council procedure that may appear to unduly force judgment on an issue without proper documentation and which the field director feels will impair the proper adjudication principles intrinsic to Field Council responsibility.'"

"You have memorized it well."

"I have been reading it all afternoon."

"You are intending to use it, then?"

"When and if I'm prepared to be a UFO."

"And you are not sure Blake is worth it?"

"I am too young, Doctor," Gregson said with a sigh, lifting his left leg to rest his foot on the edge of the bench. "Anybody who uses that clause is asking for a quick flush out of leadership. You don't contradict the vote or the mood of twenty D.S.s by the UFO unless you are very sure of yourself—and I am not that sure of Blake either."

"There are worse things than losing a field administrative job . . ."

Gregson took off his sunglasses and rubbed at his swollen eyes. "You are so right, Doctor," he said with a heavy note of the sardonic creeping in. "But I would find it hard convincing my good wife on that. If you could find the secret to getting her pregnant, perhaps. But as it is now, without a child, she seeks the only other meaningful thing in her life—being the wife of the field director, hopefully general director in three years, if I remain model . . . besides, I do not wish to abandon this office to Pat Maddigan and put the mission fifty years behind the times . . ."

"And you would make a good General Director," Barak put back, "but only if you win it by some single act of tardy justice."

"You sound pro-Blake in that statement . . ."

"He has perhaps become the issue that has brought field leadership to a critical head."

"Which is really no worry of yours, right?"

"You are wrong there, Milt. You are forgetting that the Hamaran church is the offspring of the mission . . . we still look to you for our spiritual guidance. We need leadership models as never before if we are to weather the postindependence uncertainties. Right now you are the man we must look to . . ."

"There are others above me, Doctor Merriweather for one—"

"Doctor Merriweather is my spiritual father," Barak came back quickly, almost intently then, "and I owe what I am to his years of leadership and sacrifice. But his time has passed, a new era has come to Hamara. And you must emphasize that point now."

"The real issue, as my wife says, is not to let my doubts about Blake make me commit foolishness—"

"Doubts about a man's guilt are of God as much as the assurances. Maybe you should now follow your doubts and give us a hero."

"You'll have a dead one."

"'A man could die but once; we owe God a death.'"

"Who said that?"

"Shakespeare's Henry the Fourth . . ."

"I need something from the Bible . . ."

"'In God have I put my trust: I will not be afraid of what man can do unto me.'"

There was a moment of silence then, and Gregson began to feel exposed now. "Has Blake become that important to the African church, then?"

"Perhaps not the man in the end, but the issue is. All I am suggesting is that your health is tied to the emergence of yourself, as your office demands . . ."

"And everybody else's too, it would appear . . ."

Barak did not reply, and he took to studying the seams of the tennis ball in his right hand intently. Gregson knew there had to be more to it, but he hesitated pursuing it further. It had taken some courage on the mild-mannered Barak's part to speak as he did, Gregson knew. He felt troubled now, though, that Barak felt he had to call his attention to what was obviously becoming too apparent throughout the headquarters station here, and who knew how far out across the field. He felt the urge to explain the complexities of field leadership relationships in a spiritual order where patriarchs guarded their offices close as a trust from God. But he knew it would sound like a poor defense at best.

There was that awkward silence dragging out between them, and Gregson felt some disarray. A wasp droned softly in winged limbo over the top of his sweatsock, and he watched it a long minute, seeing himself in that stalled suspension, beating the air.

"You ever hear of the 'Colonel Bogey March'?" he asked.

Barak looked at him quickly, searching the ruddy, puffy facial features for some clue to the shift in conversation. "I believe I have. Why?"

"What's it like—I mean in form?"

"It's a snappy military tune straight out of the 'Hail Britannia' class or the French 'Marseillaise.' It became popular with a World War II film, *Bridge on the River Kwai*."

Gregson savored that a moment, his lips puckering out with his meditation. "How about this other thing—'Overture to Tann—' I'm not sure what it is now . . ."

"'Tannhäuser'? You mean you have never heard Wagner at his best?"

"Meaning what?" and Gregson shifted uncomfortably on the bench again. "What does it sound like?"

"It is—well, dramatic, moving . . . not a march really, but certainly carrying the ingredients of final victory . . ."

"What does it really say?"

"Says different things to different people, I suppose. Hitler loved Wagner . . ."

"That doesn't help much in this case."

"Why?"

"Blake plays that 'Bogey' thing in the morning and finishes up with Wagner at night."

"Sounds like he goes to battle every day and cannot lay down his instruments of war at night."

"And why does he call his station 'Camelot'?" Barak let out a quick laugh, genuinely amused now. "So what is there of God in that?" Gregson added, frowning at the wasp still hanging over his sock.

"Well, you can find God in Wagner as well as in Handel or Isaac Watts, even 'Colonel Bogey,' to say nothing of 'Camelot.' It all depends on what expression you are looking for. Perhaps Blake cannot find anything in hymnody that will express what he feels . . ."

"So what is he trying to—to express?"

"Well, sounds to me like you have a general up there."

"And not a saint?"

"I didn't say that. Joan of Arc was both. But maybe you should thank God you have a general in him instead of simply a keeper of the holy incense?"

Gregson put on his sunglasses again and turned his head to look at Barak.

"You know, if you weren't an African brother, I would say you talk too much at the wrong times and opinionate too much on what you know so little about."

"Quite right, noble father," Barak returned with a quick smile, enjoying the exchange now. "But speaking of Blake's music, I remember what Henry Thoreau once said:

'If a man does not keep pace with his companions, perhaps it is because he hears a different drummer. Let him step to the music which he hears, however measured or far away.'"

Gregson did not respond, although he looked as if he wanted to. Barak could sense the mounting swirl of confusion in him then, maybe even some embarrassment in raising the question about Blake's music or maybe his own ignorance concerning it. That was what he liked about Gregson—he would never feel put down in being told by an African what he should know himself.

"I am taking your number-one assistant in surgery to Durungu tomorrow," Gregson put in then, dropping his foot back on the cement.

"Along with our number-one investor, the elder Thornhill, correct?" Barak added.

Gregson nodded. "Will Gina get along with Blake, then?"

"A beautiful woman frozen in the clay of her necessary faith."

"Shakespeare again?"

"No. I mean she is a kind of alabaster box that needs to be broken so we can all enjoy the fragrance of her true self. She is a hard, legal defender of the faith, mixed with a peculiar cynicism that doesn't fit the image of her orthodoxy. I don't know how Blake will take that."

"She a good medical officer?"

"The best. One year short of finishing medical school. As you know, she had to drop out because of her mother's illness five years ago. Both her parents were missionaries in South America. She grew up on the field but spent her teens in a boarding school. She's twenty-nine years of age, no stargazer, but she needs the challenge of the frontier."

Gregson sniffed the air again. "The smell of rain is in the air already."

"I didn't know you could smell with your clogged-up sinuses this time of year."

"You can smell anything you want to, especially when life is at stake."

Barak got up then and held out a vial of pills toward Gregson. "Take these . . . they are blood-vessel dilaters. Your nose has that blue cast again, which means your pressure is too high . . ."

Gregson took them reluctantly, for science had never fully commanded a place in his life of faith. In that moment, Barak noted the cutting lines in Gregson's face, the slashes around the mouth dragging on anything of a smile that might try to appear, the increasing bent to his shoulders. The image was becoming more fragile now, and he wondered if Gregson could rise to the hour at all. And yet, God had worked with less in history, had He not?

"I must apologize, Milt," he said then as they turned to walk off the court, "for talking out of turn. I hope this won't affect our tennis . . ."

"I told you once," Gregson came back quickly, "that you should consider taking a field post yourself here. The mission is more than ready, and I am still waiting for you to accept nomination . . . you stand a head or two taller than any of us now, David, in every sense, spiritually, educationally . . ."

"One issue like Blake would probably sink me," Barak said lightly. They paused at the corner of the storeroom, where the path branched off. In that moment, the African felt a shiver in contemplation of what was looming over this plain man with whom he had come to feel such a bond in the past months. And he was moved by a strange sense of comradeship for Gregson then, but it was accompanied by a foreboding, as if he would never know him like this again. It was as if the shape of coming events hanging over Blake stood over them too with flashing, cutting blades designed to reconstruct them all to new dimensions.

"'Sail on then, thou Mars of malcontents,'" Barak jabbed him as they parted on the path.

"Shakespeare again?"

"Of course!"

"Farewell, then, Doctor, fair surgeon who has not yet arrived at reasonable dissection!" and Barak laughed quickly, surprised at this lyrical form coming from so nonlyrical a man. "And that comes from one of your expatients. Pray for me!"

"I will! I will!" and the African watched him finally disappear around the corner of the dining room. He felt lonely then, and he glanced at the sky and sniffed. There was nothing good in the omen, more a sense of nature's disbalance and God fretting over the mixture. "Remember those pills, my good brother, remember those pills," he said out loud.

Gina Roman had spent most of an hour with Emily Stewart, just one of the many she had put in, taking the role of human catheter to drain off the piled-up waste in the young girl's spiritual bloodstream. She had decided then that she had enough of listening to the almost childlike musings of Emily, repeating over and over again the irreconcilable actions of that man Blake, as if they were some unwelcome souvenirs of a tragic voyage. For Gina now there was nothing but a rising flood of cause, a cresting of surf that had built up to an accumulating force over the past two years. All over Blake. Was he the devil incarnate, then? She had to be careful there . . . she could not ascribe the attributes of the devil to anyone within the portals of United for Life Mission. Demon possessed, then? Maybe. In any case, she was not willing any longer to concede the field to Blake, to allow him to make vegetables out of capable, dedicated people like Emily.

She had gone from Emily's room to the small chapel. Within the quiet room with its stained glass and simple mahogany altar with the picture of Christ hanging over it, she allowed her mind to come to focus. She felt no mellowness or peace or any of those emotions that people said they found in the sacrosanct velvet of church sanctuaries. A pulse throbbed in her neck now, a strange passenger in her bloodstream tripping through her arteries like some desperate virus seeking a point of refuge. She did not see the altar or the head of Christ, but her eyes fixed there, commanding from the symbolic rudiments a touch of holy flame to ignite the combustibles of her own ready spirit. She wanted the transfer to Durungu as she had never wanted anything before in her life. She told herself over and over again in the past months of waiting that she needed to get out into the African bush, to fulfill what she was sure God wanted her to do so long ago when she gave her life to missionary medicine. There was nothing here in the dull routine of doing blood cultures on missionaries, and supervising the thirty-three people on staff. She could have done that in Philadelphia. No, her cause had to be something else—and she would not rest here forever allowing her vision to be dissipated by Field Council preoccupation with budgets.

But she had to admit, sitting there now, that it was more than that too. Durungu had loomed up in her mental focus as some terrible, unholy mountain for months. She knew that what coursed within her now was a compulsion—and she knew it was of God—driving her to intersect the line of what was happening there. Every bizarre story on Blake that filtered in from people coming from the northern territories was but one more shaft of revelation. She could not fully understand the weird shape of this thing emerging so powerfully within her either. She had never met Blake, didn't even know what he looked like, except from the descriptions Emily gave her now and then or the few figments gleaned from others. But nevertheless, it was almost as if her entire Christian life was now about to rise to the vision of Mount Horeb—her burning bush that had refused to catch fire these many years was now leaping up to a hot glow. She could sense the convergence of forces that had to lead her out finally. She did not quarrel with it either. Some Christians lived all their lives holding their hands over dead ashes, content to wait for conducive atmospheres in which to do their thing for God. Not so with her. She had disciplined her life, denied herself, literally stripped herself of every pulse of human desire to be ready for what she was sure was some special event that she alone could shape and ultimately affect. Now it was Durungu. She was sure of it. So that all she could say to that altar was, "God, don't let me flinch in this solitary purpose. Try me and prove me, but find me finally tempered as gold for your use."

She left the chapel then, not content to spend too much time there for fear of missing her connections, and went to the lab to find Jonathan Bartuga there bending over his microscope. He looked up quickly as she came in, as if expecting her. Jonathan at twenty-seven was the fourth African to join the mission hospital staff, having trained for lab technician in the United States for five years. He was perhaps the handsomest of any of them, the closely sculptured facial bones of the Hamara nomad showing up in the aquiline ridges to bring out the sharp humor of his dark eyes and offer mysterious contrast to the flash of his smile.

"Did you get the message?" he said, almost with disinterest, although he knew how much she waited for it, going back to his microscope.

"What message?"

"About your transfer."

She paused in hanging up her white duster on the hook on the door, turning her head quickly toward him, noticing the Afro-American hair style he wore with some particular pride as a mark of the new Hamaran citizen.

"Don't play with me, Jonathan."

"Cranston was here," he added, not looking up. "Said to tell you to be ready at five-thirty in the morning."

"Durungu?" she asked, feeling the air go still in the room.

"Durungu." She played it casually enough, going to the sink directly across the table from him and turning on the faucet. He looked up at her then and said, "I'm going to miss our mornings in church."

She ran the water over her fingers, feeling the sharp coldness easing the fever beating in her veins. "So will I, Jonathan," she said, but her voice was dry, without feeling. She wished she could be different with him, because he had put himself on the line to play the role she wanted him to. She had used him, and she was sure he knew it. "I want to thank you, Jonathan, and I should apologize for putting you through all this—"

"Don't try to reach too far, Gina," he said quietly, but she did not look at him, busying herself with the towel in her hands. "I knew what you had in mind from the beginning . . ."

Gina smiled at him, but it was nothing more than a tug of her facial muscles. Jonathan liked Gina but yet he didn't too. She could be bold and adventuresome, but every incident was like one more spike she was driving for a grip to whatever strange goal she was pursuing. When she laughed, rarely, her eyes never laughed with her mouth, as if her several emotions ran on different circuits. She could go to church on Jonathan's arm and ignore the ripples of groundswell building over it—and yet she could crack hard on the hospital staff who didn't measure up to spiritual perfection.

She worked over patients with a cold, efficient, calculating precision—she gave injections with a mean thrust, especially to men, but whenever any man had to have a shot, he always asked for her, because she did it smoothly. She never dated any of the white personnel on the grounds that she "was choosey," but Jonathan noted that she was never comfortable around them. Jonathan "dated" her, because he felt a strange desire to help her—whatever it was that was driving her he wanted to find out. There was genuineness and beauty underneath all that façade of independence and control.

"How about escorting me to a last cup of coffee?" she said to him then.

"Go out in a blaze of glory, Gina?" he said lightly and smiled, but got up off his stool and hung up his duster. She didn't answer. He pulled on his suit coat and straightened his tie. "Why Durungu, is what I'd like to know," he went on. "That's the end of the world in more ways than one, so they tell me. Ask Emily Stewart. Or I guess you have, huh?"

He followed her out into the chilly night, seeing that posture of the cool spiritual vigilante, the hardening clay of her facial muscles, that solid rock glint in her chestnut eyes.

"I feel sorry for that man, Blake," he called after her. "I really do. Give me one of those witches of Hamlet Barak talks about all the time, but deliver me from Gina Roman, champion of righteous causes, a hallelujah lassie of the first order, the terror of all the demons, truly a lady with a big heart . . ."

But he saw that she was not listening, walking way ahead of him toward the dining room. And he pitied the man who broke her shell, who dared tamper with her.

"God help Blake," he said to himself, and ran to catch up with her, taking her by the arm, the bare skin of it feeling like a chunk of statue, hard, cold and lifeless.

# CHAPTER V

The Reverend Cletus Thornhill was dropped off at Gregson's office at 12:30 the next day by Merriweather. The plane that was to take them to Durungu was grounded that morning for mechanical problems, which meant Thornhill had the run of the compound for most of the morning. And judging by the red pockmarks under Merriweather's eyes, it had not been exactly an edifying time for the mission leader.

Gregson loaded Thornhill's two huge suitcases into the station wagon while G.D. tried to tie off the final amenities. Thornhill stood off to one side, hands behind his back, his head turning right and left as he tried to take in the entire compound. He was a short, fiftyish man, built like a lightbulb with a full mane of yellowish-brown hair that was swept back into a pile on his head, looking like hay left to stand too long in the sun. Clumps of it fell down over each ear, and he reached up every few minutes to swipe it back into place. His eyes were blue-black and dilated often, as if he were taking close-ups of everything. As they studied Gregson now, even from ten feet away, those eyes seemed to be constantly adjusting focus, as if Gregson was a blurred image. He wore a navy-blue tropical suit, white shirt and tie with an ostentatious gold cross in the lapel. He was dressed for the pulpit, and Gregson wondered if he should tell him how hot it was going to be in Durungu.

As he finished loading the gear, G.D. left in his Ford and Gregson invited Thornhill to get into the front seat. He said nothing about his son Augie in the ride to the hospital, or even about Blake. He talked mainly about his bumpy ride on the plane over from the States, and how hard it was to sleep "thirty-eight thousand feet up."

When he got to the hospital, Gregson found Gina Roman waiting on the front cement patio, sitting on one of her suitcases, arms folded, her legs crossed in a pose of patient indulgence. Gregson greeted her with a nod and a smile, and loaded her bags in back. She said nothing to him, hardly even smiled. He didn't know her that well, of course. He seldom got to fraternize with hospital staff, who were always busy, it seemed, she in particular. Now and then he had seen her come into church on the arm of Jonathan Bartuga, and he wouldn't have noticed then if his wife hadn't nudged him.

The airport was three miles away and Thornhill dominated the conversation all the way, rambling on about "dedication" and "always make sure you keep a watchman on the walls, because once you let the devil come in in sheep's clothing, or even in a Cadillac, then you wind up selling it all to him . . . right, Gregson?"

"Uh-huh," Gregson responded obediently, and he glanced at Gina Roman in the rear-view mirror to test her for some kind of expression, hoping he might bring her into some kind of conversational detour. But she sat very still in that pose Barak referred to as "frozen," a piece of statue in a blue tweed skirt, a high-collared white blouse tightly buttoned at the top, and a light-blue windbreaker over that. She was perched higher on the back seat of the wagon because of the extra-duty springs underneath, and he could see her tanned legs crossed—good, efficient, utilitarian legs. He viewed them clinically, out of habit, always checking lady-missionary legs to make sure they were wearing stockings. That was required dress for all headquarters females. But he was sure she was not wearing any today.

There was no reaction in her face toward Thornhill's long, rambling appeal about "putting on the whole armor." Her eyes were covered by dark sunglasses, but her mouth stayed in a patient line of nonexpressional tissue, the lower lip slightly fuller than the upper—and he was sure now too that she was using lipstick, for there seemed to be a pinkish-red outline to them contrasting the almost tense, lily-white of her facial skin. That, too, was a forbidden element. Somehow it did not go with her hair style he remembered Laura describing as "that straight, sleek choirboy stretch that doesn't fool anybody." Whatever that meant. It did look boyish to him now, cut evenly across her forehead and hanging straight down around her cheeks and short around the neck. It had the shape of a football helmet, a style a woman would wear when she didn't want to be bothered with it. Or maybe it was to lend some particular aura of spirituality like Joan of Arc. So be it.

Anyway, she was cool, sure, and in strange ways fascinating to Gregson, as if there was some kind of veil over her natural beauty. One of those self-sufficient nurses, Gregson mused, who had a commanding attitude in her superior knowledge of glands and corpuscles.

"So, as I say, you got to have dedication," Thornhill ran on, grinding down some now when neither Gregson nor Gina picked it up to give him fuel. "It's what I used to tell my boy Augie when I finally got him to take flying lessons when he was just sixteen, something I always wanted to do, to fly, but altitude always gave me a headache . . . so Augie did the flying for me, and I always used to tell him to put God first and flying second. And he never failed me or the Lord." In that order? Gregson wondered. "That's why Augie wrote to me, Gregson, that he thinks this man Blake up there commanding that operation may have sneaked over the wall. We should talk about that soon—"

Gregson gunned the motor then as he saw the field directly ahead and the red Cessna parked there waiting. "Here we are," he said, glad he could divert Thornhill from what could be a sticky conversation.

They loaded their gear with the help of the young pilot named McGregor. There was some debate as to where Thornhill should sit, front or back, to get the best view. Gregson would have preferred him in front to save Gina Roman further badgering, but when McGregor said the best view was from the back, that settled it.

As they flew north, Thornhill went on shouting to Gina over the sound of the plane's engine about "what constitutes real sacrifice," so Gregson asked McGregor to find any herds of elephants or giraffes he could to give Thornhill something to shoot his camera at. McGregor did that a few minutes later, and Thornhill was transported into a new dimension as his eight-millimeter zoom lens rattled on and on. Finally after five or six passes, and with his film gone, Thornhill yelled at Gregson, "Gregson, you know I told my brotherhood class I'd get some real shots on this trip, and this has to be it!"

They finally banked around and headed back on course to Durungu, Thornhill well-lubricated by now and crowing to Gina about the "glories of Bell and Howell and Super Eights."

It was nearly 4:30 when they began descending for Durungu airfield. McGregor went right on in after getting clearance over the radio. As they came a few hundred feet over the tin shacks of Durungu village proper, Gina Roman had the peculiar feeling that she was coming around in a complete life circle. For her it seemed she had seen this moment in her dreams a long time ago, as if all that was ahead of her now was a part of a divine plan, a connection she had to make. There was a sense of exhilaration coupled with a slight tremor of trepidation.

The wheels kissed lightly on the hard clay runway, and McGregor braked lightly. The buildings came into view through the fuzzy heat waves, dark, drab boxes of melancholia enduring the heavy press of the sun.

They moved into the parking area by the hangars where the other yellow planes sat in a casual semicircle, noses pointed into the gaping doors of the hangars like worshipers at a shrine.

"Looks like they weren't expecting us," Thornhill commented in a tone that reflected some disappointment.

"I didn't tell them you were coming, Mr. Thornhill," Gregson said. "I think you said—"

"Yes, yes, of course," Thornhill conceded shortly.

They stopped and McGregor cut the engine. They got out and stood around, looking for some sign of life. An African came wandering out of the hangar and stopped to peer at them. Gregson shouted to him in French, asking for Blake. The African pointed a finger toward the far end of the runway.

"Well?" Thornhill asked.

"I'm not sure," Gregson said.

"There are some people down at the far end," Gina offered, trying to help Gregson now, because for some reason she felt a sense of commiseration for him, knowing he had to put on as good a show here as possible for Thornhill.

"Yes . . . well, why don't we go up to the tower," he said. "I guess somebody has to be in the radio shack . . ."

They walked across the engulfing swarm of heat off the runway toward the tower, Gregson and McGregor carrying the suitcases. There were two people sitting in the sand in front of the tower—one was an African wrapped in an old army overcoat, a spear leaning against the wall next to him. A few feet away a little boy sat cross-legged with a tray of empty sardine tins on his head. The tall African stood up as Gregson approached.

Gregson put the cases down and began conversing with him in French. Thornhill moved in small circles, kicking at the sand, looking around at the rather shabby lumps of buildings. Now and then, as Gregson paused in his French, he would say, "What'd he say, Gregson?" But Gregson did not acknowledge, going on in slow, ponderous French again.

And then Gina saw the man come out through the door of the tower to their left, and Thornhill, facing that way, almost at the same instant bellowed, "Augie!" She saw that the man who had come out was bare to the waist, bulging muscles gleaming with sweat. He came forward uncertainly, almost reluctantly, as if he'd been caught at something. He took the embrace from his father, rather than giving too much back, his arms held almost tightly at his sides as his father pounded his bare back.

"You all right, boy?" Thornhill kept repeating. "You look a little peaked . . . you eating right?"

"Sure," Augie said a little sheepishly, conscious now of his bare torso as he saw Gina standing there. "Wait till I get my shirt on . . ." He retreated back inside quickly.

"That's my boy," Thornhill boomed back at Gina, as McGregor put the cases down quickly and moved back to lean against the tower wall to be out of the coming scenes as much as possible, squatting down near the tall African in the blanket who was laughing at some private joke.

"He looks good," Gregson commented hopefully.

"I've seen him fatter in the face," Thornhill contradicted.

Augie came out again then with a blue sweatshirt on and the gold letters indistinguishable in the loose folds.

"I didn't know you were coming," he said to his father, and there was a note of near disgruntlement, perhaps at being caught like this.

"I wanted to surprise you, boy," Thornhill returned with a quick laugh. "Catch you right in the action, how's that?" And Thornhill put his arm around Augie, who half smiled at the ground.

"Would Mr. Blake be down there somewhere?" Gregson asked, moving away from the African toward Augie and his father. He shook Augie's hand, and then introduced him to Gina. Gina sensed that

Augie's eyes were too intent, too guarded, and he seemed considerably out of sorts. He simply nodded at her but said nothing.

"Yes, sir," he said to Gregson. "Mr. Blake is down there . . ."

"What for?" his father asked, his voice carrying some ingredients of accusation.

"Well, every afternoon when the pilots get in, Blake—Mr. Blake—takes them all, the Africans too, on a run down to the end of the runway and back kicking a soccer ball. He figures it's a good way to let off steam . . ."

There was no animosity in Augie's voice, but he spoke of it like a tourist guide standing outside the meaning of it all.

"You don't go with them?" his father asked again.

"I got radio watch this week," and Augie shoved his hands deep into his back pockets and turned to look down the runway toward the others. Was it perhaps a wistful kind of look or one of disinterest?

"Oh," the elder Thornhill said, but not comprehending really.

Gina watched the tangle of dusty shapes growing larger now as they came up the slight incline of the runway, black and white arms and legs flashing in the sun, mixing with khaki and red clay, a can of worms writhing in the sun. She heard the grunts, the high-pitched yells as they fought each other to kick the ball ahead of them, now and then an exploding laugh cutting a note of discordancy against the backdrop of coffinlike buildings. She caught the smell of their sweat on the wind, sharp, pungent, rich with the chemistry of their glands. Across the way by the hangars, a cluster of young African herders forgot their cattle to watch, leaning on their sticks to stare at the scene with the intentness of people who couldn't understand such combat.

And as the cavorting line of straining young men came abreast of her, not more than thirty yards away, moving in a jerky kind of dance, the rank opened to let two men break off like two boxcars unhooking from a speeding freight, gliding toward her on a spur. The rest of them continued, oblivious of anyone else.

Gina didn't have to be told which one was Blake. "He never buckles his boots," Emily had said over and over again to her as if this was so important. But Gina would know anyway. Even though her view was not so much tied to those physical dimensions that seemed to set him apart—she noted the purposeful stride, almost a swagger really, the wide-band wristwatch on his arm, the kind that had all sorts of dials that measured seconds and tenths of seconds.

She knew that from the time her older brother had worn one just like it during World War II flying B-17s in Europe. It was worn by men who chopped up the day in tiny time particles, weighing each piece against the length of the sun. She noted now that his khaki shirt, the tail hanging down over the faded shorts, had the arms torn off at the shoulders, leaving jagged, uneven lines as if maybe he'd ripped them off with his hands in the frustration from the heat. As he approached, he removed his sunglasses as if he were unhooking a veil in easy, cautious movements, like an act of worship. The face she noted was coarse, worldly, all-knowing—she'd seen that kind of face in the skid-row infirmaries where she had worked her internship in preparation for missionary medicine. Those knobby protrusions around the mouth and eyes were notches marking former days when he flung himself on the wheels of pleasure—and maybe he still did here, for Emily had said he indulged yet with his mind, exploring, tasting everything with his eyes. It was a face undone or purposely done for some emergency in life, a face scuffed like an old shoe that did not change even with the light gloss of polish the smile was intended to give as he moved toward Gregson and Thornhill.

But she had learned to dismiss the physical cage of a man as purely irrelevant to the final character. She had seen enough male bodies spread out on hospital beds, the cavalier and the bum, and they were nothing more than glands capable only of required function. She had slapped, probed and shoved needles into such flesh and found it quite vulnerable and incapable of casting any direct spell.

But it was the mind she sought for behind that moving bottle of chemicals—she knew, how well she knew, that the body really danced on the end of the mind's puppet string. A walk, a gesture, a smile, a slight tilt to the head—like Blake had now, as if expecting some blow from an unseen hand—these all went back to the mental factory that pounded out the impulses, a factory that worked according to the peculiar mind set that shaped it from times past. She was not so stupid as to believe in the old sociopsychological school theory, that criminals had different shaped heads than did noncriminals—but she could tell in the rhythm of the body movement combined with certain shapes of bone and muscle, even in a hairline, when a man was not totally in control of himself or that his emotions and desires were bent out of the plumb line of God's perfect will.

And it was then that she saw the hair on his arms, golden fuzz caked with dust and sweat and taking on the hue of close-cropped flame in the sun, the smell of him earthy and proud, the same hair running down his muscular legs like animal fur disappearing into the tops of loose khaki socks poking out of those unbuckled combat boots that rang the bells of sexual celebration. There was casual disarray about him, a floppiness that spoke of a certain and definite quality of lasciviousness—but hair and sweat stayed locked in her brain right then, freezing her to alarming immobility, as they moved in peculiar undulation, springing the lock on the sealed hatch of the inner chamber of her mind; and then she knew why he made the circle complete and snapped it together to enclose her in the constriction she felt so suddenly and so terribly now . . .

For in that moment of blending torment as the vision escaped the inner compartment mixing with sand, yellow airplanes, khaki and the smell of the wet sweat turning to salt—in that moment the furnace room was there again . . . the smell of ammonia and wet mops and wet coal . . . and Kortoff, who had hairy arms that sweat . . . who stood there now exposing himself to her, fumbling uncertainly . . . that gentle grandfather of a man from whom she had drawn some necessary warmth and understanding on other occasions to make up for absent parents . . . but who then showed his ugly self and punctured her fourteen-year-old girlhood illusions about life, and left her with scar tissue that never healed but remained a discharging sore all her life, kept under only by a careful spiritual discipline . . . and he mumbling apologies finally with the furnace crackling flames in laughter, and his old gray head bowed in shame over a bucket of soapy, dirty water . . . and she climbing the wooden stairs finally to her room not even able to cry, just to sit there and stare at the colorless walls of her room in the mission boarding school, where she was to "grow in the Lord" while her parents carried on the work of God thousands of miles away in another far-off place . . . to sit there for hours knowing and feeling the rise of reality shaking the fruit of innocency at last forever from her mind . . . and only then to finally pray to God alone and to set her course from that terrible fix of sweating hair and to vow then that she would never trust a man again . . . and to vow that she would put on the "whole armor of God to withstand the wiles of the devil," and one day to treat man and flesh in the only way it could be finally humbled and mastered, through medicine.

But, dear God, she would know Kortoff again anywhere . . . there he was striding up to her as if they'd never met before!

It was all wrong, then, she knew, and she wanted to tell Gregson, sensing the dead hot air suddenly. But Gregson—puffy, homely, exposed and hurting undoubtedly—was already fighting his own battle here too . . . to keep things propped up on the angle of acceptance to Thornhill. She could sense what his mental set was right now, what made him walk so flat-footed and pose so poor a silhouette against the decaying leadership horizon against which he played his uncertain and troubled role . . . what moved him was a conglomeration of faith and duty, dwarfing him into homely insignificance. She could find no source of strength there; she never could in any man. But at least in him she felt no threat. People in Talfungo talked of his leadership as purely figurehead; they referred to him as a "gentle sheep who tried to give leadership but offered nothing but wool," a man propping up his field administration with straw. And yet the Africans liked him, as Jonathan Bartuga said, "because he feels with his heart and truly loves Hamara and her people." Well, at any rate, he was not cast in the same ugly dimensions as Kartoff or even this man Blake . . . he was more a kind of father image. And she knew she would not add to his problems by contributing hers, and she doubted she would anyway when she thought about it; she never asked any man for help on anything. She would not do it now. So all she could do was stand there and wait, fighting off the sickening waves of heat that stuck in her throat and spun circles of flame in her eyes, praying for detachment from the tortured vision, seeking sweet neutrality, forcing her mind to clamp hard on that broken chamber and to make her disciplined forces dismiss the harbinger as nothing more than mere coincidence conjured up out of the tension and anxieties of this trip.

"Good to see you again, Blake," Gregson was saying and then adding, "This is the Reverend Mr. Thornhill, Augie's father . . ."

"Reverend," Blake said, and his voice was steady and riding level of masculine hoarseness from the dust, unhurried. No, his kind were all the same, so sure, taking their time, but always so sure. "This is Rudy Kipstein, Rudy the Jew as he's called here, my number one." Gina glanced at the other man, looking for relief, found it. The brim of his baseball cap was jammed up against his head, giving him a look of boyish mischief, as if he'd been peeking through knotholes in a board fence, and his jaws worked steadily on the gum as he said, "Hi!" in a youthful jubilance, as if this was a high-school reunion. No cross-dimension there either, Gina mused; he could put snakes in his pocket and frogs in his cap and still sit quietly in church.

"You run these boys pretty hard, Mr. Blake," Thornhill said brusquely, trying to command the scene now, setting himself as the main contender here. Blake smiled but said nothing and came over to Gina. Gregson introduced her, and she sensed Gregson was more nervous now too for some reason, trying to keep his twiglike cowlick down, as if something was emerging here about Blake that wasn't in his file.

She took Blake's extended hand in hers easily enough, feeling the roughness of the skin like an old piece of leather. "Welcome," he said shortly, and she looked up at him, willing herself to do so, rising to meet him head on. His smile showed good teeth, though a little dulled or faded, a small gap showing between the two front ones, the only crack in the wall of mountain. An inflamed cold sore built a puffy fire at the corner of his upper lip, and the gray-blue eyes laced with red streaks passed over her quickly, computing her strengths, reaching out to feel some touch of her perhaps—and she let her hand go slack in his so that he dropped it.

He turned back to Gregson and Thornhill then and said, "We like to work hard here, Mr. Thornhill—don't we, Augie?"

Augie suddenly looked exposed with the straight-on question directed at him, and he stared back at Blake, not knowing how to answer. "Running is the best exercise for clogged-up arteries," Rudy added when Augie didn't pick it up fast enough, and then he laughed and looked quickly at Blake, then at Gina, his sunglasses taking on orange centers from the sliding sun, "the best fitness in the book . . ."

"I guess you didn't get our message we were coming," Gregson offered, clearing his throat, wanting the conversation to go more direct.

"Sorry, we didn't," Blake said. "If we had known Mr. Thornhill was coming—"

"Well, it was a last-minute decision," Thornhill boomed back. "A lot of prayer goes up for this operation, Mr. Blake, and I suppose a lot of money from a lot of people. So—well, I figured the best way to represent them was to come while I had the chance . . . to kind of

*123*

check up a little." He laughed then, because he didn't like the sound of that either. Everybody was dropping a laugh all of a sudden, Gina sensed, falsetto sounds hurled around the air like artificial flowers. "You know, I haven't seen my boy Augie since more than three years ago in Boston when I saw him off on the plane . . . just two months before that he won the Kiwanis Air Medal for the cross-country, all the way from San Diego to New York in just seventeen hours . . . how's that?"

There was a long moment of silence, and it was Rudy who finally said in a jocular tone, "Well now, Augie, you never did tell us about that air medal . . . shame on you! Mr. Thornhill, I do believe you have a most humble son here . . ."

"Well," Thornhill laughed, rising on his heels to peep over the compliment, not sure how it was directed, then clamping a big hand on Augie's shoulder, who stared at his feet and hunched up his shoulder as if the hand pained him. "I figure I raised a God-fearing boy who puts God first in all things . . . right, boy? By the way, Augie, which one of those planes is yours?"

Augie looked quickly up toward the row of airplanes across the way and then gave a sidelong glance at Blake. "Augie's on radio watch this week, Mr. Thornhill," Blake said evenly. "He's not taking his regular flight turn . . ."

Thornhill looked at Augie for confirmation or elaboration of that, so Augie nodded to the ground. "That's right, Dad."

"Oh." Thornhill returned with that uncertain sound, and now the conversation was beginning to run into a peculiar sludge, so Gregson said, "Mr. Blake, maybe we ought to get to our quarters and freshen up some . . . it's been a long ride . . ."

"I could use a shower," Thornhill cut in again.

"The only shower we got is an old rain barrel behind the pilots' Quonset," Blake said simply, putting his sunglasses back on. "If you want, I can have Joseph fill it for you, won't take long . . . we don't have all the conveniences here . . ."

"No showers?" Thornhill said, looking from Blake to Gregson as if to say that all the money he'd raised to put in here should have at least bought showers.

"Yes, well, I'm sure it's on the list," Gregson soothed, wiping at his eyes now with a crumpled white handkerchief.

124

"Hmmm, yes," Thornhill acquiesced grudgingly. "Well, I guess I can sponge-bathe or something . . ."

"In that case, then, Augie can show you to your quarters, Mr. Thornhill," Blake said. "We didn't have much time to clean up things, but maybe it won't be too bad . . . Rudy, you can show Miss Roman to the infirmary, and Mr. Gregson, I guess you can stay with me in the tower here . . ."

They dispersed rapidly as if each was eager to run to some particular shelter to think it all over. Gina walked shakily beside Rudy, not yet fully recovered from the strange backtrack in time, listening to his gum crack, smelling the odor of spearmint. "I'm not really much of a wheel around here," he said with a laugh, hiking her bags to a firmer position under his arms, refusing to let her carry any. "Though Blake—Mr. Blake—says I'm his number one, there are no number ones to him. He's good at everything. All I do is pour water, work a grease gun, fly a plane now and then, and even take my turn at cooking . . . but Gregson—Mr. Gregson—must be mad to send his best lookers up here . . . you have to be an answer to all our prayers, sister, cuz we figured we had lost any more element of beauty here when Emily left . . ."

"I'm not as genteel as I look either," she returned blandly. "I have a reputation for being one of the witches of Hamlet in one of my better moments, according to Doctor Barak anyway, and I get ugly with a hypo in my hand . . ."

"Ouch," Rudy replied with a short laugh that rang clearly enough but slightly pinched; it was enough, though, to dilute some of the dread she felt. "But if you could see who gives us hypos when we don't have an official medic—"

"You mean Mr. Blake?"

"Sure—who else? We had Emily Stewart up to a few days ago, but she left . . . so with her gone, Blake stands in just in case . . . he learned it straight out of a first-aid manual using a grapefruit. He can do a lot of amazing things . . ."

She got the sidelong commercial for Blake in that. "So I heard," she returned dryly. "Emily Stewart told me quite a few things in Talfungo about Mr. Blake . . ."

"Oh? Sure, that's right, you were in the hospital there, right?"

"Right."

"How is Emily, then?"

"As well as can be expected."

He seemed subdued by that for a moment, but perked up again as they came to the square, squat mud-brick shanty that was the infirmary. They walked into the small outpatient room that smelled of disinfectant. Two Hamaran women got up from the wooden bench and bowed to her, pulling their simple wraparound clothes around them, greeting her in part French, part Hamaran.

"They've been waiting since Emily left," Rudy explained, cracking his gum lightly. "When they know who you are they'll come back with twenty more tomorrow . . . come on in, I'll show you your room . . . it's not the Waldorf, by any means . . ."

The room attached to the outpatient section was a twelve-by-twelve with sinking wooden floors coated with sand that scraped under their feet; a single bed was pushed up against the cracked, yellowish plaster wall; there was a single wicker chair, a chest of drawers, a wardrobe made of brown canvas propped up with a wooden frame, a single nightstand with a kerosene lamp and a basin with a tarnished aluminum pitcher. A picture of the head of Christ hung on the wall over the bed. Burlap curtains hanging heavy with dust were at either window, one facing out to the airstrip, the other looking out across the runway and the sand-dune windbreak.

"It will do," she said simply and took off her blue windbreaker.

Rudy put down her bags and sat on one. "I have to warn you that some of your African patients will spill over in here sometimes . . . not always."

She gave him a quick smile, for he was trying hard not to let her down too hard. "And some probably sleep here all night, right?"

"Emily told you that, huh?"

"Some things she thought important for me to know."

"Well, you know, sometimes Emily slept with Mr. Blake," Rudy said and then coughed quickly and half laughed. "What I mean is, Blake, Mr. Blake, put up an extra partition up there in the tower off his room . . . sometimes Emily would take all-night radio watch so he could get some sleep; so he didn't see why she had to come back here to sleep with Africans all over the floor . . . she tell you that?"

She sensed he was eager now to know all she did know. "Very convenient," she said crisply, running a long finger over the layer of dust on the chest of drawers. "Do I get to share Mr. Blake's quarters too?"

Rudy laughed, inviting her to see the joke of it.

"Well, who knows? Blake—Mr. Blake—is very accommodating . . . what I mean is—well, I think I'm digging a hole under Mr. Blake with my big mouth . . ." He got up then and walked to the door, paused and looked back at her, removing his sunglasses to show his hazel eyes far too sensitive, too exposing of himself, like a child's now, unsure of where he was going. "I'm glad you're here, Gina," he said, and he might have added more on that. She felt as if she'd like to ask him why, but then he smiled and said, "Do you think molasses candy is good for the liver?"

She stared back at him, not following the shift in subject, then said, "No, and it decays your teeth." And Rudy's eyebrows lifted as he contemplated that.

"Really?" he said, shrugged and then was gone. She moved to the window that faced out front to the hangars and watched him walk quickly across the field to the planes and the pilots standing around, having finished their fitness, looking toward the infirmary, waiting for news from Rudy now as to Emily's replacement. She watched two pilots bare to the waist, in shorts, chase each other, one threatening the other with a can of what she presumed was water.

She leaned her head momentarily against the frame of the window, feeling something of the coolness of the plaster on her cheek. The sordidness of this place hung heavy now. Whatever glamor she had looked for—or maybe that sense of anticipation of a fulfilling adventure—had long since dissipated. She felt afraid, then, unsure. Now she knew something of what had destroyed Emily. But what was it really? Too early to tell. But it was there all right, that certain quality of alien presence, tipping the atmosphere the wrong way. She had the drill most of her life, how to detect the foreign elements that ran contrary to God. Maybe it wasn't all that bad—but Blake's image of Kortoff was strange, mystifying, certainly terrifying. She would not move too quickly in that direction, but she would be wary, forever keeping her vigil as she had most of her life. It had saved her pain and kept her true to God.

Then, shaking loose from the moribund feeling that seemed to hang on with insistent fingers, she turned to the two African women still sitting patiently in the next room. In simple French she began to build her bridges to them, then shifted to the Hamaran language, reaching out to lay hold of what had been her passion in coming to Africa.

Warren Larkin stopped his green camper along the dirt road and took a long drink from the canteen on the seat beside him. He was leaving the greener savannahs now that had offered some relief from the sun and headed into the sandy ridges that began the desert frontier. So far he had not been stopped by any Hamaran officials. And having reached the northern territories of Hamara, he had no reason to expect any investigations. Longstreet, the cover man from the American Consulate, in handing over the necessary papers and Hamaran license plates at the border town of Haman, assured him as much. "There are some places in Africa where law begs reprieve, and the northern frontier of Hamara is one of them."

Longstreet had handed him quite a bundle beyond the usual identification papers. The classified teletype promised under Code Name Zebra informed him that it was confirmed that the Chinese knew the satellite was in Terragona and had already dispatched a team for retrieval and would probably be heading for Durungu. But what got Larkin to swearing was the read-out of the Gamma X contraband that was supposed to be aboard the satellite. The computer aboard had fed the information back that it had scooped in a volatile microorganism highly sensitive to oxygen and capable of multiple expansion. Washington space scientists had concluded that Gamma X—which was the code name for space-chemistry contraband—had apparently ridden the latest Apollo moon capsule on its roaring path back to earth, seeding the sonosphere. The delousing of the capsule itself had not revealed any traces, but now Larkin was sure Houston would be going over that again.

But the rest of the message was what got Larkin to kicking at the sand under his feet. "What is this, Longstreet?" he said to the tall man dressed impeccably in a brown tweed business suit and carrying a folded-down rain poncho in one hand and an umbrella in the other.

"I just deliver it, I don't interpret it," Longstreet said.

"Oh, sure, sure," Larkin growled. "This Gamma X . . . they say that it is important to retrieve the satellite intact to prevent Gamma X from escaping into the atmosphere. What do they want me to do? Go in there, find the thing, reach in and cut the self-destruct before she blows? If it's so damn important to keep that Gamma X trapped in the capsule, why don't they alert World Health and even the Russians and make a united attack on the thing in the name of preserving humanity?"

"You know they can't do that, Larkin," Longstreet said tonelessly. "If the Russians find out we've got bacteria contraband on that satellite, they'll crow to the whole world that we violated the treaty on peaceful uses of outer space. They'll say we deliberately loaded the capsule with bacteria and are courting germ warfare. That could pose problems . . ."

"So what have we got right now? Just you and me and a few thousand cowherders in this desert to save humanity from a possible death worse than death?" Longstreet did not reply. Larkin went on reading. "I mean, do those mission people know anything about this, what they're up against inside Terragona? I mean this capsule might have cracked when it landed over there—"

"We can't tell anybody, Larkin."

"Well, you ought to tell the mission boys . . . it would be a lot easier and quicker for me if they knew up there at Durungu so I could get a lift into Terragona fast like."

"We can't risk it."

"Can't risk losing the cameras, you mean, Longstreet. The Pentagon doesn't want anybody to know, because all that film will go up for grabs. Same old story, hey, Longstreet? A few pictures of some damn missile silos in Russia are more important than a space bacteria that nobody knows anything about and could pollute the earth's atmosphere to negative zero for humanity." Longstreet again said nothing. Larkin went on reading the teletype. Then he said, "How much, if anything, does this man Blake or his crowd know about the satellite?" And he noticed now that the teletype had Blake's history run out on it. The CIA and the Aerospace Security boys in Houston had burned a lot of midnight oil to get all that together so quickly.

"We can't know finally," Longstreet said coolly. He was a precise, stiff, single man of forty, who had served many years under the French. "There is no reason for them to suspect . . ."

"What about this man Blake?"

"Like what?"

"Like what do I have to bargain with to get this man to let me ride piggy with him into Terragona?"

Longstreet extended the folded-down poncho to him. "There's a hundred thousand cash in 'C' notes that should make some kind of impression."

Larkin looked a bit startled as he took the pouch rather gingerly.

Somebody was very serious about this whole operation. He went to the truck and put the pouch under the front seat of the cab.

"You're so sure Blake will tumble for the green stuff?" he asked of Longstreet, walking back to him, still scanning the teletype sheets.

"He runs one step from poverty all the time," Longstreet returned dryly, almost imperiously, as if Larkin should know that. "Like all mission work, I suppose."

"God-men do not bow the knee to Baal so easily, which you also know, Longstreet?"

Longstreet dismissed the argument with a blink of his eyes. "There is some question as to how much of a mission man Blake really is . . . Washington apparently felt the same when they authorized the cash."

Larkin did not look up from his reading. "How much does the mission headquarters control the operation?"

Longstreet shrugged. "In policy and on paper, they control all of it. But going to them to ask permission to fly into Terragona is fruitless. Blake owns and controls that airspace over Terragona, and though the mission does not like to admit it, they would concede the point."

Larkin sighed. "Okay . . . now can you give me any kind of radio directional on this Terragona place so I can keep tuned in for the self-destruct signal on that satellite?"

Longstreet handed him a folded-down map. Larkin opened it and studied it. "I have circled that lake called Caha on your map . . . it is the only lagoon large enough to take a satellite that size." Larkin scribbled a few notes on the margin and stuffed the map into his back pocket and went back to reading the teletype again.

"I see here that the application Blake put into the mission for entrance would indicate that they know nothing of the medals he won as a flyer in Korea . . . and I don't see anything here either that would indicate they know about this fiasco of his with Global Airlines?"

"Our sources say that Blake does not fly himself . . . so I would conclude—"

"Yes, so would I," Larkin cut back quickly, anxious to make the point himself. "And that is where Mr. Blake will tumble finally, Longstreet . . . he'll sniff at the cash maybe, but when I drop this other shoe about Global, it will be interesting to see how he moves. In fact, I'd take odds that he won't quibble once he knows I know . . ."

"I would not hazard so presumptuous a guess about the man," Longstreet returned simply. "He is no sugar cube, you should know—"

"Trouble with you, Longstreet," Larkin replied, and he separated the teletype sheets now, taking the longer one on the Gamma X readout and the satellite information and folding it neatly down into a small portfolio at his feet. The other sheet with the information about Blake's history, he put into his back pocket. "The trouble with you, Longstreet, is that you never had to win any wars in your life—"

"That is highly classified information in that portfolio of yours, Larkin," Longstreet called after him. "You better not put that under the seat."

Larkin laughed and lifted the hood of the truck. Longstreet watched him shove the small leather portfolio into a narrow steel encasement on the roof of the hood, which looked almost like a continuing part of the hood itself. He snapped the cover shut and dropped the hood.

"We've got all kinds of tricks," he added, coming back to Longstreet. "Like I said, you never had to fight for anything in the cushion of the consulate, and maybe that's why you chose it. Not so with us in aerospace . . . we learned to fight for every orbit by every and any rule . . ." Longstreet did not respond. "Okay," Larkin went on, squinting into the afternoon sun, "is anyone else being sent out from our side?"

"Not that I know of," Longstreet replied. "I imagine they'll dispatch a team as soon as they can . . ."

"So this is a solo jaunt, hey, Longstreet?" and Larkin did not bother to hide his chagrin. "Behold the new deliverer sent to save the world . . . and not a miracle in his pocket . . ."

"I will need a record of your expenses covering that hundred thousand," Longstreet called after him as Larkin moved for the truck.

Larkin laughed as he drove off, leaving Longstreet there in the desert, holding his umbrella and looking as if he'd gotten jilted by the rain.

He smiled now as he stood by the truck relieving himself in the powdery sand, listening to the steady, pulsating, muffled beat of the drums again, thumping the steady heartbeat of the soul of Africa against the brittle rib cage of great expectation. The drums had been with him the last hundred miles or so, as he moved up the dirt road leading north to Durungu. He had stopped at various government resthouses along the way, as well as at mission stations. Nobody talked much about Blake or the air operation except one old French colonial pumping gas at a broken-down trading post, and he simply said, "When anybody heads toward Durungu, the blacks send the word ahead. Nobody knows why. But ever since that missionary air-lift's been operating up there, it's been this way. A man named Blake runs it . . . he is what you Americans call old blood and guts, *comprenez-vous?*"

"Blake?" Larkin said with some dubiousness.

The old Frenchman laughed like an excited child, and Larkin wondered how a simple leftover colonial Frenchman pumping gas a hundred miles south of Durungu could know so much about Blake. But he didn't pursue it. The only other person he had conversation with—if he could call it that—was an African dressed in French colonial whites in the government resthouse at Bungari. He called himself Belang, but he never did introduce the African with him who never bothered to speak but kept busy with his meal. When Larkin said, in answer to Belang's question, that he was on an archaeological field trip to Durungu, only then did the other African pause in his eating to take notice. From then on, all conversation slid over the edge out of sight.

Larkin turned to the door of the truck and poured some water over his head. He felt logy, almost drained. The sun never let up. The air conditioner in the truck had begun to falter some under the pressure of one thousand five hundred miles of heat, but he could find nothing wrong with it. He ran his fingers over his scruffy beard, glancing at himself in the side mirror. He would be forty-three years old next week. Seven years of manning the wilderness tracking stations, three of them in Kano, had given him a sallow, swollen, almost derelict look. And maybe too much booze? He was a scientist, not a security man. He wanted recognition for science. But what would he get now? He hated the thought of what he had in front of him . . . it was an ugly thing in the air with this satellite. GAMMA X? This was a job for the United Nations! This was a world calamity in the making! And yet Space Security would send him? Sure, why not? Losing him was not going to be expensive. They'd let him put his fingers into that cookie jar over there in Terragona, and by the time the big boys got there he'd have already blown all the booby traps. The rest of it would be comparatively easy.

He got back into the truck, checked the money pouch under his seat, placed his .45 service automatic in the clip tied to the sun visor. His head ached now, and there was a tight band beginning to pull across his chest. He shook it off.

"Well, old blood and guts," he said, rolling up the window and turning up the air conditioning, "let's see how much of that is pure legend or just plain holy bluff."

# CHAPTER VI

Gregson followed Blake through the small outer room of the tower containing the radio, a small scarred table and an assortment of cans filled with parts and baling wire. The adjoining room was not much larger than the outer. A wooden stair cut into the room at the far end near the single bed that was pushed up against the wall under an open window that gave a commanding view of the field. There was a blown-up air mattress on the bed and a single khaki blanket balled up on it. At the foot of the bed on the floor was a white porcelain pan half-filled with oil; a grease-coated piece of metal that Gregson presumed was some kind of airplane part sat in it, and parts of it were stacked neatly around the pan.

"I'll bring in a spare cot," Blake said, taking off his shirt and tossing it on his bed. "You can put your bag on the floor there, next to the box—there's a mirror there hanging on the wall . . . I can have Joseph pour a bucket of warm water over you outside if you feel gritty?"

"No, thanks, this will do fine," Gregson said and got out his toilet bag and began fumbling in it for his shaving gear. The tall African came in with a galvanized bucket and an aluminum pan which he set on the wooden crate and poured water into it.

"*Merci,*" Gregson said and Joseph laughed, poured for Blake and pattered out again on silent feet.

The two men went at their work silently. Gregson had the feeling Blake knew that his visit was not social. Each was waiting for the other to get to the pit of it all.

"I don't have much to lay on for you here," Blake finally said but not with any apology. He leaned over the pan to dip his hands into the water, the slight sag of flesh hanging over the beltline of his shorts.

"I don't mind," Gregson said, taking the tube of lather and spreading another thin gloss over his cheeks. "I lived in far more primitive quarters and with less facilities in my time."

Blake shoved his head down into the pan of water then and snorted loudly against the bite of it. The water turned an orange color from the dust in his long red hair.

"Joseph!"

"Suh!"

The tall African came back into the room with a fresh change of khakis that looked a little better than what Blake had on but not much, and also a couple of khaki towels. Blake took them, and Joseph backed out slowly, that gleam of pride there in his black eyes which said he had accomplished everything, as simple as it was, and without a flaw. Gregson caught the towel Blake threw to him.

"I hope I haven't mucked it up for you by coming without telling you about Thornhill," he offered then, drawing his razor across his cheeks, trying to hold the small mirror on the box with the other hand.

"Did Augie send for him?" Blake asked after a pause.

"I doubt it . . . Augie's been writing to him, but I think he was surprised to see him."

"Well, he's no problem to me, unless you think he is," Blake added. When Gregson did not answer, he went on, "Anyway, I might add that it's good to see you again after almost a year . . ."

The remark was not intended to be jabbing, but Gregson felt it anyway. He had come here a year or more ago to commission the eight secondhand Cessnas that the mission had purchased from an American oil company in Hamara. Gregson had apologized to Blake then that they were not new as promised, but added that he would return one day with that promise fulfilled. He never had, because he never got the necessary appropriation for new aircraft.

"I am sorry about that," he said, avoiding looking at Blake at all, concentrating on his shaving. "You really do too well keeping those secondhand machines in the air, you know . . ."

Blake grunted but said nothing. The conversation was not entirely unpleasant for Gregson. Blake was not pushing him, as he had every right to. It was almost relaxed, the sound of the flies droning in the background, the distant sound of cowbells muffled on the late-afternoon breezes. The rugged simplicity of these quarters was like a strange communion to Gregson. The harsh acrid tang of the wood-smoke drifting in from the fire in the back was so typically African, carrying the scent of the tingling wildness of the country.

But at the same time Gregson felt a sense of disbalance with Blake. It was as if Blake even now, half stripped and with shaving cream on his ruddy face, still cast a giant shadow over him. Gregson was the authority figure here, but with Blake he felt a peculiar sense of apology, as if he owed the man something. Maybe it was the view he had of all people who had the good fortune to work the frontiers in their own freewheeling style. He had had that feeling once, a long time ago, driving that book van across these lonely desert trails. And now, compared to his present, sterile, almost boring spiritual charade in headquarters, Blake had become some kind of personification of what the real sense of mission adventure was all about. Beyond this, though, it was in Blake himself—there was something of natural dominance in him, of leadership, of command, even though he made no attempt to put it on. In light of this, Gregson felt more and more on the defensive and smaller and smaller in his own role as field leader.

"I have meant to come many times before," Gregson went on, grinding the same issue, as if Blake demanded some reason. "But I really had no purpose . . . your radio reports kept me pretty much up-to-date . . ."

"But now you've come," Blake returned lightly. "I'm sure Mr. Thornhill will find the operation a bit rough on the edges . . . I should tell you I have one pigeon out yet and I'm hoping he gets in before dark . . ."

"You have a flap on yet?" Gregson asked, turning to look at him.

"He's a green kid but has the guts, flying in Augie's place. Got off late from Terragona because of some blood sample Rayburn insisted he take out with him. He's bucking a healthy headwind, so I hope he has enough gas when he gets over us . . ."

Gregson felt uneasy. Any kind of problem here with Thornhill around was going to complicate matters. But knowing Blake may be thinking the same thing, and because he felt a need to inject some point of optimism, he said, "We got fourteen thousand in field appropriation up for allocation to you next week. I guess you could use it . . ."

Blake paused in his shaving to look quickly at him. "How long have you had that?"

136

"We've accumulated it through the year, gifts people sent in at home for the operation. I think Thornhill put in a good chunk of it. It gets released by Council vote next week."

"And if the Council does not vote it in?"

Blake was already catching the possible shape of it then. "That would be most unusual . . ."

There was silence again during which Gregson could hear Blake's razor scraping on the raw skin. "I don't suppose I have to go into the fact that I'm low on gas, low on parts, our radio equipment is lousy, low on supplies for Terragona, and we could use a few shower heads for people like the Reverend Mr. Thornhill?"

Gregson half smiled, rubbed his face clean with the khaki towel and reached for his shaving lotion. "There's a catch to it," he added, deciding he might as well lay it out.

"Thornhill?"

Gregson nodded. "You haven't built up the best reputation in the mission, I suppose you know that . . . Emily Stewart hasn't helped you much either, and like I said, Augie could be the final turn in the screw." Blake did not respond, intent on finishing his shave. "Augie put in a call to me Friday, too, demanding a transfer and dropping some very legal and not too complimentary terms about you that will go into Council next week."

"Augie's words, whatever they are, don't come as any surprise . . . every man has his day in court, right? Still, if I'd known his daddy was coming I would have had my station band serenade him with 'Onward, Christian Soldiers' or something appropriate. If the band could play it, that is. They know only one tune . . ."

"You mean the 'Colonel Bogey' or whatever?" Blake gave him a quick smile but said nothing. "You ought to teach them 'Onward, Christian Soldiers' and have them play it more often than your other choices . . ."

Blake wiped his face with the towel and gave that almost boyish, mischievous smile of his again. "Emily never did like 'Colonel Bogey' or 'Tannhäuser.' Does it bother you?"

"There's this 'Camelot' thing too . . . what's that got to do with the operation?"

Blake shrugged. "Nothing to get uptight about, Mr. Gregson," he said with some detachment. "Is it all that important?"

*137*

"It all goes into the case building up on you, Blake, and the questions I have to ask that go even deeper . . ."

"How soon can I expect the money would be one more appropriate, don't you think? Or does my choice of music affect that now?"

Gregson felt uneasy. "The Council will release it as soon as they are satisfied about your spiritual credentials."

"Which means they would refuse the money if I didn't come out in the right mold?"

"These men are custodians of money, men and materials—they've got to be sure how each is used in keeping with the proper spiritual character."

Blake said nothing to that and then walked over to the porcelain pan a few feet away and picked up the airplane part. He held it out in front of him toward Gregson, the oil dripping on the wooden, scarred floor. "You see this?" and his voice remained unhurried as if he were pointing out an artifact of the frontier. "It's part of a propeller gear I'm trying to get into shape. Tomorrow one of those warriors over there will have to fly with this piece of junk. He won't know how bad it is, but I will. And now you will know, Mr. Gregson. You want to take it back and show it to the people in your Council?"

Gregson put his shaving lotion back into his toilet bag. The flies were circling the water in the pan now, dipping down to make passes at the chunks of shaving cream that floated on the surface like dumplings.

"I appreciate your problem, Blake," he said lamely, and he wanted to be done with this. "But there are the rules . . ."

"Okay, so how do you measure this thing you're after?" Blake came back, his voice sounding curious now. "By the gallon, quart, cubic meter, what?" It struck Gregson that Blake really didn't know. "What I'm really trying to say is this," Blake went on, and he reached down behind his bed and came up with a cylindrical piece of metal in both hands and dropped it with a thud on the floor so that dust rose in a small cloud. "There are some things need measuring that seem more important right now, Mr. Gregson. That there is a nitroglycerin cargo cannister. Three quarts of liquid nitro ride inside that beat-up-looking milk can in our secondhand airplanes every day. You can see that the cannister is corroded. It is World War II material the French left behind in Hamara, Mr. Gregson, and which we are now forced to live with here, but more surely to die with. Nitro, may I remind you, Mr. Gregson, will blow if the temperature of your breath on it is even a fraction of a degree the wrong side of tolerance. If we have to keep flying it, how about getting us the new fiberglass cannisters that won't heat up so fast? Beyond that, has anyone thought of what all that nitro is for over in Terragona, and is anybody asking the right questions about it?" Blake paused long enough to wave his towel at a horsefly on a holding pattern around his head. "Or maybe how about the fact that I have only three pilots with instrument ratings in this bunch and one of them has grounded himself on a point of theology? And with the days getting shorter and darkness coming earlier, these kids will have to try to come in here with only a few kerosene pots to guide them down? And the rains are coming early, so what happens if we get caught on the ground and haven't delivered enough supplies to our people in Terragona? Well, Mr. Gregson, if you'll excuse me, it's going to be the devil to pay over there if they run out of pain killers and antibiotics—"

"Every spiritual order puts first priority on the people who are in it, not the logistical problems," Gregson countered, but he knew the statement was straight out of the field manual. "You've lost three pilots, Blake . . . that's more than this mission has lost in twenty years."

Blake paused, watching Gregson, not comprehending the statement at all. "You mean God took those pilots all because of me, Gregson?"

Gregson knew how it would sound, but in essence that was the way it would finally come out in Field Council. The complexity of the judgment of God in history was not to be so easily explained here now either, especially to Blake, whose far too simplistic approach to spiritual matters would not possibly absorb it.

"If I'm going to get the money cleared, Blake, I have to come up with the answers that will satisfy the Council," he said then, wiping his face clean with the khaki towel.

Blake stood there a long time trying to button his left shirt pocket, as if it was so necessary to have everything neatly closed, his fingers looking pudgy and clumsy all of a sudden; finally the button came off in his fingers, and he threw it into the pan of water, staring at it in fixed concentration. Then, after giving his still wet hair a quick swipe back, he laughed shortly. And in that second the scarred-stump look of his face lost some of its roughness.

"Aristotle once said that misfortune unites men when the same thing is harmful to both," he said and looked at Gregson. "You think that is true?"

"I feel it, yes," Gregson returned. "I would rather it didn't occur at all."

He stood there looking at Gregson with a preoccupied look on his face. "Well, that's something anyway," he said with that short laugh. He looked terribly exposed for an instant, like men everywhere, Gregson supposed, who got caught on the horns of justice. But justice of this kind was so much harder to reconcile, even as it was hard to mete out, when done in the name of God. Because who really knew how God would rule here? Gregson never fully entered into this facet of his office—he inwardly hated it. It was really Ted's job. And it had made him ill. And yet his own leadership position rested on his ability to perform in this role too, and even more importantly in relationship to Blake.

"Well, like the good Book says," Blake went on then in that same light tone, " 'He that observeth the wind shall not sow; and he that regardeth the clouds shall not reap.' I must get my number-one cook, Ebenezer, to bring out his best bag of tricks for dinner. By the way, here's the latest report from Terragona on the caseloads," and he took the paper off his bunk and handed it to Gregson. "You might want to measure that too, Mr. Gregson."

"Thanks," Gregson said awkwardly, and he watched Blake go out of the room, wishing somehow that he could add something that would cut the atmosphere of legalism he had injected to bring back that fleeting moment when they found each other man to man. Instead he was left with the smells of shaving lotion, old parts and that overlay of stale sweat. He hunted for a mint, found it, plopped it into his mouth and chewed slowly, reading down the report.

They crowded around the small mahogany table in the ten-by-eighteen dining room, which was heavy with the heat from the overworked kitchen. Since the room was too small to entertain more than six or seven at a time, the pilots and mechanics consented to eat earlier and get out of the way. Gina found herself seated next to Blake, who commanded the head of the table from her right elbow. She hadn't planned it that way. She had come fifteen minutes early in order to pick her seat as far from him as she could. But Blake was late, so now she found herself beside Rudy Kipstein, Augie Thornhill directly across from her and still looking a little pale and out of sorts, his father next to him, with Gregson at the far end opposite Blake.

She avoided looking at Blake at all, conscious only of the smells of his shaving lotion and soap, noticing now and then through the corners of her eyes how the grease clung to his nails. She sat rather stiffly and pretended to be fascinated by the artificial-flower centerpiece that had not been changed in a long time, judging by the coat of creamy dust on the plastic leaves.

Thornhill was embarking on another long conversational tirade about "a pile of cowdung he had found in the middle of his little room behind the infirmary," to which Rudy tried a quick laugh but which no one else picked up.

"Would you lead us in prayer, Reverend?" Blake asked then, cutting into his complaint.

"What? Oh—yes, of course . . . dear Lord, we lift our hearts to Thee . . ." Five long minutes later he stopped with a crashing, sweaty "Amen," having gone from his church in California across the Atlantic and up through Africa . . . building crescendo as he traveled until he got to Durungu and began cajoling God "for the millions lost" and "Lord, what these boys have to do flying all this nitroglycerin, so what shall we say" . . . and finally concluding with "keep us from dereliction in our vows to Thee and keep us ever on the alert for the evil one who would delight to destroy Your work."

When he finished, a light rustle passed among them as if God had gotten up to go out and think on that one, and Blake reached over a few feet from Gina and turned on the Zenith shortwave. The sound of a calypso beat came into the room, tangling with the remains of Thornhill's prayer, which still hung in the atmosphere with the smells of the cooking. He pushed another button and a symphony came on after the announcer identified Radio Brazzaville. Blake left it there to take the steaming platters of rice, chicken and a big bowl of tropical fruit that came through the pass-through beyond Gina's head.

"*Merci,* Ebenezer!" he called out to the unseen face beyond the black hands, and a high-pitched laugh came back. They all laughed like that in response to him, Gina mused, as if delighted at being recognized.

"That the best music you can get, Mr. Blake?" Thornhill asked, and his eyes were measuring Blake now with a certain calculating kind of interest.

"We don't have much choice, Reverend," Blake said, piling food on the plates and handing them to Gina one at a time to pass down the line. She took each plate without looking at him, though she felt his eyes pass over her each time.

"What about the Christian radio station up in Libya that's supposed to broadcast to the entire continent eighteen hours a day?"

"In Harmattan it's hard to pick up much of anything this time of night coming from that direction . . ."

"Well, you get Brazzaville easy enough," Thornhill tossed back. "If I recall, that's a good twenty-five hundred miles from here due south, right?"

"Eighteen hundred," Augie put in quickly, and Augie didn't look as if he had much appetite right then. His smooth sculptured face seemed greasy with sweat, set in grim lines of worry. Gina had seen him earlier throwing a ball to Blake by the tower, and she had wondered then how two men rumored to be at odds with each other could engage in that act of sport.

"Not much difference," Thornhill muttered, frowning some, not liking to be contradicted by his own son.

"If you think it's bad now, sir," Rudy came in, pleasantly, "you should be here just when the rains begin. You see, I guess legend more than science has it that when the Harmattan wind blows dust down off the Sahara Desert it creates a kind of electrical atmosphere that short-circuits radio signals. When the wind shifts from the north to south, this brings the electrical storms, and when the two meet—dust and thunderheads—nothing comes through. A plane flying fifty feet over us couldn't get so much as a piece of static. The Africans call the Harmattan Wambura, meaning the god who walks with the wind and dust eating fire, or electricity, as he goes . . ."

"You believe that, Mr. Kipstein?" Thornhill said with a sniff of skepticism.

"Well, no, sir," Rudy said with a laugh.

"But we respect it," Blake put in. "So we don't fly airplanes when the rains come, if we can help it." When a plate slipped out of Blake's hands then, Gina had to look at him in reflex for a second, and she caught a slight trace of a smile around his mouth. She cleared her throat lightly and went back to staring at the artificial flowers.

"You respect that African folklore to what extent, Mr. Blake?" Thornhill went on, lifting his head as if he had caught the scent again.

"Like I said, Mr. Thornhill, we don't fly planes in those conditions," Blake returned simply. "Now that food in front of you," he went on, changing the subject to a more neutral area, "is African chop. You put chicken and gravy over your rice, top it with that fruit there, then the peanuts and finally hot pepper sauce. It's an African delicacy . . ."

"And loaded with Vitamin C," Rudy came in again, more to Gina now than to anyone else, trying to draw her into the conversation too.

"What's that, Mr. Kipstein?" Thornhill asked.

"I said a lot of Vitamin C," Rudy repeated pleasantly. "Good for preventing colds, scurvy, all of that."

"Oh," Thornhill said, not sure of the relevancy of that in the context of failing Christian radio. He put the fruit on his chicken as directed but passed up the red pepper. He sat glowering at it for a long time before trying it, then took to playing with it with his fork rather than eating much. His son, Augie, was not doing much better.

They went through the meal without much sense of fellowship, Gregson giving a commentary on Hamaran geography which was a deliberate prop to keep Thornhill on a spur in the conversation. Gina felt sweat forming on her upper lip and begin to stick to the back of her white blouse too, so that she had to keep sitting forward off the back of the chair. The collar of her blouse, up tight around her neck, was beginning to chafe her skin. The food was good, she supposed, but heavy in the heat. Once she felt Blake's knee brush against hers as he reached to tone down the volume on the radio, which was putting out the opera *Tosca* now, and she jumped quickly so that Rudy looked at her, and she smiled at him to tell him it was all right.

It was Thornhill who finally swung the conversation around to the history of the Terragona penetration, and Gina knew that the minister was making his overture now to get to more pertinent matters. Gregson took up the question, giving the full background, while Thornhill listened. But Gina could tell by the way Thornhill had his head leaning in Blake's direction that he was getting ready to break in and put something direct to the commander of the operation.

". . . and I suppose we could get a little concerned about how slim the margins are in Terragona," Gregson concluded, folding his napkin up into a small square, unmindful of what he was doing really, "but we've got to trust in the sovereignty of God in it all somewhere . . ."

To which Thornhill seemed to rise with some sense of destiny, and he added, "You are so right, Mr. Gregson," he boomed, and then he turned his head slowly toward Blake, who was just finishing up his plate of rice and chicken. "Tell me, Mr. Blake, what is your conception of the sovereignty of God?" And his jagged line of white eyebrows shot upward like a spring had been hit inside his brain.

Blake didn't answer. He finished up with the last of rice, apparently ignoring the question.

"Well, Mr. Thornhill," Gregson finally came in then, moving to get Blake off the hook.

Thornhill turned quickly to Gregson and said, "Mr. Gregson, I think Mr. Blake should have his turn, don't you?"

Gregson looked at him a little confused, his face seeming to get puffier and more red. He looked down the table to Blake then. There was a stillness now to everything, a scene being frozen for history perhaps. Even *Tosca* seemed to be fading out on the radio. Gina felt the constriction of it in her chest, and she hazarded a sidelong glance at Blake but saw no sign of shattered composure. He had put some kind of white cream on that cold sore, the only point of vulnerability that showed. He glanced back at her quickly, and she sensed she was caught at her guarded look of him, and she felt the flush of heat in her cheeks, for his eyes invited whatever query she had in mind.

"Well, you know I think that's a question I flubbed out on four times in seminary," Rudy came in quickly with a laugh, trying to disarm Thornhill.

Thornhill gave Rudy only a quick smile, as if to say he was not the issue at the moment. "How about it, Mr. Blake?" Thornhill repeated.

Blake went on chewing slowly, glancing once more at Gregson at the far end of the table as if perhaps looking for a cue. "Well, Mr. Thornhill, quite honestly I haven't the slightest idea on that really."

"Not the slightest?" Thornhill repeated, that smile growing some now, as if he had accomplished something of major significance, which, of course, he had.

"Try him on Cessna fuel systems," Rudy tried again, but Thornhill did not even acknowledge him, bent on boring in now.

"Are you a Calvinist or an Armenian then, Mr. Blake?"

"Oh, he's Bohemian," Rudy said with that forced laugh, but nobody responded.

Blake took to staring back at Thornhill now, not sure what any of this meant. "I take it that is something of importance to you, Mr. Thornhill?"

"Important—to *me?*" Thornhill said with a quick laugh of incredulity, his eyes darting quickly to Gregson before coming back in their black zoom-lens fix of Blake. "Well, Mr. Blake, the bluebook on field policy of this mission demands that every station leader pass a theological exam before taking leadership position. I read that exam before coming up here and this question of sovereignty happens to be the first on the list. How did you answer it? that's all I'm asking —I'm always curious, you see, how the leaders of this mission would cope with that. But—well, since you cannot answer it and did not even see the question, I take it you have no answers to those forty-eight questions, then?"

Blake waited for Gregson, it seemed, now. *Tosca* came on strong again and mingled with the clattering of dishes in the back so that it was like some strange world was coming down around them all here. Gregson, however, could not or would not come in with a proper response now either. So Blake said, "No, sir, I didn't even know there was such an exam."

Thornhill didn't look surprised. He half nodded, as if he was satisfied that something was finally confirmed in his own mind. Then he said, "Well, you must be a man of considerable talents to become a station manager without fulfilling a major requirement."

"Mr. Thornhill," Gregson came in now, clearing his throat and trying to get that napkin folded down into the size of a calling card, "I think I can explain it later—"

"Why later?" Thornhill countered, his own eyes narrowing some now. "I hope I'm not embarrassing anyone, Mr. Gregson, with a simple question or two on common theological questions—"

"Please, Dad," Augie cut in then, and Gina could see that Augie had a pinched look, while he kept drawing sharp lines into the white tablecloth with the end of his butter knife.

"What's that, boy?" his father turned on him with a frown. "That

145

is as much your concern as mine, remember? I always told you never to be afraid to discuss spiritual issues with anyone—"

"It's not the time, Dad," Augie insisted, folding his arms across the gold lettering of his sweatshirt and staring down at them as if he were in pain.

"Well, my word, on things like this there is no right and wrong time—"

"I think we should go see the planes now," Augie said abruptly, and pushed his chair back to stand up.

"What? Augie, what's got into you? I'm not even to dessert yet—"

"You said you wanted to see my plane, remember?" Augie went on, and he moved for the door. The elder Thornhill looked at him, then at Gregson questioningly, and finally, his face going a shade redder, said, "You will excuse me, Mr. Gregson?"

"We'll hold the coffee and dessert for you," Gregson said politely, his quick smile only a muscle spasm as Thornhill got up clumsily and moved toward Augie, who was still waiting at the door.

When they were gone, silence hung uneasily over the table. Gina would have preferred to forego the dessert herself. The food had not set too well. The collar of her blouse seemed to dig a fiery line around her neck. But she braced herself as Blake poured coffee into her cup from the white porcelain pot blackened by flames. He reached up then and took the tray of dishes filled with ice cream. He handed them to her one by one to pass down.

"We don't have full power to keep the fridge going," he said, indicating the near-melted ice cream. "Most of the power goes to keep the big reefers cooled down in the hangars where we keep the nitro and medical supplies . . ."

Nobody said anything. It was as if something had come upon all of them that left them embarrassed or intensely preoccupied. Blake, apparently feeling the strain, turned on the radio again and the clear notes of "Blessed Hour of Prayer" came on. Gina, feeling somewhat more prone to follow her own course and not wanting to remain mute forever, said, "Mr. Thornhill would be relieved." Her voice was dry, carrying just a note of the caustic, though she really intended it to be light. Blake glanced at her quickly, not knowing her exact meaning. "In the meantime, I should thank you, Mr. Blake, for the lovely dinner . . ."

"Thank Ebenezer for that," Blake said shortly.

146

"And thanks to your genius thrown in, no doubt?" she commented, unable to control the tone of the sardonic in her voice. "Mr. Kipstein informs me that you are quite amazing in all departments here—"

"I only said that—"

"Like giving injections," she finished for Rudy, wanting all of this herself, "and even arranging accommodations for the single-lady medical officer in your own quarters?"

She threw that out for Gregson in case he had any doubts, bound now to add to the fire Thornhill had kindled but not knowing exactly why.

Before Rudy could come in with that disarming bray of laughter, Blake said, "If you find yours unsuitable I will be glad to offer the same arrangement, Miss Roman." His own voice remained tonelessly flat. She caught his eyes briefly, probing hers deeply so that she went back to her coffee cup, the pulse pounding in her neck.

"It was the same as an extra room, that's what I said," Rudy offered again, making his appeal to Gregson. And Gina felt sorry that she had caught him in the webbing. "Anyway, he slept in the hangar—"

"I understand you are a doctor, Miss Roman?" Blake said, his eyes still on her in quiet surveillance, not trading blow for blow but feeling his way for a proper counterpoint.

"Too many hours short, I'm afraid, Mr. Blake."

"Well, you'll have to do and give us all our physicals which the Hamaran Aviation Department says is long overdue. We'll start as soon as we can clear the time . . . the full physical, Doctor, top to toe, all right?"

Gina was caught with a burning flush moving from her neck to the tips of her ears. He had deftly sliced to her own point of vulnerability, though he could not know it. "I am classified officially as a nurse, nothing more, Mr. Blake. If you want physicals, Doctor Barak—"

"Barak is quite out of the picture," he replied with finality, and she saw traces of hard shine in those gray eyes that made his quick, shadowy smile harden in frozen politeness.

"Mr. Blake," Gregson came in, clearing his throat and swiping at his cowlick with rapid motions of his left hand, "one thing you should understand . . ."

But before he could finish his statement, the P.A. suddenly broke in with a muffled, scratchy voice grabbing them roughly for attention. "This is field alert . . . we have a duckling on the pipe . . . we have a duckling on the pipe . . . pilots, man the pots . . ."

"You'll excuse me," Blake said abruptly, not asking, but commanding, and got up quickly to move around the table for the door.

"What's that all about?" Gregson wanted to know, half up out of his chair, looking after Blake, who had already gone.

"We got a pilot coming in, Mr. Gregson," Rudy said, and Gregson moved his ponderous bulk at surprising speed out the door.

Rudy put on his black baseball cap and jammed the brim up hard against his head and smiled at Gina. "I've got to go too, Gina. My job is to string out the fire pots so that kid up there can at least see something on his way down . . . you'll be okay?"

She wanted to tell him she was sorry she put him on the short end of things with Blake, but there wasn't time now. She smiled assuringly at him, and he left then, and she felt he was almost too eager to leave. She heard the sound of the truck screaming down on the dining room, the shout of Rudy as he mounted, and then it was gone, fading across the field. She picked up the cup, but it shook badly in her hand, so she put it down again. She sat a long minute composing herself, hearing the shouts in the distance. Then she got up and went back to the kitchen to pay her respects to Ebenezer.

Gregson caught up to Blake halfway across the field, heading for the tower.

"He's going to try coming down at this time of night?" he said, puffing now from the run and trying to keep up with Blake's long strides.

"That's the name of the game, Mr. Gregson," Blake returned shortly. "We're used to it by now."

"You expect any trouble?"

"The kid will be low on gas, and he'll have to feel his way down . . . otherwise, no sweat."

Gregson wanted to warn Blake that it better go smoothly with Thornhill here, but instead he said, "Blake, about Gina Roman . . . she's really not qualified as a doctor—"

"She's seen plenty of cases in her time, Mr. Gregson, so a few more shouldn't put her out any."

"Don't push her too hard, Blake," Gregson tried again. "It won't go over well if we lose another nurse—"

"One thing I don't need here, Mr. Gregson, is another tight-corseted warrior looking to straighten everybody out," Blake snapped back, glancing up at the heavy black curtains of the night.

Gregson didn't know how to return that one, so he said, "We should talk some more on that, Blake . . . tonight, later . . ."

Just then Thornhill appeared coming up on a ram course to the left, his short legs propelling him in an ungainly trot. Augie was a good fifteen feet ahead of him and angling for the tower door.

"Gregson, what is this all about, a pilot trying to come down this time of night?" he bellowed with the usual demand, his voice slamming sledgehammer blows at the sensitive pillars holding up the impending sense of calamity building overhead.

"Keep him out of the way," Blake said to Gregson as he disappeared into the tower.

Gregson didn't know how to keep Thornhill outside the tower, nor did he know how to explain what was coming at this point when the tranquility of the field was coming apart with the sounds of urgency. He tried to persuade Thornhill to stay there where he was, but when he went inside himself and climbed the steps to the tower, Thornhill followed, puffing and panting.

When they got to the upper porch, Blake was talking to another man, with reddish hair and wearing a light leather jacket, who held a slender microphone in one hand, the long cord running back to an outlet against the far wall.

"Where is he, Shannon?" Blake asked.

"Five miles out," Shannon replied. "I've been waiting to hear his motor."

"Well, looks like a piece of cake, hey, Augie?" Blake went on, walking by Augie, who stood with his back to the wall a few feet behind Shannon. "You always wanted to know how the rest of us live on the ground—why don't you bring Monk down?"

Augie took the mike from Shannon rather uncertainly, looking as if he might want to argue the point.

"JERICHO, this is Mother, how do you read, over?" he said into the mike, clearing his throat against the dust.

They waited a few seconds, then the sound of the motor came faintly from the east, growing in power. Almost at the same time the voice came over the speaker on the wall above Shannon's head, high-pitched like a child's, unsure of how the adventure was going to end. "Mother, this is JERICHO . . . I read you loud and clear, over!"

The motor now was coming straight for them and much too low. "JERICHO, you are too low," Augie shouted into the mike. "Pull up and do a ninety turn to the left and stay on that heading three miles . . . over!"

"Mother, you got to be kiddin'!" the voice shrilled back over the speaker as the plane rattled over them not more than fifty feet above so that Gregson could smell the exhaust, swinging away from them toward the south and the Durungu village at the far end of the runway. "You better play it right, Mother, cuz I got enough gas maybe for one pass, no more!"

Augie looked at Blake uncertainly, but Blake remained at the railing, one leg hooked over the top, continuing to stare at the sky. The motor faded away again. Augie coughed once, then wiped his hand across his forehead. Shannon moved back against the wall, arms folded, staring straight ahead. Gregson sensed that Blake was going to leave it to Augie, even though the situation called for his own command. Gregson didn't know why. Thornhill seemed to realize this too, for he said to Gregson in a raspy, scraping voice, "Why doesn't he do the job himself?" and when Gregson did not respond, Thornhill said to Blake, "Mr. Blake, how can that pilot see more than a foot in front of his face—?"

"No talking right now, Mr. Thornhill," Blake cut back without looking around, "or you'll have to go down."

Thornhill sputtered something under his breath, but he said no more.

"Okay, Mother, I'm three miles southeast—how now, brown cow?"

"Do a one-eighty, Monk," Augie said into the mike, "and ease throttle to twelve hundred RPM . . . What's your altitude now?"

"I'm at fifteen hundred . . ."

"Okay, make your turn and drop her fast to eight hundred and check back . . . keep your eyes out for the pots, Monk!"

"Roger . . ."

Gregson looked beyond Blake to the flickering globes of yellow through the dust that marked the kerosene pots. Even from here, not more than twenty yards away, it was almost impossible to see the winking signals through the blur of the dust. He felt his mouth go dry and that light tapping had begun in his right temple. This was not the time for a disaster in the making. He saw the truck coming up from the field toward the tower, its headlights nothing more than two glowing matches in a cave. It stopped below them and the pilots jumped down to stand there listening for the sound of the motor, waiting, watching.

"Crazy," Thornhill muttered at Gregson's side.

"Okay, Mother, I'm down at eight hundred," the voice came through again, sounding more hoarse, uncertain.

"Do you see the pots, Monk?" Augie prodded.

"I can't even see my prop turning, Mother . . . I'm coming down through six hundred marker . . . hold it! I think I see 'em! Hallelujah! I see 'em!"

There was a pause of just a few seconds as the sound of the motor came on stronger. "He's too far out," Blake snapped sharply at Augie. "He's coming down on those nomad fires a mile beyond the runway! Get him up, Augie!"

Augie seemed transfixed all of a sudden, unable to speak, staring at Blake, seemingly unable to comprehend while the sound of the motor got louder. Blake moved quickly then, grabbed the mike from Augie, shouted into it, "Monk, give her full throttle and pull up . . . you're over the Durungu fires! Pull up!"

Gregson heard the engine thunder in response ripping an uneven, uncertain piece out of the night, hold for ten seconds or so, then begin to sputter followed by loud popping sounds like the explosions of inflated paperbags. Gregson heard the loud crunch and squeal, then the sound of skidding tires, and Blake shouted into the mike again, "Stay off those brakes, Monk, or you'll ground loop!"

Then Gregson saw the plane come out of the darkness beyond the glow of the kerosene pots, down on the ground, but fishtailing dangerously, almost as if it was out of control. It shot by the tower, dust and sparks billowing up from its wheels, and then it began swinging until it was sliding crosswise toward the direction of the infirmary and dining room. And all Gregson could think of then was Gina Roman still over there perhaps, and even as he headed for the stairs he heard Thornhill shout, "Dear God!" And he was conscious then of a lot of running on those stairs, Blake somewhere ahead of him.

"This is terrible, terrible!" Thornhill kept yelling at Gregson as

*151*

they ran, his breath sounding like a dry pump. But Gregson wasn't bothering about him now, he was trying to see in the dust, waiting for the flash of the flames or the sound of the impact. All around him there were shapes running, feet muffled in the sand; someone had gotten the truck going, and it raced by him, the headlights poking desperately to make holes in the dust. Gregson coughed, and his chest hurt, but he kept running.

He got there to see the plane hiked over on its nose, propeller blade bent underneath, not more than twenty-five yards from the infirmary. Gina was standing by the open right door, trying to reach in to help the pilot, who was having some difficulty getting out. Blake jumped off the running board of the truck, ran to her, pushed her roughly aside, and snapped: "Get out of here! She can blow any minute!" Gina staggered back and caught the right wing strut to keep from falling. Gregson grabbed her arm to steady her.

"You all right?" he asked.

She blinked at him uncertainly and then nodded.

Blake was helping the pilot down to the ground now, and Gregson moved in with the others to help. He saw the spread of blood across the khaki shirt in the light from someone's flashlight. There was an ugly cut over the right eye too. "Get back everybody!" Blake yelled, and the tangled knot of flyers and African mechanics loosened some. "Who's got the $CO_2$?" Blake demanded. Somebody came running with the extinguisher as Blake jumped to the engine cowling, ripped it open with a savage thrust of his hands. "Come on, come on, get it in there," he raked at the man, who couldn't get the valve working. Rudy came forward quickly, snatched the extinguisher from the fumbling hands of the other pilot and hit the valve with his fist, unlocked it and turned the foam on the hot engine block. The smells of hot oil, dust and $CO_2$ mingled with the cowdung and spent gasoline.

"You all right, Monk?" somebody asked in the background, as Monk leaned against the upturned fuselage while Gina dabbed at his cut with a ball of cotton.

"Only a knot on my head, I think," Monk said, and someone else gave off a shaky kind of laugh.

"One more notch of wisdom, brother," another voice threw in, and there was more strained laughter, too tight, maybe a little pinched in the prospect of how close Monk had come to not making it.

"What's all the blood for?" Blake said then, coming up to Monk, ignoring Gina.

"Well, Mr. Blake," Monk said with some bewilderment, looking down at his smeared shirt, "I put the test tube carrying Rayburn's blood sample in my shirt pocket where I thought it would be safest. When I nosed over I rammed the control column . . . so this is all I got left." Monk took out the broken test tube with only a half inch of blood left in the bottom. Gina took it carefully, wrapped a strip of adhesive across the broken top to reseal it. "Rayburn said to make sure that sample got to the U.N. health people in Talfungo . . ."

"There really isn't enough to work with," Gina commented shortly.

"You'll have to pick up another sample tomorrow," Blake said.

"There's a bottle of water in the nitro sack," Monk came back. "At least it was there when I went over on my nose . . ." Blake opened the door of the plane and removed the pint-sized bottle, still full, and handed it to Gina. "Collins told me to send that water with the blood sample," Monk said to her.

"All right, everybody out of here now," Blake jabbed at them. "Sam! I want this plane towed out of here to the hangar and that prop removed . . . *comprenez-vous?*"

"Suh!" Sam shouted from the shadows.

Blake turned back to Monk again and lifted his voice, intending all the pilots to hear. "Now, Monk, I told you not to lay on those brakes when you came in here . . ."

"Mr. Blake, sir, I did not hit those brakes," Monk returned quickly, his eyes big in the urgency he felt to clarify his action.

"Monk, that plane could not have slid around like that without the wheels grabbing—"

"Excuse me, sir, but those wheels grabbed over in JERICHO earlier today when I landed, and I thought sure I was going over on my nose then with all that nitro ticking . . . and when I hit the runway here tonight, it was like the wheels didn't roll at all . . ."

Blake turned his head to look at the wheels. "Okay, we'll check it out," he said simply.

"And one other thing, Mr. Blake," Monk went on, swallowing first and clearing his throat as Gina continued to press that bloody cotton ball to his forehead. "There's something funny going on at JERICHO, seems to me . . ."

"Like what?"

"Well . . . I can't be sure since I've only flown in there twice . . . but they wouldn't let me in the hospital Quonset at all today. I had to stay by the plane all the time. The one guy named Collins came and got the nitro and all that, but he wouldn't say much to explain anything. Just asked me what the Boston Bruins were doing in the hockey playoffs. When I asked if I could get a drink inside, he just told me he'd bring me a drink . . ."

Gregson moved up behind Blake now and said to Monk, "Did Doctor Rayburn say anything to you when he gave you that blood sample?"

Monk's eyes blinked in the light, trying to focus on the new voice coming to him. "No, sir, just that I should get it out to the U.N. right away, that's all."

"How about the rest of you people?" Blake turned to the pilots then. "Notice anything out of the ordinary in your bases over there?"

"Doc Barth is fighting something strange too," Shannon offered. "He built a special isolation shack and he won't let me nor anybody else near the place."

"Has Rayburn reported anything unusual over the radio?" Gregson went on.

"The four o'clock report was okay," Blake returned, and then said, "Is that right, Augie?"

"Right," Augie said quietly from somewhere back in the darkness.

"See here," the elder Thornhill broke in for the first time, "just what is going on here, Mr. Gregson?"

Gregson ignored him for the moment. "I think we better check Rayburn on this on the morning transmission," he said to Blake, who nodded.

Then Blake turned to the pilots and barked, "Okay, you prop jockeys, let's clear out of here!"

The pilots began to disperse slowly, moving by Monk to slap him on the shoulder, some to rib him good-naturedly. Blake moved back to the front of the airplane.

"Was ist dis Herr Monk who flyin' das machinin' on der nosin'?" one of them, a thin, wiry man, said. The rest of them laughed much easier then, and Monk gave them a weak, hesitant grin in return. As they moved by Monk, each of them took the time to introduce himself to Gina as well, and Gina nodded to each, giving a small, ghostly smile.

"Can we talk now, Mr. Gregson?" Thornhill came in again, his voice riding a crest of anger.

"If you'll allow me a few minutes more, Mr. Thornhill?" Gregson said and, without waiting for permission, moved off to follow Gina, who was leading Monk to the infirmary for further treatment.

He came up alongside her and said, "Gina, can you check that sample?"

She gave him a quick glance. "The best blood man in Hamara is over there in JERICHO—Milford Trask," she said. "If he couldn't identify it, I certainly can't with the equipment I have here . . ."

"What about the water, then? Is there some connection?"

Gina shrugged. "They maybe figure the source of the problem, whatever it is, might be in the water."

"Their drinking water?"

"I wouldn't know."

"What do you think it means?"

"They've got sick people on their hands probably and an unclassified bug of some kind. They want the World Health to try to isolate it . . . that's only my guess."

He didn't say any more. He followed them into the infirmary to wait, hoping that he might get a few more questions into Monk. Something was beginning to lay hold of him about what Rayburn was after in that sample. He didn't like the sound of it, but he wasn't sure why. He watched Gina work, putting the stitches into the cut, closing it expertly, her movements sure, precise. She gave Monk a shot of morphine, and it wasn't long before the young flyer's eyes began to droop. Gregson was sure he wouldn't be talking any more tonight.

He finally went outside and found Thornhill approaching the infirmary in purposeful, waddling strides.

"I think we should talk to Mr. Blake," he said almost demandingly. Gregson knew that Thornhill was smarting even more now that he had witnessed Augie freeze earlier in trying to get Monk into the field.

"I'm not sure Blake is going to be available right now," Gregson tried. "It's hardly the time—"

"Everybody tells me it's not the time when it comes to him," Thornhill countered impatiently and swiped at a lock of hair that had fallen over his left ear. "This place is out of balance, Mr. Gregson, and I think it's time to find out why."

Gregson glanced at the man again, seeing only the surface features in the dim light from the infirmary, a mountain losing its proud back to the uncontrollable landslides of circumstances. A man like that shouldn't have to be running across the world trying to balance the books for God, only to have to die a piece at a time in the process.

So Gregson said, "Well, maybe we better try the tower first, then the hangars . . ."

Thornhill grunted in acknowledgment, and Gregson looked for a mint in his shirt pocket, found one, sucked on it as he walked, feeling the sand drag heavily on his feet.

# CHAPTER VII

They found Blake in the small radio room filling a bucket with spare parts. "Have a minute, Mr. Blake?" Gregson asked.

"Not really," he returned shortly, a little testy now, apparently in no mood to take either of them right then.

"I'm afraid we have to take the time, Mr. Blake," Thornhill said coolly, dogmatically, and Blake, sensing the tone, dropped his bucket of parts with a metallic thud on the mud floor. He indicated the only chair at the scarred table and said,

"Sit down, why don't you, Mr. Thornhill?"

Thornhill sat down with a decisive move like a bill collector and put his right hand down flat on the table, staring at it a long time. Gregson could see in the poor light of the kerosene lamp, which Blake was using undoubtedly to conserve power, that Thornhill's face was carrying a jaundiced tone, matching the long strands of yellowish hair hanging over either ear which he did not bother to push back now. His eyebrows twitched in a kind of furry dance, caterpillars squirming in the sun. The flesh of his jowls hung down like melting plastic, forming ugly, prickly points of fatigue. Quarter-sized circles of red rouge showed up high on the cheeks, under each eye. It was as if some monster had gotten to him in these few hours and was now beginning to bite hard on his vitals.

"Mr. Blake," he began then, studying the back of his freckled hand in front of him as if he had a moth trapped under it, "there are some things that need explaining, and I want some answers if you don't mind."

"If it's the theology exam again—"

"I'll forego that for now," Thornhill countered. Then he gave a

157

wincing smile at his hand. "I am not a witch hunter really, Mr. Blake, despite what you may be thinking." Blake did not respond to that. He leaned against the wall by the radio and folded his arms to wait, the light casting shadows like flickering bat wings across his face. "What I want to know is why these pilots have to come back so late in the day to fight their way in here? Doesn't that bother you people here?"

That wasn't the real issue, of course, but he was opening with that, laying his porch for the big concerns.

"We made that arrangement with Turgobyne, the chief of Terragona," Blake said tonelessly, but there were definite sounds of impatience there now. "We are allowed one plane a day into each of our bases. And Turgobyne keeps them there until late afternoon to make sure we can't fly back in again the same day. It's his way of protecting himself."

"Protecting himself against whom or what, Mr. Blake?"

"Against too many people coming in on him, too many for him to handle at once."

"Is it not strange that this chief—what's his name—should feel he needs to protect himself from what is purely a mission of mercy designed to save his people?"

"They don't see us totally like that."

"They know you are Christians, don't they?"

"Maybe, but as long as we carry nitro, we may not get all of the effect . . ."

"Yes, the nitro," and Thornhill turned to Gregson then, his eyes enlarging some in their red pockets. "And whose brainchild was that, then?"

"That was the mission's responsibility," Gregson came back, wondering if this was dress rehearsal for many more scenes like this in the future. He explained Hamara's prospector team being invited into Terragona by Turgobyne, along with the mission airlift. "If we were to go, we had to co-operate with Hamara or abandon the opportunity . . ."

"It's contradictory," Thornhill replied sullenly. "You are tampering awfully close with political overtones, Mr. Gregson, mixing God with mammon . . ."

"We were asked to co-operate with Hamara's request," Gregson argued. "We did not take it as political, and the Premier assured us it would not be considered as such . . ."

158

"Couldn't you find another airfield off Hamaran territory and avoid any association of this nature?"

"We are as close as we can get to Terragona that allows us the margins we need to fly," Gregson added. There was a pause during which Thornhill's fingers tapped an impatient tattoo on the table top. "It was a choice we had to make . . . we felt Terragona needed Christianity, and who knows if we would ever get the opportunity again? We counted the cost, Mr. Thornhill . . ."

"It's too much!" Thornhill cut back sharply. "Committing these boys—and I mean boys—to such terrible strain . . . why, that boy who got out of his plane out there looks like he ought to be in 4-H . . ."

"We know that . . . but all of them figured even one Terragona soul was worth it all. Besides, if we did not follow through with the operation, it was a sure thing that the Hamaran prospectors would go regardless . . . we preferred to go, making sure Terragona got Christianity before the gold and uranium fever took over—"

"And so how long does this nightmare go on, then?"

"As long as the rains hold off."

"It's still inhuman, Mr. Gregson . . . was this mainly your decision for the mission, then?"

"No, our Field Council cleared it back in 1971 after much prayer, believe me—"

"Prayer?" Thornhill countered, shaking his head so that his jowls flapped, his eyes dilating, reaching out to zoom in on Gregson. "I have serious doubts God would answer a prayer to the extent of this operational price tag—"

"The cross wasn't beautiful either, as I see it," Blake put in then, making it a blunt statement of fact, refusing to rise to the peak of Thornhill's demand.

Thornhill gave a tight smile in condescension to what he was sure was Blake's hopeful attempt at spiritualizing. "And you would know all about that, would you, Mr. Blake?" Blake pulled his baseball cap lower over his eyes and half shrugged as if to say there wasn't much point in pursuing that, after all. "And while we are at it, may I ask what all this finally costs you, Mr. Blake?" And those red spots under his eyes were now taking on a bluish shade like the color of a ripening grape. "Have you taken your turn flying with the rest of them?"

"Mr. Thornhill," Gregson came in, clearing his throat.

"Let this man talk for himself," Thornhill snapped. "Unless you feel it necessary to continually speak for him?"

"I haven't flown into Terragona, no," Blake picked it up then. "But I signed to do so if I had to—"

"And when is that exactly, sir?"

"If I lose a pilot and have an airplane to fly."

"You lost three pilots—"

"And three airplanes with them."

"My son tells me you have a Piper Cub in the hangar that is perfectly capable mechanically . . ."

"That is a back-up airplane, Mr. Thornhill, to be used in emergencies only—"

"Augie tells me you are planning to put the shell of a Volkswagen on that plane and have it flown to that pagan chief over there."

"I hope to get it in there before the rains, yes," Blake came back without hesitancy, and Gregson sensed that Thornhill was moving deliberately now.

"For what purpose, Mr. Blake?"

"It's something I promised Turgobyne—"

"And I would like to know why we are buying so many favors of a pagan chief for the right to preach the Gospel to him and his people," Thornhill replied, warming up to this now as if he was coming to the clinching third point of the sermon. " 'Can a man take fire in his bosom and not be burned?' That's Proverbs twenty-four and verse thirty-seven."

" 'Better is a dinner of herbs where love is than a stalled ox and hatred therewith,' " Blake countered. "That's in Proverbs too."

Thornhill's eyes did not waver from his intent study of Blake, but then he grunted what might have been a half laugh but which didn't materialize from his barrel-like torso. It stayed a grunt, a quiver only.

"You know Proverbs so well then, Mr. Blake?"

"I have a pilot who quotes nothing else even to compliment the cook."

"Is it necessary to go on with this?" Gregson tried then to steer a new course.

"I'll tell you why it's necessary, Mr. Gregson," Thornhill pounced back, lifting a short, fat finger to point at him. "It would seem that Mr. Blake expects his men to do what he won't do himself. That is not leadership to me. And I have doubts as to his motives here . . ."

"It takes leadership to keep an operation like this functional, Mr. Thornhill," Gregson replied, but he knew he didn't have much going for the man on that.

"Strength which way, Gregson? He has not passed the basic theological exam required of your mission for leadership. So I don't see any strengths on the spiritual side. Where is it, then? In being able to talk his pilots down to this field through a microphone? What risk is there to him in that?"

"Your son found that it has its moments," Gregson said, and he was sorry he let that out immediately, because it seemed to make Thornhill jump in his chair.

"Yes, he did!" and his eyes went bigger now, two furnace doors opening on the leaping fires of his indignation. "But as I saw it with you, Mr. Gregson, Blake did not give him the chance to finish the job. There's some kind of harassment of my son here, Gregson, and maybe Mr. Blake can tell me why?"

"Your son froze at the wrong moment, Mr. Thornhill, and it happens to the best," Blake offered languidly.

"But does it ever happen to you, Mr. Blake? Everyone has a weakness, commits a mistake, but does Mr. Blake commit any that anyone can see?"

"Mr. Thornhill," Gregson tried to squeeze in again.

"So let me add this," Thornhill went on, ignoring Gregson. "You put my boy in an awful position up there, Blake. With everybody listening and watching, you deliberately exposed him!"

The room rattled with Thornhill's grating voice, and it carried the sound of judgment. There was silence for a long minute during which Thornhill coughed once and began drumming his fingers on the table top.

"I'm afraid at this stage, in any case," Gregson said finally, moving to cut this off now while there was something left to salvage, "we simply have to go on with the operation."

"I'll suggest one better," Thornhill came back. "Get the Hamaran Government people to cut the nitro for a start . . ."

"Our flights would be grounded," Gregson replied.

"I doubt they will be quick to do that with their own people in Terragona depending on the flights—"

"But they might take the move as an excuse to mount their own airlift, too, Mr. Thornhill, without us—"

"So let them! Your pilots are taking all the risks as it is. It would seem far better for all concerned to halt operations, pull your people out and wait for a more opportune time, at least when you don't have to carry explosives for other interests. As it is now, I can hardly appreciate this kind of bad mix, and I doubt people back home would . . . how do you see that, Mr. Gregson?"

Gregson knew that the "bad mix" also referred, if not entirely, to Blake. Gregson hesitated, not sure how to carry the argument now. To abandon Terragona to Hamaran mineral prospectors was hardly the right strategy, no matter which way he looked at it. But right now Thornhill presented a powerful kind of lobby here, and there was no way to simply go around it. Gregson did not look at Blake, who remained against the wall by the radio, his arms folded, not commenting. The air was heavy with the pressure of the inevitable.

"Well, all I can do now is take it to Council," Gregson finally said rather lamely, not looking at Blake, staring down at his shoes instead.

"That makes sense for openers," Thornhill confirmed flatly. "You see, Mr. Blake, the trumpet you are blowing here has that uncertain sound. As the Scriptures point out, nobody can properly march to it . . ."

There was finality to that voice then. All that seemed left to do was pronounce the benediction. Blake stayed in that immovable pose against the wall by the radio, his arms still folded, the blond fuzz turning yellow in the lamplight. He was watching Thornhill intently now, his red-streaked eyes enlarged under the brim of his cap. He moved finally then and opened a bottom drawer in his desk, rummaged around and came up with a spool of recording tape, put it on the tape recorder on the transmitter.

"What's all that about?" Gregson asked.

"Mr. Thornhill's boy, Augie, once played this for the other pilots a long time ago . . . he was proud of it, and maybe he had a right to be . . ."

Blake threw the switch then and a voice came booming through the speaker. And Gregson knew he had come to the end of a long journey right then.

> . . . and I say to you Christian parents here this morning, will you stand and signify that you will give your sons and daughters to missions? Are you willing to give your chil-

dren to God, to die if necessary? To die, I said . . . no price is too big for the cause of Christ. I have given my son, Augie, to God, and I could ask no greater honor than having my boy blaze out for God in Africa that those people might come to know Christ . . . what will it be, then?

Blake snapped off the recorder. The sound of Thornhill's voice remained heavy in the room like sworn testimony. He sat very still in his chair, his eyes half closed, that right hand still lying flat on the table as if he had a fly still under there. He opened his eyes to stare at that hand, his face going into a kind of sag. A lock of his yellow hair had fallen on his forehead, a washed-out vine looking for a grasp up the bare wall of his skin. A ball of sweat started high on his left temple and began running a slow course to his cheek like an air bubble.

"Mr. Blake," Gregson said sharply, feeling the finality of things here now, "that is hardly the answer for this man . . . I think you owe him an apology . . ."

"Let him apologize to those pilots over there," Blake countered, his voice remaining even though carrying the first hint of storm. "As long as we are talking about uncertain sounds and all that, right? I'm sure they'd understand that all of us can get carried away at times with our own eloquence and even abide some of those flat notes we blow out once in a while?"

"Blake!" Gregson warned, but Thornhill lifted that right hand off the table, holding it out toward Gregson in a kind of feeble gesture to back off.

"Mr. Gregson," he said quietly, a little hoarsely, "if you don't mind, I think I'll turn in . . . you know, I think it's been a long day, longer than I thought . . ."

He got up slowly, and Gregson resisted the impulse to reach out and help him. "I'll see you to your quarters—"

"No . . . no, if you don't mind, Mr. Gregson, I'd like to walk it alone. Night air will do me good." He moved slowly for the door, stood in the open frame a moment, looking up at the sky. "Good night, then . . . and God look kindly on us all . . ."

He was gone then, quietly dissolving into the night. Gregson stared at the empty doorway, wanting to reach out and put the shattered pieces of the man back together. Then, as Blake turned to pick up more parts to throw into the bucket by his foot, Gregson said, "I suppose you know that was the worst thing you could have done? You know you just put the kiss of death on the man who feeds you? You just blew that appropriation—"

"Look, Mr. Gregson," Blake came back, tossing parts into the bucket, his voice controlled but building to a crest, "I don't blame him if he wants a good, clean, legitimate Christian death for his boy. No contradictory images, everything in line. But if he gets his way in that, this whole operation becomes a hopeless charade. We have to think flying every minute, Mr. Gregson, and that's what keeps those pilots alive out there . . ."

"Does that call for the shabby treatment of Thornhill?" Gregson protested. "Or what you did to Augie earlier on the tower?"

"You sent me kite flyers for pilots, remember, so if they are going to come up to the mark and win, they have to play it by my rules . . ."

"It's not all in the winning, you know . . ."

"Then, what is this all about, Mr. Gregson?" and Blake straightened up from his work to look at him directly, almost accusingly. "You want a draw? A retreat? You trying to prove how much a man can sweat blood and still say Amen . . . ?"

"No, but . . ."

"Well, I think you better get on that radio then, Mr. Gregson," Blake went on, "and get your pilot back here tomorrow. You can take Thornhill and his son out of here. And while you are at it, you can take that Gina Roman too . . . I got a feeling she's going to put water in our gasoline within forty-eight hours." He picked up his bucket of parts then and headed for the door. He stopped there, turned to look at Gregson, that boyish, disarming smile beginning to form. "The Reverend Thornhill will recover, Mr. Gregson . . . I'm sorry I blew the exam on you in front of him . . ."

"I want you to apologize to Thornhill before we leave," Gregson said to him. Blake looked at him blankly, as if he didn't comprehend. "And Gina Roman stays . . . that's the way it is."

Blake turned then without further word and went out, leaving Gregson to the flickering shadows and the night turning colder in too many ways. He rubbed his burning eyes and finally sat down in the chair at the table, hearing only the hiss of the transmitter. It was done then. Blake couldn't have sealed it any better. And yet everything the man said had its points of mad, almost beautiful logic! A square wheel on the ark of God is what somebody called him once. That struck him as strangely funny, and he laughed, the sound of it echoing flatly in the room. He caught himself quickly, feeling embarrassment, sadness.

"Lord, look upon these poor vessels of clay," he said and got up slowly to raise Talfungo on the frequency.

A few minutes later he walked across the field to the infirmary and found Gina alone stacking bottles of pills into a cupboard. She glanced at him once when he came in, maybe noting he had been in his battle, for he was never good at covering up the strains. He climbed up on the examining table to let his feet dangle a few inches off the floor. He watched her in silence, noticing again how her long, slender fingers worked with such easy grace and sureness. He found some strange sense of stability around her. There was something so sure about her, combined with that dimension of mysterious beauty hidden underneath, so that he found himself studying her intently to get a look at whatever it was that was trying to come out.

"How's Monk?" he began then, trying to will his muscles to relax.

"I sent him back to his quarters to sleep it off. He's got a nasty bump."

"Will he be ready tomorrow?"

"Have to wait and see," she returned simply, examining a label on a big bottle of yellow pills.

He accepted that without comment. Then she said, "If Monk can't fly tomorrow, who goes? I don't suppose Mr. Blake will take his turn?"

He caught the tone of accusation there despite her attempt to make it sound academic. "I leave that to Blake, how about you?"

She kept her eyes on her work, ignoring the rebuke in his voice, which he hadn't intended to come out.

"It doesn't bother you then, Mr. Gregson?"

"What?"

"That Blake doesn't fly his turn?"

"He must have his reasons. Anyway, who says he won't when he has to?"

"Tomorrow would be a good time to test it."

"Are you asking me to do that, Gina?" and he made no attempt to cover his feeling of irritation with her now. "I gave you your transfer because of the medical need, nothing more . . ."

She didn't answer. She put the jar of pills into the cupboard and stood looking at it a long time.

"Do you believe God gives insight or at least instinct about people, Mr. Gregson?" she asked.

"I'm sure He does."

"Well, I have mine about Blake . . . do you mind?"

"Such as?"

"I don't think he fits. I think he knows it. And I think everybody around here knows it too, including Rudy Kipstein. And I think you know it too. Yet you and everybody else are trying to cover for him . . . isn't that odd?"

"Are you going to be the champion of us all, then, Gina, and expose him?"

She turned her head toward him and smiled. It was wintry, lifeless, working against the classical lines of her Greek-Italian facial sculpture. Her deep chestnut eyes, enlarged in their concentration of either the outer or inner world of hers, carried a certain clinical detachment.

"Well, Mr. Thornhill had one thing right," she went on, almost lightly, "that we have to be on guard on the walls . . . if God sees fit to use me that way, well, you may just wind up pinning a medal on me, Mr. Gregson."

He smiled back at her, but he felt disturbed. Something was locked inside her all right, even as Barak had told him, something she was protecting or maybe even nourishing. He felt suddenly a strange kind of apprehension, and dropped his feet to the floor and headed for the door.

Even as he put his hand on the screen latch, the P.A. crackled to life, and he paused. The music came on then in a slow movement, almost muffled, a kind of melancholy tune but gradually moving up the scale, the horns and strings rising with it and building toward a crescendo.

"The favorite hymn of a storm trooper," Gina commented dryly.

"You know that music?" he asked, turning his head toward her.

"Wagner's 'Tannhäuser'?"

"Do you know what it means?"

"Wagner was a musician of war—that should say enough about Blake," she added with a clip. "Don't you think?"

Gregson wasn't sure. He listened again as the theme rose now to the peak. It had certain elements of hymnody maybe, or was he deliberately trying to read into it? There was storm there, conflict, and now the last run of it to the finish seemed to rise to a certain plaintive note of victory? What did Blake get out of it? Or maybe the poor man just simply likes Wagner? But it still didn't help his image much. And looking at Gina Roman then as she went on stacking those bottles neatly row upon row in the cupboard, he was sure time was running out on Blake.

Across the compound in the red Quonset, the pilots had already settled into bed. Blake had made the rule long ago that when the music came on over the P.A. they had to be turned in. At first they considered it a joke and sat around in the dark in their clothes; but when Blake caught them a few times like that and let them have it in his own style, they learned to take to the bunks before the music stopped.

Now they lay quietly under the khaki blankets listening to the music climb the gentle slopes of the melody, waiting for it to rise to its rugged mountain cliffs as it pounded out each painful step to the top. They knew every bar of it by now, every dip of the horns, every attack of the percussion, ran along with it in their minds, each man making his own interpretation, feeling the tingle of it—and even rising to it in almost personal embrace as if it had some kind of life in itself. It seemed to drive home their prayers that they had said earlier together, like the gleaming shaft of a spike into soft pine.

Shannon rolled over on his bunk, leaning his head on his arm, peering out the screen door where Mundey had disappeared with a roll of toilet paper in his hand. Mundey had been making a lot of trips like that, but only lately was he caught in the nocturnal demands. It was too quiet in the Quonset. They were not talking as they used to, and Shannon was sure they were pondering the deteriorating flying conditions. Mundey's report today of the high-temperature line in his plane, even with the air vents wide open, was a bad sign. It could only mean that the wind was swinging around to bring the southerly flow, which meant the rains were not far behind it. All of which meant they'd have to climb higher to get cooler air, and southerly air meant rougher turbulence the higher they went.

Shannon sensed that Blake was aware of this lately too. He was becoming more testy with them and even with the African mechanics. Now even his favorite music died in a rather muted tone in the night, an omen perhaps that said Blake's hold here was at last being threatened.

That fact would not have bothered him earlier. He did his job here and let the problems of solving Blake's lack of spiritual image to Talfungo. But now he wasn't sure that he could let it go by so easily. He sensed that he, too, was tied to Blake's peculiar power to weld this operation together, to drive them up every day against terrible odds. He told himself over and over before that it was God and God alone who did it; but now he sensed that Blake was playing the key role and growing larger and larger in their margins for survival. And if Gregson and Thornhill managed or were forced to suspend him on his poor theological credentials, what then? Maybe that was why Mundey found himself running out to the john at this hour of the night? Was that contemplation the reason for his own sleeplessness now?

Now that "Blake's lullaby" had ended, it was quiet in the Quonset, each of them probably thinking the same things. Somebody turned wearily on his mattress across the room and the springs creaked in tired concert.

"What happened to Mundey?" Slater asked from across the room, his voice sounding hoarse.

There was a pause. "Was ist dis Baron Von Mundey who walkin' in der moonlightin' and de dustin' mit ein toilet paperin'?" Bellinger chirped. "Yah, Baron Von Mundey bouncin' das machinin' mit ein nitro smokin' in der baggin'—"

"What?" Monk asked, not aware of what Mundey's experience had been that day.

"Knock it off," Shannon warned.

There was another pause.

"I see Augie hasn't checked in," Letchford offered from over by the door next to Augie's empty bunk.

They would be thinking of Augie now too, weighing his move to ground himself on the spiritual battle he carried on with Blake. They would be wondering if what he had done was right or wrong.

*168*

"He's running his weight-lifting kind of late, isn't he?" Slater came back.

"I think Augie's digging a hole somewhere," Bellinger came in. "I think his daddy being here has built a backfire on him . . ."

" 'Iron sharpeneth iron: so a man sharpeneth the countenance of his friend,' " Jeremy Potter intoned lyrically.

"Yeah, well, for the big man it's iron and brass running on a collision course tonight," Letchford came in through a stifled yawn.

Nobody said anything to that. It grew very quiet in the room again as each of them weighed the passing of the night against the possibilities of tomorrow. Shannon heard the tinkling sound of the cowbells a long way off across the desert. The herders were moving south to the savannahs, heading for the rain country. The air even now smelled heavy with humidity. Would Blake be on that tower tomorrow morning? The imponderability of that gave him a funny chill. He would have to pray harder, get the others to pray harder, get them fixed on God and God alone in all of this. It would not be easy though, not now. Or should they pray that Blake passes the test with Gregson?

He heard the screen door scrape and Mundey came in. Nobody said anything to him. The springs creaked as Mundey settled down into his bunk. Shannon pulled the khaki blanket up closer around his head and forced himself to think of anything but flying until sleep came in uneasy strokes.

Behind the hangars, Augie sat alone on an old packing case hugging his knees and rocking slightly back and forth. The familiar music that he had taken issue with for so long seemed to mock him, taunt him, tell him to try marching to it. Crashing, bellowing, strutting—every bar of it was Blake.

"Fly for me, Augie . . . fly for me, boy! Go on, boy, go up there and show 'em whose boy you are!"

It was his father's battle here now—again. It had always been that way. His unannounced coming had jarred everything out of balance, reversed the flow, put him into a vulnerable position with Blake and the other pilots. His father was pushing him aside again, taking control, telling him what he had always told him in one way or another, that Augie wasn't capable of rising to the moment of necessary big things by himself.

"Throw your own pitch, Augie," Blake had the audacity to tell him during that ridiculous business of playing catch today. Maybe Blake had hit it right then. Everything he had done in life was not of his own choosing—his father had been there, shaping, molding, willing, then even demanding. Was even his own concept of God molded in the image of his father, then? Was that what Blake was saying to him?

"Blake, you could never know!" he shouted now against the mocking clash of the music. It wasn't in Blake to know! And yet he didn't feel any bitterness toward Blake. He probably never did. Maybe what he fought mostly was the point of awareness that had finally struck home—he was not his own man in any sense. And maybe God Himself was trying to pry him loose now—and maybe it was throwing that ball at Blake that had sprung the latch on it all, making him measure himself by another standard?

Now that music rode high on crescendo, and it struck hard and deep inside so that he choked. There was really nothing left now but to rise as best he could to his own mountain. And he bowed his head, resting it on his knees, trying to ascend with Blake's music.

"God, let me prove something on my own, then," he pleaded as the music slammed to a halt and left him to the heavy silence of the desert.

Chief Dudanor Turgobyne, son of Caha, Prince of the Everlasting Flame, Keeper of the Destinies of Terragona, stood on the veranda of his retreat house overlooking Lake Caha. Behind him his faithful military aide waited. The word of the mysterious deaths in Caha village across the lake was not good. Reports of sick people rising from their beds to attack even their own children in a fit of frenzy added a strange new note of terror in the land. Reports of whole villages within miles of Caha fleeing the area only created increasing threats to the rule of Turgobyne himself.

Now he had this clumsy report from the yellow bird people sent by one of the men who carried thunder in his hands. It was not fully clear to him, because these foreigners did not have the Terragona language very well. He refused to believe it at first. So he sent his aide, Torendasa, to the yellow bird doctor to be sure. Now there was no mistake. Lake Caha, the home of the eternal spirit, the sacred waters that only Chief Turgobyne himself could claim as his authority and seal of power, must be shut down? Closed even to the high priests of

Caha. Caha corrupted? Would these people turn to jackals on him, then? Were they laughing at him like hyenas? *Caha carries the strange disease, they said, which causes all the sickness, and no one must use the water again until they find what it is in the waters that makes the people sick?*

Would these people not be satisfied until they had also destroyed the last, sure fortress for the Terragonans? It was one thing to tamper with the life cycles of his people—but to accuse Caha of corruption? That took courage, to say the least!

So now he straightened to his full splendorous seven feet, pulling his robes closer around him, peering down at the innocent blue waters of Caha. The long stick of wormwood in his hand, the symbol of his power, seemed so small now against the terrible shadows that threatened the land. Terragona was being torn apart by conflicts so mountainous that he could not see how he could draw it together again. There were threats of revolt among the young men who spent all their time with the men with thunder in their hands, ignoring the law of Terragona, plotting instead to take the land for themselves. Yellow Bird's people had won the women and children, who stood in long lines waiting day after day for the healing promised and even now were reported to be singing strange songs about the yellow bird's God who had sent them here. Between these two forces, the rest of Terragona continued to live, to build on the patterns of history that kept them through thousands of years in a state of happiness and unity.

But now the shaft had struck at Caha himself. The lines of age in Turgobyne's face, he knew himself, were not lines of wisdom now. They had come in the night with the spirits, who would not let him rest for what was coming to pass. His walk was slower now too. His great shoulders, symbol of the good government of Caha, were beginning to round. And worst of all, he now had to hide in the protection of his sacred retreat house while his own council members fought it out to find a way to bring order back again. Even his own loyal palace guard could not understand why he was here so early, why he did not remain in council. They, too, would be talking behind their hands about it—and that was not a sign they would be forever loyal with such questions unanswered.

He had not expected it to come to this. He had told his council some moons back, when the land was not yet visited from outside, that the men with thunder in their hands would soon bring riches from the earth so that Terragonans would not have to work so hard and die so early in their efforts to grow yam and cassava in a soil that was dying. And the yellow bird's people would heal their pain, chase away the shadows of death—as they had done with the fever—and bring a whole new prosperity to Terragona.

And so he had believed. Was it his conviction really, then? Or was he led to believe it even against his will? Even now as he stood staring across Lake Caha to the village now cursed by this strange disease, he knew what the yellow bird's people gave was good. But now to have them tell him Caha was corrupt? Could he hope to protect them from such a statement of sacrilege?

Now he turned slowly to Torendasa, who waited patiently for the word. There was no other way now. He wished he could talk to the Yellow Bird himself, the one with the bells on his feet, whose voice rose to the sound of many waters on the rocks, who breathed into the birds that flew at his command, whose eye never wavered, whose hand was strong when he gripped Turgobyne's shoulder in the greeting he gave so many moons back. He wanted to share with him what was happening here, to beg his counsel, hopefully to get some understanding.

"It is not possible to close down the Lake Caha," he would say to him, "any more than it is possible for your people to live here without the yellow bird."

The tall man might understand. His ear was open and ready.

But there was not time for that now. He took one shaky sigh, and gripped his stick harder as he spoke. "When the ceremonies to Caha are done, two suns from now . . . when the village sleeps, then you will do it."

"All of them?" Torendasa said, his voice hardly above a whisper.

Turgobyne felt the pain too but he would not show it. "All of them . . . Caha has spoken it. The people who tend Caha have displeased the sacred dwelling place of him who is everlasting fire. The law demands that corruption which is theirs be ended, lest we displease Caha even more. You will see to it that none escape to carry the corruption to others."

Torendasa nodded gravely. "And what of the men with thunder in their hands and the yellow bird's people?"

"The men with thunder in their hands have violated Caha in their promises of riches," and even as Turgobyne said it, there came a shaking rumbling out of the earth so that the veranda heaved with it. "You will see to them as well."

"And what of the yellow bird's people?"

"Do not draw from me the blood you relish, Torendasa," Turgobyne snapped then. Torendasa bowed his head under the rebuke. Turgobyne said nothing further for a long time, moving his stick across the red tiles of the veranda, hoping for a sign. Then, "Yellow Bird has not broken his promise to me . . . he has not violated the trust. He does not fill the air with many yellow birds, as he said he would not. His people have spoken rashly about Caha, but it is perhaps the foolishness of their zeal that overpowers them. We will wait."

"Forgive the clumsy words from this miserable mouth, Honorable Prince," Torendasa put in then. "But already your council has fasted many moons to find the answer of how to save Terragona and to keep you in power. If you now destroy the priests of Caha and send terror in the land, if you destroy the men with thunder in their hands and not yellow bird's people, they will wonder—"

"I must wait the sign from Caha," Turgobyne said with some impatience. "When I see the sign, I will know what to do. I will wait here by the waters for Caha to speak. While I wait, you will not touch yellow bird's people. Is that understood?"

Torendasa prostrated himself, then rose to back slowly out of the presence of Turgobyne. When he was gone, Turgobyne turned to face the lake again, removed his purple robes and lay flat on the hot tiles of the veranda. Here he would stay, even during the darkest night to come, the time of much crying and pain, until Caha spoke.

# CHAPTER VIII

Gregson came out of a heavy, stupefying sleep to the crashing sounds of a march that vibrated his eye sockets. He knew it to be "Colonel Bogey" even without his sleep-fogged senses trying to connect it. He propped himself up on one elbow, feeling the harsh beat of the music storm his brain, trip the gyro of his mushy nerve center. Then, above the demands of the music, he heard the snapping snarl of the engines. He realized then that it was still half-dark outside. His watch showed 4:45. He kicked his feet over the side of the bed, glancing at Blake's bunk. It was empty. It didn't look as if it had been slept in at all.

He dressed hurriedly, sensing the field beginning to take on a heavy beat of urgency. His head hurt and his sinuses ached. He knew he hadn't gotten to sleep before two at the earliest. The last he remembered was reading his pocket Bible and asking God to help him know what was right to do here.

He had pulled on his pants and shirt when the music stopped, and only the sound of the engines on runup remained. He was getting ready to shave when he heard someone call him from the big open window over Blake's bunk. It was Gina. She was standing a few feet back from the window, dressed in a heavy brown sweater with a green scarf around her neck and a brown tweed skirt and brown loafers. She looked in complete control of her world, as usual.

"Anything wrong, Gina?" he asked, swiping with both hands at the rebellious brambles of his hair.

"I don't mean to trouble you," she said, moving a few steps closer. He could see the classic lines of her facial sculpture now standing out in relief against the touch of the green scarf, bringing out the tones of her chestnut eyes.

"No trouble, Gina."

"Well, Mr. Gregson, I've been up since midnight trying to take care of over a hundred Africans who showed up at the infirmary for attention . . . they're not Hamaran nomads, Mr. Gregson; I'm positive they're Sudanese refugees fleeing the country and trying to get to Niger where they've been promised sanctuary . . ."

"Oh?" Gregson said. "Did you treat them?"

"I took in five complicated pregnancies and eight pneumonia cases . . . that's all I could handle. The rest of them are camped out in back of the infirmary. Mr. Gregson, you know the order Hamara has laid down that no one is to give assistance to these people if they try crossing Hamaran territory."

"Did you tell Blake?"

"A half hour ago I told him in the dining room, yes."

"What did he say?"

"He said if they didn't get help they'd have to go seventy-five miles out of their way around Hamaran territory to get to Niger. He said they'd die if they had to do that. It appears that this has been going on for some time here, and by now word is probably out to all those refugees that they can stop here for assistance."

He caught the tone of accusation in her voice, laying it at Blake's door. She was right, of course. The "boy king" didn't like the rule either, Gregson was sure; but political expediency forced the arrangement with the Sudan.

"Well, do what you can for them," Gregson said finally. "I'll have a word with Blake on it."

She didn't seem satisfied with that, continuing to look up at him as if he should pound the gavel and sentence Blake on the spot. "You also ought to know that Augie is going up this morning."

That did alarm Gregson. "Blake sending him?"

"No. Augie came in when he was having breakfast and said as long as Monk was not up to it, he wanted to go."

"What did Blake say to that?"

"All he said was that the propeller in Augie's plane was not a hundred per cent, and this was not the day for him to get a sudden attack of bravado. But that only made Augie all the more insistent. But I don't think Augie's in shape to fly . . . he looks too shaky to me . . ."

"Does Mr. Thornhill know?"

"He's over at the hangars trumpeting like a bull elephant. He's going to pray with the pilots, he says, before they go . . . it's a big day for him, Mr. Gregson, his boy is flying. But he ought to have a sedative himself and sleep it off for forty-eight hours . . ."

"Okay, Gina, I'll get right over there," Gregson said. He looked at her again, knowing she wanted him to assure her that her indictment of Blake was in order. He said, "I appreciate your concerns, Gina . . . I'll look after it."

A few minutes later, still not shaved, he set out for the hangar. The planes were going through idle now, their props turning a garish reddish-pink in the glow of the not yet risen sun, running a bloody finger across the far eastern horizon. The purples of night still held stubbornly to the desert floor, refusing to be nudged out of the way to the demands of dawn. There was no wind yet.

He saw Blake working over the dead propeller on one of the planes closest to the hangar, an African working beside him. The pilots were all inside sitting in an uncertain clump of expectancy on the steel chairs in front of the small platform that had maps and charts propped up on it. Thornhill, seeing Gregson, came to him quickly in that ponderous gait as if he were pushing a kiddie car.

"Augie's going up today, Gregson," he crowed. "My boy told Blake —really *told* him—that he was going. All you got to do is stand up to that man, Mr. Gregson . . ."

"Fine, fine," Gregson shouted back at him.

"I'm going to read the Word and pray with these fellas, Gregson," Thornhill yelled back. Gregson felt he should accompany him, so he followed him inside, giving Blake one last glance before doing so to see if he was coming. Thornhill shook hands with each of the pilots vigorously. Augie was there too, but he sat very still, his arms folded across that blue sweatshirt, his face looking almost the color of the gold lettering across the front. Gregson agreed with Gina, Augie was in no shape . . .

Then Thornhill got up on the small platform and began leafing through his large Bible. He looked the part now, commanding the elements that were his, and whatever cruel torture he had carried in the night was giving way to the new sense of excitement. He glanced around once before reading, as the pilots waited politely, and then he came off the platform, walking to where Gregson stood at the back.

"Isn't Blake coming?" he asked directly.

"Well, he's busy working on that plane," Gregson offered uncertainly.

"He should be in here, Mr. Gregson . . . it's time he learned to put God first too . . ."

Gregson watched him return to the platform, his shoulders back, taking that position in front of everybody again. The pilots began to shift uncomfortably in their chairs, glancing out toward the airplanes and Blake.

Gregson hurried out to where Blake was working, feeling vulnerable all of a sudden. He watched Blake trying to fit the propeller housing in, and when he looked around at him finally, Gregson shouted, "You have time to join us in prayer, Mr. Blake?"

Blake went right on working as if he had not heard. Gregson turned to look back into the hangar, and Thornhill was still waiting and watching, and now the pilots were looking toward the planes too. Rudy Kipstein had gotten up from his chair and was walking toward him slowly, wanting to be of some help but now knowing what.

Gregson closed his eyes against the dust blowing at him by the backwash of one of the planes and shouted again, "Mr. Blake, I know you're busy but—"

"Look, Mr. Gregson," Blake shouted back, "I got five minutes to get this prop in place and those planes rolling. You'll have to ask God to excuse me this morning—I think He'll understand!"

Gregson hesitated a minute, not knowing if he should press further. Then he turned and walked back into the hangar. Rudy returned to his seat. Gregson shook his head at Thornhill and the older man then went to reading from the Bible, his face now beginning to show those pinched ridges around the eyes and chin which said he was not very pleased.

" 'Though a thousand fall at thy side and ten thousand at thy right hand, it shall not come nigh thee,' " his voice boomed out above the rattling sounds in the hangar.

The reading was going too long, and Gregson was getting nervous. So was Rudy Kipstein, who kept looking out toward the planes. Augie was leaning forward too, as if getting ready to get up in the middle of the reading, or maybe interrupt his father, who was shouting something about "God as El Shaddai." And then a loud, piercing whistle cut through to them, echoing shrilly in the hangar, sounding almost obscene in the determined efforts of Thornhill to lay on the proper spiritual foundation. Blake was standing in the doorway of the hangar now, hands on hips in a pose of truculence.

Finally, when it appeared Thornhill was going to deliberately ignore the signal, Augie got up abruptly and said, "Dad, we're running late . . . we have to go."

But his father lifted his right hand with the open Bible in it and said, "Now, Augie, we haven't prayed yet—"

"Then pray, because we don't have the time!"

"Now, Augie, I see no reason—"

But the whistle came again, louder and even more piercing this time, and the pilots got up as one and began moving out of the hangar, a little uncertainly, not wanting to leave Thornhill standing there with his prayer not yet voiced. Gregson moved to him quickly even as he grabbed Augie by the arm, "Augie, go to it, boy . . . fly it straight. Remember like you used to fly me to all those places for services, remember, Augie?"

And Augie paused and turned to look at his father in some bewilderment or longing, Gregson couldn't tell which. For a span of a few seconds, it was father and son then, locked together by the blood neither of them could deny. In Augie's face there might have been an ingredient of confusion, as if he was trying to backtrack to other times, to pick up somewhere with his father way back when life was not half so complicated. And then with just one touch of his hand on his father's shoulder, an attempt at a caress, he walked out toward his waiting plane.

Gregson stood with Thornhill, who looked forlorn, lonely. "Come on, Mr. Thornhill," Gregson said, "we can watch them take off from the tower . . ."

So they watched as Blake guided his loaded charges on their way, the sun now up and hanging like an angry boil behind the dust so that the prop wash from the planes rose in mushroom clouds like whale's blood blown into the fine spray of misty ocean. The mechanics were out in front of the hangars, waiting. And he saw Gina over there too, with Monk, the white bandage on his head standing out like a sail.

They watched, he and Thornhill, with Blake just twenty feet down the railing of the tower, guiding each plane to the final runup, talking to them constantly through the mike, the earphones tight against his head. And then one by one they were off, making their almost frightened run down the length of the clay runway, the yellow skins of their planes burning the pure flame of the sun. And as each plane wobbled up torturously from the earth, lifting to the challenge of the sky and banking away from the hoary-headed hill at the far end, Gregson felt a rising swell of pride. He stood there clenching the rail with his hands tightly, the dust coming back to choke him, his heart going with the flimsy ghost of yellow passing by. The air clattered with the buzz of their engines, then moved to a steady rumble of sound as they each began to run up to full power. This is how God sounds, Gregson almost shouted, the air rattling with his purpose! Let Him roar and shake the earth! Let Him dig His claws into His own creation, let Him take the wings of the eagle, let Him rip the straight furrows across the fields of red and blue sky! Let Him buck the winds up there and who cared then about twenty pounds of nitro flying passenger!

And it was like all the fallen heroes of centuries past rose with Gregson in his moment of exultation, until he finally let out a yell, unable to contain it any longer, for he knew it was lost in the bellow of the planes that shot by not more than twenty yards out. And he lifted his arm in salute, wanting to reach out and touch them, to be with them, until his throat closed in the dust and his voice fell into a hopeless crack, dribbling off in the emotion that grabbed him.

And then there was only one plane left, still sitting there at the far end of the runway, prop turning that reddish-greenish color in the sun. Gregson found his handkerchief and rubbed at his eyes, watching the plane, knowing it had to be Augie, seeing the letters JERICHO on the fuselage.

"Why won't he go, Gregson?" Thornhill asked then, a few feet away along the rail.

Blake was talking into the microphone now, "What's up, Augie?"

The unhurried voice of Augie came back, sounding a little hoarse through the speaker overhead: "I can't get over 1750 RPM . . ."

"What's your cabin temperature?"

"I'm pushing up to a hundred forty-six . . ."

"Augie, you're pushing the smoke line on that nitro," Blake said, and Thornhill began edging down the porch now toward Blake. Gregson followed, feeling a rising fist of fear climb into his throat and squeeze hard.

Another pause. The plane sat there at the end of runway, nose pointed and ready . . . prop turning, rising to full power, then dying down again.

"I can get her up to 1850 on full throttle," Augie's voice came on.

"That's not enough to clear with a full load, Augie," Blake warned into the mike, and his voice was beginning to insist. "I told you that prop was touchy . . ."

"I think she'll go," Augie said. "I'll run her up once more and see if she comes up the line . . ."

"No, Mr. Blake, no," Thornhill said and reached out to touch Blake on the arm. But Blake paid no heed, watching the plane as it ran up to full power again, kicking up a long line of red dust behind it.

"Augie, what's your cabin temp now?"

A pause. "About the same . . ."

"Augie, you got to get out of that airplane, right now, you hear? She'll blow on you before you get your wheels rolling!"

"Mr. Blake, you've got to get him out!" Thornhill yelled, and he turned to make the appeal to Gregson, but Gregson knew there wasn't much either of them could do.

"I think she'll go," Augie insisted again, and his voice was resigned, and Gregson knew with terror that Augie was going to try it.

"Augie, you listen to me," Blake went on, crouched over trying to lend weight to his words, his eyes fixed on the plane, willing it to stay. "One bounce on takeoff and you've had it! Abandon that airplane, Augie, right now!"

Blake turned to Gregson then and shoved the mike into his hands, tearing the earphones off his head. "Keep talking to him," he said as he moved for the stairs. "Tell him you as field director are ordering him out of that airplane . . . I'm going to run down there and see if I can get him out!"

Gregson took the mike, but Thornhill snatched it from him in a quick, desperate move. "Augie, listen to me, boy . . . listen, you're all I have . . . don't do anything foolish now, son, do what Mr. Blake says . . . you don't have to go up now . . ."

Gregson heard Blake start up the Landrover below, but before he could throw it into gear, the plane was moving. It all came together in one welded scene, a sliding kind of movement . . . Gregson could hear Thornhill still shouting at Augie to stop it as the plane gathered speed and shot by them, its tail coming up rather slowly, sluggishly. And as it got opposite them approaching the sand dune escarpment, it lifted as if it would climb . . . then it touched again . . . now Augie had pushed his plane farther down the runway to get the speed needed, and just as he was going to lift her again, the wheels hit a flat mound of cowdung. With full power Augie could have cut through it and lifted off . . . but as it was, the plane lurched, staggered upward for thirty feet or so and then dropped.

Gregson was torn off the rail by the shock of the explosion, and flung to the wooden floor of the porch. At the same time, he felt Thornhill crushing into him. It was a while before he got his eyes open. It seemed as if the sun was gone; only a peculiar shroud was there. And the sound of falling things hitting the roof above him, like rain, like hailstones. And he scrambled to his feet, the world still rocking and fighting to come back to its axis. Beyond this there was a long, moaning sound, rising up and down in peculiar chanting pitch. It was Thornhill, who had gotten to his feet a short distance away and was half stumbling for the stairwell.

Gregson followed him down, hearing the rising cry of protest from Thornhill. He got outside in time to see Blake grab Thornhill and hold him, digging his heels into the sand as the heavier man fought to get loose, staring at the smoking crater in the runway at the end of the field. Gregson came up and put his own arms around Thornhill's, holding him, and he noticed a red sweat mark on Thornhill's neck above the line of the shirt . . .

"There's nothing left to see, Mr. Thornhill," Blake kept saying, fighting to hold the big man. "Believe me, there's nothing there to find . . ."

"Augie?" Thornhill yelled again, and suddenly he stopped struggling, as if he realized then the full import of what Blake was saying. He stood there, Blake still hanging on to him and breathing hard with the exertion, Gregson with an arm around his neck, and his eyes kept staring, not comprehending. Slowly then his eyes came to focus on Blake, only inches from his, as if begging Blake to tell him it was not true. Then his head, locks of his yellowish hair hanging limp around his eyes, nodded slowly as if it was too heavy to hold on his shoulders. And Gina came running up then, a hypo in her hand, which she deftly inserted into the muscle of his right arm.

"You know Augie . . . ," and now Thornhill was showing a glaze from the shock in his eyes, not even aware of where he was any more. "You know Augie . . . he won the cross-country." He smiled at Gregson, hardly recognizing him. "They gave him a medal, you know. I still have it. I had it mounted and put in the church trophy room. It's still there . . . he's a good boy . . . Augie is a good boy . . ."

And his knees seemed to give out. Blake let him slide down gently on the sand. Two of the African mechanics came up with the stretcher, and they put him on it carefully and carried him to the infirmary.

Gregson stood with Gina and Blake watching them until they had disappeared inside the infirmary. Then Blake called across the field toward the men standing by the hangar in knots, clotting up under the horror they felt. "Sam, bring the tractor!" And part of that clot moved, springing loose from the paralysis, dissolving under the command. Soon the tractor was coming across the runway, pulling up in front of them.

"Can't business-as-usual wait?" Gina said in that dry tone of voice. Her face was white now, her eyes luminous in contrast. Blake picked up a shovel that was leaning against the tower and tossed it up to Sam without even looking at her. He climbed up to stand behind Sam and moved off, leaving only the rude commentary of dust. Gregson said nothing to Gina. There was a terrible roaring in his head, a hammer banging a gong in his right temple. He felt faint and she said, "Are you all right, Mr. Gregson?" He caught the sharp ammonia in his nose, and he snorted, shaking his head, leaning over to grab his knees with his hands. He wanted to sit down somewhere, to try to reconcile all this. He finally told Gina he would be all right, for her to see to Thornhill. When she left, he went inside the tower and sat in the small room, listening to the hiss of the radio. Only the sound of the tractor came from outside, an animal running excitedly through the garbage, hunting for the remains of Augie.

When he opened his eyes again, he saw Joseph sitting there on the floor against the wall. It surprised him. The tall African never stayed behind when Blake was on the field. But now he sat there, clucking in his throat, his face down in that big overcoat, his eyes big and filled with a strange terror, looking to Gregson for some sign that it wasn't as bad as it seemed.

The pilots got back just after the sun went down, when night was laying hold of the day by its throat. They got the word about Augie from the African mechanics. Blake did not approach them to explain it to them. And they didn't pursue it. It was a fact of life to them by now. Their faces simply turned blank in an attempt to shut out the specter of this thing moving in on them. Letchford kept asking no one in particular how it could have happened with the wind so calm that morning on takeoff. Shannon finally told him to knock it off and for all of them to get something to eat. None of them moved to respond to that either. Later Shannon reported to Blake in the tower that they were all having wheel trouble, their brakes were mushy, and did that have anything to do with Augie's death? Blake closed his red logbook carefully and put it in his desk drawer. His face looked even more puffy now, as if he'd gotten hit by a swarm of bees. "Augie lost RPM on liftoff," he said then. That was all. And Shannon left it at that.

Around eight that evening they all walked up the narrow path across the sand-dune ridge to the big hill with the scrub of acacia and cottonwoods. Thornhill was not with them, still in the infirmary suffering shock. When they got to the small clearing at the top, they gathered silently around the shallow grave freshly dug next to the pilot named Charlie Weaver. Rudy, along with Letchford and Bellinger, lowered the small hastily constructed coffin made out of wood crates into the hole. Gregson read from the Bible by the light of the flashlight over his shoulder. It was very still. How exposed they looked! Heads bowed, shoulders hunched up against the grim reality of this kind of death, their bodies half hanging into the grave, as if a part of them was being drawn in by Augie.

"Augie gave himself to the cause," Gregson said in conclusion. "He didn't have to do it, he could have chosen some other way to serve God. Let it be said of all of us when we go that we have as much said about us. We give Augie to the Lord . . . and we take from him that good spirit that drove him to this final act of determination for the cause of Christ . . . and for the people of Terragona."

As they filed quietly out of the clearing, Gregson noted for the first time that Blake was not among them. He wondered why. Was death so repulsive to him? Was it so much for him to share in the deaths here as well as the victories? Or were there no victories, just deaths? And as he walked down the hill Gregson could see the lights blazing in the hangars and that familiar figure flinging himself again to the task of trying to beat death at its own game.

Later in the night Gregson took to walking aimlessly around the field, trying to pull it all into some kind of coherent pattern. He found himself outside the pilot's Quonset, and he listened to someone strumming a guitar softly. He went in finally, feeling he should try to share in their sense of loss and perhaps their increasing sense of foreboding over what had to happen to them. They got up quickly as he came in. He told them to be seated. Gregson sat on a chair by the door and watched the pilot pick the strings. Nobody said anything. Their faces were blank, staring at their hands clenched in front of them or at the floor. Shannon sat whittling on a piece of wood with a short blade knife, the shavings piling up by his shoes.

Gregson sought for something to say to encourage them. Instead, for some strange reason, he found himself at peace with them, entering into their communion, which seemed to transcend the tragedy of Augie's death. Finally the pilot named Bellinger began to sing to the tune he strummed:

"See the man who stands among us!
   Broken things—he mends them!
   Wounded hearts—he heals them!
  Yellow birds choking in the wind—he speeds them!

"But who can know him? He passes before we see him.
   Only a shadow, a touch as he goes,
   And we missed him, but we felt him!
  And it was the touch of life!"

How strange! Beautiful? Gregson was sure Bellinger was singing of Christ. But beyond that, were they also singing about Blake? Were they actually trying to say something to him about Blake? Was this the legend that all of northern Hamara sang to their children around the fires?

Gregson bade them goodnight with only a simple, inadequate, "Keep them flying . . . and God go with you!"

He found Blake in the hangar about eleven working the forge, bare to the waist, a wheel of one of the airplanes on the big metal bench by his side. Thunder rumbled in the distance, and the air was taking on a heavy feeling, the sag of nature and events coming down to rest hard here. Gregson watched Blake work the forge, the muscles bulging in his arms, noting the smear of grease across his face, the sweat hanging thick with it. Blake did not acknowledge his presence —he simply went on working.

"Blake, I'm sorry for what happened today," he began. "I want you to know, for what it's worth, that it wasn't your fault—"

"You have a point to make, I take it, Mr. Gregson?" he cut back abruptly, stoking the forge again with the bellows. His disposition seemed to be a cross between reflection and pugnaciousness, as if all the events here had forced him into a corner, to his smoke and fires. His face showed all the lumpy protrusions, cruel swellings cropping up under his eyes and tugging sharply at the corners of his mouth. His baseball cap held the flash of the forge to that face and brought out his eyes to points of empty reflection; and yet, at the same time, it caught a glint there that said not all of his own inner fires were dead by any means. Looking at that bare chest and the bleed of the sweat and the accumulation of his own private agonies on his face, all Gregson could think of to say right then was, "Behold the man!"

Instead he said, "Blake, you know I can't go back to Talfungo with any hope of keeping things alive for you here . . . not now."

"I understand your plane is coming for you tomorrow morning, Mr. Gregson. That's good. Rayburn put through a weak transmission about an hour ago asking what happened to his flight. He's hurting in there, Mr. Gregson, so I think when you get back you better find me another airplane . . ."

"Rayburn called?" Gregson said, perplexed that he wasn't told earlier. "I will try for another plane, of course. But I doubt Council will agree to it the way things are now. Anyway you have that Piper Cub in reserve—"

"That Cub will need some tuning up," Blake returned laconically. "Right now I got problems with wheels on what's left here . . . to put it all together is going to take time. We need planes and parts and gasoline like we never did . . ."

Gregson pondered that, not knowing exactly how to get through. "It's you I'm thinking about, Blake. The whole viability of the operation hangs on you, do you understand that? And now with Augie dead, there's going to be a lot more questions asked. So it comes down to your spiritual credentials now more than ever. I need to hear it from you, Blake—"

"You mean definitions, words, right?" Blake cut in and took the white hot piece of metal block and pounded it down to shape, the sweat spraying off his face as he did so. "Well, some things, Mr. Gregson, I feel a man ought to keep to himself, to treasure for himself . . . one is his first love making with the woman of his life . . . the other is what he and God share together that's too close to cast into a definition—"

"It's not that simple in a spiritual order, Blake," Gregson argued with some frustration. "I already told you—"

"Yes, sir, you told me," Blake replied, his voice steady, unruffled, and he shoved the piece of metal back into the forge with some vehemence. "If I remember correctly, I gave you what words I had on that application some time back . . . you had no problem with them then—"

"I know, but—"

"Well, Mr. Gregson, if the operation can only go on with the right words, then I guess you'll have to do what you have to with me . . ."

Gregson felt perplexed, almost embarrassed. There was no hostility in the way Blake spoke now. He simply stated it as fact. And Gregson could find no argument for it.

"Well," he said then with a sigh, "I guess you don't have the words. I suppose there are worse things." He hesitated, not knowing how to go on, and finally said, "Well, if it means anything to you, I'll be praying for you, Blake . . ."

Blake looked up at him for the first time and smiled that small, reluctant, boyish smile, and the touch of salve on the cold sore crinkled like a piece of crumb.

"Yes, sir," he said in a lighter tone to his voice. "I could be using some of that, Mr. Gregson." And then, when Gregson fell into an uncertain silence, he added, *"C'est la guerre,* Mr. Gregson?" and his French sounded clumsy.

Gregson grunted, shaking his head at the incredulity of that, and then smiled, *"C'est la guerre,* indeed, Mr. Blake, *c'est la guerre."* And in that moment he felt a strange kind of communion with Blake, a peculiar sense of camaraderie rising from the futility they both felt. He hesitated a moment, wondering if he should try any more with him, then decided to leave it and walked out, the sound of Blake's hammer ringing a flat chime of finality behind.

"It's a possibility," Trask said, leaning his hands on the table of crowded test tubes and beakers. He was almost making an appeal, and that was strange coming from him, a man who always dealt in categorical imperatives.

"It's far too simple," Rayburn commented, folding his arms and looking up at the design of the bacteria strain Trask had reproduced on a three-foot piece of white plasterboard. "If heat alone can affect a piece of bacteria of this potency, this appears to be—"

"Do I have to drag out Louis Pasteur?" Trask snapped, and he appeared to be agitated now. "Heat of 300 degrees Fahrenheit or more is what I'm talking about . . . up there is a design of the bacteria as I have seen on the slides and confirmed by the water specimens out of Caha. Notice the large eight-pointed flower-cluster shape of it? There's nothing quite like that in the books. In the center you see the one large black dot, right?" Rayburn grunted. "That dot is the brain center of the cluster controlling the reproduction of the bacteria body itself—"

"Trask—"

"I have been watching that cluster for twelve hours straight now," Trask went on, his eyes fixed on the design, "and I can actually see that dot moving those clusters to expand. It's—it's the fastest reproducing bacteria I've seen . . . but under heat—"

"Trask, you've got to have more proof—"

"All right," and Trask reached over to the crowded workbench and put another design of the bacteria up on the wall. "I put a piece of that stuff inside a sealed test tube and applied heat for five minutes . . . see any difference?"

"Not as many clusters," Rayburn admitted skeptically.

"Heat smeared it," Alicia added almost morosely. "That doesn't mean you killed it even yet . . ."

"Notice the dot in the center?" Trask came back sharply.

Rayburn studied it more closely. "I suppose it is smaller . . ."

"Exactly!" Trask said triumphantly. "The nerve center of this thing dies when the level of oxygen sucked out by heat is denied it." Nobody said anything. Trask, sensing their uncertainty, went on eagerly. "Brad, you remember the medical textbooks on bacteria that talked about strains that can lie dormant for thousands of years in minus-zero temperatures, usually about a hundred and twenty below or more? When brought into conducive heat of between seventy and eighty degrees, they begin to multiply rapidly. By the same token, when these strains get hit with heat beyond two hundred and more degrees, they atrophy—"

"Yes, but this bacteria has not had the minus-zero preservation in this tropical desert," Rayburn argued.

"Granted," Trask said, a little frown working between his slanted eyes. "But barring the origin for now, we may never know anyway, consider the pattern of emergence . . . the bacteria found conducive suspension in the water of Lake Caha, good temperature and oxygen base. When it entered the people up there who used the water, it also found the brain a most natural reservoir of oxygen and the most constant level of temperature, ninety-eight point six . . ."

"Then you are saying this bacteria is purely water contact, not airborne?" Rayburn asked.

Trask shrugged. "Too early to tell yet . . . but, yes, it would appear that way. Nobody has gotten sick on our staff who has had contact with those patients. I don't know the incubation period, of course, but it seems that way."

"That's something anyway," Rayburn said with a sigh.

"But will it stay that way?" Trask came back quickly.

Rayburn glanced up at him. There was nothing of the erratic showing in Trask's behavior now, except for the unusual flaring of his nostrils and the narrowing eyes, the usual signs he displayed when he was about to make a discovery strictly his own.

"What do you mean?"

"I'm saying that there is a fantastic rate of reproduction going on in that lake right now and will go on as long as that temperature remains constant. In a short time, it is going to outgrow that lake and become mobile, maybe seeking other conducive environments in which to populate—"

"Including the human brain," Alicia put in skeptically again.

"That's right," Trask said emphatically. "So consider how many people up there at Caha have had contact with it, consider how many will go into this peculiar psychopathic syndrome and how many they can kill off—"

188

"Which means the entire population of Terragona is at stake," Rayburn concluded for him. "And no way to combat it?"

"Heat is all I've got," Trask came back simply.

"So all we do is put a four-hundred-degree torch to the whole island?" Alicia chimed in. "Thank you, Jules Verne."

"You think I'm crazy?" Trask retaliated with a vehemence unlike him, and he picked up a thick volume on the crowded counter and waved it at her. "Julius S. Morgan five years ago talked about a day like this. And it is my calculated guess that we have something here totally unknown to science and that World Health will support that conclusion—"

"I'll wait, thank you," Alicia shot back almost morosely.

"What about Morgan?" Rayburn asked out of curiosity, still not willing to come up to Trask's dogmatism about this.

"It is this bacteria strain that Morgan claims is the basis for the DNA of space," Trask said flatly.

"Space?" And Alicia snorted. "You are talking about a life cycle in space? Come on, Trask, we are on terra firma in conditions nonconducive to any form of so-called space chemistry—"

"Then take a look!" And Trask picked up the book from the work bench again, flipped it open to a marked place and tore out the page, handing it to Rayburn. "Take a look at Morgan's drawing of what he theorizes is space chemistry, and then look at what we've got here!"

Rayburn took the page, studied it closely, saw the basic similarities of structure, even to the point of the heavy dot in the center of the clusters. It was, in fact, too close to Trask's drawing to argue about. Maybe too close even to accept as happenstance. He handed it to Alicia, who gave it a far-sighted look of suspicion. It was quiet in the room then, only a bubbling sound of water boiling in a test tube on the workbench. Alicia looked up from the page, frowning at the drawings on the wall. Her look at Rayburn was a mixture of continued skepticism with a trace of growing wonder.

"So?" Trask demanded as Collins took the page and looked at it. Trask gave off with a half giggle as he looked at their faces. "So who's crazy now?"

Rayburn did not comment. He had to be careful now that he did not get pulled along here on what had to be pure speculation yet.

"We still have fifteen patients down with it and under our roof," he said then. "How do we treat this thing?"

"Calls for a super hotfoot maybe," Collins interjected, trying to keep it light. "Or how do we inject three hundred degrees or so of flaming gas into the veins, right?"

"There is nothing we can do for them," Trask said with that dogmatic tone again. "But we should start thinking of how we are going to arrest the growth of it in that lake. If it starts growing beyond that watercourse—"

"So what are you suggesting?" Rayburn prodded, hungering for a moment of reprieve from the steadily mounting pressure of decision.

"Sure thing you can't freeze that lake to a hundred and twenty degrees below zero," Collins offered. "Not in this climate . . ." When nobody said anything, Collins looked up at Trask. "So it will have to be by fire, right? Quite a simple task at that . . ."

Trask kept looking at Rayburn, waiting for a comment on that.

"First, we're asking Turgobyne to shut down the lake," Alicia came in with a tone of dismissal, "and now we want to lay a fire on it . . . that's asking a lot on a wild shot in the dark . . ."

Again they waited, Trask not rising to the bite in Alicia's tone, continuing to look at Rayburn.

"We will have to wait for the World Health to confirm it," he finally said.

"So how long do you figure?" Trask insisted.

"I can't say . . ."

"So tell World Health, then, about what you think," Alicia suggested. "They ought to know—"

"Not yet," Rayburn contradicted. "Once they know we got an unclassified bacteria strain, we'll have every microbe-hunting nut roaring in here to get a sample. And right now we are still speculating, with all due respect to you, Trask . . ."

"Hear, hear," Alicia intoned again.

"You going to sit on it, then?" Trask asked bluntly.

"There's always Blake," Collins put in, sounding like Blake's public relations man.

"Of course, there's always Blake," Alicia came back shortly. "With Augie dead, no plane for us, he needs another button to sew on?"

"Did he say he'd have in a plane today, Collins?"

"Sure. You know when Blake says—"

"Okay, I'll write a note and seal it for Blake personally," Rayburn added. "Make sure the pilot gets it."

"What are you going to tell him?" Alicia asked.

Rayburn sighed, not really sure. "All I can tell him is that we have a forming deterioration pattern here—"

"And be on the lookout for an atomic bomb to drop on Lake Caha?" Alicia returned. "He's probably got one stashed in his hip pocket . . ."

"I'm not saying anything about a fire. Anyway, what could he do about it?"

"Don't ask me," Alicia replied dryly. "As far as I'm concerned, all of this sounds pretty science fiction to me—"

"If you're not going to alert him to our need for a fire, why tell him anything, then?" Trask came back.

He was right, of course. Maybe it all came down to the fact that telling Blake was more like a therapy now than anything else.

"So I'll tell him we have a bacteria count in the lake, not yet condition red but moving in that direction . . . that he should get on World Health to get us some information on that sample."

"I already told you . . . and you know, too, that if this bacteria gets out of hand—"

"There are too many lives in here hanging in the balance to start playing with fire," Rayburn replied sharply then.

"Against maybe eighty thousand Terragonans?" Trask countered.

"That's still too big a brick to drop on Blake," Alicia argued.

Again there was a pause. The air had gone heavy in the room. "What's the flash point on diesel, Collins?" Rayburn picked it up again.

Collins' eyebrows lifted. "It's probably high . . . I dunno. I could check."

"What do you have in mind?" Trask asked.

"Nothing, I guess." Rayburn rubbed the back of his neck again, feeling frustrated now. "We'll wait, Trask . . . but we'll try to keep the door open to the possibility of a fire. In the meantime, keep checking on that bacteria . . . I want to be sure every cross reference is checked, that we can rule out every possible known disease . . ."

"Meanwhile, we are running out of ways to tie those patients down back there," Trask warned, his tone sounding like he was miffed now that his will was not prevailing.

"Then we'll get more rope or whatever you need," Rayburn snapped. They waited then, not sure how to go on with it. So Rayburn added, "You all know we are the only gate swinging into Terragona right now, and I'm not going to prop it open for everybody outside to come pouring in here. Not yet. And you all know what it could mean if we push Turgobyne off the edge . . . so let's play it cool."

"Well, I can and intend to play it cool," Alicia commented rather airily, moving for the door. "I'm sure God knows all about this— this space chemistry or whatever, and I can leave it with Him. I have rounds to make, gentlemen, if you'll pardon me?"

She was gone through the swinging door, leaving her doubts behind. "Well, whatever it is, I hope God can strike his own match . . . meanwhile, I'd settle for an airplane in here with diesel oil for the light plant . . . I'm not sure we can get power to transmit much longer, Doctors."

"We'll hold on the surgery loads and help cut power," Rayburn suggested.

"Throw your flashlights in too," Collins said with a sniff, pausing at the door, "because that's how bad it is right now."

He was gone then, leaving Rayburn and Trask alone with those terrible designs on the wall. Trask turned to his cluttered table as a sign he didn't want to discuss it further. Rayburn felt alone then. Uncertain. How much time did they really have now?

# CHAPTER IX

Gina awoke to the slashing sound of airplane motors going full-power over her head, shaking the room so hard that the sand and dust showered down on her from the ceiling. It was still dark out, except for that usual reddish glow of the rising sun flooding the room with ultraviolet shadows of lavender-pink. When she looked at her watch, however, she got a jolt. It was after six! Could she have slept through "Colonel Bogey," that taunting, lilting, jabbing, obscene tune of war? Could she have been so paralyzed that she missed even the ripping snap of those planes in preflight warmup? She had been more tired last night than she would concede—it was more like three in the morning when she treated the last of those Sudanese refugees. She had done it against her will, maybe for Gregson . . . certainly not for Blake.

She got up and went to the window on bare feet, feeling the grit of the sand on her bare skin, still curious as to why it was so dark at so late an hour. She saw immediately why. Heavy, gray clouds hung over the field now, their dark undersides carrying a mean threat. Only a few bright spots on the far eastern horizon allowed the sun a crack to put its endorsement on another day.

She dressed quickly and took time to peek in on Thornhill. The bed was empty. The pillows were still propped up where he had lain all day yesterday and last night reading his Bible, shut off from sight or sound. She went outside quickly and finally saw him out by the blue airplane that sat near the hangars. He looked misshapen, almost forlorn, as if he had missed his bus, hands behind his back, staring at the ground, still hunting for some clue to what had really happened here.

193

She met Gregson coming out of the dining room. He said good morning to her but kept on walking out to the plane carrying his single bag.

"Did Monk fly today?" she demanded of him, hating to see him go, trying to delay him.

"He had to," Gregson shouted back at her as they came near the plane and the idling engine. "We lost our transmission from JERI-CHO . . . they are overdue. Monk had to go in and find out . . ."

"In what?"

"That old cub . . . Blake and Rudy were up all night working it over . . ."

She almost shouted at him that Blake should have taken his own turn at flying it. But Gregson was at the blue plane then and climbing in. He paused with one leg up and turned to look at her. He didn't look much better than Thornhill, who sat in the back of the plane, his face ashen-gray. Gregson's face seemed more swollen now, his nose taking on a peculiar blue cast. He looked at her now, almost as if he hated leaving her there.

"Take care of them, Gina!" he yelled then and gave her a game smile. Then he was inside, the plane taxied out and it was gone, climbing gently to the clouds and disappearing. She turned to walk back to the dining room, glancing once at the tower. Blake was still there on the porch, the phones on his head, one leg hooked over the rail, watching her. She walked back to the dining room, feeling his eyes on her all the way. The field remained quiet, caught in an eddy; when the fresh gust of wind slapped cutting edges of sand into her face, she welcomed it as a sign that God was still in motion.

She did nothing for most of the day. When she returned from breakfast to the infirmary, she found that the Sudanese patients had gone. She had told them she would not break the Hamaran law by treating them any further. They had taken her at her word. A law was a law, she told herself, picking up stray bits of cloth and empty food tins they had left behind. She felt relieved in not having them on her conscience now. But she felt that irritating sense of guilt at the same time, as if all the world was fleeing her, leaving her alone with the mountain of strange mixture here, and the ever present, dominating, asphyxiating awareness of Blake.

She didn't move from her quarters all day, not even for lunch, not wanting any confrontation with Blake alone. She read her Bible, drawing on its strength for what she knew she inevitably had to do here.

Later, around seven, she got a sandwich from Ebenezer's kitchen and stood outside the dining room, watching the planes come in, their red wing lights winking their anticipated communion with earth. Now only one was left in the pattern. She watched it bank around easily and come down for a quick touch. Its wheels touched lightly and then she shouted, "No!" The plane slumped to the left, and she saw the wheel fly into the air, wobbling in a low arch for the hangars. The African mechanics and pilots started running for cover. The plane spun sideways, then did a complete ground loop and slid in a screeching, digging path for the nearest hangar, the dust rising angrily from the dragging wheel-less strut. It hit hard against the corner of the far hangar, the wing being sheared off as if it were nothing more than a plastic model, and finally stopped in a smoking heap against the hangar wall.

Gina had run to the infirmary for her bag before the plane crunched to a stop, and was there at the scene right behind Blake. Rudy and some of the other pilots had already cracked the cockpit door. She recognized the pilot as the one called Potter. He was unconscious, slumped up against the controls. They carefully lifted him out under Gina's watchful eye and put him on a stretcher.

"What do you think, Gina?" Rudy asked anxiously as she bent over the still form. She heard Blake knocking around the wreck and ordering Sam to get the tractor.

"I don't know yet," Gina said. "Get him to the infirmary. What happened, Rudy?"

"Wheels," Rudy said and spit into the red clay by his foot.

Gina saw in him the first cutting lines of fatigue, the stiffness around his mouth, the heavy sags to the pockets under his eyes.

"Okay, let's get this plane into the hangar," Blake was shouting now. "Let's not stand around here wondering about it . . . come on, chow is on!"

Gina wanted to stay around and listen to what more would be said now, sure that Rudy would have something for Blake. But the pilots were carrying Potter to the sick bay, and she felt she should follow.

Rudy leaned against the wall inside the radio shack and said, "Somebody is pouring silicon crystals in our wheel housings, like I said the other night . . ." Blake didn't answer. He sat down at the radio and began working the frequency dial against the whistles and static. "We better start narrowing it down, don't you think?" Rudy went on, noticing how Blake's face appeared like a wax model's that had started to melt in the heat, all of the lines and bulges beginning to drip into blurring shapes, the beginning of final loss of identity.

When Blake still did not respond, Rudy said, "My plane didn't act so good going into Terragona today. I don't think anybody else's behaves any better."

"So we'll put a guard on the planes tonight," Blake finally returned, almost with deliberate disinterest.

Rudy moved to sit on the edge of the table, pondering the hiss and snap of the radio, debating how to put weight into his concerns. Finally he reached into his shirt pocket, took out the reddish-brown kola nut and placed it carefully on the table in the light of the kerosene lamp. Blake did not look at it.

"Who else around here uses kola nut?" he asked, putting it as gently as he could. Blake still did not look at it, his fingers remaining on the radio dial in a light touch as if he was caressing a nipple. "I found that in the parking area last night . . ."

"He never goes near the planes, he's scared to death of them," Blake insisted.

"It was right under mine," Rudy came back, playing it low key, knowing this was a sensitive point with Blake.

"He wouldn't know how to put silicon crystals in wheel housings—"

"You know it isn't that hard—"

"You want to hold court on him?"

"No," and Rudy gave a short laugh to keep all of this as neutral as he could. "But I think he should know before he starts putting his fingers deeper into the machinery—"

"If it's him, I can take care of it," Blake insisted, trying to dismiss it all now. "Anyway, he wouldn't do it on his own . . . someone is behind it—"

"That doesn't change the fact," Rudy replied. "I mean those pilots over there have to be thinking seriously how much deeper the tear is going to get in the percentages. They should be told—"

"Told what?" Blake countered, and his eyes began to show cracks of light as if the furnace of his brain had just been lit and the flames were showing through the fire door. "You want to start talking about sabotage at this stage of the game? You think they'll fly tomorrow morning not knowing how far the damage has gone?"

"You've got to tell them something—"

"They know they've got tired airplanes and wheel housings," Blake countered bluntly, even testily. "And they know that as long as those planes are waiting for them tomorrow morning, they'll roll . . ."

"You can't reline those stripped housings any more than you have. They're wobbling so bad now they're beginning to shake the structure. Tomorrow morning they may all fly off like Potter's, and then what happens with all that nitro aboard? I think I know how you feel, Skip—"

"You don't know a thing about my feelings," Blake came back with a raking snap in his voice. It caught Rudy short. He had never seen Blake lose his cool to that extent in all this time. God only knew what held him together against the backdrop of a landscape that showed the frayed edges of structural fatigue. "Everybody around here keeps trying to get a slice of my feelings so they can tell me about it. Right now I don't know what I feel, so I don't know how you can. So let's drop it on that score, Rudy . . ."

Rudy did not respond, folding his arms and looking at the floor instead, thinking about it, trying to find the right approach. Then, shifting away from the subject, he said, "Monk will probably be telling you, but he got a funny question from Collins over at JERICHO today . . . what's the flash point on diesel oil?"

Blake half-turned his head toward Rudy, but he did not say anything immediately, watching the radio silently. "Collins ought to know that by now," he said then, with some detachment.

"Collins is an engineer, a motor mechanic, not a combustion expert."

"Did he think that Monk would tell him?"

"No. I think Collins expected Monk would tell you."

"They got the radio if they want to ask."

"Which means maybe that Collins wasn't supposed to ask. Maybe they don't want anybody to know what they're doing right now. Rayburn and the others, I mean."

"You got something you think I should know, Rudy?"

"I think you know. Put that question of Collins together with the secrecy hanging over those four northern hospital bases, and you know it gets thicker every time you stir."

"Well, maybe Collins wants to build a fire."

"Like where? And why?"

"They'll tell us when they're ready."

"I think they should tell us now."

"If Rayburn wanted me to know he would have told me."

"Would it be in here, then?" Rudy extended the sealed envelope toward Blake. "Monk got it from Rayburn. It's got personal on it for you."

Blake turned his head to stare at it, took it, put it on the table in front of the radio, not opening it.

"You going to read it?"

"It's personal, can't you see?"

Rudy wondered then if the flimsy bridge he had been using to walk out to Blake for these three years was beginning to come apart. At any other time, Blake would have read it and shared it with him.

"You can't carry it all yourself, you know that," he went on. "You ought to get Talfungo in on this . . . I think it's getting too big for us."

"What will Talfungo do with it, whatever it is? You think Gregson is going to be able to act now with that big Field Council in session?"

"Better that the decision is on him than us. That's all I'm saying right now."

"What would I tell him?"

"Whatever is in that envelope." Rudy sighed, not liking to play the checkmate on Blake like this. "We got blood and water samples into World Health. Meanwhile, none of us flying into the northern bases are allowed to go inside the hospitals. Which means they got something they don't want us to catch or know about. Put that against the mud slide they're sitting on with Turgobyne, and I'd say they could be moving into a condition red."

"Meaning what?"

Rudy looked at him, at the profile of the high-ridge nose, the cut of the mouth and rounding chin, the silhouette of George Washington facing his Delaware. Rudy did not push it. They sat in silence for a long time, the posture they'd come to know with each other in the past when they'd disagreed. They had attuned themselves to each other in these pressure moments, each trying to understand the other, each trying to reach the other. They had never fully attained that. But now it seemed different, strange. Rudy realized that part of it was due to the fact that for the first time he had suggested to Blake that Talfungo be in on things. Up to now Blake had fought his own battle here, called his own game plan and Rudy had stood with him. Now Blake had to sense that Rudy's confidence might be slipping, though Rudy had not intended to convey that.

Rudy backed off that line, and said, "I picked up another one of those funny transmissions again today . . . there's no question about it, it's coming out of Terragona . . ."

"I know, I heard it too," Blake said simply. "One of those prospectors is playing with a ham operator outside—"

"In code?" Rudy cut back, keeping his voice light. "Why would they shift to key transmission from voice? Only somebody trying to cover for something or someone would suddenly switch over like that—"

"You want me to go chasing signals then, Rudy?" Blake bristled, and a muscle began tugging at the corner of his mouth. It was obvious to Rudy then that Blake had been thinking about that transmission too and could not come up with the answers either.

Rudy waited a few seconds, then reached into his shirt pocket and took out a clump of napkin, opened it and spread it on the table.

"Molasses candy," he said, indicating the three small, black squares. "With sorghum . . ."

Blake looked at it, not comprehending where that fit into all this. Then he grunted, looking back at the radio, and said, "Well, at least you've moved from liquid to solid . . . that's something for the books."

Rudy laughed and took off his cap to signal his change of mood. And even Blake had to smile then. It was a tired effort at best, pulling on the stiff facial muscles, refusing to allow any genuineness at all. Rudy watched him in silence again, only the sound of the hissing radio in the room.

"You want to read it?" Blake said, indicating the sealed envelope of Rayburn's.

"Nope," Rudy said, but glad for the reprieve now, that he was back inside the circle again. "It's personal, remember?"

Just then Mundey walked in for his radio watch, and Blake stood up. "Stay on JERICHO frequency, Mundey," he said shortly. He glanced at the candy on the table. "Help yourself to the Yom Kippur offering there . . ." Rudy smiled as Mundey glanced at the candy with some suspicion.

"There's a seven-foot African outside looking for you," Mundey said to Blake. "Looks like one of those Sudanese refugees."

Blake moved for the door quickly, came back and picked up the sealed envelope still on the table. Rudy turned and followed him out, snapping at Mundey, "That stuff is better than an apple a day . . ."

Gina found that the total damage to Potter was two cracked ribs. She taped him up tightly and helped him back to the pilots' Quonset. When she returned, Rudy was waiting at the door.

"Get your bag, Gina," he said briskly.

"What for?" She looked at the Landrover parked ten yards out, Blake behind the wheel, dimly illuminated from the infirmary lamps.

"Ask that later, okay?"

She got her bag and walked out to the Landrover reluctantly. A tall African, knees almost to his chin, was sitting in back wrapped up in a faded gray blanket.

"I won't treat Sudanese," she said flatly, refusing to get in.

Blake started the engine as Rudy went around to the other side and got in front with him.

"Is that what they taught you in medical school, Doctor?" Blake countered sharply. "Make up your mind, it's going to be a short night . . ."

"Come on, Gina," Rudy coaxed. "It won't be that bad . . ."

She finally acquiesced, tossing her bag in back, and climbed in next to the African, who simply stared ahead. Blake shot the Landrover off with a jerk, slamming her back hard against the seat. From then on it was a wild, dusty, careening drive across the desert, lightning bouncing long stabbing fingers into the ground ahead of them. Gina had to hang on all the way to keep from flying out the door or landing in the African's lap next to her.

Finally, after about a half hour, Blake began to slow down as the wink of fires showed up through the dusty windshield. As they came closer to the nomad camp, the African spoke in his own language. Blake said to Rudy, "You figure what he's saying?" Rudy shook his head, and the African, sensing their problem, leaned forward and poked his long arm between Blake and Rudy, finger extended off to the right.

Gina waited, not saying anything, coughing now and then against the bite of the dust in her throat. They moved along for another mile or so, skirting the fires and the nomad camp, until the African said, "Samba bara . . ."

"That's it," Blake said, and Gina saw the green camper come into the glare of the headlights, sitting there as a block of contradiction in the empty desert.

Blake pulled up a few feet from it, keeping it in the flood of his lights, switching off the engine.

"Just what is this all about?" Gina demanded as she got out to stumble after them, the African staying by the vehicle. "What is this truck doing out here in nowhere and what does it mean to us?"

Neither of them answered. Blake went around to the driver's side of the cab and looked in. The driver sat very still there behind the wheel, his eyes open and staring into the glow of the headlights. Blake finally opened the door and climbed up to lean in, testing the man for life. "Help me get him out, Rudy," he said. They put the body down on the sand by the truck and Blake said to Gina, "Look him over, Doctor . . . that's why we brought you along."

She felt a stab of resentment at his drollery, but she got down on her knees beside the bearded man and held her stethoscope to the bare chest under the shirt. "He's dead," she said shortly.

"From what?" Blake snapped impatiently.

"How should I know? There isn't a mark on him. Heart attack maybe. You want me to perform an autopsy out here?"

Blake climbed up into the cab of the truck again, Rudy remaining right behind, holding the door open. "A converted army weapons carrier," Blake said then, as if Rudy had asked about the truck. "Whoever the man was, he had contact with American military equipment . . ." He stepped down from the cab again, carrying a pistol in his right hand. The two of them stood in the light examining it.

"Army special service automatic," Blake said.

"Well, that's something they, whoever it was, didn't find," Rudy offered.

"Anything on the body?"

"Clean . . . not a mark of identification. But I did find this map sticking out of the sand a few feet from the truck. It's a rough of Terragona and has a red circle around Caha."

Blake took it and studied it intently. "Well, was it left behind as useless or was it overlooked?" Blake asked.

"Anybody can get a map of Terragona," Rudy said. "The government office has a good supply. But why the circle around Caha?"

Blake grunted, not too sure of that. He turned then and walked back to the front of the truck, the buckles of his boots jingling loudly in the cavelike quiet of the desert night air. He lifted the hood of the truck with a jarring, scraping sound, sniffed the engine block, then ran his fingers over the air-conditioning grates, sniffed them. He turned to let Rudy smell.

"African white lightning," Rudy said with some awe, snorting against the bite of it in his nose.

"African what?" Gina said, growing more and more irritated at what was going on between them.

"An African poison made from the bark of the thorn tree," Rudy explained patiently. "It's mixed with a colorless liquid drawn from the brain of the viper, so the story goes . . . it works like monoxide, only slower."

"So who put it on the air-conditioning grates of that truck, then?" Gina queried.

"Somebody who knew how to handle that stuff, you can be sure," Rudy replied. Meanwhile, Blake had reached up inside to the roof of the hood, feeling with his right hand. He stopped suddenly, felt around and then pulled down a flat cover of steel hinged onto the surface. "Jackpot?" Rudy asked.

Blake took the bundle of papers from inside the compartment and began leafing through them. He handed Rudy a small piece of paper from the stack. Rudy looked at it, holding it up to the light. He whistled softly. "A voucher for a hundred thousand in C notes? Just who was this guy?"

"It's a U. S. State Department voucher," Blake said. "The number on there probably corresponds to the man who owned the truck."

"You think the money is still around?"

"I doubt it." Blake was busy scanning the yellow sheafs of paper. Finally he stuffed them all inside his shirt.

"It all falls into place so neatly for you, doesn't it, Mr. Blake?" Gina put it to him almost snidely. "It's almost like this is a stage prop and a scene you've been over many times before."

Blake pulled the hood down with a slam and turned to move to the rear of the truck. "The trouble with you, Doctor," he said over his shoulder, "is that you don't know anything about the great fraternity of the military. Once you're in it you never forget a face or how to get the most out of a piece of equipment like this . . ."

He was at the rear of the truck then, playing his flashlight up over the back doors. The lock had been sprung and hung loosely in the hasp like a dead spider. He jumped up on the tailgate, swung open the heavy steel doors, moved inside. Rudy followed, turning to pull Gina up after him. There was not much inside the back of the truck. A cot, a small bolted-down hotplate, a portable cooler, that was all. There were papers scattered on the floor. Blake bent over to look at some of them, then stood up and played his light around until he spotted the piece of equipment bolted down in the far corner toward the front.

"That's some piece of radio equipment," Rudy offered. "Big enough to pick up the sound of a bird flying at a few thousand feet at least."

The equipment had been smashed in, and Blake picked over the broken parts slowly. "It's a tracking beam oscilloscope," he said, more or less to himself. "Or *was* . . ."

"So is my Uncle Louis," Rudy quipped and tried a grin on Gina, who did not rise to it, feeling cold from the desert night air and strangely apprehensive in the musty darkness of the camper.

"It fixes on supersonic radio beams," Blake went on. "People in aerospace use it often to track orbiting satellites."

"So what was this poor man using it for, to get Guy Lombardo from the Waldorf?" returned Rudy in some awe. "I mean we don't have any tracking stations within a couple thousand miles—"

"Let's go," Blake cut him off and pushed by both of them for the door.

"Shall we look for the money?" Rudy called after him.

"What is he talking about?" Gina asked in some exasperation as Rudy helped her down off the tailgate. Rudy did not reply.

Blake had walked out a good twenty yards back of the truck now. He swung his flashlight beam close to the ground, then farther out. Rudy and Gina came up to him and stood there watching until Rudy said, "Somebody else was here all right . . . you can see the camper's tracks there . . . see that . . . but it looks like it was moving most of the way up here without a driver—"

"The driver was probably just about out by then," Blake commented simply.

"But what about those other tracks?" Rudy indicated.

Blake held the light on them. "Limousine," he said. "Parked right here . . . there's the footsteps in the sand, shoe marks, not bare feet of desert nomads."

"They, whoever they are, were following him all the way," Rudy went on. "Do you suppose the green-camper guy was on his way to Durungu?"

"Maybe. It's a sure thing the limousine is on its way . . . see there, the tire tracks go on angling southwest, curving back in toward Durungu . . ."

"Well, if we get a sedan riding into our camp tomorrow, we should kind of know who's who?"

"In whose hall of fame?" Gina poked in dryly. "I don't see what all this has to do with a mission. There are crimes committed on the desert frontier practically every day, and they say it's the smart ones who don't ask the wrong questions. It's something strictly for the Hamaran desert patrols, or am I reading that from the wrong rules of the road?"

"That Sudanese who took us out here figured we ought to know," Blake said laconically.

"He's also illegal—"

"No, Doctor, he just figured he owed us a favor . . ."

Blake turned and moved on quickly to the Landrover and came back with two shovels. He tossed one to Rudy and moved off a few yards to start digging.

"What do you think you're doing?" Gina snapped at him.

Blake turned a shovel of loose sand. "I'm going to bury the man . . ."

"You can't do that!"

"You want us to carry him back to Durungu?" Blake asked, continuing to dig. "You got someplace to stash him back there until you find a government man willing to get involved?"

"It's against the law!"

"Lady, you sure have the law on your tongue," Blake came back. "The only law on this frontier is courtesy and expediency . . . you know what that is?"

204

"I know the latter is to cover the evidence, and you are pretty good at that in all departments, aren't you, Mr. Blake?"

"That's right, Doctor," he replied indifferently, going on with his shoveling.

"Whoever owns that truck, besides that poor dead man, is going to send someone to ask questions," she went on, trying to dent him.

Blake shrugged. "That will come later, a much more convenient time. Meanwhile, Doctor, if you will stand out of the light and button up for once, we will continue to do what is a real kindness to our friend here, who would not appreciate your arguments about law when the desert buzzards will be around to pick at him tomorrow . . . now, if you don't mind?"

"I mind," she protested, looking to Rudy for support. But he did not look back at her now, going on with his own digging, very intent all of a sudden on his work.

In a half hour they had finished burying the body. They put the shovels in back of the Landrover. Blake put the gun he had found in the cab of the truck under his seat. He walked back to the site of the grave and stuck a long shaft of aluminum that he had found in the back of the truck into the ground, marking it. Then he came back, got in and moved the Landrover across the desert to the nomad fires.

When he got to the first tents, he braked and got out. There were people coming toward them from the fires and the tents, gathering in a loose knot of uncertainty around them.

"Okay, Doctor," Blake said to her when she did not move from the back seat. "This is your hour to shine . . ."

"I said I wouldn't treat them," she insisted adamantly.

Blake looked at the ground. "Doctor," he said then, with some sharpness, "this man here gave me the information on that dead man that could prove valuable in some way before too long," and he indicated the tall African beside him, who peered toward Gina, not comprehending either why she did not move. "He did that, risking his own neck, to get something back for his people . . . now are you going to treat them, or do I?"

She did not move from her seat. Blake came over to her and snatched the black medical bag from its place by her feet. "You can't diagnose without knowing the language," she called after him.

He did not respond. He walked over to the big fire, dropped down on one knee and opened the bag. The growing group of mostly women and children began to form a scraggly line under the prodding of the tall African. "He'll kill them," Gina said to Rudy, who continued to stand there waiting for her. Finally she got out to move quickly to where Blake was pawing through her black bag.

"Sulfa works anywhere," Rudy said encouragingly from behind her. Gina snatched the bag from Blake and looked up at the woman a few feet away carrying the nursing baby in her arms, her shriveled breasts offering no life. "There's no way I can dispense without a diagnosis," she argued then.

"This is not the outpatient clinic of New York General or whatever," Blake returned bluntly. "Besides, it's not *what* you give them but *how* . . . what they need most of all is to know somebody cares."

Gina glanced up at him quickly, feeling the rebuke, then at the woman, noting the look of expectancy, almost desperation. Every eye behind her in the line was the same. Well, she would not let him, of all people, prod her into an unwilling act of humanitarianism! "All I got is aspirin, some sulfa, and worm medicine," she said petulantly.

"That will do," Blake came back.

"So how are you going to find out what her problem is?"

Blake turned to the tall African and said something staggeringly clumsy in the language. The woman hesitated, then pointed to her lower abdominal area. Gina did not look at Blake, who she was sure was giving her that small, thin smile of his.

"That could be anything," she said hopelessly. "Tumor, infection, complications of the bladder—"

"What do you give for infection?" Blake said.

Gina sighed, poured eight yellow sulfa pills into her hand and reached up to extend them to the woman. She took them eagerly, as if they were the negotiables for eternal life, smiling back at her, bowing. "May God have mercy on me for that," Gina said, more to herself.

It went like that for hours, with patients pointing to head, ears, throat, knees or stomach. Gina hardly waited for the peculiar charade. She moved from one bottle to the other as each emptied far too quickly. Finally there wasn't anything left to dispense. She stood up on aching legs and closed the empty bag, feeling the grating sense of guilt for violating her medical profession so crassly.

As they stood there, the tall African walked to his tent and came back a minute later with two young women wrapped in tattered blankets. They stood in front of Blake, heads down, their large silver earrings glittering in the light from the fire.

Gina cleared her throat and fumbled with her medical bag, feeling the pulse suddenly began to beat in her neck. She glanced up once at Blake, who was staring at the two women.

"Are you enjoying yourself, Mr. Blake?" she flung at him indignantly.

"Gina, it's the chief's custom to show his thanks some way," Rudy said from behind her. "He doesn't have anything else to give . . ."

"Well, what are you waiting for, Mr. Blake?"

"I can't decide which one," Blake returned without a look at her. Rudy tried the disarming laugh. "He's pulling your leg, Gina . . ."

"Is he, Rudy?" she said for Blake. "The look on his face is hardly that of sheer pain . . ."

"To not show satisfaction is the worst of insults," Rudy tried again.

"Oh, of course," Gina mocked. "What interesting community relationships you two have established here in the name of the mission . . . I see now that what you have exchanged here is my medicine for gratification of your own lust . . ."

Blake continued to disregard her. He finally pointed to the young woman on the left. The chief clucked his own agreement. The other girl, visibly disappointed at not being chosen, turned and walked back to her tent in dejection.

"So now you intend to take that virgin back to Durungu for the long, lonely rainy season ahead, Mr. Blake?" Gina barked at him again, her face burning now in the swelling sense of outrage she felt.

He turned his head to her slowly, and he smiled. "You have a point there, Doctor," and he turned and started for the Landrover, the young girl following obediently.

They drove back in the same careening, wild rocking of the vehicle under Blake's mad, vicious driving. The young African girl sat in back with Gina, her blanket pulled up close around her. Gina did not look at her. All she felt was a peculiar choking pocket in her throat, and her stomach began to contract into painful spasms. After fifteen minutes of the dusty driving, Gina finally told Blake to stop by a clump of wild thorn scrub. She got out and went behind the screen and vomited. She wanted to cry, but she had long forgotten how to do that. She could only stand there, half crouched over, gasping against the heave in her stomach, feeling the pain strike deeper. What was it in this brazen night that cut through to her inner chambers of insulation against the bizarre or the sensational? Was it the savagery or the raw beauty of a simple people? Or was it the view of young girls given over to a man of capable intent? It was as if all her dormant nerves had been ruthlessly raked into a pile like dead leaves and set afire, leaping to the touch of the flame. It had all lanced home to the deeper recesses of her inner emotions, cutting into the dry, unused glands she had kept numb all this time by the careful application of spiritual Novocaine. The primitive had broken it open, crudely, painfully. And now confronted with herself, with what she had lying in her which had never been acknowledged before, coming up with the burning bile, she almost felt betrayed by this side of Africa she had not seen until now. And at the same time she felt peculiarly bonded to it, as if the secret was out but kept between her and this people. And Blake. Did he know too? What kind of diabolical spirit possessed him?

And then the spasm stopped and she stood there quietly, feeling nothing. The flame in her was slowly coming under control. And then Blake gunned the engine, letting her know it was late. She refused to move. She would not play his tune like everybody else! She found a Kleenex in the pocket of her denim jacket and blew her nose. The pink of the dawn, she noticed, was beginning to smear in big patches across the eastern horizon, bringing out the twisted arthritic bones of the rocky ridges in the distance. Finally she walked back to the Landrover and got in without a word.

It was nearly 5:30 before they got to the airfield, coming in between the pilots' Quonset and the infirmary, moving up the runway. Blake hit the brakes quickly as the field came into full view. It had rained, Gina noted, and not too long ago, leaving the runway looking like slick, pinkish-red paste. The clouds still hung in gray pallor overhead, but there were patches of blue now and the sun came through in stabs of orange-red. Something else had definitely changed here. Across the field, directly in front of them by the tower, sat a half-dozen official black limousines and three huge equipment trucks. Over to the left by the hangars were two red airplanes standing in striking predominance over the yellow Cessnas. There was also a silver-colored twin-engine plane that looked like an old Dakota with the words "Texas Oil" painted in orange on the side. The entire character of the field had been changed now from one of marginal strength to a dimension of almost awesome power.

"Well, I said we'd know who's who," Rudy said in wonder. "Take your pick. It looks like the circus has finally come to town. How'd they all fly here in the middle of the night anyhow?"

"Looks like they came in at daybreak, judging from the fresh marks on the runway there," Blake said factually.

"So who are all these people?" Gina demanded.

Blake said nothing, leaning his arms on the steering wheel, studying the scene. "Well," Rudy said, turning his head halfway toward her, "we always figured the word would get out sooner or later. The big industrial boys have had their eyes on Terragona too and had hired their own personal spies to keep watch on our operational health. Now with Augie blowing up and Potter going in last night, the word must have gone down the line that we are beginning to break up . . ."

"So all the so-called spies used the local telephone booth?" Gina quipped rather sourly, still feeling the disarray of her experience of the past night.

"No, Gina, it's the drums," Rudy countered with a quick laugh. "You notice they've stopped?" Gina did sense the unnatural silence hanging over the field. "This country still depends on the drums to get the word through the fastest. It's a smart industrial cookie who makes certain he hires an African who can beat out the word and interpret it that way. Yes, sir, a hot hand on the drum is ten times the weight in gold out here . . . and probably will be till Hamara gets a sophisticated communications system . . ."

"So what do all those people want, then?"

"Want?" Rudy turned his head to look at her. "Tea, rubber, bauxite, tin, uranium, oil, copper—all that Terragona is hiding, of course. It's the gold rush taking shape out here, Gina, and it could get bigger and more ugly than the one we had in California . . ."

Gina would have asked more, but Blake threw the Landrover into gear and moved to the tower. He pulled up in front and got out quickly. Rudy followed, reading the titles on the limousine doors or the bumper flags, like a little boy excited by all the company that had come to his house: "Texas Oil, Japanese Trade Commission, American Borax . . . hey, the Hamaran tricolor is out there too, Skipper!"

Gina got out of the Landrover too, the Sudanese girl remaining in the back, pulling her blanket around her, trying to shut out the confusing sights and sounds. Gina saw the limousine doors open almost as one, and a curious array of important-looking people came toward them. They were decked out in business suits or bush khaki, each trying to present the image that would come closest to what Blake would respond to.

"Sam!" Blake called across the field to where the African mechanics and pilots stood around the two new red airplanes there.

"Suh!"

"Get our airplanes loaded and warmed up!"

Sam looked confused, as if he expected something else today with all these important people around with their expensive equipment. He looked up at the gray sky, then at the wet clay by his feet. This was not the day to fly, he was saying.

"You hear me, Sam?" Blake shouted again, his voice bouncing off the hollow shells of the hangars.

*"Oui,* suh!" Sam finally yelled back and turned to run toward the hangars. The pilots stood where they were, however, hands in their pockets, staring back across the field toward Blake, still uncertain.

Blake turned to Rudy then and said, "Get over there and start them moving, Rudy. I want them rolling in twenty minutes . . ."

"It's pretty wet and slick, Skipper," Rudy offered diffidently. "With those wheel housings—"

"You know what happens if we don't get in the air today of all days?" Blake snapped at him. "You'll have all these people here swarming over Terragona by noon!"

Just then a tall man in a big white Stetson hat moved up on Blake and shoved a blank check at him. "Fill in any amount, Governor," he boomed in a southern drawl. "Texas Oil pays its way all the way . . . on top of that, you can have that Dakota over there that'll land anywhere in Terragona. Appears to me, son, you could use a generous Texas hand in this place . . . you got a dry tit, here, son, a dry tit . . . McChurson is my name, by the way . . ."

"We're not buying today," Blake said indifferently, not even looking at the check extended to him, his eyes still on the activity around the hangars. "All you people can get back in your limousines and head back to Talfungo," he added.

210

"American Borax will put a million over to you on your permission to ride to Terragona, Mr. Blake," somebody called out from the group.

"We will double it," a short, bespectacled Japanese man said, bowing toward Blake.

"Don't let them corrupt you, son," McChurson insisted.

Just then Dirk Shannon came out of the tower door a few feet away, studying a small scrap of paper he had in his right hand. He looked in some disarray now, a bit pale and unsure of himself.

"Mundey took the ten o'clock transmission last night from Talfungo," he began.

"Not here," Blake warned, and took Shannon by the arm to lead him out of earshot of the others. Rudy, who had not yet moved to go across the field to the hangars as ordered, followed; Gina, uncertain how far she could get in on this, moved with him.

"Okay, let's have it," Blake said to Shannon.

"Well, Merriweather, the General Director, sent the word"—and Shannon dropped his voice, and there was a kind of trembling in it—"that your gas requisition will have to wait pending Field Council decision on this operation . . ."

Blake frowned at Shannon, not comprehending, looking almost confused. He squatted down slowly and picked up a handful of clay, squeezing the paste slowly between his fingers. "Who is Merriweather again?" he asked then.

"The top man of the mission," Rudy offered.

"I thought Gregson controlled the field . . . ?"

Rudy shrugged. "It's Council time . . . the General Director is in Talfungo, and he has the right to send in the plays from the bench. Anyway, with the operation on the agenda, it's not unusual for headquarters to delay the paperwork on supply until there's a green light . . ."

"Except we're not running on paper," Blake responded, unable yet to understand. Then, "How much gas we got left in the hangars?"

Rudy thought a minute. "Maybe two hundred gallons with what's in the barrels . . . less after today's flight . . ."

Blake sniffed, opening his left palm to study the ball of clay there. "Another day or two at best," he said, more to himself than to them. "How long do you think we'll have to wait then?"

Nobody responded. Shannon looked at the paper in his hand as if it were a summons. Rudy found a stick of gum in his leather-jacket pocket, suddenly wanting to be busy with something, unwrapped it and folded it into his mouth. "They could pass on that tomorrow even," he said, trying to stoke up a fresh head of optimism.

Blake said nothing. But he knew by now that the Council would not act that fast with so much doubt about him. They would debate his right to lead here first.

"There's something else too," Shannon went on. "We only got a few minutes of a weak transmission from Rayburn around three . . . he says he's lost three patients in the last few hours in the hospital, other bases are reporting fatalities too. He says it's beginning to get tight especially on the northern end of the island. One other thing I'm not sure I got straight . . . I think he asked what the flash point was to ignite diesel and would it burn in water."

Blake grunted, squeezing that clay in his left hand, the water dripping out from the closed fist.

"You better not load your plane today, Rudy," he said then. "I want you to fly to Trader Joe's down in Myagunde later . . . if anybody's got high-octane gas, he'll have it."

"You think it's wise to go over the big man's head?" Rudy put it to him dubiously. "That might put Gregson's hand in a bind—"

"It appears Gregson has no hand," Blake returned bluntly. "You got a better idea on how to keep things alive?"

"Try obeying orders for a change," Gina put in quickly, unable to remain outside the exchange.

Blake kept his eyes on that closed fist and the water still coming through in painfully slow drops. "Lady, how is it you lived so long busting in the doors where you don't belong?"

Before she could retort, Rudy cut in and said, "How shall I pay for that gas?"

"Somebody here I'm sure will offer to pay for it," Blake countered.

"In exchange for what?" Gina snapped, and Rudy shot a quick glance at her in warning.

"Shannon," Blake continued, ignoring her, "you better eat chow and get on the flight line."

Shannon hesitated, as if he wanted to say something else. "There are two men inside from the Hamaran Government waiting to see you privately . . . they brought those two Cessna 206s over there . . ."

212

Blake glanced at the clouds, which seemed to be breaking up some. "We'll have to hold our takeoff time, Rudy . . . ground is too wet."

"Shall we unload the nitro?"

"No. She'll sit for a while. In a few minutes we'll get some sun to dry up the field a little . . . but keep your eye on the temperature line, she could jump fast . . ."

Just then the two Africans stepped out of the tower radio room and walked toward them. Blake rose from his haunches, throwing the clay to the ground at his feet. The lead African was dressed in blue-striped white ducks, white shirt, maroon tie and blue blazer with the Hamaran coat of arms on the left pocket. The dress was a distinct hallmark of the National Liberation Party. He moved in quick strides toward Blake, as if destiny was always just one elusive step ahead of him. Behind him, the shorter, fatter African with the goatee, wearing the white shorts and shirt, maintained a discreet distance. He smoked a long, thin cigar which he held firmly between his teeth, but which was not lit.

"Mr. Blake?" the tall African said, his voice smooth, the English riding heavy on the French but very clear and crisp, flowing on a crest of diplomacy. "My name is Felix Mentaya, Minister of Mines. This is Timothy Belang, Government Information Officer," and Gina noticed that he did not even turn to look behind him at the man.

Blake nodded and said, "Mr. Belang and I have met on other occasions . . ." Mentaya did not respond to that. Blake did not bother to introduce either Gina or Rudy. He had turned and was making his move to walk across the field to the hangars.

"I'm happy to be the bearer of good news," Mentaya went on, reaching out to restrain Blake with his voice, which had command to it. Gina noted that his dark eyes, deeply set in the sockets, seemed to glow like black water in a deep stone well, belying the easy, disarming smile.

"I am pushing a flight line, Mr. Mentaya," Blake said shortly.

"Of course, of course! And I have two new airplanes to put on that flight line, Mr. Blake, a gift of the Hamaran Government." Mentaya took out a sheaf of papers from inside his coat. "All you have to do is sign here under that of your own field director, Milton Gregson." He pushed the papers out to Blake, and the viewing audience of VIPs moved in closer to get a look. A sudden gust of wind, heavy with moisture and carrying the smell of southern grasses and thunderstorms, caught Blake's cap and tugged at the brim. Blake turned and took the papers from Mentaya without much interest. He scanned them quickly and handed them back. "You see there the official seal of the Premier," Mentaya insisted, not taking the papers extended to him, "authorizing me to give you these two planes—"

"And your pilots to go with them, Mr. Mentaya?"

"But of course, Mr. Blake," Mentaya returned with some surprise. "I cannot trust government equipment to pilots who are used to flying older aircraft—"

"I deal strictly with the Premier," Blake said flatly, turning again to look across the field. "By order of the Premier himself . . ."

"The Premier is in Madagascar for ten days," Mentaya insisted, and Rudy reached out and took the papers from Blake's hand, still extended toward Mentaya. "That is why I am authorized on his behalf—"

"I'm sorry, Mr. Mentaya. I cannot allow another aircraft over Terragona except our own, and anyway yours are the wrong color . . ."

"Color?" Mentaya looked both confused and irritated then. "What has color to do with it?"

"Yellow is what Chief Turgobyne recognizes in airplanes, no other. You land in Terragona with those red jobs and you'll be dead five seconds after you roll to a stop . . ."

Belang let out a short laugh then, as if Blake had pulled a joke, and Mentaya gave him a mean look. "Very well . . . I can have my pilots paint our aircraft immediately," Mentaya said in a turgid tone.

"It will take a few days to dry in this building humidity, Mr. Mentaya," Blake countered. "If you try flying those bigger jobs with full loads on this short field, the resistance of wet paint to aerodynamic flow—"

"Do not play with me, Mr. Blake," Mentaya cut in sharply then.

"Skip," Rudy put in then, "Gregson did sign these papers," and he held them out for Blake to look at again.

"You have very little choice now anyway," Mentaya went on. "Your so-called airlift is in bad shape . . . you are short of planes, petrol and equipment. Besides, I have steel landing mats over there, Mr. Blake, something you are going to need if the rains come early as expected. Now I can save face for you and your mission and save your people and ours in Terragona at the same time. In any case,

214

either you accept it and sign, or I fly anyway, since I have your mission chief field officer on record authorizing me to do so—"

"Sam!"

"*Oui,* suh!"

"Wind them up!"

"*Oui,* suh!"

"It will have to wait," Blake said, ignoring the papers. "The wind and sun will not. I will turn my mechanics to painting your planes, Mr. Mentaya."

"You are defying a government order!" Mentaya shouted against the sudden snap of the airplane engines kicking over, and he snatched the papers from Rudy. "This will go hard on you, you understand that, Mr. Blake?"

"I am not defying anything," Blake came back blandly. "Once those planes are painted yellow, we'll talk again. I am trying to save your life right now, Mr. Mentaya—"

"Do not stall with me, Mr. Blake!"

"Skip, maybe—"

"I thought I told you to get over to those hangars?" Blake barked at Rudy.

Rudy hesitated, then took off his cap and scratched his head in a gesture of frustration. Then he showed a disarming, almost embarrassed, grin. "Well, yes, sir, I guess you did just that," he said and moved on by Blake and Mentaya and headed across the field to where the pilots stood waiting.

"Something more we can do for you, Doctor?" Blake said to Gina, who stood a few feet away, arms folded, computing and measuring it all, not quite believing what was happening. She savored the atmosphere, only vaguely conscious of all the moving parts. The acid taste of bile was still in her mouth, her head pounded, and there remained that certain constriction as if the air had gone too thin all of a sudden. Blake's image of defiance was looming higher and casting longer shadows now. To her the composite of the past night's wild ride and his own mocking blend had been enough; but now his deliberate resistance to Mentaya and the mission's authority on top of it, was perhaps the final dimension to dispel anybody's doubts about where he stood. Even Rudy seemed confused. Couldn't Gregson have seen all this? She took a deep breath then to cut down the pressure pushing on her throat that demanded she scorify him, to return his blatant effrontery with as much of the same.

"Not really," she said to him coolly, her voice rising in sardonic tones over the rumbling sound of the engines that had subdued now to a mumbling idle. "You seem to have done quite adequately in all respects."

"Then you better get your beauty sleep," he replied brusquely. "You're overdue. And don't forget to take care of my little flower . . ." She would not let her eyes drop from his steady gaze, though that pulse hammered in her throat. He turned then and walked away from Mentaya, who lifted the folded papers in his hands as if to make further appeal, then dropped them in disgust.

"They won't fly for you today, Mr. Blake," he called after him. "Not today!"

But Blake apparently had not heard. He moved on in that rolling swagger of his, and she was sure she could hear those buckles jangling their discordant tune, while the little boy with the tray of empty tins on his head ran to get in front, like a court jester, the king's fool.

Blake was working over one of the plane's wheel housings when Rudy came out of the hangar, walking slowly toward him. Blake looked up, noting that Rudy's face seemed to be sagging heavily against the facial structure. It was the first time he had seen Rudy in any kind of shadow at all.

Rudy came up to him, spit out his gum and handed the half sheet of paper to him with obvious reluctance, as if it were an eviction notice. The crisp, large, clear boldface of the teletype hung out in front of him. He didn't look at Rudy as he folded it slowly and put it into his shirt pocket. He said nothing, but his face now took on a kind of vacant look, almost resignation, like maybe he had come to terms with death.

"So now you know, Rudy," he offered then, his voice just barely hanging over the sound of the idling engine ten feet away.

Rudy shrugged. "It doesn't make any difference," he said. Blake looked up at him, not really sure. Rudy tried a smile, which didn't come off too well.

Blake savored that a long ten seconds. "The rest of them know?"

"Well, Mentaya told them earlier . . . when Shannon said he didn't believe him, Mentaya gave him that teletype . . ."

216

Blake spit into the dirt by his feet, staring down at his boots, his hands buried deep in his back pockets. "Maybe now we know who hit the guy in the green camper," he said, but it sounded as if he was really thinking of something else, mouthing words that were meaningless in the enormity of this other thing. Rudy didn't answer, not getting the connection between the teletype and the truck or the man who had died in it. Blake finally tossed the wrench he held in his left hand into a bucket by the plane in front of him, a gesture of finality.

"I think you better talk to them," Rudy said, moving to close with the immediate situation. "They're pretty shook up in there—"

"And why shouldn't they be?" Blake flung back, and he gave a sharp, explosive kind of laugh that sounded strange as it mixed with the sound of the engines. "So what have they got going today for them? Stripped wheel housings, a twenty-mile-an-hour gusty wind out of the east to crosscheck them on takeoff, clouds maybe up to seven thousand feet to bump them all the way to Terragona? And now on top of that, they got an imitation general for a wing commander?"

"I still think you should—"

"What do you want me to tell them? Not to hold it against me? That every man has his right to his past, his mistakes? You want me to stand in front of them and hang it all out for them to see and then send them maybe to their death today when I won't do it myself? You want them to forgive me, Rudy? Well, they may forgive me, but they sure won't fly for me—"

"So maybe it's time they learned to fly it for God and Terragona," Rudy shouted back.

"Tomorrow maybe," Blake retaliated. "When they got time to think about it and get it straight in their minds. But today, they fly for me, like any other day. You tell them I'll be on that tower like any other day, you understand me, Rudy?" He was glancing around the ground by his feet then, as if he was looking for a rock he wanted to throw at someone, something. "You tell them just like that! But they got five minutes—only five—to make up their minds. Because the temperature line is shooting up fast in all this humidity, and that nitro is ticking!"

His voice rang to a kind of shrill pitch, catching on the high notes straining above the sound of the motors, and he turned abruptly and started across the field, heading for the tower, his city of refuge, the steam rising from the wet airfield enveloping him. His head was down, his khakis flapping around him, posing the figure of a man who had just stumbled in off the desert, torn by the elements of his long journey. The forced, rigid lines of his back were bent to the gusty wind that whipped up the heat from the sun which had broken through the clouds, the cruel, cutting lines of the exposure slashing him to a degradation of a fallen gladiator with a knife at his throat . . .

Rudy wanted to run after him, tell him it was all right, that it *didn't* make any difference. Instead, he turned finally and walked into the hangar, not really sure now either.

It was the longest walk Blake had ever made here, away from the flight line before his planes were even moving. He saw those limousines and the men standing by them watching, Mentaya and Belang studying him intently. He wanted to say something to Mentaya—but what would it be now? It was done. He stepped inside the radio shack and leaned his hands on the table, letting his weight drop on them. Sweat poured from his face and fell on the table to lie there by his fingers like melted wax. He felt the burn in his chest, the sting in his eyes, the thumping beat of his heart rattling in his ears, signaling that the tired circuits were on overload. His legs felt heavy, drawing the muscles tight in his calves, turning the knees to paste. He wanted to sit down, but he knew he could not, because once he was down he wasn't sure he could get up again . . .

He waited. It was 6:35. Three minutes gone already! And they weren't out yet. JESUS, IN THIS HEAT, IT WILL BE WORSE IF THEY DECIDE TO GO! AND YET, WORSE IF THEY DON'T! Worse on whom? Not them! On himself, then? On Terragona? He prayed now they wouldn't go, debated running back across the field and scrubbing it today, hoping to get that testy nitro back in the coolers. He couldn't wave them off today, not now . . . to stand up there on that tower playing God? Now when they knew why he wouldn't go himself?

He felt the hot wind boil inside the room, hiss at him with its rasping voice, flinging sand against the transmitter in derisive mockery at the sounds that matched its own.

Now he straightened slowly, pushed himself off his hands. It was nearly 6:40! *We'll have to unload that nitro!* It's too late!

Then he heard the sound of the shouts across the field, the sudden rip of full power to the engines.

He leaped out through the doorway, opening his mouth to yell to them to get away from those airplanes, let them blow up. But he saw

Shannon's plane SUGAR LUMP already moving out of the parking area, heading down the strip to the runup line. The others were already in their planes too, goosing the engines, swinging ponderously around to follow Shannon. He ran to the Landrover parked a few feet away, hopped in, started the engine and shot down the runway toward the runup circle. He saw Rudy running across his path, and he slowed for the big Jew, who grabbed hold of the door frame and vaulted into the back seat.

"We should have scrubbed it!" Blake yelled at him. "They took too long . . ."

"They weren't sure what to do," Rudy shouted back, leaning forward over the back seat, his breath hot on Blake's ear. "Then all Shannon said was that maybe today was the most important flight they ever made . . . and no matter, Terragona was still there and you were on the flight line, so what were they waiting for . . ."

"Okay, forget it!" Blake returned and braked the Landrover, jumping out before it came to a full stop, Rudy bolting after him.

Shannon was swinging his plane up on the field, positioning to run up his engines like always before starting the roll. Blake ran up to the propped-open side panels and shouted, "What's your temperature?" Shannon glanced at his gauges.

"One sixty-three!"

"You don't have the time to run her up! Roll her, Shannon, right now!"

He leaped back from the windows then and stood by the wing tip, lifting his arms as if he was putting the blessing on Shannon, hanging there between sky and earth in a pose of willing crucifixion. Then one hand began circling over his head to urge full throttle. Shannon lifted his thumb in acknowledgment, and for one block of no more than three seconds he peered at Blake through the plexiglass, the look maybe that tried to say a thousand things that had been forgotten or overlooked all this time. Maybe it was the look of a man who knew he could die in the next sixty seconds and suddenly realized there were many gaps to fill, so many strings to tuck back in.

And then he fed full power, and the plane moved out in a protesting squeal as the stripped wheel housings fought the cargo weight and the new speed. The blast of prop wash tore at Blake, and he fell to his knees, hanging on to his cap, lifting one arm against the blast of wet dust pouring over him.

The plane took too long to get up, Shannon ruddering hard against the easterly crosswind that tried to walk him off the runway, the sun now pouring down on him in murderous fury, one giant silver-liquid eye turning the torch his way, reaching out to fuse that nitro. He staggered peculiarly off the ground, his left wing bobbing, and he fought her back to finally lift uncertainly like a glider on a string, banking away from the ugly cotton hair and pushing for those heavy clouds that had not broken up enough to offer any reprieve from turbulence.

Blake had gotten up before Shannon had lifted his wheels, bent only on getting them all running from that sun, swinging his right arm furiously for the next plane in line, which was Mundey's ROUTE 66, urging him forward, shouting at him to roll it. Mundey, always quick on the throttle anyway, gave it the goose. His face was only a blur as he shot by Blake, but Rudy could see the flaming patches of his acne standing out like raw burns on his cheeks. Blake didn't wait to watch him go either—his right arm kept pumping like a traffic cop's, moving the others up to the line while circling one hand over his head to tell them to throttle out and get moving. By now they had gotten the message too, kicking in the juice before they had even swung into position, streaks of their faces shooting by, the arc of white wings touching the last visible mark of permanence before the uncertain sea ahead.

Over by the line of limousines, Belang turned to Mentaya and said, "You said they would not fly, Felix, today of all days?" Mentaya did not answer. He stood stiffly there in front of the radiator of his black government special, arms folded, watching each plane go, watching them like a chicken hawk eyeing a grouse running in a field. Belang chuckled, removing his cigar to study it intently. "You and Monsieur Faber said he is not Napoleonic?"

"You find that fool who was supposed to work over those wheel housings," Mentaya snapped. "No money for him . . ."

"Can't find him," Belang returned, still half-smiling. "He won't be caught taking money from us in this place anyway . . ."

"At any rate," Mentaya went on, looking out toward the runup line then, "Our day may not yet be finished . . . as you can see now!"

It was Tim Slater's COFFIN CORNER Mentaya indicated, moving up to swing into takeoff position, its wheels giving off smoke even as Slater began to ease off the brakes for the quick takeoff. Blake was pumping his arms for Slater to go full out, and then, seeing the smoking wheels, Blake threw up his arms. Slater hit the brakes hard so that they squealed, and the wheels looked like they were about to cave in right then. Blake ran to the door of the plane, yanked it open and yelled, "Get out of there, Slater!" Slater, sensing the problem, jumped down quickly to the ground. Blake then hopped into the plane, as Rudy ran a few steps toward him, gunned the motor and turned the plane around to run it jerkily across the clay tarmac toward the open space a hundred yards beyond the hangar. By then the mechanics were running for cover, knowing what could happen. Blake finally stopped the plane, cut the engine, jumped out and began running back across the field toward the runup line where Monk still sat in his Piper Cub, not sure what to do, the engine turning over and sounding as mute as a lawnmower, compared to the others. Blake, sensing Monk's hesitation, ran up to the plane and slammed his palm against the fuselage under Monk's window and yelled, "Go, Monk, go!"

Monk let off the brakes then and hit full power, the plane jumping off down the wet clay runway, its motor rattling a false pride like a pup's growl. He went all the way, running scared, and finally lifted up that first agonizing step to the sky, banking too sharply away from the ugly finger of the cotton hair and then staggering up that uneven path to the higher altitudes in pursuit of the others.

Blake turned then, hopped into the Landrover, and tore off across the field toward the parked Cessna. Not more than thirty yards away from it, he jumped from the cab and sprawled flat out on the ground. The Landrover went on and hit the parked Cessna a jarring, crunching blow broadside. The explosion sent a shock wave across the field, knocking some of the VIPs down by their vehicles, followed by the usual drizzle of falling debris.

Rudy, his ears still ringing from the blast, was up and running with Slater toward Blake, who was still prone on the ground but now beginning to stagger uncertainly to his feet. "You okay?" Rudy asked as he stopped by him, resisting the urge to reach out and help him. Blake stood up in a half crouch, hands on his knees, as if he had run all the bases himself and was now trying to get his wind, staring at the ground. Rudy glanced at him. The wet clay dust had left a coat of red on the skin of his face, sticking to it like plaster, outlining the eye sockets, the nose, the mouth. Rudy looked away toward the plane now burning in an angry red-orange plume. The clouds closed in on the sun again, and the shadows rode across the field as if thousands of birds had suddenly passed over.

Blake straightened slowly, wiping at the dust on his face, smearing it, blurring the image. He found his sunglasses on the ground and put them on carefully, as if it were makeup for the next act. Then he began walking slowly across the field to the tower, passing the silent line of VIPs, who wisely said nothing to him.

"Like I said, monsieur," Belang commented to Mentaya, brushing the red clay from his white shift and shorts, "a flea under the belt can worry an army—"

"Nevertheless, he has lost another aircraft," Mentaya countered quickly, watching Blake disappear into the tower. "He knows now he cannot run this alone. Now he will sign! Yes, he will sign!"

# CHAPTER X

Milt Gregson was back in Talfungo by ten o'clock that Tuesday morning. Ted and Merriweather were there waiting. Merriweather embraced the sagging figure of Thornhill as they met. Neither man said anything to the other. G.D. had lost two sons himself in the spiritual wars, and his right hand that tapped lightly on Thornhill's shoulder was trying to communicate that.

They drove to the hospital first, though Thornhill insisted he was all right. But even in Standish's care, G.D. did not leave him. Thornhill would want to talk now, and G.D. wanted to give the chief benefactor of the mission every courtesy at this point.

Gregson and Ted hung around the waiting room for fifteen minutes, neither man bothering to converse. Finally Gregson told Ted he wanted to go home and shower. Ted hesitated, not knowing if he should leave without telling the General Director. But when Gregson went out, he followed a few minutes later.

"Anything yet on those cables you sent?" Gregson asked him as they drove.

"Too early yet," Ted returned, hunching over the wheel to ease his constricted lungs. When Ted stopped in front of Gregson's red brick prefab, he said, "G.D. wants the word on Blake on his desk by this evening . . ."

Gregson got out of the Ford station wagon in slow moves, slammed the door behind him and walked around the front of the car to climb for the cement step to his walk.

"You do have the statement, Milt?" Ted called to him, his voice sounding like the bleat of a sheep.

Gregson paused and half turned, not looking at Ted but instead noticing that his lawn looked as if it had been rained on in his absence. He crouched down and stuck his finger into the topsoil. It was a good quarter-inch wet. He thought of the Durungu airfield turned mushy like that. When he straightened, he felt a new tangling thread around his already strangled sense of direction.

"Tell him I won't be ready until morning," he said to Ted. That cough of protest followed him up the walk even as Ted gunned the motor and moved off.

Nothing happened all day. The compound seemed to hang in suspension, caught in the eye of the storm. Gregson ate lunch with Laura, but she was strangely subdued. They never had too much to say to each other lately, but she always had plenty to comment about Blake. She, perhaps more than anyone else, except for G.D. maybe, had more riding on what he would do to lead the suspension on Blake. He glanced at her now and then, noticing how thin she looked, her blonde hair washed out to a tired brownish color, done straight back in a severe pull that intensified the narrowness of her face and eyes. The five years here had been hard on her, maybe even harder than on himself. They had once, a long time ago it seemed, shared the burdens of their service in the simpler areas of the bush. Here he had been forced to keep confidential field matters to himself. It had strained their relationship to times of uneasy silences. He couldn't remember when they had prayed together last about the problems here. Now as he looked at her across the table, sensing the enormity of the crevice Blake was directly or indirectly widening between them, he felt the first real sense of honest terror. For he could not reach out to her now, to communicate his dilemmas, when he needed her understanding. And she, as helpless as he, could not find a way either.

So later that evening he decided to walk, with the sinking sun sliding behind the ominous cloud in the west, the wind turning slightly cool with the coming promise of rain. It was hard to find familiar ground as he walked. Now and then he passed people in the shadows, but they were just faces. They skittered away from him after uncertain greetings, seeing in him perhaps a figure of contradiction, a prophet of no sure revelations. He sensed nothing but dark corners everywhere, filled with peculiar shapes.

He did not know how long he walked. But sometime in the night he found himself in the compound chapel, sitting in the darkness. The odors of mahogany and cement mixed together, smelling like a carpenter's shop. There was a dim light coming off the painting of John the Baptist baptizing Jesus in the Jordan high on the wall behind the choir loft. All he could think of then was Archimedes' law of mathematics that he had memorized a long time ago in school—that there was a relationship between the diameter of a circle and its circumference. John the Baptist was the diameter for the extension of the circle of God's love for Jesus maybe? Was Blake the same for Terragona? Was he, Milton Gregson, in fact, in the same critical relationship to the furthering of the history of United for Life Mission? Was the altering of the diameter going to affect history that much here? Could one single action of one man so finally affect human and organizational destinies? Tomorrow morning the Field Council was expecting him to alter the totality of events in Durungu to every dimension . . . one way or the other.

"Behold the lamb of God who taketh away the sin of the world!" He read the line under the painting done up in scroll. He knew that line well from his boyhood in Christmas cantatas. How almost utterly meaningless those words were now! In that other life, a world of kite string, fishing line and pimples, there was no great pressure to believe. But now they sounded too simple, even almost irrelevant. John never had it so good? He could plow his furrow and say of the One following: "He will make the crooked places straight!" Would Jesus still do that for Milton Gregson if he plowed a crooked furrow tomorrow morning?

He sat back on the bench with a sigh, mulling it over, wondering if he was making more of a case out of this than actually existed. If he did choose to go with Blake finally and stood up to his own Field Council and G.D., the worst that could happen would be a vote against his attempt. The fact that he argued for Blake would not certainly have that much effect on his office with the other men. But if he did make a case, then on what grounds would he make it for Blake? Yes, there was the real shape of the disaster hanging over him then. He could hardly argue on the basis of Godly intuition, which was really all he had finally. That would hardly hold up on so large an issue that Blake now posed for the entire field. And yet, maybe he had no argument for Blake at all really, but was now simply refusing to own up to his own bad judgment in enlisting Blake in the first place on so poor a statement of his spiritual credentials. God help him, if that's all this was about in the end!

So maybe he did not have a case for a man who was, on the surface, so far out of step with the mission. He could argue about maintaining the finely tuned operational balances in Durungu until after the rains, or the need for patience in what was an operation of obvious significance. Some of the men would go along with him on that undoubtedly. But in the end the decision would swing with Merriweather and Maddigan, the mainsprings of the organization; their case was laid on the need for preservation of the spiritual order that could not afford departure from policy or practice. And Gregson knew they were right in that. So all he would have then when it was all done was a rather empty gesture at best, a meaningless charade almost, that could only sink him deeper into the bogs of ineptness and build a larger question mark in the minds of his field superintendents about his capacity to judge and rule rightly. If he ever had.

He wanted a mint then, and he reached into his jacket pocket and came up instead with a piece of paper folded over twice. He remembered Rudy shoving that into his hands earlier that same morning in the dining room in Durungu just before he took off. He opened it now and peered down at the clumsy block letters done up with a faulty ballpoint:

IF BLAKE DOES NOT HAVE THE FAITH OR ONLY EVEN
HALF OF IT, AM I NOT MORE RESPONSIBLE FOR HIM
THAN IF HE HAD 100 PER CENT?

—RUDY

That was all. Gregson slowly folded the paper and stuck it into his pocket again. The absurdity of the simplicities! In a spiritual order sustained by careful legislation to guard the purity of the faith, could he move on so inadequate a piece of truth!

He felt deeply troubled then, so that he leaned his head on the top of the bench in front of him, feeling the coolness ease the flush of his skin. Maybe now he knew finally . . . it wasn't that Merriweather or Maddigan were wrong on Blake . . . maybe it wasn't even Blake in the end that became the critical point now. Maybe, as Barak tried to tell him, it was God's way of making him face what he had feared all this time in the field office, that moment of loneliness, of standing alone, of having to put his life and position on the line for something he believed in, even though he was not able to fully articulate it. Well, maybe for himself he could do it, reverse the flow of judgment on Blake and take whatever was in the offing with it. But there was Laura too . . . and Ted, and all the others who could go with him. If the issue was as strong as it appeared, he could lose the office all in one sweep . . . if Maddigan got elected, it was sure he would pick his own field staff, men from the north mostly. That meant Ted was headed for the deadly jungles to choke on mold and fungus . . . and for himself and Laura, back to the desert frontier and a book van . . . but was Blake that critical in the end? He would never know on this side of the decision he had to make. Only God knew.

"Take your burdens to the Lord and leave them there." He hummed the melody then, the echo of it almost terrifying him in the empty dark place. But all he heard really was the sound of airplane engines, the stink of exhaust and the image of Blake's reddish-blond head bent over that pan of oil and parts caught in the red glow of the forge.

Nothing happened. This was one burden he couldn't unload on God. He would have to take it with him now, because it was his and his alone to shoulder.

So be it!

He was up at 6:30 the morning of the twelfth, feeling strangely refreshed even though he knew he hadn't fallen asleep much before three. There was a funny kind of tingling going through him now even as he dressed, his nerves stretching some with the adrenalin. He glanced over at Laura in the bed. Though she breathed easily and relaxed, he knew she wasn't asleep. Nobody in this compound was indulging in that luxury this morning.

He got on the phone in the kitchen and made four calls. In each case, the phone was yanked off the hook before the first ring was half through. They were sitting pretty close, probably anticipating something, though they did not expect it to be him. By now Merriweather had probably filled their horizon, or else Maddigan.

By the time he got to the office at seven, lights were on in the main office, since the heavy cloud cover had cast a dark shroud over the damp morning. He walked inside and met Ted, who looked as if he'd dropped his main bearing. Gregson gave him a cheerful good morning, and Ted coughed, avoiding the amenities, having no capacity for it now. Gregson moved on down the corridor, feeling as if he were climbing up into the cab of a stalled freight in the railroad yard.

"Charlie?" he said to the man sitting behind the desk in the supply office, who was looking rather frayed, sleepy and out of sorts. "I want those gas trucks rolling for Durungu right away . . . and the same goes for all the other supplies on Blake's requisition . . ."

"G.D. hasn't released any of that yet," Charlie returned, sitting up quickly.

"I'm releasing it as field director, Charlie . . ."

"But . . ."

"You heard it, Charlie . . ." Charlie Bryan threw a quick glance of alarm at Ted. But Gregson turned now and began walking down the corridor toward the Operations office, Ted on his heels.

"Milt"—Ted reached out his hand to touch Gregson's shoulder, trying to restrain him—"G.D. already talked to Durungu around five-thirty . . . he told them he was holding up the supplies pending Council action today . . ."

Gregson did not acknowledge. He went on to turn into Frank Mason's office. Frank was mixing freeze-dried coffee in a porcelain cup. "Frank, I want two Cessnas pulled out of the transport pool along with two pilots and sent to Durungu as replacements . . ."

Frank put his cup down quickly on his desk, so that the spoon rattled against the porcelain. Frank's fiftyish face turned a shade of alarm. "Can't do that, Milt," he said. "Besides the embargo G.D. set, all of our planes are out running our kids back to the schools down south . . ." Gregson remembered that the two-week Easter vacation had just finished.

"Alert them for first thing tomorrow morning then, okay?"

"Well . . . I guess so . . ." Frank looked as Charlie had, as if someone had just told him a bomb was somewhere in the building.

"And get on Joe Blayne at the airport," Gregson went on, Ted's wheeze next to him sounding like a sludge pump sucking on a mud-bank. "I want a shipment of Cessna parts heading for Durungu on those same planes tomorrow . . ."

"I'll have to have a signed release . . ."

"You'll have it!"

"So what kind of parts, Milt?"

"A double portion of every piece you got in Cessna stock over there, how's that for openers?"

"A double . . . ?" Gregson turned away to go back up the corridor and Frank yelled after him, "Who do I charge it to?"

"Operation Shoestring, what else?"

228

Ted now reached out and pulled on Gregson's arm, but Gregson kept on going. "Milt, what are you going to tell G.D.? He and Maddigan were up late last night talking about curtailing the Durungu operation . . ."

Gregson turned into the Field Policies and Procedures office. Edna Wright looked up at him politely, her sixtyish face cast in clean lines of wisdom and patience. Edna was the legal expert on all field policy procedures.

"Edna, cut me an order to go to all field superintendents on the compound," Gregson said. "It is to read that I am canceling Field Council sessions indefinitely on prerogative of Clause 490 . . . how much time do I have to work with on that clause?"

"One week," Edna returned without so much as a blink.

"Milt, are you—are you calling up the UFO?" Ted asked with a kind of moan riding his voice. "Milt, you're not calling up the UFO!"

"That's exactly what I'm doing, Ted," Gregson replied. "Edna, take care of the paperwork and see that the D.S.s get that order within the hour, okay?" Edna was already turning to her typewriter.

As Gregson turned to head back to his office, he saw Frank Mason and Charlie Bryan leaning their heads out their office doors, watching and listening, disbelief written on their faces. They ducked back in as Gregson moved back toward them. A few seconds later, the typewriters were snapping out the work. For Gregson, the freight was beginning to move out of the yards now, and he had to admit to a feeling of exhilaration as he held on to the throttle. How long he could hold it was a question, of course, but for now it was his; what would come later he refused to think about. But already he could hear someone on the telephone down the corridor in the direction of Frank Mason's office talking low but hurriedly. Was Frank telling his wife to start packing?

"Ted, get Durungu on the radio," Gregson went on, "and tell Blake what we're doing . . ."

"I can't get Durungu till noon," Ted countered in a kind of wounded tone. "Blake locks in his transmitter all morning to stay in touch with his pilots—"

"So get him at noon, then . . ."

"Milt." Ted continued his appeal. "G.D. won't stand for the UFO, of all things, on Blake. And the rest of the superintendents—"

"Did that fresh blood sample get down here from Durungu?" Gregson went on, moving into his own office now. "And the water?"

"We sent it to World Health already—"

"Get Doctor Yammanaka over there on the phone and tell him we suspect an epidemic building in Terragona and we need a report on that sample and if possible identification of the problem."

"You know that G.D. told me last night to contact Colonel Jamison at the U.N. helicopter base and ask him about the possibility of stand-by for evacuation of Terragona—"

"Don't put that through," Gregson said flatly.

"But—Milt, you can't fight G.D. like—like it's a kind of Indian wrestling—"

"I don't want anything going out of this office to the outside that even gives a hint we've got a panic on about Terragona. When Rayburn wants an evac he'll let me know through Blake." Ted swallowed, unable to respond, and Gregson added, "I want you to call the Hamaran Office of Mines and inform Felix Mentaya that we are no longer going to carry nitro into Terragona on our aircraft, as of today—"

"You'll shut everything down, Milt—"

"Maybe, maybe not. Last night I looked at the cargo charts and there's already twelve thousand pounds of nitro that we've delivered in there. Anybody in his right mind knows that a team of ten mineral prospectors can't use that much in five years just to prospect. I think the Premier would wonder about that."

"Mentaya will get nasty—"

"We'll just have to let him."

"You know how G.D. is about antagonizing rules like this, especially government—"

"I'll take that responsibility with Felix. You can tell G.D. in the meantime that I've called up the UFO and am appointing a commission to go to Durungu to hold court on the spot."

"You'll have to have pretty good reasons."

Gregson sighed and swiped at the bramble of his cowlick with his right hand. Ted's voice was trembling now as he began to see the shape of things, and the smell of the jungles was already too close. "And, Ted," Gregson went on, "I'm ordering you to keep everything under the lid in the next twenty-four hours on Blake or Terragona . . . do you understand that?"

Ted's eyes dropped to the floor, and he dug for a limp handkerchief to dab at the glistening patches of sweat on his forehead, around his mouth. Finally he reached into his shirt pocket and walked to the desk to toss the cable by Gregson's right elbow in a gesture that said, "Try this one if you dare."

Gregson opened it and read:

YOUR QUERY ALEX BELL STOP BELL DIED LEUKEMIA THREE WEEKS AGO STOP NO WORD LEFT ON MAN CALLED BLAKE STOP WILL CONTINUE SEARCH AND NOTIFY STOP Walker, Seaman's Mission, NY

"Well, that's that," Gregson said, feeling the cold hand of uncertainty grab him. He had counted on something positive coming from Bell to back his move on Blake. His one "gamble" had lost. Ted, sensing he might want to change his mind about the events he had set in motion here, waited. "If Renfro calls from Boston, let me know, Ted," Gregson concluded.

Ted knew there was no point in pursuing it. He hesitated another minute, wanting to make another appeal, then turned and walked out. But Gregson knew Ted would delay that phone call about the UFO as long as he could. He would hope Gregson would change his mind.

Now Gregson knew the weight of his decision was his. He heard the thunder roll in a staggering pitch outside. The first drops of rain were already on the windowpanes. He got up and went to the window to look out. The dark gray held no promise of anything but an all-day rain. He wondered if it was raining in Durungu. But it was Terragona finally that he thought about. He sensed the disaster building there, but he couldn't put his finger on the shape of it. And he felt helpless to know what to do. All he could finally do was to hang on as best he could to that thin hope—one man, one man's pluck, added to his own uncertain, staggering moves to cover for him. How long he could hold his own end here was questionable. Because even with the UFO, Merriweather would still hold the balance of power. "Lord," Gregson said out loud, "do it your way in the end . . . your way . . ."

It was at that same hour, early Wednesday morning, when the Hamaran stumbled into the hospital base at JERICHO. Collins got Rayburn out of surgery. When Rayburn got to the outpatient area, Trask and Alicia had gotten the mutilated body up on the examining table. Rayburn shut the door on the line of Terragonans waiting just outside, craning to see in. Even as he did so, he ordered the other two nurses, who had come running, to get back into surgery and wrap things up there.

They left, and he turned to the prospector on the table. There were over twenty spear holes in him. Rayburn went to work on him, but he knew there wasn't much he could do. Already the man was in a semiconscious state, and sliding fast.

"What happened?" he asked as he began to work the sutures over the gouging wounds.

Nobody said anything. Finally Collins offered, "All the poor man kept saying before he passed out was that Turgobyne's palace guard is killing off the Caha priesthood up there . . ."

Rayburn looked up at him quickly, noticing the paleness of his face now. "Killing?" He frowned toward Trask, looking for sign of contradiction. Trask instead looked resigned to the fact, his arms folded across his dirty white smock, peering at the face of the dying man with some clinical interest. "What about the prospectors?"

"Well, Barth just called in five minutes before this poor man stumbled in here," Collins went on. "Two prospectors were blasting near him. They were killed not more than a hundred yards from his back door."

"What for?" Rayburn put it to Trask again.

Trask shrugged. "I told you that was a possibility earlier," he said shortly. "What did you expect?"

"Since you asked," Alicia cut in from the other side of the table where she was checking the dying man's pulse, and Rayburn could see that it had gotten to her too, the frayed ends of her nerves tugging spasms at the corners of her mouth, "I would have expected that any man, Turgobyne included, who has any humanity at all would realize that you don't destroy sickness by killing the patient—"

"He's reacting the only way he knows how," Trask countered flatly. "Somebody has to be blamed, so it's only natural that the priests of Caha would get it for allowing the corruption—"

"Why the prospectors?" Rayburn asked, working the sutures swiftly, trying to project what this was all going to mean to them now.

Trask sniffed. "They've been blasting up there . . . the chief has no choice but to lay the blame on the foreign elements—"

"So we are next in line?" Collins put in. "After all, we're the ones who told him the lake was loaded—"

"How long was this fellow on the trail, do you think?" Rayburn asked.

"Well, he came in on the back of a bush cow . . . he kept saying the roof fell in last night . . ."

"Turgobyne had plenty of time to land on us, then," Rayburn came back, trying to get in an element of hope. "It may be he won't . . ."

"So why is he holding off?" Alicia asked.

She put the question directly to Rayburn, but it was Trask who said, "He still may think our miracle medicine will hold the popularity for him . . ."

"But he doesn't know that we've lost five people in here during the last twelve hours, all to that bacteria of yours," Alicia reminded him.

"News like that has already traveled up the line probably," Trask replied.

"And if you look outside, our popularity is fading fast," Alicia went on. "I don't think there are ten people waiting to get in . . ."

"I am not worried about the ones who died here," Trask came on again, "from that bacteria, I mean. It's the ones who have passed the crisis and are now moving into that totally new, strange and, frankly, terrifying dimension of personality emergence, quite unlike anything that resembles the human mode of behavior—"

"You sound worse than Dracula, Trask," Alicia snapped then, "or like maybe God is nowhere around—"

"All right, so let me tell you something, then," Trask fired back, his eyes going to narrow slits. "When those surviving patients reach that point of total mastery by the bacterial cycle, they're going to break what restraints we've got on them—and then I'll let you tell them to get some sense, because they are going to be murdering everything that is unlike themselves—"

"You know there is no such screwball space life," Alicia shot back. "If there was, God would have said something about it in the Scriptures! When those patients come out of it, they will be hungry, that's all, Trask. They will have recovered from a bug which is probably a rare strain of meningitis. Anyway, what would you have us do to them, kill them now before they unveil their new—their new personality, for crying out loud?"

"Okay, hold it down, you two," Rayburn warned. "Trask, is there any way to verify that Turgobyne is killing those people other than what this poor fellow said?"

"It's probably true," Trask said dogmatically, feeling quickly again under Alicia's barrage. "And that also means, if anybody survived that slaughter, they'll be heading for Doc Barth's and us for refuge. We're the closest of any of the northern bases."

"And Turgobyne's hit squad won't be checking in their weapons at the door when they follow them in," Collins added.

They waited on Rayburn then while the Hamaran began to give off staggering coughs in his breathing. Alicia reached over and held the oxygen mask over his face.

"What about the radio, Collins?" Rayburn asked, continuing to work the sutures.

"Well, I dunno . . . I put in that new condenser that Monk flew in yesterday. The transmission seemed stronger for a while in our earlier call to Durungu, but I doubt they got half of it. Something is cutting into our transmission, some stronger signal of some kind . . ."

"Keep working on it . . . we're going to have to depend on it in the next few hours." Alicia swabbed at the open wound he was working on. She looked at him and shook her head. The Hamaran was not going to make it. "Well," Rayburn went on, continuing to close up the jagged flesh anyway, "I better try to sum up the options here. For one, the logical thing to do would be to ask for an evacuation." He paused to let them think about that, not sure himself what he would do now. "But then, you already know that only an armed military escort could successfully get in here and get us out—and that would mean a deplorable end to everything here . . ."

"What about that lake?" Trask cut in immediately, intent now only on the one primary concern of his.

"Well, I really don't see how anything can be done with that lake, Trask—"

"You talked about trying to fire it with diesel—"

"The logistics are impossible, Trask. We'd have to get enough diesel in here to start with, then try to transport it to that lake, and you know we aren't allowed off this perimeter. Anyway, it's time we need right now, and firing Caha won't increase that in our favor . . . at least not now with what's happened up at that lake."

"So what's the point of sitting here at all, then, if we leave that lake to grow its own special brand of hell?"

"I have to wait for verification of that sample—"

"It probably only just got to Talfungo! That could mean a week or more!" Rayburn did not reply, so Trask added, "I'm warning you, Brad, that if the culture starts moving, and if we have to call a fire bomb to wipe out the island just to kill that bug to save the outside world from contamination, then how do we add that up?"

Rayburn looked down at the black flesh of the Hamaran on the table, the white powderpuff bandages standing out like truce flags asking for amnesty from death. He wanted to dismiss Trask's fears as ridiculous. And yet he had spent a few hours the previous night reading Morgan's space-chemistry text. It was too close to play with. And yet he had to entertain the one hope that Trask and Morgan were both wrong—or at least that what Trask claimed was wrong.

"I see your point, Trask," he said wearily. "But if I blast the sacred watercourse of the Terragonans on what I presume is at best a speculation, then I bring it all down on seventy-five people here in my charge. I'll have to call for evacuation before I decide to do that."

"Evacuate?" Trask countered sharply. "I thought you said once that we were going to hold on here come what may? You going to leave the Terragonans to fight this themselves?"

Rayburn did not pick up the argument. The weight of truth was on Trask's side. Though it was odd for Trask to be so argumentative on the basis of spiritual commitment all of a sudden, he was right. Rayburn stitched up the last of the Hamaran's wounds and stepped back to look at his work. Alicia and Collins did not comment, waiting on him instead. The options were not easy. Rayburn knew they were aware of the spear holes in the dying man on the table, deep, gouging slashes in the flesh as if he had been the object of some frenzied attack. They had to be thinking of what it was going to be like dying that way. And yet they had to appreciate Trask's wisdom too, that jumping out was no honorable way either, though the flesh would find it tempting right then.

"I'm going to sit tight for the next twelve hours," he finally said. "If we can hold that long, chances are we may go longer. By then maybe we'll have word from the World Health." He knew it was a cautious statement, maybe too cautious. He was playing it safe and close. To Trask, more than Alicia or Collins, it must have sounded like an attempt to stall in order to maintain the idealistic vision for Terragona Rayburn would not let go—to hold and anchor a base for Christianity at any cost. At this point there was nothing to leave, no Bible, no solidly Christian foundation, no converts. Trask, who never did agree with the ideal in the first place, would think the protecting of it now a bit ludicrous in light of the bacteria threat.

"Well, never turn your tail to the heat." Collins came in then, picking up the tone of things an octave, and Rayburn had to bless him for the timing of it, "because a blister there is hard to explain. That's what my daddy used to say." He paused to look at each of them, and scratched his close-cropped head, sensing he had spoken out of turn again. "Not very biblical, I guess, maybe too simple?"

"We love you anyway, Rick," Alicia commented dryly, but when Rayburn glanced up at her he thought he saw a trace of tears in her eyes.

"Well, you all know Blake has the message I sent about a deteriorating pattern in here," he went on, trying to stitch in some hope, but he knew the gesture was empty. Until he told Blake what he wanted, it would remain so, even as Trask had tried to tell him earlier. "In the meantime, Collins, get on the radio and inform the other northern bases in particular to be ready for possible refugees fleeing from Caha. Tell them"—and he paused, weighing it, wanting to be sure, conscious of all their eyes on him—"tell him to take in anybody who wants protection and treat any of them who are sick and to use tranquilizers or anything else they've got . . . also tell them to rig the fuses in the nitro boxes and if they see they are coming under attack, to get out and blow that nitro before the Terragonans get their hands on it . . ."

"Okay," Collins said. "Shall I tell Blake to drop the nitro on those flights now that the prospectors have had it?"

"No . . . Blake has to log the nitro weights every night with Hamara by radio . . . what's Hamara going to think when he tells them he's riding without it?"

"So they cut our flight plans?" Collins offered.

"Worse yet, they could get suspicious enough to jump in here for a look-see with helicopters full of marines—"

"Well, they're going to know something's up anyway," Collins argued. "Those prospectors sent out a signal every night to Talfungo by their own radio . . ."

"Voice transmission?"

"No . . . strictly Morse code all the way. And it makes no sense either, letters are all scattered . . ."

"Why would they do that?"

"Well, maybe one of their guys likes to play Scrabble with somebody back home," Collins quipped, and Alicia gave off with a groan. Collins grinned at her, then went on, "So what happens when the code doesn't go through today? The guy on the other end may be waiting for those new letters to make a triple-word score on his board—"

"They're bound to come and check anyway," Trask put in impatiently. "So let's get on with the problem of the lake while we have the time . . ."

"They won't jump right away," Rayburn went on, uneasy now about the fact of the prospectors communicating to the outside in Morse. "Talfungo will figure they had a breakdown or something and couldn't get through . . ."

"Which reminds me, Doctors—you, too, Alicia, dear—" Collins went on, "we've got a major sending and receiving problem of our own building up on a nasty weather front over Durungu . . . a lot of static electricity is shorting our transmission almost totally . . ."

"Is it on all channels?" Rayburn asked.

"Well, funny thing, I picked up a ham operator east of Talfungo an hour ago, fairly clearly . . . but when I start to swing back toward Durungu it's hopeless . . ."

"We've never had a signal to Talfungo yet," Rayburn said.

Collins shrugged. "Weather can do that sometimes . . ."

"Keep trying," Rayburn returned. "Meanwhile, Collins, you better clean out that back shed to make room for refugees that may be coming out of Caha . . ."

"That means moving Blake's VW out," Collins replied.

"Good riddance," Alicia put in shortly.

"Okay, so I spent a lot of time putting that car together," Collins protested. "Now all I got left is the shell—"

"You won't get that now in the little Piper puddle-jumper of Monk's," Alicia countered.

"If Blake wants it here, he'll get it here. Anyway, who knows what Turgobyne might do for us once he sees that VW all in one piece? He could give us a medal, Royal Order of the Garter, or something?"

"More likely he'll tie it around your neck and dump you in Caha," Alicia retorted, trying to make a quip, but it came out flat.

Rayburn checked the pulse of the dying Hamaran again. Staring down at the eight or nine bandages covering the jagged holes, he wondered how many bodies were lying around like this up in Caha right now. He wished that he had not tried to get Turgobyne to shut down that lake. If he hadn't, maybe now those prospectors would still be alive. And in that instant he felt a sharp bolt of resentment toward Trask for his dogmatic conclusions about the unknown bacteria strain. And yet maybe it was because Trask had thrown in the bomb that jarred his own urge for a smooth ride to a medical missionary triumph then?

Alicia moved from the table to the door and then came back again. "They're all gone," she said simply, looking at Rayburn in some puzzlement. "Maybe they saw this poor man stumble in here bleeding and all . . . or maybe the word is out that we've lost our yellow bird magic?"

Trask turned then without a word and walked out of the room in a quick, catlike movement. He came back a minute later.

"All the patients back there are gone too," he said. "Except for the ones we got tied down in isolation, of course," and he sounded now as if he knew that was going to happen too.

"*All* the bed patients?" Rayburn asked in some awe. "Postoperatives?"

"All of them," Trask said. "Just us now . . . and twenty-two violent psychopaths plus what we can expect coming our way in the next few hours . . ."

"They'll die running with incisions hardly healed," Alicia protested, her hands hanging down helplessly at her sides.

"They figure they'll die quicker in here," Trask countered dogmatically.

Rayburn leaned his hands on the table, trying to take the weight that tore at his back muscles. He was conscious then of the terrible quiet, an eerie, almost uneasy silence.

Then he realized that the Hamaran on the table was dead.

Alicia took off her rubber gloves with a sound of tearing tape, almost derisive in commentary, dropped them into the can by her foot. She turned and moved out of the room without a word. Collins hesitated, sensing there was little he could do now, or say, and finally moved out mumbling something about the radio.

Rayburn took off his gloves slowly. Trask did not move, continuing to stand against the instrument table with his arms folded.

"So what are you thinking, Trask?" he began, even though he knew.

Trask hesitated. Then, "I think you know we have to get word out . . ."

"To Blake?"

"No, I mean you ought to pour every ounce of juice we got left in our power plant and try to wing it straight to Gregson in Talfungo . . . Blake doesn't have the equipment, he'd only have to try to get it from Gregson. And if the rumors are right about Blake's popularity in Talfungo, you know he couldn't borrow a cup of sugar from there right now. Gregson could maybe get a copter to Durungu . . ."

"You're so sure the fire will do it?"

Trask shrugged. "I'm ninety per cent sure, the ten per cent doubt is on how well whoever does it, does it. I'd trust Blake doing it, but will he be allowed to stay around for it in light of what's been going on? We will have to have a good burn on that lake, is what I'm saying . . ."

"You know that's going to pull the manhole cover down tight over us?"

Trask studied him carefully for a few seconds. "We pulled the manhole over us the day we landed in here, Brad. There isn't a missionary on this island—including your own staff here—who doesn't know it's Custer's Last Stand . . ."

"You should go out at least, Trask, and share your space discovery with the world of science . . . World Health ought to know about it . . ."

"Don't think I haven't been thinking about it," Trask returned. "But do I get it that way, leaving everybody else in here to die with the Terragonans?"

Rayburn did not respond to that. Finally, "Not much to show for it in the end, is there?"

"You mean no Bible in Terragonan, no church, no converts?"

"Something like that, yes . . ."

"I see nothing demeaning in dying to save an entire nation from extinction from an unknown bacteria strain . . ."

239

"What a way for a virologist to go, right, Trask?" Rayburn tried playing it light then, though he had no particular feeling for it.

"And not a surgeon's?" Trask came back.

Rayburn shrugged. "Well, maybe I had visions of a more glamorous death, I don't know . . ."

"Don't we all," Trask said shortly. After a pause, he went on, "If you need a rationale for it all, just remember God knew this place was going to get hit by this bacteria; so He sent us in to intercept it, trace it and kill it in its den. Thus we save Terragona and maybe the whole world . . ."

Rayburn looked up at him then, sensing a new discordant element suddenly. "The world?"

Trask ran a hand through his short hair and scratched his scalp, as if he were struggling now with something elusive.

"Well, I told you that lake was crawling," he went on, suddenly examining a fingernail on his right index finger. "And that sooner or later, if we let the epidemic get out of hand, some of those Terragonans would start running to the outside. Which would mean seeding the main traffic streams of the civilized world . . ."

Rayburn shook his head, refusing to come up to what he was hearing. "Trask, what are you talking about? The world?"

Trask took his time, playing it out for effect, and finally said, "I mean, Brad, that our lovely anesthetist, Sylvia Pratt, who came down sick yesterday? Well, her blood shows she's got the crud . . ."

Rayburn took a full minute to absorb the enormity of the statement, feeling something slide out from under him suddenly.

"Trask, you said the bug was not airborne contagion, that it was purely water contact—"

"I said I didn't know for sure, remember—?"

"Well . . . Trask"—and Rayburn found it hard now to keep his control—"what's the point of talking about a fire on Caha then if the people who survived Turgobyne's slaughter up there may right now be running to relatives or friends, carrying that bug that is airborne contagion? What—what good was it for Turgobyne to be told he had to shut down that lake and then for him to kill off those people—"

"Those survivors won't go anywhere but to us," Trask cut back sharply, sniffing in that disdainful way of his whenever anyone challenged his judgment. "And to the other northern bases. We're all they've got now, Brad. No relative or friend will take them in, the curse of Caha is on them. And I already told you the fire is necessary to kill that bug, which is half the battle in whipping any epidemic—"

"And the other half, Trask? What about the other half?"

"All right," and now Trask's nostrils were pinching and his eyes were going into those tight slits, his voice beginning to take on that element of invective, "so maybe we better start praying seriously about a fire on that lake *and* that Turgobyne's assassins get here in time to do in our patients back there before they break loose and make us do it!"

Rayburn studied him intently, not really sure yet what Trask was saying. "That's no way to stop an epidemic, Trask, and you know it . . ."

Trask shrugged. "Okay, so you want them running loose instead to seed the rest of the island? When you come right down to it, we can't even risk Turgobyne's executioners' coming in here doing the job, lest they get contaminated as well . . ."

"Is that all we can leave behind, then?" Rayburn cut in sharply. "After all this, that's the best we can do?"

"You got time now to debate the options?" Trask replied almost disdainfully. "That bug we got locked up in the back room isn't going to wait long, you can be sure!"

Rayburn didn't respond. He felt tired, worse now, the feeling of everything turning to jelly from his knees up. He took to walking around the small room slowly, arms folded, his eyes on his feet. Finally he stopped at the table again, frowning at the torn flesh of the body there.

"How much time do you think we have?" he asked, shifting gears now, realizing there really wasn't time to debate it.

Trask shrugged. "I don't know how soon Turgobyne's palace guard will get here . . . but as to our patients out back, some of them are ready to break the barriers anytime. But it's hard to say . . . an hour, two, maybe twelve . . . our supply of tranquilizers is down to nothing, and I don't know how long that brain in there is going to stay under to that stuff. I imagine the other northern bases are facing the same thing. If we get a rush on refugees out of Caha now, we could be in a mess . . . either way, time is the factor now, yes . . ."

Rayburn ran his right hand over his face, rubbing at his burning skin and eyes. "We'll ask Blake to run in more drugs on the flights," he said simply.

"And the lake?"

Rayburn hesitated. He glanced at Trask again, noting the sharp lines of intensity in his face. For Trask it was all that mattered, that lake, regardless of the consequences. But, of course, he did not have to live with the decision; he owned the luxury of finally being detached when it was done. And yet, on the other hand, maybe he had the most to lose too. He had made a discovery, if it was finally proved he was right, of unprecedented significance to science. He had every right to ask to go out—instead he was willing to stay and take whatever came with the rest of them. Rayburn could hardly deny him on that count.

"I'll ask Collins to try to get through to Talfungo," he said. "If he gets through to Durungu I'll tell him to inform Blake as well. It'll take some time even then, you know that. Gregson has a Field Council on this week with a lot riding on the line. He won't be quick to mount a fire team for us, you can be sure . . . he knows what that can do to us too . . ."

Trask said nothing more. Then he turned and moved for the doorway to go back to his lab. He hesitated there, looking back at Rayburn. "Sometimes it costs more to love than to make war, right, Brad?" Just a trace of a thin smile came across his small mouth, and before Rayburn could comment, he was gone.

Rayburn looked down at the torn body of the Hamaran again, then pulled the sheet up slowly over the face. Then he walked out into the corridor and caught Collins just heading down toward the radio room.

"Rick, did you rig the fuses in those nitro boxes?" he asked.

Collins nodded. "All set, except I have to run the hot line outside so you can blow it from out there—"

"I want all doors bolted and shutters battened down on the windows," Rayburn said.

Collins looked at him closely. "You going to crash-dive it?"

Rayburn looked at the floor. "I'll let you know later, Rick . . . don't panic anybody. And try to get Talfungo on the radio . . . let me know when you do . . ."

Collins hesitated as if he wanted to add something. Then he simply nodded and turned and walked on down the corridor, which was strangely quiet now with no patients in the wards. Rayburn glanced at his watch. It was 11:10.

Rudy ate a sandwich before taking off for Myagunde. It was 11:15 A.M. Gina came out of the kitchen while he was eating, noting that his baseball cap and sunglasses were still on, flecks of egg salad on his upper lip. He did not look up at her, intent only on eating, as if it was a necessary chore to finish.

"What are you going to do about him?" she put it to him straight on.

"Who?" He played it dumb, chewing slowly, studying his eaten sandwich as if he wasn't sure what was in it.

"The man, who else?"

"Blake?" She did not answer, studying the sun-beaten leather of his face, which was cast in shadow like an eclipse from those sunglasses. "What do you want me to do, Gina?"

"Well, it's obvious the man is going to destroy every living thing here. I should think you'd see that yourself and move accordingly to assume command. I'm sure Gregson would be relieved. Anyway, you've been with him long enough—"

"That's right, all of three years now," he came back, still chewing, not looking at her, his voice riding a dull, flat edge. "So I guess I know Blake better than most . . ."

"So?"

"Do you know him, Gina?" and he took a sip of coffee quickly.

"Nobody knows him. I doubt certainly that God does. That's the problem, isn't it?"

"You really want to finish him, don't you, Gina?"

"Don't exaggerate the terms, Rudy, please." Rudy did not answer. "You simply won't admit what you know to be true—he's out of joint here, Rudy, he doesn't own one identifiable image of the faith—"

"Maybe God doesn't cut the cloth to fit everybody the same."

"You're covering for him again, Rudy."

Rudy shrugged. "I figure that's the least I can do."

"He defied Felix Mentaya!"

"Ask the African mechanics over in the hangars about Felix . . . even his own people don't trust him . . ."

"He's still government as far as the mission is concerned, Rudy . . ."

"And Blake handled him quite well, I thought, completely in line with a government request . . . anyway, Blake has every right to check it back with the Premier's office. Beyond that, he figures his word to Turgobyne counts more anyway . . ."

"The Scriptures warn about binding ourselves to an oath to an unbeliever. And promising that VW car to him—"

"Now you sound like the Reverend Mr. Thornhill," and Rudy tried to smile but it got lost in the shadow of his sunglasses.

"You know what he'll do in the end, Rudy," she went on. "He'll sell himself to the highest bidder out there just to fulfill those stupid promises. Then where are we? Where is the mission? Where is God?"

"Well, God will be in Terragona, that's for sure," Rudy returned, his voice light. Gina turned her back to him to look out the window across the field. "Look, Gina," Rudy went on, "it's taken a lot for him to refuse their offers already, especially when we're short of everything just to keep operating—"

She turned quickly and sat down opposite him, trying to reach out to him with the rightfulness of her position. "Rudy, you're just as worried as the rest of us . . . don't sit there with such perfect aplomb as if all is right in this world!"

He reached out by her hand and took a toothpick from the holder there and began digging at his teeth as he looked at her, not sure what he was after.

"Did you put my fudge on?" he asked, and she blinked at him, not comprehending how that fit the conversation.

"It's cooling."

"Better hurry it up, I'm off to Myagunde in fifteen minutes." She didn't move though, and he didn't seem eager to push her. He put the bent toothpick down and leaned his elbows on the table, reaching up to dig a finger in his right ear. "Okay, Gina, I'm worried, but not about the things you are." He gave her a quick smile, trying to be easy on her. "I'm more worried about what Blake thinks about the rest of us, us purebred saints. He's trying to play this by the rules he set up with Turgobyne, the honorable game—"

"Rules without the consent of his mission—"

"Maybe so. But there weren't many people willing to advise him in those early days, Gina. All anybody cared about then was that he get into Terragona—"

"Honorable? You call his way honorable? Honor for whom? For himself! He wants this all played his way, nobody else's. I think you know that too!"

"That's all you know, Gina?"

"That's what I see!"

244

"In three days, you got it all figured out? I've been here three years watching this thing develop, watching Blake, and I still can't be so sure as that—"

"The Spirit of God, Rudy, just listen to the Spirit of God, the discerner of the thoughts and intents of the heart."

"Yeah, well, sometimes I don't sleep good, I have to admit," he came back mildly, resting his chin on his fist. "Sometimes I find myself running down a long tunnel with doors on either side. I try the doors, nobody answers. The headshrinkers would say I'm looking for answers to questions I ask all day. Maybe. Maybe I'm looking for the things in Blake everybody else is—what Augie felt he had to have to prove Blake, what Gregson looked for, what you think. We got to have it all spelled out on the chalkboard—"

"It's the rule of our life, Rudy," she insisted. "Why should we expect him to be different? Is he something special?"

He pondered that a minute. "You know what I really wanted to ask you when I sat down here to eat?" and she felt a pocket of sweat on her upper lip, but didn't know why. "I wanted to ask you to help me prepare him for the big theological exam Talfungo Field Council will put to him pretty soon. All he needs is a crash course in the right definitions—"

"Is that all, Rudy? You think that's all it is?" and she got up again to walk to the window.

"Look, that's all anybody wants right now," he appealed to her. "The right words . . . he never went to school, seminary or anything like that, so he doesn't know the terms—"

"And what about experience? Does he know God, Rudy, that's the critical point!"

"Did you ask him?"

"No, did you?"

"I never felt I needed to."

She turned to look at him. "Why not?"

He shrugged. "Well, I figure for any man to come out to this place he has to be driven by something other than vocational guidance." She didn't bother to give him a reply on that, it was far too inadequate. Rudy sensed it too. He sighed. "Besides, this place is a divine miracle when you stop to look at it. And a big part of it is through Blake's sweat and a strange way of making old airplanes run and kid pilots fly—"

"Come on, Rudy!" she cut back at him. "The devil himself could put it all together in the same way, and you know it! The man hasn't the foggiest notion about spiritual posture and the necessities of devotional habit and prayer! So don't try to get him off the hook with his aeronautical genius and certainly not with a theological cram course . . ."

He studied her for a minute and said, "That's what robs you of your beauty, you know that, Gina?" She turned away from him quickly to stare out the window, feeling a flush burn her ears, boil to the roots of her hair. "You are beautiful, Gina, but it's hid under all that legal complex. You got the rulebook straight, Gina, but love is lost on page eight hundred of Appendix Z—"

"Don't preach to me, Rudy," she countered, her voice cold and sharp. "You are smoke-screening for him again. To answer your original question about him, I won't be a part of any collusion to further the spiritual camouflage over him. It is both unspiritual and unethical—"

"And unloving?"

"I don't make love cover for justice—"

"And what does law cover, Gina?"

"It keeps us from being phony!"

"Well, there's a pilot out there named Slater who'd give you quite an argument about how phony Blake is, especially after what the big man did to get that crippled airplane off his back—"

"You are confusing the issue," Gina retorted flatly.

Rudy had no comment for that. He paused to listen to the airplane engine running up outside. He got up and put his cap on. "How about that fudge?"

She went into the kitchen, got the pan and came back out to put it on the table in front of him with quick, decisive moves.

"It's not hard yet," he said, looking down at it. He dipped a finger into it, put it to his lips like a boy sneaking a dip of cake batter. "You know, one time I went home—you know what they say about never being able to go home again—I went home anyway ten years ago as a new Christian to celebrate Yom Kippur with my parents. I just wanted to let them know I loved them and that my following Christ didn't change that. But you know, my daddy didn't know me, refused to know me—he looked at me like I was a vacuum-cleaner salesman. They buried me two years before, you see, in effigy kind of, but not in the Jewish cemetery. I was dead to them the day I chose Christ, and Jewish ground was too good for me. But I'll tell you, Gina," and he dipped his finger into the fudge again, sucking it gingerly, "you don't know how it feels to be in your own house where they don't even ask you—your own people—to hang your hat." He paused again, listening to that airplane engine. "I think that's the way Blake feels —after three years of pouring out his guts here, nobody has yet asked him to put his shoes under the bed. So . . . love is harder to fulfill than the law, Gina. But if you ever get the order straight, you'd be hard to beat . . . hard to beat."

He got up, took off his sunglasses and gave her a quick wink, and headed for the door. Suddenly she felt a terrible sense of pressure in her chest, and she said, "Rudy?" He paused at the door, digging for a stick of gum in his jacket pocket. "How far is it to Myagunde?"

"Five hundred miles or so."

"You'll be coming back tomorrow, then?"

He grinned, folded the stick of gum into his mouth, put his sunglasses back on. "Nope. Got a schedule to keep in Terragona tomorrow. Be back sometime tonight, Gina, depending on the winds."

"In this kind of weather? Why don't you wait until tomorrow—"

"Got a flight on for Terragona tomorrow, remember? Anyway you forget I have the best homing beacon in aviation up there in the tower, and he doesn't miss very often. But light a candle for me just in case and add a prayer, okay, Gina?"

She stayed there by the table, feeling the peculiar prickling chill up her legs and running up her spine. "And while you're at it," he called back to her through the screen door, "say one for Blake too—if you can bend the law a little! And maybe Gregson too—he's in a squeeze himself right now. Keep the fudge on, Gina!"

She didn't go out to watch him take off. She sat at the table and sipped coffee, waiting, listening to his engine build and then come marching down on her, going over the dining room with a swishing sound that shook the room. The quiet came again—and the wet, gray heat. The fudge in the pan in front of her was taking on a wrinkling hardness, freezing the shape of Rudy's finger.

She grabbed up the pan quickly and hurried back into the kitchen to put it into the small icebox. Then she heard the thunder again, a reverberating bounce off the sky. Ebenezer looked up at the ceiling, pausing in his work with the bread dough, his eyes big.

Felix Mentaya leaned against the hangar door peering out at the eerie afternoon darkness, sniffing at the damp wind, sensing the mounting charge of the elements. Lightning slashed at ground level in bolts of blue that hissed with power. The thunder that followed slammed with meteorlike force into the earth, shaking it, making the hangar tremble with the vibrations.

He pulled back in to gain the partial protection of the hangar doorframe. He was not fully emancipated as yet from the strange mixture of nature, the peculiar powers mustered there in one long charge against earth. The gods of his childhood still hung in the empty rooms of his spiritual cave, faces to the wall maybe, but there nevertheless. In times like this, they would crowd him, remind him, warn him, not to ignore his ancestral spirits. Though he gave no credence to those voices, he felt some fear yet, though he reminded himself that he had dumped all such superstitions at the Cathedral of Notre Dame. Even the Christian God had gone that way. Religion in any form was a detriment to his political destiny. The Party had drilled him long in that. And yet the dual dimensions of this unusual weather, together with Blake, seemed to jolt him, put him in inner disarray.

"When it does rain finally, we'll need an ark," Belang commented in an offhand way from behind him where he sat on a pile of old burlap bags. There was always the sound of smothered laughter in Belang's voice. It irritated Felix. Why did he need him anyway? He seemed more in sympathy with Blake than with the Cause, and in the end could prove to be a liability.

Felix did not respond immediately. "The fool," he finally said, almost shouting it to the wind, staring across the field toward the tower. "The field will wash away, and he sits over there thinking he can bluff me! Have you put the pilots to painting our planes?"

"No, Blake insisted his mechanics do it—"

"To stall for time, of course."

"Well, do you want to fight him on it?"

Mentaya said nothing, deciding to let it go.

"We will go in the morning, without the signatures," he finally said.

"Blake is the key man here, you know that. That man Gregson doesn't count in the end. The Premier dealt with Blake on this operation. If anything should go wrong in Terragona and if the Premier figures out that those papers of yours are a forgery of his signature—"

"Shout it to everyone while you're at it!" Felix turned to snap at him. "Whoever named you Information Officer named you well, monsieur!" He turned to the doorway again. "Besides, Blake will sign . . ."

"Maybe—"

"No maybe! He has nothing left here—nothing! When the rain comes, he will run here to sign. He will not want to be stuck with the lives of his own people and ours . . ."

"You said he would not have flyers today after what you told them about him," Belang reminded him in that slightly mocking tone. "Still they went, wheel housings and all. He may be a flea of the first order, Felix, but that took a bit of doing—and any man who can turn down Texas Oil, American Borax and the Japanese Trade Commission, especially the way he's hurting in here—"

"I am warning you for the last time!" Felix turned on Belang again, who had taken off his left shoe and sock and was examining his big toe carefully. "He will yield," Felix went on, taking to walking back and forth in quick strides in front of Belang. "I know his kind. I spent ten years with missionaries, don't forget. They will pray just so long, and when there is no sign of divine miracle they choose the next most expedient route . . ."

"You ought to know, Felix," Belang commented, but not with any conviction. "But I doubt Blake and God have the same arrangement . . ."

Felix stopped his pacing abruptly to stare at Belang, who kept his eyes on his big toe, then turned and walked back to the hangar door to lean against it to watch the wind and clouds building up. He was not really that sure of Blake either. The uncertainty made him feel exposed. There was more to this than just getting that signature, though Belang did not know that. He had no idea how that figure of Miss Drew walking that mile and a half to his campfire every night just to coach him in math could hang on to his brain. That old woman with tired, gray eyes and white boiling hair and a stoop to her shoulders. In his long journey from God, he had never been able to completely destroy that image of her drawing those equations in the smooth sand around the fire and smiling as he put the answers underneath with a stick.

No, he had never fully been able to bury Miss Drew . . . He tried that day, a year after he had returned from London, fully committed to politics. He faced her in the dusty yard of that orphanage with the papers he had worked six months to get, authorizing him to give her 150,000 francs in government subsidy as a part of the new national socialism. She simply stood there looking small and frail, the orphanage falling in, her orphans in rags, the school sagging. She lifted her head, looked beyond him and said, "No, thank you, we will manage quite well as God provides."

As God provides! A year later that orphanage killed her! He had sat by her deathbed, then, almost willing her to die, to be free forever of her, watching her mouth sag open, her eyelids turn purple. And only once she opened those eyes, studied him a long time and then said, "Don't sell your soul to the highest bidder, Felix, give yourself to God . . ." Suddenly, then, he couldn't let her die! He argued, shouted, swore and finally fell by her bed pleading to let him go. She didn't. She was dead.

So here it was again! Like Miss Drew had risen again to taunt him. Blake! How dare he keep the world waiting here as if he had jammed a chair up against the door! Was he, Felix Mentaya, to have one more God-figure to taunt him and haunt him?

No. He would not go on with that. He would die first! Tomorrow he would make his move. He would go without the signature then. Faber had warned him not to move without all the corners tucked in. He insisted that the penetration to Terragona be done as under Hamaran Government sanction. Those signatures, all of them, would prove the point and show the world that it was not an act of deliberate aggression. And yet Faber also warned him not to delay if there were any hitches to his getting into Terragona with the guns . . . the timetable had to be kept. The prospectors inside Terragona were getting nervous. And the Chinese warned that they wanted Terragona at any cost.

So what did Blake matter, then? Felix had enough on paper with Gregson's signature under the forged one of the "boy king." So now why did he stand here a victim of Blake's arrogance like all those other fools? Only the color of his airplanes held him now . . . he had not anticipated that technicality. He couldn't chance dropping into Terragona at the main hospital base with any jarring element. So it would have to be in the morning, then . . . and at last his dream of political ascendancy would be realized!

And yet he could get no sure sense of satisfaction in that now. He hated himself for it. But Faber could not know what it meant to have a haunting God image crowding his sense of political destiny. Blake had to yield! Otherwise he was stuck forever with Miss Drew! How stupid it all seemed! But nobody understood this kind of thing—nobody!

He felt the wind gust again. "The wind will talk the will of the gods," his mother had told him. "The wind bloweth where it listeth, and thou hearest the sound but canst not tell whence it cometh or whither it goeth . . . so is everyone that is born of the Spirit." Miss Drew had made him memorize that well. But he knew how the wind blew, always at his back, carrying him to power! That's where he intended to keep it!

He turned and stared at the empty shell of the VW sitting in the corner looking like a head without a body. Like that damn piece of junk there, that's how he would have Blake in the end, and Miss Drew and even God! Yes, even God!

He glanced again at Belang, who was smiling around that long cigar as if he knew all that was going on in Felix's mind.

"We should have taken that high-powered radio out of that man's green truck out there," Belang said then. "We could be monitoring just about everybody's calls and even that satellite—"

"Shut up, you fool!" Mentaya snarled at him. Slowly he turned back to the field again. Belang would have to go too, sometime before tomorrow. He did not have to carry that swine into Terragona! Or . . . if he did, it maybe would be easier to do it in Terragona . . . yes! Now it was just a matter of time . . . but not too much . . .

Ted Cranston took his time calling Merriweather, as Gregson figured he would. Ted would hold out to the last, hoping Gregson would change his mind about the UFO. Even then, G.D. should have heard about it, the way the rumors were flying. But the Director was in caucus all morning with Maddigan, so it wasn't until 11:30 that Ted finally got to him.

He came straight into Gregson's office like a tidal wave, pushing everything aside. Ted quietly slid in behind him, ducking for a neutral corner.

"It is true then, Milt?" he began, shoving the door shut with his left foot. No pleasantries today for the older man. There were color marks high on both cheeks, under the blue eyes that held a polished luster.

"About the UFO? Yes, G.D."

The older man moved into the room slowly, his eyes on the floor as if he were examining it for hidden flaws.

"You could have told me, Milt. I mean pulling the UFO is a last-ditch, desperate kind of move . . ."

"It was all *I* had, G.D. I felt I had to have the proper legislative backing to get that gasoline moving—"

"We would have moved that gasoline in plenty of time, Milt. We weren't about to cut it off completely. You didn't need to call up the UFO for that . . ."

"It wasn't only that, G.D. I felt I had to keep Blake in the operation up there, and the UFO was the only way . . ."

"Then you must have a good report on him to substantiate the move?"

"That's just it, G.D., I don't."

"Then, what . . . ?"

"I know he's probably out of line, and maybe he should be removed. But I feel strongly, for some reason I can only charge to God in me, that I must give him the time to finish the job before the rains . . ."

"And you know it is the strong feeling among the field superintendents that God is now judging us for what we've allowed to happen in Durungu, all those deaths, don't you see?" the older man came back, his voice sounding perplexed.

"There's the other side of it too, G.D., that God may be judging us for putting it together with secondhand equipment and laying the whole burden on Blake," Gregson replied, and he got up to stand behind his swivel chair, using it as a shield. He never was good at arguing with Merriweather sitting down.

Merriweather blinked at him, as if he did not understand. "It sounds to me as if you don't know the latest on Blake," he said, and he turned to Ted, frowning. "Have you given him that cable, Ted?"

Ted came forward shakily, fumbling in his shirt pocket and coming up with the yellow cable, giving Gregson an agonized look, as if the final sentence had been passed. Gregson took it and read it quickly:

FAA CHECK ON BLAKE STOP BLAKE CRASHED
GLOBAL JET OUT OF KENNEDY 1968 STOP HE ONLY

SURVIVOR STOP RULING PILOT ERROR REPEAT PILOT ERROR STOP MORE LATER STOP—Renfro.

"How long have you had this?" Gregson asked aimlessly of Ted. "It came about an hour ago . . . I was going to bring it in, but . . ." Ted did not finish it.

Gregson put the message back on the desk top. Nobody said anything. Gregson finally turned and walked to the window to stare out at the gray drizzle. All Gregson felt now, besides the weight of the message itself, was that he had really met Blake for the first time. All the other contacts with him were mere shadows, wispy shapes. Suddenly the man was fully cast in bold relief against the tangled landscape of his role in Durungu. PILOT ERROR? This was no time for that to land on Blake, certainly not here at this precise moment! Whatever point he had now for his UFO was pretty well flattened out, nothing more than a legislative dodge.

"That puts your UFO a little after the fact, doesn't it, Milt?" Merriweather appealed then.

"Because of his past?" And Gregson knew it was futile to try to keep up the defense now. "God knows all about our pasts—"

"You want to tell that to the Reuters News Agency man who has been camped on my step for two days?" G.D. snapped back. "The word is out, Milt, and he's going to get it like everybody else. Maybe you want to tell that to Thornhill, who has lost all he's got up there at Durungu? You think Maddigan will buy that, or the Field Council?"

"So maybe Blake needs us now more than ever . . ."

"And when his pilots find out," G.D. went on, "what will happen then? He can't lead them after this, if he ever did really . . . but even if there was a chance he could, it would be a cruelty on our part to demand that he do it, right?"

"I believe the Lord has forgiven him," Gregson went on doggedly. "I'm afraid the Lord won't forgive me if I don't allow him to make his journey complete."

Merriweather did not respond to that. He finally sighed heavily and then went on in a businesslike tone, "You know then, Milt, that in the light of the circumstances here, what you are forcing on me now," and he was still carrying appeal in his voice too. "You know that the constitution of this mission provides emergency powers for the General Director whenever any field executive action constitutes a case of clear and present danger to the spiritual health and survival of the order. Unless you withdraw the UFO and allow the Field Council to take necessary and fitting action on Blake—and it is incomprehensible to me that you insist on so drastic a move on a situation and a person so miscast for leadership—then I have no other course but to assume those powers and relieve you as field director . . ."

Gregson turned slowly, rested his hips on the window sill and folded his arms, staring down at his shoes. Well, there it was. G.D. knew the bylaws better than anyone. And, of course, he had the weight of truth on his side. And yet, as Gregson sat there pondering it, he could hear the clatter of noise coming from the outer offices. The freight was rattling along at full steam now. New orders were being cut, his orders. There was a kind of excitement building out there. If he threw the brakes, reversed himself on the UFO, he would tear up a lot of track. God only knew why he felt this way about Blake, and he could only hope God would reveal it to him before too much longer . . . but right now, he knew he had to work for time, to hold Blake in the operation regardless.

He rose off the sill and walked to the chair again, stopped behind it. "Don't make me do it, Milt, don't put me into this kind of spot," G.D. pleaded with him. "Think of the larger picture, the mission, the people at home who are going to have every right to ask why. If, God forbid, Terragona should tear apart, we will have to own up to keeping Blake in command . . ."

"People at home may be more compassionate than we think, G.D.," Gregson replied wearily, although he knew it would be hard on the older man if that did occur.

"But this is hardly the issue on which to test that, is it, Milt?"

Gregson waited a long minute again and then said, "I have to stand by the UFO, G.D.—"

"Don't throw away your leadership, Milt!"

"Up to now I haven't displayed much, G.D., and you know it, so does everybody else around here. Beyond all that, I'm thinking about Blake in this. He must have had a little bit of hell himself up there, trying to face up to his past, people dying on him—"

"Milt, you know that the long haul does not allow us to coddle any one individual who stands in the way of the will and purposes of God!"

"Like you once said, G.D. I was always the short-haul adminis-

254

trator, and maybe that will be my undoing here now when it's done."

Again there was that moment of heavy silence. Gregson did not look up at him. "Then you are aware of what it all means to you?" Merriweather finally said, his voice heavy now.

"As I remember it," Gregson said, sitting down in his chair now, knowing it didn't matter anymore, "it will take forty-eight hours for Boston to clear your suspension of me. I'll take that time as my bid to hold Shoestring together in its most critical hour."

Merriweather simply stared at him, disbelieving even yet, those pink spots on his cheeks rising to full red, then draining off. The boyish façade had yielded to the tearing mudslide of reality, gouging, ripping away at the mask to leave the stark erosion of time. In that moment, Gregson sensed that the older man had gone through his own long night of indecision over Blake, even about the continuance of the operation.

Then the older man took off his glasses in a slow, almost painful movement and ran his right hand over his eyes. "I do not consider myself a man lacking in compassion," he began, his voice almost meditative, even groping. "God knows I have been careful not to hurt a single hair of any man's head under my charge in forty years, even when I have had to serve justice. And God knows that includes Blake now too, do you understand that, Milt?" Gregson nodded at the floor. "So now I have to believe that what you have done in this single act on his behalf must stand unless proven wrong. And I will convey that to the Field Council too. You are my man even yet, Milt, remember?" Gregson did not look up at him, for he caught those tones of appeal there, and in that moment he would rather have yielded toward him, wanting his blessing, sensing the deep love he felt for the older man as the gulf began to widen between them. Then, Merriweather cleared his throat, straightened his shoulders and added, "At any rate, you have called it your way, so we will have to live with it, Milt. You have picked your commission for Durungu, and when do we go?"

Gregson wanted a mint. He knew it was final now, the argument ended, the mold fully cast. He named the seven-man commission, including G.D., suggesting that perhaps Thornhill should go too. G.D. nodded.

"Will he be ready?" he asked.

"Not until tomorrow . . ."

"Then we go tomorrow," he said shortly. "You better notify Blake.

And I'm going to insist on two other things, Milt; one, I want Durungu shut down tomorrow, all operations, while we convene the investigation. I want those pilots on hand for questioning. Second, I am going to call Colonel Jamison of the U.N. and alert him for possible evacuation . . ."

Gregson opened his mouth to argue the point. It was all too premature to alert the U.N. But he sensed that the older man needed that for the record now too—because he alone perhaps would have to stand against the pressures of inquiry at home later on.

Gregson shrugged and found his handkerchief to blow his nose. He still did not look up at G.D., not wanting to view the broken ties that had held them together these years. The older man hesitated. Then, his voice sounding weary, he said, "May the Good Lord overrule whoever is wrong in this, Milt." Then he turned and went out.

Ted coughed once in the silence that followed, smothering it quickly as if it might sound irreverent in the heavy atmosphere.

"Ted, are those gas trucks rolling?" Gregson asked.

Ted paused, not able to shift gears that fast. "Well . . . it's taken time to get it all straightened out with supply. G.D.'s order had to be countermanded, and I wasn't sure how things would come out here—"

"I want those trucks rolling right now."

"Well . . . they can't really get far today anyway, Milt, with the weather closing in and on those roads up north . . ."

"They better be in Durungu by tomorrow morning when I get there, Ted, is that understood?"

Ted cleared his throat painfully. "Sure, Milt, just as you say . . ." Gregson looked up at him, felt again that pang of compassion for him. Ted had tried to hold things off here, keep the message about Blake from him . . . there was in that single act some kind of gesture, feeble as it was, so Gregson said: "Get some coffee, Ted . . . and . . . maybe later around three you might want to join me in prayer about this . . ."

Ted looked at him quickly, a bit surprised. They hadn't prayed together in a long time. He hesitated, as if he wanted to say more, then simply nodded and went out of the room, his harsh, fitful cough following him down the corridor.

Gregson sat there a long minute staring at the desk top, then turned slowly in his swivel chair until he was facing the map of Terragona on the wall. He was trembling yet, feeling the full force of the encounter with Merriweather. He counted the blue pins that indicated the mission hospital bases, adding up the totals of people there again. He had altered the diameter of the circle, hopefully on their behalf. In so doing he had also cut the circumference of his own here in Talfungo. The price of administrative decision, even in a spiritual order, was high, higher than he thought. And even now, on top of that, he was not fully free of doubt. Merriweather's arguments were strong and rightful. He had exposed himself for a man who now carried almost hopelessly crippling credentials on the points that should matter the most to a mission administration. He wondered how long it would take for Blake's pilots to find out about that pilot error . . . well, maybe the radio problem was a blessing in that sense . . .

He heard a knock on the door and said, "Come!" The man who poked his head through the half-open door had curly black hair, probing brown eyes against a black face.

"I am Albert Banqui," he said as if he had just driven up in a Cadillac. "I am from the Reuters News Agency. Dr. Merriweather said you would have answers for me on the Terragona operation."

Gregson sensed then the first move of G.D. to put the full responsibility in his lap. "Come on in and sit down," he said. Banqui sat down in the wicker chair in front of the desk, crossing his legs. Gregson sensed no ready friendship in those brown eyes which seemed to say "the whole world is watching." But he detected no deliberate hostility either.

Well, the hour of truth was at hand. So be it! Better to manage the news than to have it come out from under a rock. He hoped! But he knew it was not going to be easy, even as Banqui took out his notebook.

# CHAPTER XI

Blake came out of his sleep in a slow climb through cotton fuzz, peeling his way through it layer by layer until he felt his body as a solid thing in the chair. The sweat had soaked his khaki shirt through. The remnants of flame and smoke hung in his brain like the burning rafters of a barn. He was staring at the radio transmitter, the one red eye of POWER-ON staring back at him like some solitary vestige straight out of hell. Time and place remained alien forces around him. The room seemed tilted, loaded with blurring shapes.

Then he heard it. Short, stabbing notes like a bird sensing the enemy close at hand? He listened, slanting his head sideways to the angle of the room. Bleep . . . five counts . . . bleep . . . five counts . . .

He shook his head, fighting off the cotton that kept wrapping strand after strand of gummy punk around his brain. He reached out his left hand and touched the frequency dial. It stayed there . . . the steady, perfectly timed signal coming strong off the Terragona band.

When did that come on? How long was it jabbing him here, calling to him as he slipped deeper into the well of exhaustion? He wanted to go back to that cotton fuzz, that protective layer that would seal him off from any more of the problems here. That signal held no reprieve for him, he knew it. It had to be the final confirmation of all that he had put together in his mind the last few torturous hours. It was again the final, mocking enlistment of him to lay his hand to death. He listened again, rubbing his right hand over his face, feeling the grease of the sweat, tasting the salt of it. He wanted to refuse that sound, ignore it, but it continued with a kind of throbbing pain, firing jolts deep into his brain.

He leaned forward, pulling his sweat-soaked shirt off the back of

258

the chair with the sound of a long tear. The dials of his wristwatch swam up to him. It was fifteen after three. Sometime, how far back, he had sat down here waiting for the Talfungo transmission which was due around noon. It had never come, lost in the garbled weather build-up. He had swung back to Terragona frequency again, hoping Rayburn might be trying to get through. All he had there was that jarring signal, jamming anything else that might be coming through. Finally he had swung off to try to raise Rudy, who was flying the southeasterly leg to Myagunde, to check on him in the weather build-up. He didn't get Rudy . . . but he got that other thing . . . that other transmission that had to be Collins' voice trying to raise Talfungo . . . So now he looked down at the shaky block letters he had written down off that transmission . . .

REQUEST PETROL FIRE ON CAHA . . . URGENT . . . CANNOT CONTAIN EPIDEMIC WITHOUT IT . . . SUGGEST YOU GET COPTER FOR THE JOB, NOTIFY BLAKE . . .

There had been no reply from Gregson. Not yet. He had waited on that frequency . . . and then he had fallen into the doze, sliding into the hole, pulling the cover of darkness over his head. But the vision of fire and smoke came anyway. And there were faces hanging over it now, faces he didn't recognize, some he did . . . like Rayburn and Collins . . . hanging up there in midair without bodies, like balloons on strings . . .

Now he got up from the chair, feeling dizzy, the mush coming into his knees. He stared at the frequency, wondering if Gregson had replied during the time he was out . . . he reached down and twirled over to the Talfungo frequency, tried to raise them . . . only that maddening static and the leftovers of that steady, beating signal. He came back on the other Myagunde channel, held it there . . . would Gregson clear a fire on Caha? Should he try a relay through Bungari to get to Gregson in Talfungo? He didn't really want to talk to Gregson then . . . He didn't want to be told he had to lay that fire . . . and yet it had to be laid. He knew it. He knew now from reading the teletypes taken out of that green camper that he had a countdown signal coming from that lost satellite. The whole tie-in with Lake Caha and the GAMMA X was there after he matched that with Rayburn's personal note to him about a bug polluting Caha. Now he knew what

Rayburn and Barth and the others were fighting. Now he knew, too, why Collins had asked for the flash point on diesel. They wanted a fire to try to burn the bug out! How sure were they it would work? They couldn't know that that contamination was connected with the lost satellite. If they did, would they still try a fire? He should tell Gregson about that satellite . . . would it make any difference to the field director, even if he knew? Gregson had other problems hanging on him in Talfungo . . . the right leadership here, for one? More than that maybe . . . how to keep it all together without a disaster to his own people? He needed to talk to Rayburn now . . . to be sure . . . but the radio on Terragona frequency was useless with that signal jamming it . . . wait for Gregson, then? What else?

So what would that man—Larkin was his name read out on the teletypes—have done with the satellite if he had managed to get in there and find it? Try to dismantle the self-destruct first and save the cameras—yes, a few hundred feet of Peeping Tom celluloid for the Washington boys, that had to come first! Then maybe try to keep it from blowing up to prevent GAMMA X from spraying into the atmosphere? Maybe. But Turgobyne would never let him get within ten miles of that lake . . . only an army shooting their way in had any chance. And maybe that's what was bothering Rayburn now? Somebody might just jump in there with guns blazing?

Now he walked to the door and looked out. He needed Rudy. The Jew had that certain godly intuition about things. The clouds, he noticed now, were jamming up in black array in the sky. Lightning cut at the soft underbellies and the thunder came tumbling down the slopes like a drunk thrown out of a bar. It was not going to get any better here . . . another day and the field could be under water . . .

So he might have to do this himself, then. How? He needed a copter, even as Rayburn was frantically trying to tell Gregson. Would Gregson make the big leap? When he knew a fire was going to lock in his own for good? Well, if he didn't it would be up to the pilots. Would they do it for him? Hardly. They wouldn't be the same. He didn't blame them for that. They would try, go through the motions, but their knowledge of him would forbid them seeing him as their general again. Would they go for Rayburn . . . for Terragona? Too late to throw that at them now . . . God, it's come down to this, they'll go, only maybe if I go with them? God, help me! I am not going to send them to divebomb that lake with me standing here watching their white faces flash by telling me they understand! I don't want to be "understood," as if I were a glandless cripple!

He glanced at the two Cessnas of Mentaya's over by the hangar, carrying the first coat of yellow paint. Mentaya. So it was clear enough what he was after here now too. Clear enough who had done Larkin in. So Mentaya wanted that satellite then, but what else? He had to have something else in mind for Terragona . . . and maybe now the reason for all that nitro was clear . . . but he still wanted to know what was in those crates he was carrying . . . he'd have to get hold of Slater and Sam on that bit . . .

He turned back into the tower and walked shakily to the rear, looking for Joseph. The walls appeared slanted to him. His breathing seemed to come harder. He jumped now at every flick of shadow. He was sweating hard, even though the breeze was cooler. Joseph was not there. His lean-to was empty, and there was no fire. He glanced up at the ridge of the escarpment and saw the thin wisp of smoke curling upward, just a breath on glass to show he was up there. He had put himself on the other side of the ridge now, refusing to view the mounting carnage here which he had been a part of. Right then he wanted to confront Joseph, help him to save face here. But there wasn't much he could do. Joseph had brought his own design of death here . . . the African law said death for death. Though nobody had died yet on those wheel housings, Joseph had to carry the burden of the destruction nevertheless . . . "he who thinks death is as guilty as he who commits it," said the Hamaran proverb.

He turned back into the room again to the demanding signal, which was as irritating as a hungry child's cry in the background, trying to resist it. He stopped at the radio, tuned in the marginal frequency that would tune out the signal some and bring in the Myagunde channel just in case Gregson was still going to talk to Rayburn . . . GOD, I DON'T WANT TO DO THIS TO RAYBURN! He stared at the chair where Augie once sat, how long ago? The baseball mitt sat on it like a bird's nest, with the ball nestled in it like an egg.

JESUS, FOR AUGIE TO DIE LIKE THAT, FLYING THAT BOMB, RISING TO THAT ONE GREAT MOMENT OF MANHOOD FOR GOD! JESUS, I PRAY I MIGHT RISE TO THAT, TO A DEATH THAT HAS MEANING LIKE THAT. BUT MAYBE NOW I WON'T GET IT . . . MY DEATH IS TO LIVE HERE, TO DIE A DAY AT A TIME IN THE EYES OF THESE

PEOPLE I KEEP CUTTING DOWN! JESUS, MAYBE AUGIE WAS RIGHT, YOU ARE JUDGING ME NOW!

He sat down heavily at the radio again. He found his red logbook, opened it and picked up the stubby pencil, began writing clumsily, the page blurring in front of him. God, there just wasn't much time left!

It was nearly 7:00 P.M. now, and Gregson had finished all he was going to eat of the supper Laura had brought him on a tray. Now he had pushed most of it aside and was trying to work Archimedes' Law out of Scripture when the phone rang.

The man on the other end identified himself as Olude of the Office of Interior in Hamara, a personal aide of Mentaya's. In crisp French Olude stated that they had not had radio contact with their prospectors in Terragona and that it was already twelve hours overdue. Did Gregson have contact with his own people there? Gregson said he did not, that he had to go through Durungu relay and that was down because of the weather build-up.

To which Olude said, "If we do not have contact in the morning, monsieur, we will have to decide on what action is necessary to find out."

Gregson felt a shaft of alarm. If Olude decided to jump into Terragona with helicopter rescue, that would complicate matters considerably. "I would ask your indulgence," he said quickly. "I expect Felix Mentaya has already gone in with his planes—"

"We have not heard from him either, Mr. Gregson," Olude came back almost accusingly.

"I will notify you as soon as we make contact," Gregson assured. The line went dead.

Gregson hung up only to have it ring again. The voice on the other end identified itself as that of Dr. Hiroshi Yammanaka, Director of World Health in Hamara. Gregson had met him only twice, but he liked the soft-spoken Oriental who used precise English that had a tendency to slur into accent when he got excited or tried to tell a joke.

"About that blood and water sample, Mr. Gregson," Yammanaka began, "we have put it through all one hundred and thirty-two possible classifications in our computer . . . we have not been able to identify it. But this much I can tell you: It is a highly potent strain that resembles encephalitis and meningitis—"

"Is it curable, Doctor?" Gregson cut in.

"Well . . . until we identify it or find combinations of drugs that might show some effect—"

"How long do you anticipate that will be?"

"We just can't tell . . . we injected a small unit of the strain we isolated out of Trask's sample into two mice and now—"

"They died?"

Yammanaka paused. "Mr. Gregson, death would have been—shall we say, simple? Actually what happened is that one of the mice went into a violent trauma and killed the other one . . ."

Gregson waited as Yammanaka paused. "Are you trying to tell me this is what is happening in Terragona, Doctor?"

"We still can't be sure—"

"Well, do you suspect it can?"

"There is a very close association in the chemical responses between mice and humans in some diseases, Mr. Gregson. Although it is most abnormal for any known bacteria strain to act so fast and produce such erratic manifestations—"

"Dr. Yammanaka, excuse me, but I have seventy-five of my people in Terragona eyeball-to-eyeball with this thing . . . now, what is the danger to them and to Terragona?"

"Well, Mr. Gregson, a primitive culture unaccustomed to fighting strange bacteria strains like this, and if that aggressive syndrome manifests itself in humans, it could wipe out Terragona in a month. My concern now is whether it can be contained *within* Terragona. For that reason, I am prepared to ask for voluntary medical teams to go in and help—"

Gregson hastily explained the ban on flights other than the mission's one-a-day with only one pilot, as Turgobyne insisted. "To break that is to ask for a worse disaster," he added. "Perhaps we better pull our people out of there and set up a quarantine village up at Durungu?"

"Of course, that is a decision you must make, Mr. Gregson," Yammanaka came back rather coolly, "but it means leaving the Terragonans to fend for themselves, does it not?"

Gregson knew immediately that he was too quick on the trigger with that, so he said, "Yes, of course . . . Rayburn probably wouldn't consent to that anyway . . ."

"Do you intend to fry to Durungu soon, Mr. Gregson?" Yammanaka asked. Gregson detected the "fry" instead of "fly," which meant the cool, precise Japanese was beginning to get a little frayed now.

"Tomorrow morning, yes."

"Could you arrange a fright yet tonight?"

"Not in this weather, Doctor . . ."

"Mr. Gregson"—and Yammanaka's voice had gone to a tone of sharp urgency—"I strongly recommend that we fry to Durungu as soon as possible . . . if not tonight, at dawn. It is important that I talk to Dr. Rayburn about this. In the meantime, it is important that you tell him to keep the situation stabilized in there as best he can until we can come up with something that will work on the bacteria . . . correct?"

"Certainly, Doctor . . ."

"Can we plan to fry around shree then?"

"Three?" Gregson corrected, not meaning to. He listened to the thunder outside sliding off the edges of the clouds building to a landslide. "Well, if weather permits, Doctor, we'll go . . ."

"Sank you, Mr. Gregson."

Gregson wanted some coffee now as he hung up, but the door opened and Ted stuck his face in. "We just picked up a transmission out of Terragona . . . you want to take it?"

Gregson got up quickly and followed Ted down the hall to the radio room. "We never got Terragona direct before, how come?" he said to Ted's back.

"It's on a relay with a ham operator up at Tulasi station on the escarpment east of here," Ted replied as they moved into the radio room. Merriweather was already there, his face set in worried lines.

"Rayburn is asking us to lay a fire on Caha," he said to Gregson, and Gregson took the yellow paper from him to read it.

"This just come?"

"No, the ham operator says he picked up something like that earlier today but he couldn't identify the call letters or the message," Ted came back.

"What is this fire business all about, Milt?" Merriweather asked.

"Dr. Yammanaka just notified me that they've got a bacteria strain of unknown classification that is proving to be quite lethal . . . apparently Rayburn feels he can contain it by firing that lake—"

"We daren't comply with that," G.D. snapped back. "Not until we are more certain of what we are dealing with. A fire will be the worst thing for our people in there—"

"Rayburn must know that—"

"You will be pulling the house down on those Hamaran prospectors as well, Milt, and that means you've had it with the government! I will not permit it, and don't push me on this one, Milt!"

Gregson knew then that he could not carry this too far in the use of his limited power without taking on the aura of recklessness. He really wasn't sure now either, and G.D.'s advice had the element of truth in it. They really didn't have enough on the bacteria yet and Rayburn certainly didn't. If it turned out to be something curable later, he knew he would not forgive himself for a premature act now.

"Send a message," he said to Ted then. "Tell Rayburn we will not comply with the request for a fire on Caha until World Health verifies what the bug is and if fire is advisable. Meanwhile—tell him to avoid any acts that might antagonize Turgobyne . . . keep the situation stabilized until we have word. Repeat it to him . . . no fire. And when you get through to him, get on to Blake and tell him the same thing in case they've already tried him . . ."

"Durungu is totally locked in," Ted advised then. "Our other transmitter, the bigger one, can't get a thing . . ."

"Keep trying . . ."

Ted nodded and Gregson glanced at Merriweather, who had turned his back now to look out the rain-smeared window. The older man was not going to engage in the amenities now.

Gregson walked out of the room and stopped at one of the offices to ring up Charlie Mason in supply to ask if the gas trucks were rolling yet. Charlie howled long and hard that it was impossible to roll three thousand gallons of high-octane in the dark, in weather like this and on those roads, and did he want to kill those drivers?

"You'll do it, Charlie," Gregson cajoled.

He moved on down the hall to his office and found Laura there, preparing to take his tray out. She moved now with characteristic indifference, telling him she was not interested in what he was doing really but playing her role out of duty. By now she had been blitzed by the news of his UFO caper, and for her she had already seen the beginning of the end.

"Colonel Jamison just called," she said coolly to him. "He just got back from dinner and found Merriweather's note about a copter stand-by . . ."

"Thanks," he said to her, but she moved on by him without even a glance and out of the room.

Thunder rattled the room then as Gregson exchanged greetings with Jamison, whom he had entertained for dinner twice in the past year.

"Your man Blake drop both shoes up there at Durungu?" Jamison asked.

"I don't know yet, Henry . . . what I wanted to know is if you could get your copters off to Durungu without filing the flight plan with Hamara Interior Control?"

"I hardly think so, old man . . . stand-by is one thing, but lift-off is another. Why?"

Gregson explained about Olude's possible move to try for Terragona himself to check on his own men whom he had not heard from, and how he might go in even quicker if he knew the U.N. was called in to check.

"They wouldn't jump Terragona with military escort without the 'boy king's' approval . . ."

"The 'boy king' is in Madagascar," Gregson cut in. "And I can't get Durungu to talk to Felix Mentaya, who's up there trying to get into the airlift himself . . ."

"Well," Jamison came back, "I'll have to kick this one up to command. Take some time, but my weather ops don't show a break until around four in the morning anyway. If I do get cleared—and it's a big *if*—I'll need to refuel at Durungu. My reserve tanks drink a lot. You prepared for that, old man?"

"Of course," and Gregson thanked him and hung up.

What was there left to do now? He didn't even know what he would do with Jamison's helicopters even if he did get them to Durungu. Could he chance an evacuation of his own in Terragona with the way things were in there? No, what he was doing was instinctive but not practical. And now, as he looked up at the map of Terragona on the wall, he wondered what was going on in there. Yammanaka's description of that bacteria's effect on the mice still hung in his brain.

"God, give us time," he said to the map.

The planes came in around 7:30, and it was already dark, the heavy clouds closing down on the field, putting a heavy, sagging curtain over it. A peculiar ground fog had begun then from the little half-drizzle of rain that had hit the hot clay of the runway. They were landing now against the continuing easterly gusts of wind that occasionally pushed from the southeast, forcing them to rudder hard against it to make the touchdown. Gina was in the kitchen helping Ebenezer prepare supper. As each plane touched down with that characteristic ripping sound of the wheels hitting the clay, she held her breath, waiting for that other sound, resisting it, of a wheelless strut dragging a long, gouging furrow as it drove for a crash.

Her shoulders sagged in relief then as she heard them taxiing into the parking area and she said, "Thank You, Lord."

After what seemed a long time, they trooped into the dining room, their voices subdued now, not boisterous as other times when they were anxious to let off steam after a long day of the strain. Finally she went out to them with a tray of cups and a coffee pot and set it down in front of them.

". . . so we load a twenty-five-gallon drum of petrol into the cargo bay, run a length of hose out of the cap down through the right doorframe and control it with a safety cock," Shannon was explaining to them, a big sheet of paper in front of him on which he had a design of airplanes following a track over what looked like trees. "Two men to a plane, three planes; Rudy might be able to go and operate the drum alone . . . one man flies, the other operates the fuel valve . . ."

"Only seventy-five gallons?" Letchford said. "We ought to use that Texan's Dakota and we could get more in . . ."

"That Dakota is too clumsy to skip over the lake," Shannon countered.

"Come to think of it, even for us," Mundey commented in a meditative tone, staring at the design, "it's going to be like shooting a toboggan down into a saucer anyway. I crossed over that lake once, and it's ringed with seventy-foot palms . . ."

Now Gina saw the drawing in front of Shannon as she put the cup down in front of him. She saw the name "CAHA" blocked out on top, and she knew then what they were planning.

"You don't mean you are going to try to blow that lake, Shannon?" she asked, a note of incredulity in her voice. Nobody responded.

Shannon did not look up at her, continuing to study the drawing in front of him. "You know what that will do to our people in there—"

"If Rayburn and the others are willing to put their lives on the line for a fire, then we figure the least we can do is try it," Shannon replied shortly.

"You or Blake?" she put it back to him bluntly.

"What difference does that make?" and Shannon was working at his own control now, which meant he knew very well what she was asking.

"The difference is that Gregson is the only field officer with the power to take that kind of action—"

"Rayburn has been on Talfungo all day to get Gregson to move—"

"And?"

"Gregson turned it down . . ."

"So now Blake orders it?"

"He didn't *order* anything. He simply laid out the facts of the situation which all of us knew were emerging. Anyway . . . he's still officer-in-charge here . . ."

"Not over Gregson's head! This is not your decision, and not Blake's, when so many lives are involved. You should wait—"

"Wait for what?" Shannon brought his voice down now to an even pitch, not wanting any dragged-out fight here in front of the other pilots. "Like Blake said, it will take too long for Talfungo to make up their minds about this—"

"So you let Blake decide for all of you again?" Shannon did not reply. Sensing they might all be rethinking that, she added, "Hell and destruction are in his path, Shannon. You follow him, all of you go the same route . . . it's here, the whole operation reeks of it!"

"And hell and destruction are what await the Terragona people if we don't move on what Blake suggests—"

"Suggests?" Gina's voice was barbed now as a flush of heat poured through her. "Since when did he *suggest* anything here? He's driving you, Shannon, like he's driven all of you these months, driving you to play his war games, to do *his* bidding, to dance on his string like puppets—"

Just then the sound of the plane came on strong from the northeast, swished over the Quonset, drowning out Gina's voice. There was a pause as the sound faded, and the sharp rip of the wheels hitting clay said another pilot was down.

268

"That's Monk," Mundey offered.

"Late again?" Bellinger added.

An awkward silence came into the room again, and all of them were now suddenly preoccupied with their fingernails or the cracked lines in the table. Like children waiting for scoldings to pass? But they weren't children, not any more! The jagged pieces of conversational shrapnel still hung in the room, and Gina, not wanting to lose the momentum, was about to continue when Shannon said, "Did Slater yank those magneto cables out of Mentaya's planes?" putting it to no one in particular, bent only perhaps on changing the subject.

"He got them," Bellinger confirmed. "He put them in the drawer under the radio bench in the tower . . . but Mentaya's fit to be tied . . ."

Shannon nodded. Gina savored that a minute, trying to understand, to draw it from their expressionless faces. Then, "You know you can't get away with that, Shannon . . ."

"We are protecting his life," Shannon retaliated. "And our own in Terragona, plus how many Terragonans? The minute he drops on our airfield over there in the morning, it'll be war and whatever we thought we could do to save that territory is shot out the window . . ."

"You concluded that all by yourself?"

Shannon opened his mouth to reply, but just then a sudden gust of wind made the Quonset lean and creak, and particles of sand fell down from the ceiling to the table.

"Wind just swung south," Mundey said offhandedly.

The screen door banged open, letting in a fresh swirl of heavy, humid air, and Monk stood there, blinking into the light, his freckles standing out of the yellow paleness of his face, his blue eyes carrying the wonder of a child. But there were stronger lines to his chin now too, a harder cut to his jaw. Boyhood was long gone, maybe too quickly . . .

"Where's Blake?" he asked in his high-pitched voice.

"Up at the tower," Shannon replied. "You're late out of JERICHO again, Monk?"

"Man, Shannon," and Monk looked at Gina, not sure maybe whether to talk in front of her. "It really fell apart over there today . . . one of those patients down with the crud broke loose and almost tore the hospital apart with his bare hands . . . he threw Rayburn and Trask across the room as if they were made of plastic . . . it was Collins who finally managed to deck him with a piece of two-by-four, but—but Shannon, the guy still tried to get up . . . I mean, it was hairy! They're asking for more tranquilizers to try to hold the rest of them . . . but I never did see anything like that in my life . . . they've been trying to get through here all day, even tried Talfungo . . . but we got some kind of funny signal jamming the frequency all the way . . . I couldn't even make contact with the ground when I was a mile out of touchdown—"

"That's the Wambura," Mundey said solemnly.

"Not this, it ain't," Monk protested.

"We heard it coming in, Monk," Shannon said.

"Well . . . what is that signal, Shannon?"

Shannon did not respond.

"Ask *Commandant-en-Chef* Blake, he knows everything," Gina broke in almost snidely.

Monk looked at her quizzically, then said, "One other thing you should know, and Blake better know . . . Rayburn wants Blake to tell Gregson that they need a fire on that lake over there . . . they been trying Talfungo all day—"

"They got through," Shannon said patiently, and he took the sheet of paper with the design from Bellinger.

"They okayed it, then?"

"No . . . they refused the request . . ."

Monk stared at him, his tongue darting out to lick his dry lips. "Gee, Shannon . . . ?"

"You could at least wait for Rudy," Gina said.

"Rudy hasn't been heard from all day . . . he might have laid over in Myagunde with this weather . . ."

"Not Rudy," Bellinger chimed in. "He'll fly through a hurricane to keep his schedule with Terragona tomorrow—"

Just then the screen opened again, and Slater walked in, hands deep in his pockets, looking at all of them in some perplexity, his face sagging. They waited for him, sensing he had something now.

"I just got off the radio," he began, his voice cracking some. "I was trying to raise Bungari station for a possible relay to Talfungo for Blake . . . suddenly we hooked into this transmission from way over at the Tumbasa game reserve two hundred miles southeast of here . . . they said a light plane went in about an hour ago . . . it burned to a crisp . . ." Slater swallowed, cleared his throat and went on, "They want to know if we had any planes in that area coming on a leg for here . . ."

"That's Myagunde direction," Mundey said.

Nobody said anything. The silence was even more heavy now. "Not . . . not Rudy?" Gina protested then in a half whisper.

"We can't be sure," Shannon came back quickly. "Sometimes government border patrols chase around at night in their planes . . . Does Blake know?"

Slater looked back at him. "He was there when I took it," he said almost in awe then. "He—he looked like he just got poleaxed . . . like something fell out of him or on him . . . I dunno . . ."

They sat there in their several isolated islands, unable to fully coagulate around this thing emerging here, trying to piece the possibility of Rudy's death to the awful specter of their own hanging too real in the room, coming out of that paper Shannon kept in front of him.

"It was Blake who sent him," Gina came in again condemningly, feeling the bitterness begin to swell up in her now. "Blake ordered him on that run against mission orders and in a weather build-up—"

"That won't help now, Gina," Shannon warned her.

"No, it won't, will it, Shannon?" she countered. "How many more times will you have to write that epitaph in this place? Augie, Charlie Weaver, Doc Kelland—"

"Look, if you have a mind to talk about it all, I'll be glad to see you in your quarters," Shannon snapped back at her.

Gina felt the cutting shaft of his rebuke, pushing her off now, dismissing her from any more incriminations of Blake in front of the others. The rain came harder then, hitting the pan roof in rising staccato, and they all, as one, looked up at the ceiling, resisting the complication of that now. They did not look at her. They were beyond reach, she knew it. Blake had already shaped them and molded them in his own image. The immensity and finality of that left her numb. Their faces now remained in deliberate protective anonymity toward her, unwilling to rise with her in her vilification of Blake. Even now, as they were preparing to do his bidding again, perhaps flirt with death in an entirely new dimension and to seal the fate of the very ones they had served in Terragona, they would still refuse to sort it out in her terms. So now all she wanted was to be out of there, to go and cry for

Rudy and pray too, to withdraw then if she could from the steady rise to disaster growing here.

Inside the infirmary the Sudanese girl stood up uneasily as Gina walked in, holding her blanket close around her, staring at Gina with sleep-laden eyes, traces of confusion and fear still there.

"Your hour will come too, my dear," she said dryly, but the small, round face and fawnlike eyes did not light up with understanding. She was holding the gray blanket close with one hand, the other held out from her body, closed into a fist. Gina reached down and gently unclasped the palm. The small square sat sticky and black in the moistness of her palm, looking like a black ruby.

It was Rudy's molasses candy "with sorghum." She folded the palm back gently into the fist again, closing it over the candy.

Oh God, she cried now in her inner torment, let Rudy be alive!

# CHAPTER XII

Blake felt the rigors grab his back muscles, run up through his neck and dig into his scalp. The sweat ran from him now, emitting the smell of the salts of his body. He folded his arms and leaned forward in his chair to get the purchase of the table on his chest, which seemed to flutter strangely. There was hardly any feeling in his legs, only the same weak quivering. He kept his eyes on Mentaya, but there were double images there, the yellow rainslicker Mentaya wore gleaming in a peculiar golden sheen like the sun, stabbing at his eyes, building new, torturing distortions in his brain.

"I want those magneto cables, Mr. Blake," Mentaya repeated, with that no-nonsense tone in his voice, "stolen by your pilots . . . and which puts this operation in jeopardy with the government."

"We pulled those cables for your own protection, Felix," Blake countered.

"Do not fool with me now, monsieur . . . I am empowered to take whatever course of action is necessary to fulfill what I was sent here to do . . ."

"And I am not sure what that is exactly," Blake went on.

"Look, Blake, here are ten one-thousand-dollar American notes—"

"Mr. Mentaya, I know you took that money off a man named Larkin out there in a green camper in the desert. Larkin is an American space agency man chasing the same American satellite as you—"

"The point being what, Mr. Blake?" Felix cut back impatiently.

"I also found the teletypes in Larkin's hiding place under the hood of his truck, the place you missed. Those teletypes tell about the Chinese being the only ones who had tracked that satellite into Terragona, besides the Americans. That can only say how you got the information about it in this country that does not pick up any kind of highly classified information like that—"

"Felix," Belang interjected with some concern then, "the Chinese? Is Faber with the Albanian militants, the Chinese wing?"

"And there's this too," Blake went on, reaching under the table and coming up with the gun, which he placed carefully on the table in front of him. "That is a Czech Mauser automatic machine pistol my men found in your aircraft under a lid called mining equipment. That kind of weapon does not go with mineral prospecting, right, Mr. Mentaya? In fact, the only place you can get that kind of gun is through the rebel trails in Africa that the Chinese operate, or am I wrong?"

"This is none of your affair, Mr. Blake," Felix said calmly, but with a warning note in his voice now.

Blake paused, feeling his legs turn pasty, unable to brush away the peculiar shadows across his eyes.

"So it isn't. Your politics are your own affair. But the Premier warned the mission and me in particular not to allow anything to happen in Terragona that would embarrass Hamara or cause tension with the bordering countries. If you try to take Terragona your way now, a lot of innocent people are going to die—"

"I am not here to argue, Mr. Blake," Mentaya warned again.

"The point I'm getting to," Blake went on, "is that every man should have his chance to consider or reconsider the big gambles and be sure it's worth it all. For one thing, there's that satellite you are after. It's on a countdown to self-destruct, so there probably won't be anything to find over there tomorrow—"

"And I take your word on that, Mr. Blake?"

"I have the facts, the ones you missed in Larkin's truck . . . if you want to see them."

"I will determine the validity of those facts when I get to Terragona, Mr. Blake," Mentaya said flatly. "You have delayed me long enough. I demand those magneto cables."

"And then there's the matter of the signatures," Blake continued, hoping he could yet box Felix in, hold him off. "If anything went wrong before you got into Terragona, you would have the signatures of the top mission brass showing our willingness to cooperate in an act of aggression. That would make us all appear to be partners in your move to take Terragona, and the Premier would see us as involved in a political move after all we've done to keep ourselves clean on that point. Or maybe you had that in mind all along then, Mr. Mentaya?"

"The magneto cables, Mr. Blake—"

"But there is something else about the signatures, mine in particular," Blake insisted, hurrying now, because he felt the darkness coming down on him heavier then. "Why did you wait around here for mine so long? You must be on a countdown yourself for Terragona, and you could have gone in without my signature. Could it be that you are not really sure that blasting your way into Terragona is right? You know, Monsieur Belang told me when he stayed with me a few months back that you were once committed to the Christian ministry and there is a missionary lady named Miss Drew you can't quite shake from your past—"

"Belang, you fool!" Mentaya barked, and Belang looked alarmed and then mystified, still not getting the full import of this.

"Don't blame him, Mr. Mentaya," Blake said, wiping at the sweat rolling down into his eyes now. "We all have our past, and I've got my reckoning with God yet too. But you know my signature won't change the doubt you may have about the way you are planning to take Terragona—"

"If it's the money you want, Mr. Blake," Felix cut in with a cajoling tone, "you can have it . . . all of it. It will take you a long way from this Godforsaken place . . ."

"Money doesn't mean a thing right now, Felix. What matters is that you change your mind about making a blood bath of Terragona just to give the Chinese a prize—"

"What is your price then, Mr. Blake?" Felix interjected sharply.

"No price tags, Mr. Mentaya. All I'm saying is that the peace of God comes far less expensive than what you are laying on the line—"

"You're offering me peace?" and Mentaya let out a shrill laugh. "Look at you, Mr. Blake! Your field is washing away! Your planes are smashing up! And you, Mr. Blake, are an impostor, running from the shambles of your past, hiding behind the skirts of a religious order!"

"You're probably right in all of that," Blake replied, taking a shaky breath, trying to keep Mentaya in focus. "You and I are alike in one other way too . . . we are both avoiding the big scene with

God, and there is never a more desperate soul than one refusing to turn around and face Him—"

"You offer me no choice now then, Mr. Blake," Felix interrupted with warning, "but to take what action now appears necessary . . ."

Blake saw him move, or maybe just his yellow rainslicker shifting a bit. He lifted the gun in his right hand from under the table, laid it on the table top, laying his right hand over it. "You might as well note exhibit C then, Mr. Mentaya," he said, forcing himself now to control the spasms running through him. "This is a .45 service automatic with U. S. Space Agency serial numbers matching Larkin undoubtedly. Put all this together—the money, teletypes, the Mauser —and the evidence spells out a betrayal that will destroy Hamara, let alone Terragona. All I'm asking you right now is to back off—"

"Felix, you can't drag Hamara in with the Chinese—"

"So you are asking me, Mr. Blake?" and Mentaya laughed in that same raucous sound, ignoring Belang altogether. "You make propositions to me? You don't even belong in this country, you don't belong in Terragona—and you are offering me an opportunity to back off? Look at you, Mr. Blake, your hands shake. Is it malaria, monsieur? Or is it that the battle has become too hot now? Is it now that you suffer the malady of all God-men, unable to rise to the big test in the end? Whatever your view of God, Monsieur Blake, it is not strong enough now. Do you think one meaningless blob of geography called Hamara, which threatens to blow away with one good wind, will absorb a man of my destiny? You think I care in the least about these stupid cowherders and date growers in the end? Do you think even eighty thousand Terragonans over there are anything more than grist for the wheels of political and social progress? You and your stupid values of the individual in the sight of God! You think the 'boy king' of Hamara makes any difference to me either? All the legions of hell won't protect him now that I am on the move. So now behold the great God-figure—Yellow Bird indeed—that all the cattleherders sing about, now unable to control his demise! Right, Belang? So who needs your signature, Mr. Blake? Your collapse into oblivion is enough for me! Keep the magneto cables, monsieur, we will improvise! And keep your charity! And may God speak a good epitaph over you, for surely no one else will!" He paused then, his voice rattling off the walls. "Belang," he snapped, "you can make up your mind now, go with me or die right here . . ."

"Mr. Mentaya," Blake cut in, deciding to make one last attempt, "there is a name on the list of Hamaran prospectors who went into Terragona . . . that name is Mentaya, too. Would that be your son then?"

"So?"

"Well . . ." and now Blake felt the veil of blackness come hard over him, "you ought to know that satellite is leaking a deadly bug into Lake Caha over there . . . your son's chances of surviving that are tied in with our people staying on the job over there—"

"Another of your tales, Mr. Blake?" Mentaya shouted back in derision. "Well, it won't work! *Au revoir!*"

Blake did not see or hear them go out. A peculiar fuzz came across his eyes. The gun under his hand felt sweaty, clammy, like a sponge; then as he pulled his hand back, it fell to the floor with a clatter. Now he could not move! *God, I'm crying! I feel the tears with the sweat!* Am I still afraid of the dark then?

JESUS! HELP ME! SOMEBODY IS ON THAT RADIO! RUDY? GOD, IS IT RUDY? LET IT BE RUDY! SOMEBODY HELP HIM! I CAN'T MOVE! RUDY, THERE'S NOBODY TO HELP YOU NOW!

Gina had stood there a long time leaning her head against the wall by the window of the infirmary, watching the rain chase in directionless rivulets on the glass. She was caught between dull ache and numbness, unable to rise to the loss of Rudy. She felt void, unable to pray even, the crest of her holy cause against Blake flattening out. The accumulated stink of death was everywhere here, in the wind that blew its fitful shrieking derision. It was in the rain that struck hard but did not cleanse or refresh. It was a dry rain born out of a freak of nature, swept along by that confused wind. Wind and rain, fog and dust, swirled in twisted courses in bizarre and tragic concert with the events. All seemed to testify to the absence of God in this place. The whole operation was like a top spun into being by the single sovereign act of God but then suddenly commanded by some other diabolical hand, whipping it into a murderous gyration that cut a wider swathe of blood as it built its insane revolutions.

She tried to focus on Blake objectively, to see him as an element victimized by it all as any of them, to see him maybe as Shannon did, or as Rudy did. She willed herself to have some feeling of compas-

277

sion, but found it an alien emotion, unable to form and maintain a proper shape with respect to him. Well, one thing she knew: if this spinning top with its murderous designs was to totter, wobble and finally halt, it could come only by some form of spiritual resolve. She had to get to that radio, try to get Talfungo. Not only because of what Shannon and the others were planning with that fire in the morning, but because Rudy could not be dead because of Blake. Where would it end? Gregson had to know! The bag had been sprung here to let loose seven worse demons! Maybe, then, this was her moment! All the disciplines of her life, like all the refusals to her flesh, she had endured, waiting for the one solitary act that God alone must have her perform. She could not deny herself!

"You could be beautiful . . ." She remembered what Rudy had told her. *Could* be? Oh, she knew! She had asked herself that many times in her life, even studying her nudity in the mirror, fascinated by the instruments that would not function. *Could* be . . . but it was not for her! She left all that behind as medicine gave her a new command of her life, of proper function—and with that had come holy resolve to make war for God, to strike the pennants of godlessness, to hold up the standard of righteousness and holiness. God put His trust in women, because they kept their vows!

Well, she would keep hers now. There would be no more unholy designs for death in this place! She picked up her bag, the credentials for her custodial role in life, the instruments she used with such dexterity and skill that gave her the right to disembowel if necessary. Blake wanted physicals for the pilots? Well, she was about to start with him! Now! Top to toe! There was more than one way to humble a man, how well she knew!

She put her hand to the doorknob, closed her eyes, felt the pounding in her neck, her mouth tasting dry. "Lord, I put on the whole armor, the helmet of salvation, the shield of faith . . . let me not waver in this Thy holy calling!"

She was halfway to the tower when the "Tannhäuser" music came on the P.A. with a jarring kind of blast. She stood still in the rain, pulling her tan raincoat closer around her, looking up toward the tower, wondering why he would put it on now, so close to midnight. She listened to the slowly building tempo of it, sounding weird in the rain and the ground mist, its melancholy strains seeming to lend an awesome pall against the background of death here.

Then it stopped, but she could hear the ridges of the tape thumping, meaning no one was controlling it. The tower was dark as she approached, standing there like a ship beached on the shore. The door to the radio room was closed. She tried it. It was locked. She knocked but there was no response. She could hear a voice coming over the radio, but she could not make it out over the sound of the rumbling thunder and rain.

She moved on to try the window leading to Blake's quarters. It was locked too, as was the back door. She played her flashlight over the doors, the walls, looking for answers. Finally she turned and walked across to the dining room and found Shannon and the others outside looking toward the tower, trying to figure it out.

"Blake's locked himself in the tower," she said to him.

They went back with her. Shannon pounded on the door, called to Blake. Finally he backed off and looked up at the floor of the porch two feet beyond his extended hand. He jumped, caught hold and pulled himself up as Mundey and Letchford gave him a boost. They watched him disappear down the open stairway to Blake's quarters.

A minute or two passed before the latch on the radio-room door was thrown and Shannon opened it for them. "Get in here quick," he said, and they moved into the dark, musty-smelling room lit only by the dim light from the radio transmitter dial. "All right . . . throw your light around . . . somebody get on that radio . . ."

"Nothing but that weird signal," Mundey commented lamely, but he moved over to it to go through the motions anyway.

Gina played her light around the room, paused as she saw the gun on the floor. Where had she seen that before?

"Over here," Shannon said then. Gina played the light toward him into the corner nearest the door.

"Mr. Blake?" Shannon asked politely. Gina saw what looked like a bundle of wrinkled khakis, then the familiar combat boots. She played the light up slowly. He had his knees drawn up under his chin, his arms folded tightly across his middle, as if he was cold. Now and then spasms shook his body. His eyes stared back, not seeing them. She knew that look. Those eyes were two dead-end tunnels in the side of the sand-colored hills of his face. "Mr. Blake, it's Shannon . . ." No response. "Somebody shut off that tape recorder . . ."

Letchford moved over quickly and hit the switch, and the thumping sounds of the machine died.

"There's something here, Shannon," Mundey said from over by the radio, and he came over to Shannon with a half sheet of yellow paper in his hand. "Blake must have taken this from Talfungo sometime lately . . ."

Shannon took the paper and Gina put her light on it for him to read. The words were in pencil done up in severe block letters, with wobbly, shaky lines. "Gas okayed," Shannon read. "Gregson coming with World Health . . . morning . . . the word nitro? And halt operations tomorrow . . ."

"About time," Gina said brusquely.

"Get back on the Talfungo frequency and see if you can raise them," Shannon told Mundey. "If they're getting through, they might be receiving . . ."

"Not on our equipment," Slater commented pessimistically, but Mundey went back to the radio to try.

"You can wait now, Shannon," Gina went on. "As long as Gregson is coming in the morning—"

"Maybe," Shannon replied doubtfully. "Blake was pretty insistent we go in the morning—"

"For what reason?"

"I don't want to argue about it, Gina," Shannon put back shortly with some irritation.

"What do you want, Shannon?" Blake's voice reached out to them, sounding strangely harsh. His eyes had gone wider, a blind man suddenly aware of sounds around him. Shannon hesitated, not sure how to handle this. "You got that vigilante sawbones with you, Shannon?" Blake asked.

"She's here, Mr. Blake," Shannon said, and he gave her a quick glance.

"You mean she's everywhere, Shannon, don't forget," Blake returned. "Keeper of the flame and all that, hey, Doctor?" and he laughed then, leaning his head on his knees, his body shaking until it sounded like a giggle. "God's angel of justice . . . right, Shannon?" and he laughed again, throwing his head back against the wall, his face twisted in the light of Gina's flashlight. Shannon reached over and took the light from her, as if he didn't want to see his leader exposed like that.

280

"You'll have to hold him until I can get the needle in," Gina said casually.

Shannon moved closer to him, but Blake suddenly looked up at him, his eyes wide, and he threw a punch. Shannon backed off. "Okay, you guys, lend a hand here." The rest of them moved reluctantly to do his bidding, not too sure of what was going on now. "Just be careful with him . . ."

As they crowded into the small space between the table and the wall, Blake looked up at them, his eyes carrying a wild, mad look.

"What do you want from me, you crumbs? You put me in the dock once, remember? Why don't you tell them, those eighty-eight people you killed? You chowder heads who cut maintenance schedules, who put electrical systems in backward! Fly Global, the safest way to go! Safest, my eye! You glorified grease monkeys who don't know an engine cowl from a toilet seat! So it's pilot error, is it? So what do you want from me now, blood?"

Gina looked at Shannon in the half-light, wanting some explanation of that. But Shannon was moving then with the others, finally landing on Blake, trying to do it gently, merely trying to hold him to the floor. Blake fought them with maniacal strength. Gina waited, standing over them, looking for a bare arm or leg to get the hypo into. The walls pounded with the struggle, and the pilots grunted with the effort. One of them was half crying, a strange, terrifying sound, like a child who was inflicting pain on a dumb animal and didn't want to.

"Keep his head down, keep his head down," Shannon kept repeating to them, panting heavily himself with the struggle, his voice shaky. "What are you waiting for, Gina?"

And then there was the bare arm held flat to the floor, and she slipped the needle in quickly just as someone kicked the flashlight aside.

"What did they pay you screws to keep your mouth shut?" Blake kept yelling. "You'll get yours, you'll get yours! 'Vengeance is mine, saith the Lord.' You screw up an airplane so people die, you'll get yours."

He went on like that for a full minute or more, and then the sedative began to take over and his thrashing began to die, his words coming in a half-whimper through puffy lips. She picked up the flashlight and held it on his face, noting the cold sore still on his upper lip beginning to scab over. He was the giant tumbled off the towering beanstalk now, lying there in abject helplessness. The pilots stayed where they were beside him, getting their wind, not looking at each other, almost as if they were ashamed for what they had done.

For Gina, it was finished—and she was glad.

"You better get him to the infirmary," she said crisply. "I can't work on him here . . ."

They got up slowly, silently. Four of them picked up Blake, two at the shoulders, two at the feet. "Out the back way," Shannon said. "I don't want Mentaya or any of those other VIPs to know . . ."

They got to the back door, and Shannon swung it open. The wind and rain hit them with a jarring assault. They stopped suddenly. The tall figure stood there framed by the flashes of lightning, the spear held straight out an inch from Shannon's leather jacket, chest-high.

"Joseph," Shannon said in some awe. *"Bon soir,* Joseph?"

"Wow," Mundey said in a half-whisper, and they put Blake down, not wanting to move against that threat.

"Who's got the French?" Shannon asked, continuing to stare at Joseph.

"Let me try," Gina said. She put the words out slowly, mixing in a few Hamaran phrases with it, trying to convey to Joseph that his *commandant* was sick and needed to get to the hospital.

Joseph did not move for a long minute or more. "Where did he come from anyway?" Letchford asked in some wonder. "I thought he had gone for the bush long ago . . . ?" Gina tried speaking again. Slowly, then, the spear came back from Shannon's chest, and Joseph turned slowly and went out, taking the lead, making certain they would go directly to the infirmary. The pilots picked up Blake and started the long slippery walk to the infirmary.

"Monk, stay on that radio," Shannon said. "Keep trying Talfungo for another half hour, if you don't get anything, get back on Terragona . . ."

So it was Shannon, Letchford, Bellinger and Slater carrying Blake in the rain and mud. They fell down once in their walk, and Blake's unconscious form fell into the slimy clay. Joseph turned quickly and was down on his knees to lift his leader. But Bellinger had Blake's head in his lap already, holding it protectively off the muddy ground until they could get their footing and lift him again. Gina leaned over to see what she could do; when a lightning bolt flashed over them, she caught the twisted lines of agony in Bellinger's face. He was trying to wipe a smear of mud off the forehead of Blake with his right hand, as if soothing a bruise on a child. *It can't be, Gina thought, they're suffering with him, even* for *him!*

They finally got him into the infirmary and put Blake on Gina's bed as she had commanded. "Take off his shirt," she said shortly. Bellinger did so. "Now tie his wrists and ankles to the bedposts with this adhesive." They looked at her, perplexed now, resisting such an act, as if they were being asked to bind him up like a mad animal.

Gina lit the kerosene lamp and put it on the dresser. The Sudanese girl got up uncertainly from her place in the corner. "Look, your leader has had a complete breakdown, mentally, emotionally and physically," she explained clinically. "He could get violent, hurt himself and others . . . so tie him down."

Shannon finally took the rolls of adhesive she extended, giving one to Letchford. When they had lashed the wrists and ankles, Blake was laid out in spread-eagle fashion. They had never seen him that way before, and now it left them subdued, unsure, bewildered.

"It's like he was on a cross," Mundey commented.

"Is he going to be all right?" Bellinger asked.

"Who can say?" Gina returned with detachment. "Maybe it's the end of a long nightmare for him, for you, all of us. Now, do you mind if I work on him alone?"

They all looked at her quickly, almost suspiciously. But finally Shannon prodded them out of the room. Only he and Joseph were left there. Gina prepared another hypo.

"What was he babbling about in the tower, Shannon?" she asked. "About eighty-eight people dying and that thing about pilot error?"

She turned to look at him. He was looking at Blake, frowning. "How soon can you get him up?"

"Don't be ridiculous! He won't even know his own name for weeks—"

"We'll need him on that tower in the morning—"

"What was he shouting about, Shannon?" she flung at him again, her voice slashing in the small room, so that Joseph looked at her quickly in some wariness.

Shannon licked his lips. "He crashed a jet at Kennedy International in 1968 . . . eighty-eight people died, he alone lived. They called it pilot error . . ."

She stared at him. "Be sure your sin will find you out," she said dryly. "That explains him well enough . . ."

"It only explains his problem—"

"Three years of living the lie," Gina came back.

Shannon hesitated, maybe not relishing going on with that argument, which he probably figured he couldn't win. Then, "Those kids won't fly tomorrow without him on the flight line—"

"Which proves you weren't supposed to fly tomorrow," she countered. "The message read to halt operations, remember?"

"Talfungo doesn't know what's going on in Terragona," Shannon went on doggedly.

"But you seem to know it all," she came back sharply. "You said Blake knows . . . so what is it, Shannon, that drives you to keep flying tomorrow, to blow that lake against your own field office orders?"

He shook his head wearily then. "Blake said not to tell—"

"Blake said! Blake said!" she almost mimicked him, and she slammed the door of the medicine chest. "Must we all play the secrecy game for him, Shannon? Is he locking you to information that is the concoction of his own distorted sense of—of mission, if we can call it that for want of a better word?"

"It's no concoction!" his voice shrilled then, his face exploding in the subsurface eruptions of his anger. She hesitated, sensing that he himself was close to the edge. Joseph had turned from his place at the end of the bed to study them both in the same way, catching the mounting battle here. Shannon sighed and ran a shaky hand over his face. "The signal jamming our frequency is a countdown from a satellite the Americans lost out of orbit a week ago," he went on then, his voice flat and almost toneless. "It landed in Caha and is probably leaking a contraband bacteria picked up in outer orbit. The signal is a self-destruct . . . timed for twenty-four hours from commencement. Blake isn't sure, but he figured the signal began yesterday morning early . . ."

Gina put the loaded hypo syringe on a tray on the side table by the medicine chest. "So you better wait for Gregson then and tell him—"

"For the love of Pete, Gina, there isn't time!" Shannon countered, bristling again. "You ought to know, if that thing blows over there, we have no idea of its potency once it is diffused into that lake and even into the air—"

"So what's a fire supposed to do?"

"We can only hope, as Blake says, that the burn-off will kill what's already in the lake and prevent the exploded body of the bug from making a link-up with the rest of the crud—"

"Blake knows so much about it?"

"No. He's having to guess at it too. But it ties in with Rayburn's urgent demand for a fire on Caha . . . only he's thinking of the possibility of checking the bug as it is in the lake, he knows nothing of the satellite connection . . ."

"So how does Blake know about that satellite?"

"He found the teletypes on a truck last night out there in the desert on a man, supposedly an American space agent, sent in here to get into Terragona after that satellite . . ." Gina knew then what Blake had taken out of the green camper.

"You haven't told the other pilots—why?"

"Blake said to keep it close . . . he doesn't even want to chance talking about it over the radio to Talfungo . . . too many people listen in on the frequency. Once that news gets out, we'll have this place crowded with a lot of curious people . . . and who knows who'll try to go into Terragona?"

Gina shook her head. "World Health is coming tomorrow, Shannon . . . those people are supposed to know what to do—"

"We've got to get into the air at dawn, Gina," Shannon went on with insistence. "And if Mentaya makes us load nitro and we have to go through the maneuvers over that lake, I can't be sure our guys will have the nerve to try that—"

"Blake can't do you any good," Gina snapped. "You can see that for yourself . . . he won't mount his war chariot in this place any more . . . so make up your mind, whatever you do, and I hope you get sense and wait for Gregson."

"You don't understand—"

"And do you, Shannon?" she returned with intensity. "God has dropped judgment on your noble leader here, and maybe you ought to thank Him for that! Blake was wrong to con you into flying for him on this crazy mission! I don't care what's in that lake, it's not a decision he or you or anybody here can make when you have seventy-five of our people in there hanging in the balance!"

Shannon sighed then and walked to the door, paused and said, while looking at the floor, "We need a miracle for Blake, whether you want to admit that or not . . . if you've a mind to pray, pray for that, for Terragona, for the rest of us . . . maybe he's all the Terragonans and we, and who knows who else, have right now in the time that's left . . ."

"I fail to appreciate your measure of him," she replied coolly, sorting out her medicines again. "I believe in signs that indicate the will of God, and what you see lying in that bed is a pretty clear design of God to me . . ."

He glanced at her, a look that said he was unable to grasp her analysis. Then, without further comment, he went out. She picked up the loaded hypo, walked over to the bed and hit the muscle in the left arm. She sensed the satisfaction of the needle piercing the flesh, seeing the hair on his chest gleaming with fresh sweat, seeing the image of Kortoff in that furnace room . . . it was done.

She was sitting by the dresser when Mentaya came in, his yellow rainslicker crackling as he walked. He went over to the bed, looked down at the unconscious form, then over to her. She wondered how he knew about Blake being here like this.

"And you are?" he demanded sharply.

"Gina Roman, medical officer here . . ."

"What is your diagnosis of this man?"

"Complete nervous and physical collapse."

"Hmmm, yes. And how long will he be like this?"

She shrugged. "A long time, I expect." He did not answer, so she ventured, "Mr. Mentaya, do you still want that signature?"

He hesitated, his eyes gleaming like a cat's. "What do you have in mind?"

"I can get him to sign those papers of yours . . . but only if you agree to waive any more nitro loads for our pilots."

Mentaya continued to watch her carefully. "You are asking a lot . . ."

"When I give you the signature, I expect a written order on the nitro."

Mentaya nodded. "All right, I will agree, but you must provide the signature PLUS the magneto cables for my aircraft . . . you know where they are?"

She hesitated now, not sure of how much to give. "Yes. But—"

"You tell me where they are, the nitro order could be yours."

"In the drawer under the radio transmitter . . . it is hard to see, but if you feel underneath—"

"How would you know?"

"I overheard them talking . . . the pilots . . ."

"Very well . . . the cables I will get, the signature I will wait for. When I have both, you will get your desire . . . goodnight, madam, and guard that—that poor piece of flesh well!"

# CHAPTER XIII

She sat stiffly in that chair a long time, listening to the storm dilute itself outside in a hopeless frenzy. Now and then she jerked as Blake rose up against the binds of the adhesive strips, and his voice rode a jagged line of terror and appeal:

"Hold it, Brock, keep your hands off that throttle, you'll stall her . . . May Day . . . May Day . . . Kennedy Tower, this is Global one seventy-four . . . we've lost number-one engine . . . fire warning in number two . . . rudder and trim sluggish . . . Jesus, we're going in!"

She knew now what it was he was shouting.

"Pilot error, pilot error," he cried again, sounding like a protest. She was only eight feet or so from his bed and could watch his body heave, the sweat gleaming on his chest, turning the reddish hair dark like wet corn silk. His face was puffy, those lumps of facial tissue standing out like boils, torn by the pain shooting through his mental recall and blown up by the enlarged focus of the past. She noticed his feet, those two big toes poking out of the holes in his khaki socks, the most glaring point of humanity in any man. When did he lose his boots? She saw them on the floor by the bed. Those toes sticking out bothered her, because they gave him the dimension of commonality instead of giant similitude as she had known him and wanted him to be in this point of total dissolvement. She would be certain to put his boots back on before they carried him out.

But as he jerked and swore on into the night and fought the binds that held him, she could find no point of satisfaction in his torture. She attempted a kind of objective view. She had seen many men die in her time and viewed the fight with some clinical detachment. She wanted that here now too. She did not want to feel any rise to his call or alertness to his cry or any sense of commiseration for his plight. He had scraped her soul enough in his snide kind of way, and now it was his turn! And yet she was trembling now too, not knowing why. And she found herself rocking back and forth in the chair, hearing his cries and yet not fully able to charge them to the sound of the demons in hell. And she found herself in that terrible position, for as justice was served, another voice kept her from the moment of triumph and begged for some other meaning to all this.

It was near three o'clock and the crosscurrents of the struggle had begun to wear her down. Once she was conscious of Joseph stepping inside the door to look at his fallen leader, then at her, maybe to be sure she was doing everything right. The Sudanese girl had fled from the room earlier, unable to absorb the strange and terrifying sounds coming from the giant lashed to the bed. Now and then fits of rain hit the pan roof overhead drowning out his cries, giving her some reprieve.

But now she wanted desperately to be free of him. She wanted to leave him to his thrashing and babbling. But for some strange reason that was even more terrifying to her, she could not move. She prayed for release, until her hands hurt from clenching them so tightly in the intensity of her prayers. She wanted someone to come who knew what to do, silence him even. She prayed for detachment more than for anything else . . . but it would not come.

So it was only he and she now. In one moment she actually could look on the naked torso caught in the tangle of the sheet, jerking with his tortured images and see nothing more than neutral flesh suffering the bite of nature. At other times she could sense a feeling of vindication, a moment of smug spiritual achievement, like all that twisting and turning was the devil himself caught on the rack of God and begging to atone for all the havoc he had flung into the world in the name of the angel of light.

And then again there was that point of terror too, when the paralytic part of her lifted a terribly feeble hand and tapped on the empty chambers of her soul, knocking on the dry and dusty timbers that carried the weight of unused charity and threatened to tumble down into her immaculately swept rooms of legal finery. "Love for you is on page eight hundred of Appendix Z," Rudy had said, and it shot a reverberating echo through her, a seismic rumble even. And it was so loud and threatening that she shouted at Blake when his voice rose in agony, "Take him, whoever owns him! Take him!" And hearing herself screaming it above the sound of the rain on the roof, she clamped her hand over her mouth in fright, biting her fingers to keep back the words still in her throat.

She knew she had to leave it then, to protect herself from a blasphemy that would forever judge her in the end. She would get the signature first. She prepared the hypo just in case she would need it. She would release his right arm from the adhesive bind to allow him to use the pen. If he became violent, she would slip him the injection. She could count now on the fuzziness of this thinking, and move his hand, if necessary, to the deliberate act.

She got up then and saw his eyes flutter, stare emptily toward the ceiling. She went over and looked down at him. He was breathing hard yet, the sweat rolling heavily off his chest and down to the sheets to soak into dark designs. Though he looked at her, she knew he did not see her. Gingerly she reached up and cut the adhesive holding his right wrist to the bedpost. The arm fell to the bed like a club, lying alongside his body, the wrist showing puffy from the constriction of the tape.

"Now, Mr. Blake," she said pleasantly, calling out the familiar tone of a nurse on duty, seeking to disarm him, keeping her head up from his body as if she could not tolerate the sight of his sweat, "it's time to sign the order of the day . . . you hear me, Mr. Blake?"

He did not respond, so she went around the bed to work with the limp hand directly. She lifted it and put the pen between the pudgy fingers. He seemed to grip it, as if he knew perhaps? She guided it up to the papers she had nailed down on a clipboard. She felt no real pleasure in this, but she told herself now that it had to be done for the salvation of this place . . .

And then the pen fell out of his clumsy fingers. She made a quick move to snatch it up, but at the same instant his hand flashed out like a snake's head and caught hers in such a vice that she cried out in pain and terror. Not loud enough though, not as loudly as she wanted, not loud enough to carry to Joseph outside. His eyes were not on her, though. He was looking at something deep within himself, something beyond time and place . . . the grayish sheen to his eyes went to the shade of gun metal, then dissolved to a softer tone of bluish mist.

She fell to her knees beside the bed, the pain in her hand forcing her down, and all the time she tried to fight the grip, tugging to free herself.

"Oh, Jesus," she gasped, hanging there, half off the floor, her knees bent, wanting to touch the floor but unable to, her arm held up to that hand caught in that vice. "Don't do this to me . . . don't do this to me, Lord . . . I can't go any further with this man . . . I can't go any further than You've taken me . . . don't let me fall now into the pit . . . don't let me be swallowed up like this . . . You know I can't do more than I've done . . ."

She wanted to cry out for Joseph then, but suddenly the hand gripping hers relaxed. She could feel the rough calluses of his palm, the swollen contour of his fingers. But he was holding hers, like a child who has found assurance . . .

She waited. She could not sort out her feelings or the meaning of them. She felt the sweat of his hand in hers, the warmth of it, and she tried to remove it slowly, but each time it squeezed tightly, telling her to leave it. So she lay there, her knees finally touching the floor, her eyes now on the level of the mattress, staring at her hand lost in his, feeling the awesome immensity of the moment. She was not controlling him now! She had maneuvered every man to a position of humility before, either with a hypodermic or a stethoscope. Male flesh had remained a supple thing under her command, moved when she bid it, jumped when she pinched it. Such authority had kept her erect, functional, sealed off from debilitating disarray!

But it was his hand that held hers now. And into her mind of exploding images rose Kortoff to a point of wide-angled exposure . . . to the point when it seemed he stood over her in the ghastly array of throbbing glands and blue veins and dirty pockets on his knees . . . and she closed her eyes as the scream caught in her throat, and she tugged fiercely at the hand again. The hand tightened, and she heard him say, "Leave it."

And she stared at him, but his eyes were not open, yet his voice was so clear. It was not torn by his ravings now but modulated on a tone half between sleep and wakefulness. And then it seemed that the image of Kortoff took on a double vision, multiplying images until he was not easily recognizable, dissolving slowly off the center of her brain . . . and all that was left of it was empty buckets and mops and an open furnace box that burned in soft blue flame, harmless heat . . .

The hand tightened on hers again, an embracing feeling of solidarity, not demanding, not searing hot lines of ugly passion across her already tormented vision . . . it was instead a touch of communion, of need, a hand reaching to hers from the black waters of some tormented nightmare, depending on her to lead him out. And she opened her eyes again to see her hand lost in his, as if she had reached into a cookie jar . . . she felt the pulse of him there, something beyond what she had ever picked up through stethoscopes or the wires of a cardiogram. She felt life . . . for the first time in her long walk in the desert, she felt life!

And now he said, "Thank you . . . thank you for coming . . . it's been a long dark night . . . thank you for giving me your hand . . . I can't find my way out of here . . . Mr. Bell said you'd come sometime . . . when it was darkest . . . he had you right on this . . . 'the light shineth in the darkness and the darkness comprehended it not' . . . I've been waiting a long time . . . all alone . . . except for Rudy . . . you know Rudy . . . thank You, Jesus, thank You . . ."

He heaved a sigh then, his chest rising against the light as if he was bursting some hidden bonds within himself . . . and his eyes closed, and he fell into an uncertain but true sleep.

She stayed where she was, down on her knees by the bed, staring at his face, watching his chest rise and fall, noticing now the easy respiration. Only now and then his mouth or his leg would twitch—apart from that he was in easy tranquility. And as she felt the flesh of his hand on hers and stared at it again as if it were an apparition that needed careful interpretation, the full impact of what had occurred struck her deeply. And the waves of feeling widened within her, rose to a crest in her throat, and all the carefully constructed dikes within her seemed to collapse at once. She fought it all the way, for her years of building the layers of indifference to human emotion still held intact—she swallowed in harsh gulps, her body beginning to convulse with the pressures. And then it broke, coming with strange sighs and half-moans, that monster deep within her finally rising to the surface. She felt the hot tears, pouring salt into her mouth, gushing in uncontrollable torrents to fall on her hand, then in his, dropping there like wax to seal whatever strange and redemptive act they had shared together.

She woke up with a start. Her eyes caught the hand first in front of her. It was not her own. She raised her head slowly, staring at the hand, at her own inside it. She glanced up at him quickly.

He was looking at her, down the length of his bare chest. His eyes in particular were different. They seemed bluer, cleaner. The lumpy bulges of his skin were there yet on his face, but seemed subdued some, cut down, shrunken, taking away the cutting lines of pugnaciousness.

She felt embarrassed then and got up, forcing her stiff knees to straighten under her. The movement removed her hand from his, and she felt the cool air on it, but it left her feeling a sense of abrupt disengagement. It was almost like being pushed out of the nest.

"You handle all your patients that way?" he said, his voice quiet, lazy.

"Not all of them," she returned simply, not looking at him, gathering up a few bottles of pills on the side table.

"What time is it?"

She glanced at her watch. "Four-thirty . . . in the morning."

"You better get to Rudy and tell him to get the guys on the line . . . we'll have to go early. Is it raining?"

She looked around at the window. She could see traces of pink from the not yet risen sun mixing with the drying drops on the pane. "No."

He waited, his eyes staying on her face, as if trying to identify her with memory. He was not yet fully on track. The part of his brain that had shut out the possibility of the death of Rudy would not function for a long time. That news would have to be given to him at the right time.

"Was I sleepwalking?" he asked, glancing up at the adhesive strips that still held him.

"A little. You passed out . . . total exhaustion." She hesitated, wondering if she should tell him it was worse than that. "We had to make sure you didn't hurt yourself . . ."

"Section eight?" he offered, looking at her steadily.

"Something very close to that . . . yes."

She continued to stand there by the bed giving him furtive glances, sensing some kind of strange fusion had occurred between them and not fully knowing what. She wanted time to analyze it.

"Is Joseph around?"

"He's been outside all night."

"I'd like to see him."

"You can. I'll go over and get some breakfast," she said, wanting to be away from him now, to pull herself together. "You have to stay in bed . . ."

"Tied?" he said, his voice trying to lift to a bantering tone that had been his hallmark, but subdued now by the low energy flow.

She cut away the strips with a scissors and picked up her sweater to move for the door.

"Hey," and she paused to look at him. "Black on the coffee . . ." She sensed he wanted to say something else. She felt a flush in her cheeks but not knowing why.

"As you like it," she returned lightly and went out to tell Joseph he was wanted by his *"commandant-en-chef."* The tall African jumped to his feet eagerly. As she moved out the door, she heard Blake say to him, *"Comment von votre femme et familee?"* And Joseph's giggle sprayed in response, and he gleefully returned with:

*"Oui! Très bien, merci!"*

She paused outside the infirmary to take deep breaths of cool, damp air. The field had patches of water here and there, but most of it was already drying off. She put her hands to her cheeks, still felt the heat there. Something had happened, something strange, maybe even awesome! It was not only that he had come out of a completely hopeless pattern of collapse—although that was in itself a cause for wonder. But, beyond that, something had definitely altered inside her —some of the crackling, brittle rightfulness of cause had broken off somewhere deep within. So now, standing there in the fresh morning air, it was almost like being introduced to the world all over again.

She felt disturbed by it, even confused. And yet she had that strange feeling of peace! Then she heard the airplane engine kick to life out by the hangars. She couldn't tell for sure, but it looked like one of Mentaya's bigger Cessnas. Then suddenly she remembered what she had told him the night before. Oh, not now! She did not want Mentaya to get off the ground because of her complicity!

She ran to the dining room and found Shannon and the others

sitting there. They all looked as if they hadn't slept at all, nursing coffee cups, faces smudged with uncertainty.

"Shannon?" she said, and he got up quickly to move toward her, expecting bad news on Blake. "Is Mentaya warming up?"

"I guess so . . . he held a gun on Monk last night and walked straight to that drawer under the radio where the cables were hid. I don't know who told him. How's Blake?"

She glanced out the screen door toward the sound of the plane warming up, wishing now she knew how to undo it. "He—you asked for a miracle and you got it," she said simply.

"You mean—he's out of it?"

"He can take nourishment, and he's lucid—"

"Well, that's enough!" And Shannon ran out the door, the other pilots taking the cue and chasing out after him. Gina stumbled after them, trying to hold them back. When she got there, Shannon was already talking to Blake, who was up leaning on his elbows.

". . . we loaded the gas drums as you said," Shannon told him. "But Mentaya is out there insisting we load the nitro too . . . Mr. Blake, to fly nitro over that lake—"

"I put ten empty cannisters inside the reefer box number six," Blake said then, his voice hoarse with fatigue. "Mentaya won't know the difference, if you act as if they're the real thing when you load them . . ."

"Okay, sir," Shannon said with a quick grin. "But Mentaya has one of his men out there carrying a machine gun, saying we won't go until he gets gas for his planes . . . we loaded the last gallon in those drums on our planes—"

"He doesn't need full tanks," Blake came back quickly. "He's on a one-way trip into Terragona anyway. He's trying to squeeze the last ball of sweat out of you this morning, Shannon . . . just don't worry about him . . . get out on the flight line and start warming it up . . ."

They hesitated then, wanting to go, but hanging back, unsure. Shannon looked at them, then back at Blake. Finally Shannon said to them, "Move it . . . I'll see you out on the line in a few minutes . . ."

They continued to look anxiously at Blake, and Gina sensed now what Shannon meant when he said the previous night that Blake had to get out on that tower, or they wouldn't go. Seeing him laid out now, looking pale and still a bit in disarray against the sheets, the image had cut into their resolve.

"Let's go," Mundey finally said, and they turned to walk out reluctantly.

Only Shannon remained. He licked his lips uncertainly and said, "One thing, sir . . . when we get over the lake, after we dump the gas . . . how . . . how do we fire it?"

Blake looked at him as if he didn't comprehend the question. Then, "Just don't worry about it, Shannon . . ."

Shannon hesitated, wanting some clarification. Then, clearing his throat, he said, "They're hanging back today, Mr. Blake . . . the other pilots. It's not an easy piece of cake for them to divebomb that lake . . . I mean, it's not been easy flying nitro either . . . but none of them has ever skip-bombed a Cessna over seventy-foot palms—"

"Did you tell them why they have to do it?" Blake asked, and he sank back onto the pillows, as if he was unable to hold himself up on his elbows any longer.

"Yes, sir . . . I finally had to tell them early this morning. It—well, it put new pressure on them . . . they know they have to do it now, but—"

"They maybe want to wait for Gregson, to be sure?" Blake finished for him.

"I—I guess they don't like the idea of dropping the brick on Rayburn and the others in there—"

"Get out on the line, Shannon," Blake said then, trying to put command in his voice, but it trembled some in the effort. "You know what you have to do . . ."

Shannon nodded, put on his black baseball cap carefully and turned and walked out.

"Lie down!" Gina scolded him as Blake made a move to get up on his elbows again. She reached for another hypo that she had prepared.

"No drugs," he said quickly to her.

"You have to sleep now—"

"I said no drugs," he insisted. She looked at him, noticing the hard light in his blue-gray eyes. She put the hypo back on the table. "Now . . . there's a boy named Duka, you know him . . . every morning he comes to the tower about this time with his tray of ground nuts

. . . would you give him some money for them? A few francs will do it . . ."

"Certainly," she said.

He said nothing for a long ten seconds. Then, "Where's Joseph?"

"Last I saw him, a few minutes ago, he was heading for the hangars . . ."

He nodded. "Good," and he sank back down into the pillows with a sigh. "Which way is the wind blowing?"

She walked to the window and looked across the field toward the red windsock. It was beginning to flutter a little. "South, maybe a little southwest," she said and walked slowly back to the bed. "You shouldn't send them on this business of bombing the lake," she finally said, but she didn't press it, finding that she did not have the same sense of intensity about it any more. Besides, she knew it was a little late to argue it. "It's an awful burden for them to carry on their minds . . . especially when you can't be sure the fire will do it . . ."

He looked at her, a slight creasing between his eyes beginning to show, as if maybe he hadn't thought of that or maybe that the appeal was not in contempt. Finally he said, "I'll take that coffee now . . ." She folded her arms and pulled her sweater closer around her shoulders, turned and moved for the door. "One thing more," she stopped to look at him. "Did you drop this?" He extended the clipboard with Mentaya's papers still attached. She went back and took it from him, averting her eyes. Just for a second or two she hesitated, wondering if she should try to explain that. She felt his eyes on her, waiting? But she was unable to rise to it; the years of making sure everything she did was always rightful, thus forbidding apologies or explanations, would not permit her to now either.

"Lie down," she said crisply to him, and walked to the door quickly, her heart hammering strangely, suddenly craving the anonymity of the outside, unable to face the closure with him lest too much of herself be forced into the open.

Blake waited until Joseph came back. Whatever it was that had intersected his spirit during the long night had left him in a state of elevated peace. The hard knot that had hung in his chest for months was gone. The roaring of the forces of collision that had tortured his brain for years had stilled. He could hear the birds now, the first time such a sound had ever crossed over the threshold of his ears

297

and found lodging in his mind. The incessant crashing of surf that he had awakened to for so long was silent. He wanted time to dwell on these sensations, to drink it in, feeling the tortured glands of his body rise to partake of it hungrily.

He thought of Gina Roman, trying to analyze the contradictory posture of her by his bed, her hand, small and moist in his. He had lain there a good half hour looking down at her, at the hand lost in his, her face neutralized to innocence, the sharp lines of her facial structure now softened to bring out the striking lines of beauty there. He would not be able to explain what had brought her to that position, but he knew it had to be a part of the strange clashing of the elements that he vaguely remembered of the night before.

So now his drained senses began to build again. He lifted his head off the pillow and saw the shafts of pink growing larger. He put his feet over the side of the bed, feeling the room rock some, waited for it to correct itself. He pulled on his boots, found his shirt. His breath came short with the effort. He got to the window and looked out. He saw Joseph coming then, his tall, thin postlike figure moving in disconnected rhythm.

It was ready, then.

He began to sweat. The test was here, and if he could not do it now he never would. Joseph stepped into the room and nodded to him. It was a matter of time. If he was to do any good at all for Rayburn and the others, he would have to move fast—and he would be late even if he did pull it off . . .

He walked out of the infirmary, shaking his head against the dizziness and the blurring vision, refusing to give in to it, following Joseph toward the hangars. The sun was up now, slashing the remaining grays of the night with long shafts of red, giving no quarter. He saw the pilots standing around their planes, still not sure of what to do, the props still standing cold. Beyond them Mentaya was arguing profusely with Shannon in angry gestures. The two Cessna 206s were standing off to his right, props turning over in idle. No one was inside the planes . . . the pilots were busy elsewhere, hopefully preoccupied for another five minutes. He glanced at the 206 nearest him and noticed the end of the red hose sticking under the right door. The fifty-gallon drum of petrol was loaded now too, as he had instructed. He glanced at Sam and the other mechanics standing off to his left . . . Sam nodded, telling him all was set to go. Blake looked around one more

298

time. He could not see Belang anywhere now. He glanced at the line of black limousines over by the tower, like stabs of ink flung up against the white shale of the escarpment, coming to a peculiar lavender in that red sun. There was movement over there too, which meant the VIPs were up and anxious to make a move today if events afforded.

He saw the pilots turn his way then, watching him, wondering what he was doing there. Blake knew he had to move quickly now before Mentaya turned and saw him too. Sam and the other mechanics backed off slowly, leaving it to him, as if they knew he had to go the rest of the way alone. And maybe they knew too, even as he did, that maybe the only way those pilots were going to go today was by this one certain act of his own . . . A man could die for less! So it was down to him now, five years of accumulated hell boiling down to one piece of action . . . just he—and God? *Lord, look upon this poor child now as never before!*

Now he saw Mentaya turn away from Shannon and shout back into the hangars, "Belang!" Blake made his move then, knowing he had probably waited too long already. He had covered ten strides to the 206 and was reaching up to grip the handle of the door when he shot a quick glance over his shoulder. Mentaya was running toward him, closing fast, that .45 service automatic in his hand, the one Blake recognized easily as the one he had dropped a long time ago in the tower . . . he pulled on the door and started to climb up.

"Stop right there, Mr. Blake!"

Blake looked back. Mentaya had stopped not more than twenty yards away, lifting the gun to take aim at him. Blake was sure he would shoot, because for him there was no tomorrow. At the same instant, as he waited for the shock of the bullet, he saw the move to his left, coming as a kind of shadowy blur. The spear flew through the air in a flat line, a mere zipping fleck of substance caught in the uncertain rose-purple of the awakening day. It caught Mentaya high in the chest, going deep into the lungs. For a few seconds he stood there, absolutely still, staring at the shaft hanging out of him, trying to get his hands up to pull it out . . . then he dropped slowly to the ground, taking his time, as if he wanted to make sure as he landed that he would not lose any of the creases in his pants.

Blake ran back and stopped to lean over him, noticing that the spear had gone deep. The pilots were there too, not sure what to do.

Mentaya's eyes were larger now, as if intent on what had happened to him, but the piercing glow of them was subdued. His lips moved but nothing came. Finally, in a voice thick with pain and rising fluid in his lungs, he said, "The wheels of God grind slow but fine, Mr. Blake?" and a faint smile tugged weakly at the corners of his mouth. And there seemed to come over him then a strange pose of peace as if he was glad his struggle was ended. Then, turning his eyes to Blake, he added, "My son . . . Mr. Blake, don't forget my son . . ."

Blake knew there wasn't time to linger if he was going to climb his own mountain then. He stood up, turned and ran for the plane, shouting over his shoulder, "Get those planes in the air, Shannon!" Then he was up in the seat, running his eyes over the gauges, licking at the sweat forming on his upper lip. He gave throttle and moved the plane slowly down the wet clay toward the dining room, all the time conscious of the pressure rising in his chest, laying hold of his throat, forcing his hands to tremble, building that terrifying mental block. He didn't want to take the time here on the ground to let that monstrous hand squeeze him any harder, so he clumsily kicked the plane around by the infirmary, even as he saw Gina Roman standing there by the door, a tray in her hands with his black coffee . . . and he caught the almost delicate pose of her there, looking at him with a somewhat jilted expression, something he had never seen in her before, as if he had broken a promise to her . . .

Now he was pointed toward the far end of the runway, and for a few seconds he hesitated, looking down the smooth surface of the clay. No man can go home again! That's what Rudy always said. Well, then . . . take the highway! And he jammed the throttle all the way in and let out the brakes. The plane bit into the soggy clay, and she started a reluctant roll and seemed to shoot out from under him. He saw the hangars whip by and the pilots and mechanics standing there in a long line abreast. The mechanics had their closed fists in the air, their mouths open and shouting what he knew it had to be: *"La jour va être long!"*

Now the plane bucked on him, wanting to rise to its natural instinct of flight but held to that wet clay. It seemed to fishtail hard on him, threatening to slide off its run . . . and for that instant he was at Kennedy International again, the terminal buildings sinking away from him . . . and all the warning lights were on, and he could not pull up the plane!

He saw the windsock go by, bending its red bag out of the south, waving mockingly at him. God, was there a point when the mind would not rise above the accumulated debris of a burned-out soul? And now he could see the rim of the runway flatten out in front: He was running out of airfield and would in a second or two be going over and down the slope straight into the Durungu village . . .

The plane would not rise!

God, make it a good crash, then! And he yelled, "God, don't let me come out of this having to look at empty faces again! Put wind under this bird, God! Put wind under her!"

With desperation then he yanked back on the wheel. The plane came up, staggering under the prod but yawing in a sickening slide to the left. He felt a fresh spurt of terror as he overcorrected, and the plane went into a crablike glide not more than twenty-five feet above the tin shacks of the Durungu market square. People starting to set up shop began to scatter . . .

JESUS, THIS PLANE ACTS LIKE A COW! NO, IT MUST BE ME, GOD! JESUS, MUST IT ALWAYS BE ME?

Then he managed to get the plane off its cockeyed angle downward, and at the same time he grabbed his left knee, which was shaking so violently to keep from clamping on the rudder. Then the stall alarm began to squeal at him, and the red light was on!

DEAR GOD, ANOTHER WARNING LIGHT! His nose was too high for the power! He shoved the control column forward, and the ground came up at him. A herd of cattle began stampeding in front of him, the herders chasing after them . . . he fought the urge to yank the nose up again and willed himself to ease it . . . *Dear God, help me to ease it!*

Now he was careening around in a sloppy turn and heading for the hangars again, no more than a hundred feet up, and he knew he was going to pile into them . . . the stall alarm was on again . . . the images of flame were sucking at his brain . . . his eyes swept frantically over the gauges . . . then he saw it . . . the horizon indicator showed him tilting up and sliding off, totally out of trim! He forced himself to let up on the controls, allowing the nose to come down off its disastrous pitch . . . he felt the lift immediately as the engine grabbed firm chunks of life and passed it on to the tired wings

. . . he was over the hangars by then but not clearing them by much
. . . one glance down showed him the other three planes with their
props turning, moving out quickly to follow him . . .

GOD OF WIND AND FIRE AND SPIRITS LAIN DORMANT
BY THE REFUSAL TO RISE TO ONE SINGLE ACT OF COUR-
AGE! SOMEBODY SAID THAT SOMEWHERE A LONG TIME
AGO . . . NOW, RUDY, FOR ALL THE SWEAT YOU LOST
OVER ME . . . BEHOLD! AND AUGIE SHOULD HAVE
LIVED TO SEE IT! AND FOR ALL OF THEM NOW, WHO
WERE WILLING TO DIE TO PROVE MY PAST HAS NO TER-
ROR OF JUDGMENT, THIS IS FOR ALL OF YOU TOO! JESUS,
NOW LET THE DEED ARTICULATE THE WORD! I'M FREE!
GOD, I'M FREE AT LAST!

# CHAPTER XIV

Gina did not want to move from her place by the infirmary wall, her body pressed into the mud brick, her face turned away from the dust and hot breath of burning grease the planes poured over her as they took off after Blake. It was a long time after silence had come down on the field before she lifted her head, taking in the turned-over tray at her feet, the coffee pot lying like a useless tin can a few feet away. She knew she had to move, to rise to the instincts that her medical training had drilled into her. The other feelings that lay a heavy hand on her heart and left her in a strange void, precipitated out of the disappointment she felt at seeing Blake's face flash by in that airplane, she forced aside now.

She got up, stumbled back into the infirmary, grabbed her black bag and half ran out to the hangar, where Mentaya still lay with that spear sticking up from his chest. She examined the wound, saw that the spear had cut through a pulmonary artery; the bleeding was profuse. Mentaya remained unconscious, and she sensed that his chances for life were feeble at best. She called to Sam and the others to help her remove the spear, cautioning them to be careful as they removed it a half inch at a time. When it was out finally, she went to work, knowing she was not fully equipped to handle this kind of emergency, yet knowing she would have to put all her powers to work if Mentaya was to have any kind of chance at all.

She didn't know how long she worked over Mentaya, feeling the mounting sense of alarm, even panic, at losing control of the bleeding. After a while she sensed Timothy Belang crouched down a few feet away watching her, chewing on that long cigar, saying nothing. It all seemed a peculiar blur of time, blood and membrane. Once she remembered going back to the infirmary for fresh plasma, there to find the boy.

*"Bonjour, madame,"* he said in a small, timorous voice, the smile faint, uncertain, while he adjusted the tray of ground nuts on his head.

*"Bonjour, Duka,"* she said softly, sensing the clinging odor of Blake's sweat yet in the room. She reached into her jacket pocket and pulled out the coins, extended them to the boy. He looked at them, then at her, then around the room. He was not going to accept the purchase except from Blake . . . to do otherwise was to accept the finality of Blake's disappearance. She withdrew the coins and leaned a moment against the wall to watch him as he looked around the room aimlessly and finally went out with a feeble, *"Merci, madame . . ."*

She remembered crouching over Mentaya again, suturing the wound, rigging the plasma bottles with the help of Belang and Sam. She heard the plane overhead once, circling, then landing, the squeal of the wheels against the clay. She did not look up. That would have to be Gregson's plane then coming with the World Health people. When the plane rolled into the parking area behind her, she turned her head once to glance at it. In that instant she saw the familiar ROUTE 66 on the yellow fuselage.

"Rudy!" and she ran to him as he jumped down out of the plane, feeling the shout of sheer exultation rise in her throat; and as she ran, she cried, because it was no longer difficult to do. She saw Potter hobbling across the tarmac, hanging on to his bruised rib cage as he half ran to meet Rudy. Sam and the other mechanics were already at the plane, pounding Rudy on the back.

"Gas her up, Sam," Rudy said. "I'm late for my appointment . . ."

Gina ran up to him and threw her arms around his neck and buried her face in his leather jacket. "Rudy . . . never have I had such a wonderful answer to prayer . . ."

"What's this?" Rudy said to her, backing off a step to look into her face. "Don't tell me Gina Roman, the last of the dry-eyed warriors, is shedding a tear?" She wiped at her cheeks hurriedly, embarrassed, still not used to showing any such emotion, trying to laugh up at him at the same time.

"We thought you had crashed . . ."

"Naw, that was some gamewarden," Rudy came back, looking toward the canvas shelter half that shaded Mentaya on the ground, "on a drunken spree. I had to lay over at Myagunde last night to ne-

304

gotiate for a copter with a cargo of petrol . . . I tried calling in but nothing, I mean nothing, was riding the airwaves last night. The copter'll be here in a couple of hours. Where's Blake, and what's up with Mentaya?"

She blurted it out to him, trying to keep it in the order of sequence, explaining finally that she could not chance moving Mentaya to the infirmary with the bleeding and all. When she finished, Rudy's face had taken on a shade of tightness. He took off his sunglasses with both hands and stared a long time toward Mentaya's prostrate form on the ground.

"Blake flew?" he said finally, his voice caught between a growing note of wonder and pleasure and cautiousness. "I'll be . . ." And he shook his head at the ground. "I would have liked to have seen that . . . you want to gas me up, Sam?"

"No can do," Sam came back quickly. "All petrol gone to Terragona with boss man . . ."

"What about that 206 over there?"

"It's got less than half a tank," Potter interjected.

Rudy glanced at him. "You got a proverb for that, Potter?"

" 'The prudent man looketh well to his going,' " Potter came back quickly.

"You tell that to Blake or the rest of them?" Rudy countered, frowning now. "Skip-bombing that lake is like diving a bald eagle into a gopher hole." He paused then, his voice beginning to sound dismal, and he looked at Gina steadily: "So what plane did he fly?"

"The other 206," she said.

He nodded, as if he was afraid of that, and he put his sunglasses back on slowly over his eyes like they were a shawl of mourning.

They all looked up then as the two red planes passed over the field and banked around over the cotton hair to make the landing.

"And who might that be?" Rudy asked, almost indifferently now, for all events here were paled into insignificance compared to what was going on in Terragona.

"Gregson," Gina said simply. "He said he'd be here today with the World Health people . . ."

"Too little and too late," Rudy commented. "Well, Gina, you'll have to spit it all out again . . . only this time for the record . . ."

"Do it for me, Rudy, please?" she appealed to him then. "I've really got to go back to the infirmary for some things . . . I . . . I just can't go through it again . . . will you, please? Jeremy here will fit in the pieces . . ."

She didn't wait for his reply, but turned quickly and walked, almost ran, back to the infirmary, desperate now for withdrawal, unsure of herself, of her emotions.

Gregson got out of his plane and walked over to the unconscious form of Mentaya, ten feet from where Joseph sat on his haunches against the hangar wall.

Rudy joined him there as the five-man, slack-jawed commission gathered around. Rudy repeated the sequence of events as Gina had given them, Potter chiming in now and then with the missing pieces. Gregson kept staring down at Mentaya, trying to weigh the enormity of all this against the mission.

"Will he live?" he said when Rudy paused.

"Gina says it's going to be close . . . but she thinks so . . ."

Gregson nodded. Beyond the weight of Mentaya's still form on his mind now, he felt the throbbing of bafflement in the fact of Blake and the other pilots having gone to lay the fire on Caha, even when he was sure he had gotten through to someone here last night the order to halt operations. When Rudy mentioned the lost American satellite and Blake's apparent insistence that it was leaking bacteria in Caha, Gregson interrupted, "I am not following you, Rudy . . . what satellite and where?"

"Lake Caha," Rudy answered. "Blake apparently had information taken from the truck driven by a U. S. Space Agency man . . . in fact, I was with him when he found it . . ."

"Could that be true, Dr. Yammanaka?" Gregson turned to the Oriental at his side. "That lost satellite possibly in there and leaking the bacteria?"

Yammanaka took off his glasses to frown at the ground. "It is, of course, possible . . . yes . . . but we have little or no information on any space contraband classifications, nor have we received word that there is any aboard—"

"Would American Space notify you?" Gregson asked.

"Not necessarily," Yammanaka said. "The State Department will hold any information to be sure of the political factors first—"

"And supposing it is space bacteria in there, then?" Gregson continued.

306

"Then, of course, it is even more serious, Mr. Gregson. We do know that space chemistry of a particular strain will multiply so rapidly that the containment possibilities are almost impossible—"

"Milt, whatever is going on?" G.D. cut in irritably. "We better be thinking about what we are going to say to the Premier about Mentaya—"

"A fire on Caha makes sense then, Doctor?" Gregson ignored G.D.

Again Yammanaka took his time. "Who can say? It is always possible . . . and I think Dr. Rayburn must have reasons for asking for a fire, then . . ."

"In any case, we should try to reach our pilots and order them to return before they lay that fire, Milt," G.D. argued. "We cannot put our people into jeopardy to that degree!"

Gregson glanced over to where Timothy Belang stood at a discreet distance, watching them with some detachment, his arms folded across his chest, chewing on a cigar. "I take it you saw what happened here, Timothy?" Gregson called to him.

Belang pulled at his scraggly goatee thoughtfully and walked toward Gregson, glancing only once at Mentaya on the ground. "I had no reason to resist what happened to that—that patriot there who is pinned to the soil he was willing to betray," he said solemnly, removing his chewed cigar slowly and tossing it on the ground next to Mentaya. "As for Joseph? The Africans have a proverb which says, 'He who carries fire in his hand cannot wait.' So he who brings death suffers death, *comprenez-vous?*"

"I don't understand, Milt," G.D. interrupted impatiently.

"As for the lost American satellite in Caha, it is true," Belang went on. "I and my colleague there were on a mission to retrieve it, at least that was part of our assignment. It is true that an American space agent in a green truck was, in fact, done away with in accordance with the cold-war nature of things . . . he did have teletypes about the satellite, and your man Blake did have that information . . . in any case, Monsieur Gregson, I am trying to say I wish to be of service to you if I can, hopefully . . ."

"Thank you, Timothy," Gregson said, not knowing what else to say.

"This is something for the American Government people, Milt," Merriweather insisted. "We have no right tampering—"

"The tampering has been done," Gregson replied bluntly. "A satellite carrying contraband bacteria has landed in Terragona—"

"It is not our responsibility!" G.D. countered. "We are dealing with an unknown, unclassified bacteria strain and taking drastic action that we don't even know will affect it. In the meantime, that puts our people—and the Hamaran team in there—in a critical situation. I demand you raise Blake and insist he return—"

"They're beyond recall now anyway, sir," Rudy put in politely. "I expect right now they are approaching the lake . . . I doubt you could raise them on the radio with the kind of signal jamming the Terragona frequency, which appears to be a self-destruct countdown signal from the satellite . . ."

"Nevertheless, Milt," Maddigan intoned for the first time, "Blake was completely out of line taking that decision on himself—"

"It is not a mission decision," G.D. jumped in quickly, almost as if he were speaking to Albert Banqui, then a few feet beyond him. "We must make the attempt to communicate that to our pilots—"

"Rudy, there's a transmitter in my plane," Gregson said then, knowing he had no choice, that the record should be served. "Will you get it up in the tower and have Potter try to get Bungari on it and see if our gas trucks passed there yet?"

"I have a copter coming with petrol," Rudy said to him hopefully. "In about an hour and a half—"

"You got petrol?" Gregson turned to look at him.

Rudy looked embarrassed then. "Well, when you froze any more petrol on Blake, he asked me to try for some in Myagunde . . . that's why I'm still here and the rest of them are gone . . ."

Gregson nodded. "We may all be too late now anyway," he said to no one in particular. "But if our trucks passed Bungari, there may yet be time for something . . . Bungari is only forty minutes from here . . ."

"What do you have in mind, Milt?" Merriweather asked, his question almost an appeal.

Gregson didn't reply, because he didn't know honestly how to answer that. Gas was perhaps nothing more than a symbol of hope now anyway. And so instead he told Rudy to try to get Terragona on the other radio. "Dr. Yammanaka needs to talk to Rayburn about the progress of that bug," he explained.

"I doubt that signal will allow us through," Rudy warned.

"Okay . . . just see what you can do . . ."

As Rudy turned to run ahead, Gina Roman came up and knelt down beside Mentaya, listening to his heart with her stethoscope. Gregson noticed that her face was pale now, bringing out the sharp points of her face . . . and there was something else, but he couldn't tell, something maybe trying to come through the careful composure. Or had something come out already?

"Can you save him?" Gregson asked then.

She didn't answer right away and finally dropped the stethoscope back around her neck, continuing to look at Mentaya's face. "I'm going to try," she said simply. "There is a government doctor at Bungari . . . you might do well to get him up here . . ."

"Shouldn't we try to get as many of our people out of Terragona as we can?" G.D. asked again as Gregson turned to walk toward the tower across the field.

"How about using that plane over there?" Maddigan suggested, indicating the two-engine Dakota behind them by the hangar.

"Any plane that size trying to get into Terragona will cause more trouble than anything else," Gregson corrected.

"So get the Hamaran Army to go in with you," Maddigan countered morosely, and there were a few murmurs of approval from the other members of the commission walking behind Gregson.

Gregson did not respond. It was not a reasonable suggestion, he knew, but mainly emotion, a protective instinct for their own and maybe for themselves as custodians of those lives. He knew evacuation was impossible now. If this was a fact of space bacteria, Rayburn would not allow any of them in Terragona to go out for fear of carrying the highly volatile contamination to the outside. Rather, Gregson began projecting what his moves should be in the next hour or so, since the rapidly diminishing element of time was going to force some kind of action.

He glanced once at Albert Banqui, who walked beside him writing in his notebook as he moved. He wondered then if he was wise in bringing the journalist along, now that events had taken such a turn. But even beyond that, he was concerned even more about whether he was right in delaying that fire on Caha that Rayburn had asked for last night. If he had cleared it and gotten a helicopter from Jamison, he might at least have some sense of vindication in knowing he had moved fast enough to affect that bug before it had gotten out

*309*

of hand . . . because now he wasn't sure if there was time to get it done. And he thought of the irony here, that they had come to hold court on Blake, who now was probably, for all anybody knew, the only man left with a chance to stop that galloping bug from spreading beyond Terragona. He hunted for a mint but could find none . . .

Blake saw the lake coming up under his left wing, glistening blue in the morning sun, lying in its garb of innocency that centuries of peacefulness had given it. He eased the throttle back for the descent, glancing to his right to see the other three planes cluster in a holding pattern, waiting for him to lead on as had been agreed.

He was reluctant now to have the flight end in an act of violence. He was still experiencing the warm feeling of having finally mastered the five years of nightmare. Even though he felt unsteady at times yet, especially when pockets of turbulence bounced the plane, he knew he had control again and would have liked to fly on and on.

But the lake was there . . . whatever feeling of peace and sweet victory he had in the climbing of this mountain God had seen fit to give to him, the lake was there, and with it he felt the clutch of the old fear grab his stomach and tell him this would not be that easy. He went down easily, nose forward, knowing he didn't have that much time to indulge second thoughts or nurse the doubts. He made his exploratory pass, saw the seventy-foot palms that encircled the lake, computed quickly what he would have to do to get over them, all the time conscious of that bleeping signal on the plane's radio, stronger now, chopping off the seconds to final destruction . . .

He made his circle of the lake, feeling the 206 ride heavy in the bank with a tendency to slide off. Once he got down over that lake, he would have to stay down over it. It was not more than a half-mile long and maybe an eighth wide. Since he did not have an extra man to work the flow valve on that hose leading out of the barrel and down through the doorframe, he would have to stay down over the lake until it was emptied. That would mean doing 180-degree turns over the trees and diving back down over the water again, all the time keeping the plane down close to the surface so the gas would hit its target. At least the other pilots, with that extra man, could make their run, shut off the flow valve and go back up over the trees, make their turn and come back, avoiding those tight circles . . .

Well, at this point, his was not to envy them the extra margin. He

took ten seconds to remind God that he was still the unsure pilot
even yet, that the maneuvers he had to make now in this plane
were not those a man suffering from flight shock from former days
should undertake. He thought of Turgobyne then too, wishing he had
the time now to explain to the old chief why all this was necessary
. . . but would he ever really understand? Then he took one more
last, almost longing, look at the clear skies above him and the shim-
mering blue below, and put his left wing down quickly and let the
plane slide off down the cliff of sky to the lake. He let out a yell once
as he felt the plane jerk away from him too soon, and the tips of the
palms flashed under him so close that he could see the patches of
moisture on them . . . *too close!* He fought the plane out, its engine
almost stalling, nose up, side slip, straightened her out over the water
and kicked hard on the left rudder as the trees at the end of the lake
rushed at him . . . the 180 turn sucked the wind out of his stomach
and the seat belt jammed hard into his middle . . . but he was around
now, going back, not fifty feet above the water. He reached back of
the seat with his right hand, felt for the flow valve, opened it . . . he
disregarded the sweat stinging his eyes, the dryness in his mouth, the
steel fingers pressing on his throat . . . he kept his mind on that signal that kept up its maddening, monotonous bleeping, warning him
that he was on the losing end of time . . .

He lost track of how many runs he had made across the lake, how
many looping, terrifying tight turns he made over those trees and back
down again, all the time talking to himself and God . . . until finally
he reached back of the seat and tapped the barrel with his knuckles,
hearing the hollow sound feed back to him . . . he pulled the nose up
and climbed out of the perimeter of the lake, to wiggle his wings at
the pilots still in the waiting pattern.

He watched them put their noses down together, heading into that
straight-on glide downward, a mere hundred yards apart. Shannon's
plane slipped into the stalling-off dive over the lake first, then the
other two. Their wings wobbled uncertainly as they leveled out over
the lake, trying to hold their speed and keep their noses down to prevent the stall, the stream of gas pluming out behind them in a silvery,
misty cloud . . .

He watched them, for five minutes or more, make their passes,
pull up, do their swinging turns over the trees, like herons diving for
fish, rush back down to the lake again. And Blake, watching from a

thousand feet up, felt a growing sense of pride in them, a welling up of communion with them as he never had before, watching them narrowly miss each other in those turns but never hesitating in their haste to get the gas dumped before that satellite blew . . .

And then they were pulling up, climbing for the sun, away from the lake, their yellow wings flashing. "Act three," Blake said to himself, licking his dry, cracked lips, reached under his seat and pulled out the flare pistol, checked the chamber to be sure the shell was in place, put four more on the seat beside him. He leaned forward and saw the light line in the window where Sam was supposed to have used the glass cutter. He found the acetylene-torch goggles on the seat next to him, put them on carefully. Then he reached over with the flare pistol and tapped lightly on that eight-inch square in the window. The glass fell out after the third firm tap. The wind rushed into the cabin, and Blake eased back on the throttle to cut down on the flow of it.

Then, clearing his throat, as if he were getting ready to make a speech, he tipped the plane over again in that sliding kind of dive, forcing himself to ignore the galloping of his heart. He came over the lake again, did a steep ninety-degree turn not more than fifty feet over the lake, catching only a brief glimpse of a cluster of Terragonans watching from behind a swampy scrub on the shore. He stuck the pistol out the hole in the window and fired. The yellow magnesium flare arched out too far and lost most of its heat before it reached the gas-soaked water. He went up again, did a tight turn over the trees and down again. The same thing happened. He knew he would have to stand the plane all the way over on her wing and fire straight down if he was going to get it done. This time he dropped lower, watching the water carefully, computing the distance, then dropped the left wing in the screaming 180 turn. He was so close to the water now that he could see scraggles of seaweed. He fired. The flare hit the water from not more than thirty feet up. He saw it disappear into the water, dissolve, and then the gas ignited under him with a blinding kind of orange-yellow flame, reaching up with its heat, engulfing him. The plane bucked on the updraft of heat, bounced him into an almost uncontrollable slide . . . he hit full throttle, skimming the trees just barely and shot skyward as fast as he could.

Now he was up and turning to get a look down. The lake was a mass of orange-yellow flame with black, billowing smoke boiling upward. He felt an acute pang of regret then, even sadness, for Turgobyne, the Terragonans, for Rayburn and the others. And even as he watched, waiting, he saw the explosion at the far end of the lake. It plumed up into an angry pillar of white water and debris, then settled into a white-bearded froth. The satellite had blown. The bleeping radio signal was dead.

Now the other three planes came abreast of him, banking eastward for home. Blake glanced at his gas gauge, then up at the dials of the reserve tanks in the ceiling. He was about out. Nobody said anything over the radio. There was nothing to talk about. What they had done took a bit of flying courage to say the least; but right now each of them had to be thinking more about the totality of their act, hoping that what they did was right. But in any case, they knew that for their colleagues down below, they could only reap the whirlwind for it.

Finally Blake picked up the mike and said, on the now open channel, "Shannon, take them home . . . I've got to make a call into JERICHO. When you get back to Durungu, report to Gregson . . . tell him to wait for any further messages from JERICHO. Fly it straight, gentlemen . . . and well done . . ."

There was a long pause, and then Shannon's voice came on, rather subdued, maybe an element of question mixed with it, as he said, "Roger . . . out." Nobody had to tell them that Blake was just about out of petrol. They knew that he knew the margins when he decided to take the 206. And nobody had to tell them that it was useless for them to hang around on their own low tanks.

Chief Turgobyne stood a long time on the porch watching the flames on Caha leap to a frenzy, boiling up a heat that reached to him and Torendasa, who stood next to him. Now and then Torendasa hid his face in fear of the wrath of Caha, but Turgobyne never let his eyes waver. The flames burned deeply into his mind, dictated the will of Caha. Then the sudden thunder in the sky shook the porch, and it brought a new moan of terror from Torendasa. Turgobyne, his heart running wild like a child's in the night, saw the pillar of white-yellow flame across the lake. Then it died and sank into the flames.

It was done.

When the flames began to diminish, Turgobyne glanced up into the murky sky where the yellow birds were disappearing into the far horizon. He finally dropped his eyes to the tiles on the porch, poking at them with his stick. He was reluctant to speak even yet, though the anger in him burned with a fierceness that threatened to consume him.

"Purge the land, then, Torendasa," he finally said, his voice barely above a whisper. "Send the word by the drums that Caha has spoken his will by fire. None of them shall live. Do you understand?"

Torendasa bowed. Turgobyne said no more. Torendasa waited to be sure. Then slowly he backed away from his leader. The shoulders of the tall king seemed even more bent now, and his head remained bowed. How would he now stand against the land, his own people, after this? Even if Terragona spears claimed all of Yellow Bird's people this day, would that satisfy the people who had suffered their long night of pain?

Torendasa did not know. But he feared for the tall king now. And he knew even now that the chief felt no pleasure in his ordered vengeance—he would have yet trusted Yellow Bird, the one who walked with bells on his feet, in spite of it all, except there was no way to defy Caha.

It was going on 8:30 A.M. when Rick Collins reported the blowing of the lake to Trask and Rayburn in Trask's lab, and that it was Blake who did it with his planes. Alicia had just come in with a Silex of coffee and stood there staring at Rick, then at the other two. Nobody said anything. It was done.

"What about the radio, Rick?" Rayburn finally asked.

"Well, that jammed radio signal is gone, for what reason I can't say . . . Durungu should be open now, except we are so weak on power after all that transmitting yesterday and last night—"

"You better try to get Talfungo," Rayburn added. "Gregson should know what went on in here . . . maybe you ought to try to raise Blake, too, and see if World Health told him what they found—"

"You can ask him direct," Collins replied. "He's heading in here right now on his last gallon of gasoline . . ."

Alicia moved to put the Silex on the workbench and said, "You mean at last I get to see my hero?" She tried to play it light, but it got lost in the atmosphere that carried the weight of final things.

"You better get on that radio, Rick," Rayburn advised.

"Right," Collins said and left the room.

"And I, Doctors, must see to our patients," Alicia added, moving for the door in that swaying walk. She hesitated at the door, one hand on the doorknob, as if she wanted to say something more. But her face showed the perplexity of the moment, because there seemed no point now in commenting on the inevitability of the end. Yet, like all creatures of dust, Rayburn sensed, she wanted to touch them in some expression of durability, maybe to get one last encouragement that death was not going to be too painful. Then, as if sensing the irrelevancy of words, she opened the door and went out.

Rayburn and Trask drank their coffee in silence, each of them preoccupied with the larger, emerging event.

"Well, how much time now, Trask?" Rayburn finally asked.

Trask took his time as usual. "Hear the drums?" Rayburn listened and caught the faint beat of them in the distance. "They're probably sending the word straight out of the Imperial Palace at Caha . . . they won't wait any longer now . . ."

Rayburn nodded, downed the rest of his coffee and put the cup on the workbench carefully, as if every move was now calculated to save time.

"Blake picked the wrong time to come calling," he said almost whimsically. "Or maybe the wrong time to run out of gas . . ."

"Or maybe he knows it's the right time," Trask replied, staring into his empty cup, not bothering to amplify.

It was 8:35 when Blake saw the JERICHO strip coming up through the blur of his prop. He eased throttle and began his descent, knowing he had to get around fast and down before the last of his gas went. The field was still open, but he could see a lot of movement in the brush near the hospital Quonset. As he passed over the hospital, he saw two people standing out in front, waving up at him. They did not appear to notice the activity in the jungles near them, or maybe they were resigned to it anyway.

He tried the radio again and Collins' voice chirped, "Roger, big man, did you bring the body beautiful?"

"Roger," Blake replied and glanced over his shoulder at the VW shell sitting in the cargo bay, the leather cargo belts holding it securely to the floor. He switched off the frequency then, wanting to concentrate on the landing.

The VW was all he could do for Turgobyne now, what little gesture there was left in it. It maybe wouldn't make up for what he did to the lake, but maybe it was the one article left that Turgobyne really wanted in all this. Maybe when it was all over, the old chief would have to start picking things over. Maybe in the end it wasn't medicine he wanted and certainly not the nitro. Maybe the yellow bird "magic" in the end was at best not a good price to pay for all that had happened to him. So maybe the car would make up for some of the loss?

Now Blake was beyond the strip, over the jungle again. He saw the clearing below him, just off the end of the runway, looking like a yam farm. There were Terragonans there too, standing still, looking up at him.

He passed on and made a wide turn to come into the final approach, glancing at the gas gauge that was bumping the empty peg, the prop sound easing into a fine whisper as he throttled down and applied half flaps. The trees skimmed under his wheels, rolling by him like a carpet of green velvet. The sun stroked the leaves with the splash of life-giving communion, and the gentle, peaceful south wind made them nod at him in lazy approval. It was as if the entire galaxy of angelic armies were watching, waving their arms at him! And even as he saw the field coming up, he could see those figures at the far end, near the Quonset, waving him in, reaching to him for the welcome embrace.

And in that rich moment, he forgot the stink of death that had burned his body and mind over the years; he forgot the rage of those long nights when he fought those images of flame, trying desperately to negotiate some kind of peace with them. He forgot all, caught in this magnificent moment of sheer balance, hanging between heaven and earth in a long, easy drift to the ground, those people waving him home and watching each tree, each leaf growing larger as he descended.

JESUS, IT IS ENOUGH! He said it out loud, for want of something to express it all: "Amen! The long day is ended!"

He did not see the tree at all as it fired off its sling below, but he felt the crush of it on his prop and under-carriage. He knew he had not scraped the tree himself, though he wasn't sure if he hadn't run out of gas. But then, the sound of the motor was still strong, and he knew in that single instant that what had hit him had come from the ground.

It jerked him around once, jarringly . . . he hit the throttle instinctively to get power back, but he knew the bird was mortally wounded. He had only one impression as he saw the ground come up —the plane was going in easy, almost gently, as if God would not allow death its unholy design or violence any more.

Now he could even see the spot where he was going to hit, near the end of the runway in the brush. It looked soft, specially prepared even, cushioned by the heavy green ferns. He rose to meet it as the whining of the wind in the broken structure of the plane shrilled to a protesting scream.

And now he felt no regrets.

Kumako felt no rising point of triumph even as the yellow bird staggered under the crush of the tree. The months of waiting, hoping, had ended in the sound of that palm roaring like an animal in its up-ward spring. He heard the shouts of his people there in the clearing as the yellow bird faltered, parts of its feathers flying into the wind. But he did not shout with them. The big bird came down in a sliding drift, seeming to fight gamely to right itself, then faltering in a struggle it knew it could not win . . . when it disappeared beyond the trees, he waited for the sound of it striking the earth. There was none. He stayed where he was as his warriors ran through the forest to find it . . .

He could remember only one time before in his life when he had felt such contradictory emotions . . . as a boy when he had wounded that deer and followed it for days, never allowing it to rest to lick its wound dry and perhaps heal itself . . . until he found it at last having died by a small stream, too weak to go on. He had no satisfaction in that death then, and he would not eat the meat his mother prepared from it . . .

What was it in this death of the yellow bird that made him stand alone in the clearing when he should be the first to drive his spear into the flesh, the first to tear the yellow body apart, the first to raise its skin for all to see? He had outfoxed it, trapped it, destroyed it. The honor of final victory was his now! Terragona was still possessed by Turgobyne, and the glorious one could continue to rule. Soon they would come and carry him to Turgobyne's Council Chambers, the yellow skin riding with him as proof for all to see what Caha had won! Soon the robes of purple would be on his shoulders, hung on him by Turgobyne himself, and the pain in the land would end.

But it was not a good death the yellow bird had met this day. His stomach did not feel warm over it. Like the deer, he remembered, it had died choosing its own way and its own place by a stream of life, mocking him in the end, that the victory was not all his.

So he sat on a stump, stuck his spear into the ground beside him and waited for them to come. No birds sang. No frog croaked. And now there was no wind.

It was going on 8:41 when Rudy, straining to catch the radio message coming in, picked up his pencil and began writing on a yellow piece of paper in big block letters. Gregson leaned over his shoulder to watch the letters unfold, sensing Rudy's hesitation as he wrote until he stopped writing altogether.

"Milt?" Merriweather prodded him impatiently then, and Gregson picked up the paper from under Rudy's hand, glancing at the big Jew quickly, who simply stared at the radio dial, his face drawn tight against the high cheekbones, his wide mouth pressed into a thin line.

Gregson cleared his throat and began reading the message aloud for all of them: "Lake Caha successfully fired . . . all airfields in north and south reported blocked with brush by Terragonans, impossible to get into by our planes . . ." Somebody sucked in his breath shakily in the room, and Gregson paused before going on. Then: "Blake was killed five minutes ago in a crash trying to get into JERICHO . . ."

"Oh, Jesus," somebody moaned in the room, and the faces seemed to go blank then, frozen in poses of incomprehension or maybe withdrawal from knowing how to react toward the man they had come to investigate. Merriweather, his face gone suddenly ashen, took off his glasses slowly, like they were too heavy for his face. Gregson felt a heavy sag inside, clamping down hard on his heart. He had wanted more than anything to talk to Blake once more . . . maybe to tell him he had prayed for him. It seemed so important that he know . . .

"Rayburn says they got to the wreck," Rudy said, his voice subdued, "and got Blake out, but he was already dead . . . the Terragonans got there first and tore parts of the fuselage off and disappeared . . . he says he also got the VW shell out which came through okay," and Rudy's lips tightened again in the irony of that. "They got out and back and weren't molested in any way . . . he says his field is still open, but there is sign now of activity in the jungles around him . . ." And Rudy reached up then and touched the dial, trying to bring in the voice, and suddenly it was there, coming over the speaker now, sounding a long way off but unquestionably that of Rayburn . . .

". . . repeat . . . we suspect space bacteria . . . contraband space chemistry . . . repeat . . . space chemistry . . . report to World Health immediately . . . no prognosis . . . impossible to treat . . . am trusting to the fire on Caha to do its work to contain it . . . losing power rapidly now . . . must blow the nitro . . . while there is still time . . . patients tearing loose . . . cannot control . . . am blowing the nitro . . . no time . . . pray for us—"

The sound of that empty static came on again, cutting off the voice abruptly. Rudy worked at it, but he finally shook his head at Gregson, meaning there was no more contact.

"I got Talfungo!" Potter sang out then, but nobody turned to him at all now, not even Merriweather. They simply waited, tolerating the intrusion on their hardening preoccupation with what was happening in Terragona. Potter turned toward Gregson then, waiting.

"What have you got?" Gregson said wearily.

"Colonel Jamison of the U.N. says he cannot commit rescue squadrons without notifying Hamaran Control," Potter repeated. "What do you want him to do?"

Gregson looked at Merriweather, expecting the older man to give the order. But there was in his face now that look of resignation to the inevitable. It was, after all, too little and too late.

"Tell him to file the flight plan with Hamara and get here as fast as he can," Gregson said then. He could only hope now that Olude would not follow suit, that he would wait. He stood there helplessly then, feeling the constriction of the room, the white faces leaning toward him almost like a jury gathering in the final evidence for the verdict.

"Helicopter from Myagunde is five minutes out," Rudy said from what seemed a long way off. "We'll have gas pretty quick . . ."

Gregson didn't respond. He finally got up from his half-sitting position on the table and moved to the back door and stood there against the frame, staring at the gray shale of the escarpment, feeling the grief grip harder around his heart.

# CHAPTER XV

It was 10:45 A.M., and as the first of the three U.N. helicopters descended on JERICHO, the visible carnage rose to meet them. Gregson, who had insisted on going with the rescue flight despite G.D.'s argument that what was left in Terragona was strictly U.N. business, could see that the sixty-foot-long Quonset had been blown apart, debris strewn everywhere.

He scanned the grounds around the Quonset even as they descended, looking for signs of Terragonans who might have died on the outside trying to get in when the blast went off. He saw no such sign. If there were dead Terragonans inside, then they could have blown it accidentally themselves . . . was he now hoping that was the case? Maybe this was why G.D. wanted him to let it alone, to leave it to God and history then—and avoid a lot of more complicating questions? Maybe he was right, even as Gregson sensed Albert Banqui pressing up behind him at the helicopter door to get a better view.

As the helicopter touched down, Gregson held them on board—Banqui, Shannon, Rudy, and the other pilots, who had arrived from Terragona on a stiff tailwind in time to clamber aboard the copter with him—looking for signs of Terragonans lying in wait to rush. He saw none. But he knew they were there, waiting, watching maybe for one armed military escort to jump off. Gregson was grateful that Jamison had not insisted on an armed rescue.

Finally Rudy jumped down to the ground and started running for the Quonset before Gregson could hold him, and then they were all running. "Keep the rotors turning!" Gregson shouted up at Jamison, who had his head out the cabin window, looking dubious.

Then Gregson was pushing through mounds of rubble inside the

Quonset, twisted sheets of steel, plaster and pulverized equipment. "Look for the medical logs!" he yelled, for it was most important now that Yammanaka have that record to determine, if possible, just what it was Rayburn and the others had fought in here. Or was it that he wanted the logs himself to settle in his own mind just what Rayburn's final act here really was?

Someone shouted from inside the blown-out building, and Gregson moved forward quickly, coughing on the plaster dust. The inside section that had been the main wards had not been as totally demolished by the blast as the front end. Here they found the bodies of Trask and Alicia Davenport under the debris, along with others of the staff.

"Well, they didn't die from Terragona spears," Shannon said quietly, as if he were asking the same questions as Gregson, looking down at Trask's body lying face down in the broken glass and plaster.

"They died tending their patients," Rudy added simply, "like they were supposed to . . ."

Gregson swallowed against the pain of it all as Dr. Yammanaka came out front, holding a wallet in his hands. He gave it uncertainly to Gregson. It was Rayburn's.

"It was under all that plaster in front," Yammanaka said. "Nothing else I'm afraid remains . . ."

Gregson nodded and tucked the wallet in his back pocket. They went on searching for the logs with no trace until someone called from the back, and he moved and half stumbled there to a back room where Shannon and the other pilots stood around. Collins lay face down, a piece of Quonset metal sticking out of the back of his skull. The radio transmitter lay in a tangle of wires and metal in the corner. He had one arm thrown protectively across the body of Blake, who had a gray blanket covering him up to his chin. Gregson looked at that face which seemed so unfamiliar in the neutralizing pose of death. The lumpy tissue of skin around the eyes and mouth were gone; the face had sunk into an anonymity except for the crusted cold sore on the upper lip. The jutting aquilinity of the jawline, which had given him that look of impregnableness, had dissolved. There was almost a look of serenity there now. At any rate, death had searched him clean and gone away the poorer.

"It appears the nitroglycerin was triggered accidentally by someone," Banqui offered then, almost in the form of a question, his voice sounding a bit mystified and even awed by all of this. Gregson did not comment. Banqui would judge it all himself in the end anyway . . .

It was Letchford who called from outside the back door, and they moved out to see the VW parked against the crumpled wall. It was completely assembled, except that the body had not been fully welded into place, so that it hung rather crookedly on the frame. It sat there posing a comical image or even one of grotesqueness against the backdrop of the destruction.

"I found this on the front seat," Letchford said, and he handed over the brown logbook that had Rayburn's name on it.

"Well, looks like he figured we might come in here," Gregson said. "Come on, we better get moving out of here . . ."

"We'd like to take Mr. Blake back," Rudy said. Gregson looked at him and the other pilots standing in a loose collection of uncertainty, unable to reconcile all of this as belonging to them. Gregson knew they would want their commander buried on that hill overlooking the Durungu airfield.

"You better hurry it," Gregson said. "There are people in the jungle over there . . . and we got the other bases yet . . ."

Only eighteen missionaries were found alive in the nine hospital bases. The three northern rim bases on the fringe of Lake Caha had been blown apart in the same way JERICHO had. Banqui took it all in again, but Gregson added nothing more. The eighteen who had survived were all from the southern rim bases.

They took on the living quickly as Gregson prodded the pilots to hurry while the other copter pilots kept urging them on, not sure of the movement in the jungles around them. Finally they were all aboard and the copter was lifting again, straining with the load, the other two coming up behind. Gregson stood by the cargo door watching the gouged land fade from view, the torn blisters of hope, a dream, left behind. And then there was only the desert, the caramel sheet of it passing underneath, the unmarked, faceless sea of sand offering mute, unspotted contrast to the cruel sores of Terragona.

It was near 10:00 P.M. and Gregson still sat in the tower radio room, mulling it over, still pursuing that elusive element in the twisted fabric of the events that would lend some credence, if not vindication, for his own actions and certainly those of Blake and the others in Terragona.

He had since been informed by Timothy Belang that, after he radioed into Hamara control about Mentaya's surcease, Olude wisely chose to stay out of the picture, not wanting to risk identification with what Belang told him, "activities beneath the dignity of Hamaran national purpose." An official inquiry into it all would come when the Premier returned.

Sometime during Gregson's preoccupation with those nagging questions still hanging over him, Merriweather had come in and sat down in the chair opposite him. He looked older now and more pale, even unsure maybe, evidence enough that he, too, had been poking around in the dead ashes. After sitting a long time in silence, he finally said, "Did we do it all wrong, then, Milt?" and he took off his glasses to rub at his swollen eyes with the fingers of his left hand.

Gregson did not expect that question from the older man, who had lived his years on the presumption that everything he did was right as ordained of God. Gregson simply looked at him, tempted to begin listing the things he had wished he could have done over in the past few days. Some of them he would have dropped in the older man's lap too. But by now the need to do that had passed.

And even now he knew he would have to be accountable for his own failures in not rising to the critical moment as he should have as field leader; but beyond that human frailty, which, of course, had to be reckoned with, there was something else emerging through the haze that kept him from giving vent to his impulse. Because Gregson was sure now too that what had gone on here in the past few days, maybe from the very beginning, as well as in Terragona, was somehow beyond their power to control in the end. Nobody would really know in the end maybe, but it was as if God alone moved every action, set the timing and completed on His own what perhaps He alone knew had to be done.

"Well," he finally said, taking a long sigh to relieve the heaviness in his chest, "I guess some things in life cost more than others, G.D. . . . it's no different in God's work . . ."

It was not a very adequate answer for a man who was willing to open himself up like he did, but it was all Gregson had right then. Merriweather simply stared at the floor in silence, perhaps wanting something more than that too; then he put his glasses back on slowly,

323

almost painfully, got up and moved for the door. He paused there a long minute looking out into the night and then said, his voice subdued, "And how about Ramsey Blake then? Did . . . did we do anything right by him?"

Gregson hesitated, not really sure how to answer that one. But when he looked up at the bent of the older man's shoulders in the doorway, caught the image of fragility there, maybe even humility, he said, "Well, G.D., we let him finish his journey . . . maybe that's all we were supposed to do . . ."

Merriweather did not move for a long time, thinking on it, and then he said, his voice hoarse, "Goodnight, then, Milt." And he was gone.

It was nearly midnight, but Gregson was still there in that small room, at the scarred desk used by Blake, listening to the night slowly wind down. The storms had gone, but in the distance he could hear faint rumblings of a new assault gathering not too far away. He knew he was no longer in command of the field here. The suspension order was now in effect, and Merriweather would assume command pending Field Council action on whether to appoint a new man to fill out the term or allow Gregson the reinstatement. Gregson was almost sure, in light of all that had happened, that Pat Maddigan would take over.

But that did not disturb him all that much now. He was looking for that other thing here, that which had been nagging at the back of his mind for most of the hours he sat here trying to pull it all together. And all of a sudden, because his finger had been playing with the knob, the drawer of the old desk was open. He saw the red book lying there. He picked it up, tried the clasp, found it locked. But the key was lying in the bottom of the drawer. He unlocked the book, opened it, saw that it was the daily log of Blake's. There were the teletypes folded in front, which he opened and read carefully, then put them aside. Then he turned the pages and sensed the first stab of awareness ripple across his tired heart as he began to read.

He went through each entry carefully, shaking his head as he read, conscious then of the fantastic battle one soul had carried on with himself and with God in this place.

Finally he came to the last of the entries, still seeking, groping:

God! I've lost Rudy! Jesus, don't punish them any more for my sins . . .

And, again, only two fragments of Scripture this time:

For none of us liveth to himself and none dieth to himself . . . whether we live or die, we are the Lord's . . . for without the shedding of blood there is no remission . . .[1]

Gregson pondered the power of that in context for a long minute before he turned to the last page. There he found the folded letter stuck between it and the cover. He picked it up, unfolded it, and saw that it was from Alex Bell of Seaman's Mission, New York, dated March 19, 1970, just about the time Blake had applied to the mission:

. . . Mr. Blake, I want you to know that I understand completely your resistance to words as words having final authority in themselves. Your unfortunate disaster with Global Airlines which, as you say, was "full of great words about careful maintenance and safety checks which turned out to be a crock in the end" was bound to build suspicion about all systems and even ideologies that own up to words as mere slogans. Christianity must face the same test for you. I believe God welcomes it! In the meantime, you must let the deed articulate the word. The proof of words, definitions and terms in the lexicon of God is through their final verification in experience. God delights to prove Himself to you in this way. It is a pursuit worth all of your being; it is even worth dying for, but I know of no more glorious death. And then, too, the day you climb into an airplane again and face the mountain of your past, perhaps only then will the words of Christ and of God begin to have singular meaning. I pray only that you will find kindred spirits in your quest who will make your journey short!

Gregson folded the letter back into the book and closed it slowly. So be it!

[1] Romans 14:7, Hebrews 9:22